PRAISE FOR SUSANNA CRAIG

"With *Who's That Earl*, Susanna Craig is off to a great start in her new Love and Let Spy series. The settings and characters come alive, the romance is full of spark, and the prose is as smooth as the best Scotch whisky." —**Sherry Thomas, author of the Lady Sherlock series**

"Evocative writing, a delightful Scottish setting, and fully realized characters made this a joy to read. This spy hero and writer heroine touched my heart." —*New York Times* **bestselling author Sabrina Jeffries**

"Susanna Craig creates a delightful story full of wit and intrigue." —*USA Today* **bestselling author Ella Quinn**

"The marvelous first Love and Let Spy Regency romance from Craig offers an author and a former soldier a second chance at love in the midst of a gripping mystery. Craig delights with a fast-paced, intrigue-filled plot and expertly developed characters. Regency fans will eagerly anticipate future installments." —*Publishers Weekly,* **starred review on *Who's That Earl***

"With gorgeous, contemplative phrasing, absorbing characters and a clever and unpredictable story line, *The Duke's Suspicion* is a remarkable must-read." —**Kathy Altman,** *USA Today* **bestselling author, on *The Duke's Suspicion***

D0954345

Also by Susanna Craig

THE LADY KNOWS BEST

GOODE'S GUIDE TO MISCONDUCT

Susanna Craig

ZEBRA BOOKS
KENSINGTON PUBLISHING CORP.
www.kensingtonbooks.com

For Clare,
who inspires me more than she knows—
keep playing; keep writing; keep dreaming!

CHAPTER 1

London, late May 1810

Daphne Burke had not called anyone an eejit for a very long time.

At least, not aloud.

But on the day Eileen escaped her confinement—the basket in which Daphne's younger sister, Bellis, had insisted upon carrying the sleek white cat, like a living fashion accessory, as they strolled down Bond Street—Daphne's streak broke.

"Ladies do not hurl insults," Bell had the nerve to remind her, in a perfect imitation of the first words spoken to them by their one and only governess.

With a roll of her eyes, Daphne stepped around her sister to follow the cat into Porter's Bookshop. "Then I guess it's settled: I'm no lady."

Porter's specialized in the old, rare, and unusual. No gothic novels or fashionable volumes of sentimental poetry here. It was dimly lit, a little musty, and on this particular spring morning, empty, despite the crowds of shoppers on the street. Not even a clerk was in sight.

Just over the threshold, Daphne paused to draw a calming breath, the scents of paper and ink and leather far better at restoring her spirits than anything bottled in a lady's vinaigrette.

In exchange for a few moments' peace and quiet, she almost didn't mind going on a wild goose—er, cat—chase.

"Eileen?"

The stacks and shelves of books absorbed her whisper. She strained to pick up any familiar sound: claws against a wooden table leg, the crinkle of paper beneath a paw, a delicate feline sneeze.

Silence.

The cat could be anywhere.

"Here, puss-puss-puss."

Nothing.

Peering into every shadowed corner, Daphne made her way deeper and deeper into the bookshop. Nearly at the back, she spotted Eileen's long white tail as it whisked through the crack of an open door. A storeroom, perhaps, or an office. Daphne sent a glance over her shoulder, but still no sign of a clerk.

The door opened wider at the slightest pressure of her hand. Her view, however, was obstructed by another tall, overstuffed bookshelf. Hearing voices, she paused and peered into the narrow gap above a row of books.

The room beyond was larger and brighter than Daphne had expected, with a tall though grimy window beside the shop's back door. A desk, strewn with papers and ledgers, was tucked into the corner near the window, and on the floor next to it were more books, stacked even more haphazardly than in the shop, if such a thing were possible.

An oval table filled the center of the room. Around it sat several women, most of them quite young, none of whom Daphne recognized.

All of them started when Eileen jumped onto the center of the worn oak table.

"I didn't know Porter's kept a cat on the premises," said the youngest of them, who could not have been much more than fifteen, her hair arranged in perfect blond ringlets. Her fingers gripped the edge of the table, as if she were restraining herself from reaching out to pet Eileen.

"Probably to keep away the mice," declared another, snatching up a stack of what looked like magazines, apparently to save them from the cat. She was some years older, twenty-six or -seven, Daphne guessed, with frizzy, ginger-blond hair and a scattering of freckles over the bridge of her nose, just visible beneath her spectacles. "But we still have one more item to finalize," she went on, determined to otherwise ignore the distraction, "before the next issue of the *Magazine for Misses* goes to print tomorrow."

Daphne sucked in a breath, and the effort of staying silent while doing so made her eyes grow wide. The woman could only be referring to *Mrs. Goode's Magazine for Misses*.

Daphne had read every issue of the new publication and admired its philosophy immensely. Rather than diminishing the capacity of young women and trivializing their dreams of something greater, the periodical offered knowledge and education of a different sort than most ladies' magazines.

Under the guise of a staid cover and imbued with the respectability of the author of the famous book, *Mrs. Goode's Guide to Homekeeping,* the *Magazine for Misses* provided young women with information on much more than the latest fashions: columns about politics, legislative matters, and the war with France; reviews of interesting books and scandalous plays; satirical cartoons . . . all penned anonymously, of course, to keep safe the identity of those who risked their reputations to tell young women things most of society believed young women ought not to know. The *Magazine for Mischief,* Daphne had often heard it called.

When Bell had caught Daphne reading the second issue, Daphne had bribed her to secrecy.

How was she to explain her intrusion upon a meeting of the magazine's staff? She should go, before she was noticed. Except . . .

In seeming compliance with the order to get back to work, Eileen sprawled across the table and began to rasp her pink tongue over one front paw. Papers rustled beneath her as she washed behind her left ear.

At the head of the table, with her back to the door, sat a woman whose dark hair was highlighted by a distinctive streak of silver. When she cleared her throat, all eyes turned to her, including Eileen's. Could she be Mrs. Goode?

"Yesterday afternoon," she began, "when I collected the post addressed to the magazine, I found a letter from a reader seeking advice." She reached out and carefully slid a folded paper from beneath the cat. "She signs herself 'Aggrieved in Grosvenor Square.'"

Grosvenor Square was large enough that the detail did not provide much of a clue as to the letter writer's identity. But it still made Daphne's ears prick up with interest. Grosvenor Square was the neighborhood in which Daphne and Bell lived when in London, at Finch House with their eldest sister and her husband, Cami and Gabriel, the Marquess and Marchioness of Ashborough.

"The young lady writes that her father has arranged a match for her," the woman continued, glancing down now and then at the letter, "with a well-to-do man who has a rather notorious reputation, it would seem. As so many unfortunate young women do, she hoped and believed she could persuade the man to change his ways." A murmur of sympathy rose around the table, and several of them shook their heads. The woman with reddish hair clutched the stack of magazines tighter to her chest and fixed her mouth in prim lines of disapproval at the letter writer's credulity. "And on the very evening of the dinner party to announce their betrothal, the young woman happened upon her husband-to-be in the dark with another woman . . ." The older woman paused in her recitation, as if reluctant to finish the sentence, and her voice dropped to a scandalized whisper as she glanced down and read the words: ". . . playing chess."

The collective gasp that rose from the others muffled the sound of Daphne's. She wasn't sure exactly what playing chess might be a euphemism for—wasn't sure she wanted to know—but she could guess that Aggrieved in Grosvenor Square had seen something shocking indeed.

"She must call off the wedding," Daphne declared before she could stop herself.

A wave of alarm spread through the room's occupants, which the older woman stilled with a motion of her hand as she rose. "Who's there?" she demanded. "Show yourself."

Squaring her shoulders, Daphne rounded the corner of the bookshelf and stood before them on trembling legs.

"Why, it's Miss Burke," the older woman said.

Facing her now, and free of the bookcase's shadow, Daphne recognized her as Lady Stalbridge, one of the women who regularly attended her sister Cami's literary salons. "Yes, ma'am," Daphne confessed, and curtsied.

When she rose, every eye in the room was fixed on her, but none more shrewd than Lady Stalbridge's, which were a considerably brighter shade of blue than Daphne's own. "I'm so pleased you were able to accept my invitation to join us here today," the countess said after a moment, in a tone that brooked no contradiction, though of course there had been no such invitation.

Daphne glanced toward Eileen, who had curled into a tighter circle, preparing to sleep. One of her pink-hued ears flicked, as if dismissing her own role in dragging Daphne into this situation.

Why would Lady Stalbridge lie to cover up Daphne's eavesdropping?

"Miss Burke is sister to Lady Ashborough, the authoress,"

she explained to the others. Eyebrows shot up around the table. "It would mean a great deal to our little magazine to have your sister's approval," she went on, and suddenly Daphne understood why she hadn't been driven away in a huff. "And of course I would be most delighted if your other sister, the Duchess of Raynham, could be prevailed upon to contribute a piece about women and natural philosophy. I'm sure our readers would find it inspirational."

Daphne smiled weakly and nodded her understanding. Of course. How foolish of her to imagine, even for a moment, that Lady Stalbridge had been willing to fabricate an invitation to today's meeting because she wanted Daphne herself.

Daphne was the only ordinary member of an extraordinary family.

Five of the six Burke children had been blessed with good looks, genius, and daring. Cami and Erica were as different as chalk and cheese, but both striking in appearance and brilliant. Cami, the Marchioness of Ashborough, wrote famous political novels, while Erica, the Duchess of Raynham, had earned renown for her botanical discoveries and had once even addressed a meeting of The Royal Society.

Paris, the eldest Burke brother, was a respected barrister and an MP. Galen, her other brother, had written three volumes of poetry so profound and so popular the word *laureate* had occasionally been bandied about by the reviewers. And all of them, together with their parents and spouses, showered pretty and vivacious Bellis, the baby of the family, with attention and praise.

Daphne had grown up in their shadows. Nothing about her stood out, no streak of brilliance or burst of artistic passion. She was the sort of young woman for whom adverbs had been invented: *reasonably* intelligent, *tolerably* musical, *moderately* pretty. All except for her hair, which was a shade of brown for which modifiers were not needed. Neither light nor dark. Not golden brown, like Bell's. A far cry from Cami's raven tresses or Erica's fiery red curls.

Over the years, Daphne had learned to make her peace with it. Her spot in her siblings' shadows was comfortable enough—or, if not precisely comfortable, then familiar, which amounted to much the same thing.

What more than her family connections could Daphne Burke possibly have to offer the *Magazine for Misses*?

Nevertheless, Lady Stalbridge took a step backward and, with a sweep of her arm, welcomed Daphne into the room. "Join us, won't you?" she said, nodding toward the remaining empty chair. "Allow me to introduce you to the others."

Daphne glanced around the table at the fresh faces studying her in turn. Evidently, it was a magazine not just *for* misses, but almost entirely *by* them. With a vague nod toward the two young women nearest her, she perched uncertainly on the edge of an unforgiving wooden seat.

Resuming her own chair at the head of the table, Lady Stalbridge nodded toward a young woman about Bell's age, with coffee-colored hair and a pert nose. "Miss Julia Addison shares with our readers her exceptional knowledge of the theater, while Lady Clarissa Sutliffe"—the one with the blond ringlets waggled her fingertips in a wave of acknowledgment—"has a passion for books and music. Miss Theodosia Nelson writes about matters of national importance." Here a brown-skinned woman with dark eyes smiled in greeting. "And of course our artist, Miss Constantia Cooper"—the ginger-haired woman with freckles grudgingly tipped her chin—"has a keen eye for fashion."

That last revelation was the most surprising; Miss Cooper's dress was plain to the point of severe, and her coiffure appeared to be anchored in place by a pencil. From behind her spectacles, Miss Cooper was eyeing Daphne, too, and there was something unsettling about the penetration of her glare, as if she knew Daphne had no business being there.

"I take it from your outburst, Miss Burke," Miss Cooper said, "that you are no unfortunate victim of a conduct manual education."

Conduct manuals urged a young lady to control her body, her words, her thoughts, even her dreams—in short, to shrink, even sacrifice herself—all in the service of appealing to an eligible man who was, by his very nature, unworthy of her notice and yet, somehow, necessary to her livelihood.

Daphne proudly shook her head. Such lessons had not been a feature of anyone's upbringing in the Burke household.

"So, tell us," Miss Cooper went on, "why do you think the letter writer ought to break off her engagement? Rather a risky proposition for a young lady."

Daphne refused to shy away from Miss Cooper's sharp look, though she had to swallow twice before she could speak. "Because I . . . because I believe in love."

The other woman choked back a huff of derisive laughter. "You would do well to remember, Miss Burke, that one of the aims of the *Magazine for Misses* is to promote rational conduct."

That phrase even appeared on the magazine's masthead, which proclaimed a mission *to improve wisdom and promote rational conduct among young persons of the fair sex.*

"Scoff if you will," Daphne replied, favoring Miss Cooper with a patronizing smile, "but I have witnessed the power of a love match firsthand, and many times over." She had seen it in her eldest siblings' marriages, and in her parents. "This man"—she gestured toward the letter Lady Stalbridge still held—"does not love his bride-to-be. I doubt he even is capable of it. And I also question whether any father who could arrange such a match truly loves his child. She will be better off a spinster than yoked forever to a cad."

A murmur of approval greeted her speech. Miss Nelson nodded. "Well said."

"I wonder, ma'am," said Miss Addison to Lady Stalbridge after a moment, "whether we oughtn't to consider making an advice column a regular feature of the magazine?"

Lady Stalbridge's lips curved in an expression of thoughtful interest. She weighed the matter for several minutes while the others looked on. At last she said, "What say you, Miss Burke?"

"Consider the sort of advice she is prepared to offer," Miss Cooper objected. "Worse than 'listen to your parents.' *Listen to your heart,*" she sneered.

"Personally, I prefer to use my head," Daphne replied evenly. "And I should recommend that others do the same."

Someone at the table, perhaps Miss Addison, choked back a triumphant giggle.

"If you join us," added the young Lady Clarissa, "and if there's time, perhaps you could round out your first month's column by advising someone how to persuade her papa that a young lady can pursue a career as a concert pianist without any loss of reputation or respectability."

Daphne could easily guess the identity of the young lady in need of guidance on such a subject. But she could not help but wonder about her father, who was unlikely to be persuadable on such a point, though Lady Clarissa was perfectly in the right, as far as Daphne was concerned. "I would suggest changing the instrument," she suggested with a nod of encouragement. "In your letter. Just to preserve anonymity."

"Yes," agreed Lady Stalbridge. "Outside this room, we guard everyone's identity strenuously, including that of Mrs. Goode. As I'm sure you know, the *Magazine for Misses* does not always receive a warm welcome. Sadly, too many still believe young ladies incapable of forming—to say nothing of expressing—sensible opinions on matters of both education and entertainment."

As a girl, Daphne had wished to become a teacher. Gradually, however, she had come to understand that teachers were most often impoverished young woman with no other choice. To choose such a profession might be seen as a slight to her family, as if her father and brothers and brothers-in-law were incapable of supporting her in comfort. It might be taking a situation from a young woman desperate for the sort of respectable independence a teaching post afforded, as her sister-in-law Rosamund, Paris's wife, had once been.

But she hadn't given up entirely on the dream until the day Bell had looked her in the eye and exclaimed, "You just want an excuse to order people around!"

"So, Miss Burke," Lady Stalbridge prompted, "what do you say?"

Daphne still suspected that she was wanted primarily for the possibility of persuading her famous elder sisters to participate in the venture. Or that the offer was merely a means of ensuring her silence.

But joining the *Magazine for Misses* as an advice columnist would finally give Daphne an opportunity to make her own mark on the world—if anyone listened.

"Daph?"

Bell's voice. From inside the bookshop, though not yet close enough to have overheard anything.

"I accept," Daphne said, leaping to her feet and snatching up Eileen, who squeaked in protest. "But I have to go. I'll be in touch."

Lady Stalbridge stood, too, and handed her Aggrieved in Grosvenor Square's letter, even as she laid a finger across her lips to remind Daphne of the necessity of secrecy.

Daphne bobbed her head, tucked the letter into her reticule, and left. The swish of her skirts nearly toppled a stack of books as she hurried back toward the front of the shop.

"Careful now, miss." The clerk, who had at last deigned to make an appearance, paused in the act of helping another customer to admonish her.

"I'm sorry, sir," she replied without slowing her steps.

Bell, who was standing just inside the door, turned toward the sound of her hurrying feet. "There you are! Were you hiding?"

It took several moments for Daphne to realize her sister was speaking to the cat.

Bell lifted Eileen from Daphne's arms, deposited her once more into the basket dangling from her forearm, and tapped her pink nose. "You naughty girl. You made Daphne get all dirty."

Daphne glanced down to discover a streak of dust down the front of her skirts and a goodly collection of white fur on her dark green spencer.

"I'm sorry it took so long. I was—" she began, though uncertain what explanation she could offer. But Bell was already off. After a few fruitless swipes at her clothing, Daphne followed her sister out of the bookshop and into the bright spring morning.

Daphne had spent a great deal of time in England since her three eldest siblings' marriages, but she had always preferred Dublin to London. Now, however, the prospect of being able to meet regularly with the staff of the *Magazine for Misses* gave the city a fresh appeal.

She imagined the friends she would make among its writers, even Constantia Cooper—all of them dedicated to the prospect of improving wisdom and promoting rational conduct. She, Daphne, would advise other young women how to make good choices and attain their dreams.

And unlike Bell, they might even listen!

Cautiously, she wended her way into the throng of shoppers, trying at least to keep her sister, and the Finch House footman who had accompanied them on this excursion, in her sight. Bell never moved more quickly than when she'd been given permission to purchase a new bonnet.

The milliner's was only slightly less crowded than the pavement outside. As Bell pushed her way to the counter, Daphne hung back, content to daydream as she pretended to examine a display of gloves. A few moments later, her attention was caught by a gentleman who, though standing on the street, appeared to be looking right at her through the gilt-lettered shop window.

Fashionably and expensively dressed, Viscount Deveraux was the sort of man who always carried himself as if he knew how handsome he was, with his brown eyes, straight nose and sculpted jaw, and careless waves of dark blond hair just visible beneath the brim of his tall beaver hat. If the gossips could be believed, his looks were not all he had to offer the women who were willing to brave the scandal of being associated with such a rake.

He was accompanied this morning by his friend, the Earl of Ryland, who was dark-clad as usual and somber-faced. Lord Ryland was every inch the gentleman, surely a better friend than a man like Lord Deveraux deserved, but rumored to be too indebted to pursue a bride who did not bring a fortune.

Daphne had been introduced to both of them in passing at some event early in the Season. Lord Ryland had been flawlessly polite; Lord Deveraux, she was quite sure, had forgotten her name the moment it was spoken. He had hardly even met her eye.

So why was he now looking her up and down while wearing an unusually pleased expression?

When Lord Ryland spoke to him, drawing away his notice, she belatedly realized he had been studying his own reflection in the glass. His warm smile of approval had been all for himself.

Rolling her eyes, she dragged her gaze back to the gloves and began to make mental notes on her answer to Aggrieved in Grosvenor Square. This afternoon, she would find some way to send a draft to Lady Stalbridge.

"People call him 'that devil Deveraux,' you know." Bell appeared at her elbow with a hatbox in each hand. At Daphne's raised eyebrow, she laughed and gave a little shrug, as if to say, *I couldn't possibly be expected to choose.* "They don't even bother to whisper when they say it. I pity the girl he is going to marry."

Daphne bobbed her head in agreement. The story sounded familiar, and why shouldn't it? That particular affliction—a loveless, faithless union—was a common one around Town. At one and twenty, Daphne had hoped to avoid the indignity of the marriage mart entirely. But she couldn't very well leave Bell to navigate the rake-infested waters of a London Season on her own.

Daphne followed her sister from the shop, eager to get home, review the letter from Aggrieved in Grosvenor Square, and begin writing out her answer. In her head, she tried out a few particularly cutting phrases sure to put the chess-playing rogue in his place. Occasionally, she caught her gaze wandering to the broad shoulders of the fair-haired gentleman several yards in front of her. Just the sort of devil she had in mind. . . .

CHAPTER 2

A few days later

Miles, Viscount Deveraux, did not look up as booted footsteps approached and came to a stop beside his chair. Nor again when the fellow to whom the boots belonged said with an exasperated sigh, "I feared I'd find you here."

Alistair Haythorne, the Earl of Ryland's voice. Just what was needed to put the cap on this overflowing chamber pot of a day. Miles lifted his glass to his lips, intending to toss back another swallow or two.

But no brandy seared the back of his throat. When had he finished his drink?

Unrumpled as always, Alistair called for coffee, signaling to a waiter even as he plucked the empty tumbler from Miles's hand with a grimace of distaste. Before Miles could curl his fingers into an answering fist, Alistair slapped a magazine against his palm, in place of the drink.

Miles blinked at the tattered paper cover, trying to bring the print into focus. "What's this?"

"The explanation for your present misery."

"If I *am* miserable at present," Miles retorted defensively, pushing himself more upright in the deep leather chair, "blame the lack of brandy, not . . ." He squinted, blinked, squinted again. The letters danced before him. ". . . *Mrs. Goode's Magazine for Misshus*—er, *Misses*."

A ladies' magazine? He could just make out some folderol about *rational conduct* and *wisdom*. He peered at Alistair in disbelief.

They'd known one another for . . . well, Miles's head was in no condition to do sums. A very long time. Since they'd begun at Eton together. Three days into their first term, an older boy had made some snide remark that had caused Alistair's slight shoulders to slump and tears to spring into his eyes. Miles—bold and comparatively brawny—had instinctively come to the smaller boy's defense.

They'd both been soundly thrashed, first by the older boy and then by the headmaster. But out of their shared misery had sprung a lifelong, if unlikely, friendship. Alistair had seen to it that Miles passed most of his classes and, in recent years, took his seat in the House of Lords, at least on occasion; Miles had made sure Alistair hadn't been picked last for every game of cricket and even coaxed him to indulge in a spot of fun, once in a while.

Miles prayed his old friend was having him on now. "And here I thought I was bearing up reasonably well under the latest news about bonnet trimmings for this season," he said, tossing the ladies' magazine onto the table. It knocked the empty tumbler onto the carpet before skidding to a halt.

Alistair didn't smile. "You're hiding in your club and drunk before noon." He snatched up the magazine as a servant arrived with the coffee tray and deposited it on the table between them. When the servant bent to retrieve the glass from the floor, he and Alistair shared a glance that could only be described as commiseration. As soon as he'd gone, Alistair added in a lower voice, "And everyone knows why."

"Word's abroad that Miss Grey won't have me, eh?" Miles blew out a breath and slumped low in the chair again.

He supposed it was inevitable that a notice in the morning edition of *The Times* calling off the wedding of the Season would spark chatter, no matter how small the print.

"Worse," Alistair declared, making no effort to soften the blow. "Word's abroad *why* Miss Grey won't have you. And worst of all"—he gestured with the rolled-up magazine— "the news is circulating among the young ladies them- selves."

Miles eyed the magazine more intently, even as he wished Alistair would stop waving it about and making his head spin. "A gossip column can hardly be considered *news*." He'd been the subject of tittle-tattle too often to muster anything like fear.

"If I were you, Deveraux," Alistair cautioned, "I would not be quite so dismissive about this particular publication. *Mrs. Goode's Magazine for Misses* may not have been around for long, but it's earned quite a fearsome reputation." His voice dropped lower. "It promotes freethinking and rule breaking among young ladies. *Magazine for Mischief*, people have even taken to calling it. Or worse, *Goode's Guide to Misconduct*."

Mrs. Goode, the formidable persona behind the popular if controversial book of domestic advice, *Mrs. Goode's Guide to Homekeeping*, had evidently lent her name to the periodical. "*Magazine for Misses* . . ." Miles mused, recall- ing what he'd read on the cover. He leaned forward and sloshed some coffee into a cup. Ordinarily he would have added milk and sugar—he liked things sweet, especially his women—but today, the bitter draught just suited his mood. "Misses . . . misses' conduct . . . misconduct—heh!" He laughed darkly.

Alistair was clearly not amused by the pun. Miles, how- ever, was reluctantly intrigued. As someone who derived much of his pleasure from the company of women who were willing to defy society's strictures, he generally approved of the magazine's philosophy.

"Why does that particular copy look as if it was dropped in the bathtub and then run over by a mail coach?" he asked, with a nod toward its tattered and curled pages.

"It might well have been," Alistair answered with a shrug. "The thing is handed about in secret, among girls whose parents would lock them up if they were caught."

It never ceased to amaze Miles how few people understood that forbidding fruit only made people long for a taste. "Where did you come by it, then?"

"My sister Harriet was hiding it inside her arithmetic lesson book," Alistair explained with an aggrieved sigh. "Her governess brought it to me—scandalized, of course—and I promised to give Harry a talking-to. But first . . ." He thumbed through the magazine. "I wanted you to hear this: 'Dear Miss B.—'" he read, when he'd found the page he sought and folded the cover back. "'Recently my father accepted on my behalf an offer from a gentleman who has, I will admit, a less than sterling reputation. But I persuaded myself that his proposal was a sign he meant to return to the path of virtue himself.'"

Miles snorted. "Are we pretending I'm the only recently betrothed chap to whom that could refer?"

Alistair sent him a sharp but knowing glare over the top of the magazine before continuing to read aloud. "'Then, at the dinner party hosted by my parents to celebrate our engagement, he slipped away to the library, where I found him with another woman. . . .'"

That did sound like him. "Well?" Miles prompted. "What's the charge? What does she claim to have seen me doing?"

"It doesn't say. There's a row of little stars, as if something had to be redacted."

Miles snatched the magazine from his friend's hand and

scanned the page. A sketch of a honeybee filled the upper-most corner, the insect's flight path indicated by a dashed line looping around a banner of text: *Trust Miss Busy B. for Good Advice . . . Even if It Stings!*

Eventually, his gaze came to rest on the damning ********.

Oh, very clever, inviting readers to fill in the blanks with whatever salacious details their imaginations could concoct. He took a slurp of scalding coffee and grimaced.

"Mrs. Wellcroft and I were playing chess," he said in his defense. He and the widow were old friends. "We'd both grown bored with the conversation over dinner, and neither of us fancied cards."

One of Alistair's dark brows lifted into a skeptical arch. "*Playing chess.* Is that some new lovers' cant I haven't heard?"

It was true that Miles wasn't very good at chess. Certainly not as good as he was at . . . other things. "I didn't tup her, if that's what you're implying. At least," he added, a little sheepishly, "not on that occasion. I've turned over a new leaf since my engagement to Miss Grey."

"One might expect to find a nine-day-old leaf still fresh and green, barely unfurled. Not crumpling into dust at the slightest touch. And yet . . ."

Miles hardly heard him. He'd picked up reading where Alistair had left off.

I overheard the pair of them laughing together over something—a wager, of which he is a party, pertaining to whether he would find a bride this Season! Humiliated to think I had merely been the means of winning a bet, I slipped away undetected and cried off from the rest of the party. Since then, I have pleaded various ailments to avoid everything to do with the wedding—especially him. After three

*visits from the physician, my mother is beginning to
suspect. If I keep my promise to marry him, I'll be
miserable. If I don't, my reputation will be in tatters.
What should I do?*

The letter was signed *Aggrieved in Grosvenor Sq.*
"Bloody hell," Miles muttered.

The trouble had started when he'd arrived in Town at the
start of April and mentioned to a few fellows, in the strictest
confidence, that he thought it might be time for him, at the
advanced age of eight and twenty, to give some thought to
marriage.

The next evening, a chap whom Miles hardly knew had
remarked over a hand of cards that Miles was unlikely to
have his pick, as some of the best families had instructed
their daughters to avoid *that devil, Deveraux.* Miles had only
smiled. Someone else had asserted that if he weren't careful,
he might find it difficult to make any match at all. And
somehow—Miles was never quite sure how, though he'd
been getting himself into scrapes all his life—the evening
had ended with him standing on his chair, vowing to wed a
young lady of quality before the end of the Season.

Every gentleman present, except for Alistair, had bet
against him, their wagers duly recorded in White's infamous
betting books.

Miles had been astonished by their lack of confidence;
after all, he'd never lacked for female companionship
before. But as it had turned out, a rakish reputation was no
benefit when it came to finding a respectable bride. He'd
succeeded in the end only because Edward Grey had squandered what little fortune he'd had on bad investments and
had spotted a lucky chance to improve the family's standing
with a gentleman who did not require his bride bring a
dowry. And because his daughter was a naïve, biddable sort
of girl—or so Miles had thought.

Writing this letter—well, and breaking their engagement—
were the first and only signs of spirit he had seen in Arabella
Grey, the first and only things about her that had roused his
interest, even a little.

Not that it mattered. Men like him didn't marry for happiness or companionship. Certainly not for love. They married to carry on the family name and to forge alliances. They
married because it was the expected, respectable thing to do.

Now, thanks to that wager, if he didn't take a wife within
the month, Miles stood to lose a great deal more than his
self-respect.

"I don't suppose you had a peek at the betting book
before coming in here?" he ventured.

Alistair shook his head. "The crowd around it was too
great." Was it Miles's imagination, or did his friend sound
ever so slightly amused? Alistair nodded toward the magazine. "It would seem that all the young ladies of marriage-
able age in five counties aren't the only ones who know
what sort of rogue you are."

"Nonsense. There's nothing here about *me*. Surely people
have better things to do than pretend to parse the identity of
a man in a letter sent to a stranger for bad advice."

Alistair poured himself a cup of coffee, adding a dollop
of milk and two lumps of sugar with the ease of a man who
did not have the sword of Damocles hanging over his head.
He stirred the concoction, then rapped the tiny spoon against
the edge of his cup—its chime rang in Miles's head like an
absurd tinkling death knell—and paused to drink before
saying, "I recommend you read Miss Busy B.'s reply."

Strictly speaking, he already knew the advice Miss
Grey must have received. The visit from Mr. Grey and his
unctuous solicitor yesterday afternoon had been more than
sufficient to make clear where things stood. But curiosity
niggled at Miles. Along with a thread of hope that he could

yet find some way to manage the situation to his advantage. He focused once more on the page.

Dear Miss A. G., the answer began.

<u>A</u>ggrieved in <u>G</u>rosvenor Square.

<u>A</u>rabella <u>G</u>rey.

A muscle twitched near his eye, and the fine thread of hope, the one by which the sword of Damocles was suspended, began to fray.

> *It has long been the fashion to insist that a reformed rake makes the best husband.*
>
> *Miss Busy B. disagrees.*
>
> *The platitude is illogical. It presumes rakes are capable of being reformed. But in the whole history of mankind, what evidence to support such a claim has been offered? Certainly, the so-called gentleman who sought your hand has provided none.*
>
> *Dedicated readers of the* Magazine for Misses *know it has always been our view that young ladies must seek and welcome the truth, the better to know and speak their own minds. As to the question of what you must do, we feel it is far preferable to be a contented spinster than a miserable wife. If you are determined to marry eventually, however, fear not for your reputation or future prospects. A true gentleman—and we feel sure one still exists, even in this day and age—will not resent the strength and wisdom you have shown in turning your back on the devil himself.*

The thread of hope snapped as Miles brought his teeth together with an audible click. *That devil, Deveraux.* He'd borne the epithet almost as long as he'd borne the title. Its appearance in the pages of the magazine was unlikely to be a coincidence.

If Alistair was right, every eligible miss in London for the Season, and most of their parents, would now feel themselves within their rights to give Miles the cut direct. A title, a fortune, and a handsome face had smoothed many a rough path for him—paths his own bad behavior had roughened, to be fair.

But it would be some time before society was prepared to forgive him for what he'd done to Arabella Grey—and driven her to do, in turn.

And time was the one thing he didn't have.

"Who the hell is she?" he ground out, clanking his cup onto its saucer, still resting on the table. "This Miss Busybody . . ."

"Miss Busy *B*.," Alistair corrected, gesturing toward the illustration at the top of the page with the tip of his spoon. "A play on the clever, industrious insect, one presumes. And to answer your question: no one knows. According to my sister, this column is the first of its sort to appear in the magazine."

Despite his throbbing temples, Miles began to thumb through the pages, uncertain what he sought. Surely there must be some clue as to who wrote and published the thing? But everything looked so . . . ordinary.

Only upon more careful inspection did he begin to see what Alistair had meant. The reviews were more sharply critical and opinionated than would generally be expected, given that they purported to be written by young ladies. And he rather suspected that the pattern for an embroidery sampler would spell out something shocking if any young lady ever bothered to complete it. Even the fashion plates were . . . well, cartoonish, somehow. Mocking.

Squinting, Miles tilted his head one way, the picture the other.

Alistair twitched the magazine from his fingers and closed it.

"Say," Miles protested, "that looked an awfully lot like—"

"Find a promising new biscuit recipe, Deveraux?"

"It *was* you. But why did the artist draw you with a stick up your—?"

"Coat?" Alistair interjected. "I haven't the faintest idea. Someone identified only as Miss C. sketches the 'Unfashionable Plates,' as they're known. Apparently, she enjoys making people appear ridiculous."

In spite of his own predicament, Miles struggled to repress a grin. Alistair had always been rather . . . dull, in matters of dress particularly. His bevy of sisters, elder and younger, had been trying to coax him into better choices for years.

"Enough about me," Alistair said, folding the magazine and tucking it into his breast pocket. "What will you do?"

"Do?" Miles poured more coffee into his cup, though he was already more sober than he wished. "Why, I shall accept my invitation to Lady Clearwater's ball this evening, of course. It would seem I'm in search of a bride."

"But . . ." Astonishment made Alistair's objection catch in his throat.

"But first, I believe I'll write to Miss Busy B. and thank her. Somewhere out there is a silly, romantic-minded young lady who read that letter and fancies herself up to the challenge of taming that devil, Deveraux."

CHAPTER 3

Had the phrase *devil-may-care* been invented to describe Lord Deveraux?

Daphne knew better. Still, he entered the Clearwaters' ballroom with a smile and a swagger that defied every gasp, every whisper.

Tall and elegantly dressed in crisp black and white, he paused in the doorway just long enough to let every eye take him in. Then he dipped his head to acknowledge the crowd's attention, as if they had intended to convey some honor by it. The movement made his golden-brown hair gleam beneath the light of several hundred candles; a careless kiss or two more from the summer sun and it would be blond, dark blond, the color of sun-ripened wheatfields or polished oak.

In the fraction of a moment between the lowest point of his sardonic bow and the straightening of his spine, the ball-goers shifted their notice to Miss Grey, like a flock of starlings wheeling as one, guided purely by instinct.

All but one of them, that was. However appalled she might be by his audacity in coming tonight, wearing the scandal of his broken engagement like a badge of honor and exposing poor Miss Grey to further distress, Daphne once more found she could not look away from the despicable Lord Deveraux.

Thus, when his head rose, his eyes naturally met hers. Or so it seemed to her, anyway. Standing as they were on opposite ends of the long room, one could not say for certain whom or what he might have seen or why both his brows and his lips curved in something like amusement. Or was it admonition?

Daphne jerked her gaze away, first to the floor and then to some greenery in a tall urn. For perhaps the first time in her life she wished she had been listening on one of the many occasions her sister Erica, the botanist, had tried to teach her something about plants. Because then she might have been able to occupy her mind as well as her eyes.

If she were thinking about horticulture, she would *not* be thinking about how devilishly handsome Lord Deveraux was, in spite—or perhaps because—of his rakish reputation.

If she could have mustered some curiosity about leaf patterns and shapes, she would have something to distract from the warmth that had settled low in her belly and now seemed determined to simmer there.

Desire?

She would deny it to her sister, all her sisters, anyone who thought to ask—not, of course, that anyone would. Desire was not something about which young ladies spoke openly. On the rare occasion someone as level-headed as Daphne *was* bold enough to admit desiring a man, she was expected to choose a more suitable object than Lord Deveraux.

Miss Cooper would call it irrational to deny one's feelings to oneself. And Daphne knew she was hardly the first—if the tales of his numerous conquests were to be believed—to find the notorious viscount appealing. Attractive.

The danger lay in acting on those feelings.

Which, of course, she had no intention of doing. Even if she were foolhardy enough to consider it, Lord Deveraux would not—not with her, at any rate. Without any firsthand knowledge of the particulars, Daphne understood that courtesans, actresses, and young widows all had charms that the only moderately pretty and frequently pedantic daughter of a Dublin solicitor did not.

A small knot of people—though not small enough to be discreet—had formed around Miss Grey, ostensibly to support her through the ordeal of being in the same room with her former betrothed, and particularly to prevent the two of them from coming within speaking distance of one another.

Shrieking distance, however, was another matter. The cluster of guests was not quite thick enough to muffle the shrill, incoherent gasps of Miss Grey's rising hysteria, which floated along on a steady undercurrent of whispers:

"How dare he show his face here? The nerve of some so-called gentlemen!"

And farther from the unfortunate young lady in question:

"He may be a scoundrel, but she's the one who'll suffer . . ."

"Imagine calling things off with a man who looks like that . . ."

". . . a man who kisses *like that . . ."*

And almost at Daphne's elbow:

"I heard it was all down to that horrid magazine. Where else would a girl get such wretched advice?"

The ball of warmth in Daphne's belly hardened into a lump of cold lead.

That horrid magazine?

No, surely not. Though the coincidence *was* quite extraordinary. This month's issue of the *Magazine for Misses*, containing Daphne's advice to Aggrieved in Grosvenor Square, had come out the day before yesterday. And word of Miss Grey's broken engagement had followed hard on its heels.

Daphne still had not fully reconciled herself to the possibility that people—strangers—might actually value her opinion and take her advice.

Wretched advice.

Breaking an engagement was never a matter to be taken

lightly. Had Daphne spouted off without thinking, written without reflecting on how her answer might affect the young woman in question? Oh, she had understood there were those in society who would choose to cast such a decision in an unfavorable light. Doubtless the young lady's family was embarrassed, even displeased. It might be some time before the scandal died down enough for another gentleman to be willing to make her an offer.

But *wretched*?

Wasn't Aggrieved in Grosvenor Square better off not bound in wedded misery?

And misery it would surely be. Particularly if Aggrieved in Grosvenor Square was actually Miss Grey. Because that would mean that the gentleman who'd made the scandalous wager was none other than . . .

Refusing to risk another glance in Lord Deveraux's direction, Daphne grabbed her sister's hand and dragged her toward the crowd of commiserating matrons, determined to see for herself. Daphne took some consolation in the certainty that Miss Grey's letter had not been that of a broken-hearted woman. In fact, the gossips said the two had hardly even spoken to one another. Why, if Mr. Grey had not insisted his daughter *get right back on the horse,* as Daphne had heard one ballgoer explain in derisive tones, or if Lord Deveraux had simply chosen to find his entertainment elsewhere this evening, everything would have been fine.

But as Daphne and Bell pressed closer, the sight of the young woman's tear-stained face was not exactly reassuring. Miss Grey looked, well . . . *wretched*. And Mrs. Grey was standing next to her, waving her fan and scanning the crowd with narrowed eyes as if hunting for the person who had advised her daughter to do such a shocking thing.

Had Daphne made a terrible mistake?

The lump of lead in her gut began to roll about until she feared she was going to be sick. "Bell," she ground out from between clenched teeth. When that produced no response from her sister, presently craning her neck to get a better view of Miss Grey, Daphne jerked Bell's arm and began to drag her in the opposite direction. "Bell, please. Let's find Cami and leave."

Bellis planted her feet. "Leave? The ball? I think not, sister dear. Need I remind you that my dance card is full?"

Dance?

It took Daphne a moment to recall that, of course, people would eventually resume all the ordinary activities planned for such an evening: dancing and flirting and gossiping about people other than Miss Grey and Lord Deveraux. And of course Bellis would want to be among them, enjoying every moment of her first London Season and the attention it had rightfully brought her. In her heart, Daphne did not want to rob her younger sister of the experiences she'd dreamed of.

But her stomach had other ideas.

Something of her distress must have been evident on her face, for Bell's expression changed, softened. "Daph?" Concern wrinkled her brow. "We can go, if you want. The gentlemen will wait."

Daphne would not have described her sister as selfish, exactly. Selflessness, however, was unexpected. Or maybe it wasn't selflessness. Maybe Bell still had enough faith in fairy tales that she believed a handsome prince was simply her due.

And perhaps she was right.

Suddenly Daphne couldn't bear to be responsible for delaying Bell's happiness, certainly not on the heels of possibly destroying Miss Grey's. Out of the corner of one eye, she spied French doors leading to a back balcony that ran the width of the house. "Air," she gritted out, praying it would be enough to set her to rights.

Rimmed by ornate wrought iron railings and lit by a half-dozen torchiers, the balcony was blessedly empty at present.

"Shocking, really, what Miss Grey is being expected to endure," ventured Bell as they stepped into the cool evening air. "I don't blame you for wanting to get away from such an unpleasant scene."

Daphne moved closer to Bell and the meager warmth of one of the flickering lights, but she did not speak until she'd taken another look around to make sure they were alone.

"It's all my f-fault." She was no longer sure whether she'd locked her jaw against the roiling in her belly or the chattering of her teeth.

"Nonsense," Bellis reassured her airily. "I didn't really fancy having my toes stepped on by Lord Cowell, anyway, and Mr. Bennett has already told me he'll be at the Moncrieffs' dinner party. I can explain then."

"I m-mean," Daphne hiccupped, "m-my fault about Miss Grey."

Bell's amber earbobs danced in the light as she shook her head. "I declare, Daph. It's one thing to feel an over-developed sense of responsibility for your younger sister. Quite another to fancy you bear some blame for a stranger's poor choices."

Daphne drew a shaky breath. "You think it a p-poor choice, then, for her to refuse Lord Deveraux?"

"Well . . ." Bell rubbed a gloved fingertip over her chin as she pondered the matter. "It might not have been a poor choice to decline his offer. But to accept his proposal and then cry off? It won't make her life easier, that's for certain."

"I refuse to believe that a se'enight scandal is more difficult than being married forever to a notorious rake."

"Our sister married a notorious rake," Bell pointed out after a moment, "and she's never been happier."

Daphne knew it was true—knew, at least, that Cami was happy. She'd always found it more difficult to imagine Gabriel, Lord Ashborough, was really as bad as people had said; after all, he had played tea party with Daphne and Bell when they were young, and later with his own daughters. Impossible to imagine a true rake, like Lord Deveraux, sacrificing his dignity to please a child.

"Worst of all, people say her mind was changed by some silly advice column in *Goode's Guide to Misconduct*."

"Don't call it that," Daphne snapped, before she thought better of it.

"*Everyone* calls it that," her sister countered. "See here, I've kept my promise not to tell Cami I caught you reading the thing, but surely you can't expect me not to poke a little fun?"

Privately, Daphne felt certain that her eldest sister would be willing to concede the necessity of occasional misconduct—Bellis seemed to be the only member of the Burke clan likely to make a match by following the rules. But as Daphne's secret was rather larger than leafing through the magazine, she hadn't wanted to put the matter to the test.

"What if it wasn't silly advice?" she insisted. "If he's willing to lay wagers involving ladies, Lord Deveraux is a worse scoundrel than anyone suspected." *He may be a scoundrel, but she's the one who'll suffer.* . . . "What if the person who answered Miss Grey's letter truly believed that telling her to call it off was the best thing?"

Daphne hadn't realized she was gripping the iron railing with both hands until Bell laid her fingertips along her sleeve. "Daph?"

All at once, her thin kid gloves were no barrier to the cold metal, and she shuddered. "I d-did believe it. I *do* believe it. Lord Deveraux is nothing more than a tomcat. Faithless, amoral . . . Why, I might well have saved Miss Grey from the pox!" She felt as though she had shouted the final word, though in truth her voice had dropped to a whisper.

Bell's fingers bit into her forearm. "*You?* You wrote that answer?"

Daphne nodded uncertainly. "That day I followed Eileen into Porter's, I stumbled on a staff meeting. And now, I— I'm Miss Busy B."

Bell blinked.

"You won't say anything?" Daphne pleaded belatedly. In the rush of guilt over Miss Grey's grief, Daphne had forgotten Lady Stalbridge's only hard and fast rule: tell no one.

Her sister was studying her face, and Daphne looked back, searching for some sign of her childhood co-conspirator.

A frown darted between Bell's brows. "I can't believe you think you need to ask." Then she linked the little fingers of their right hands and shook them, at the same time giving a decisive nod, their long-ago sign of an unbreakable sisterly vow. "You always did like ordering people about. But what are you going to do now?"

"Do?"

"I mean, are you going to tell Miss Grey you made a mistake?"

"It wasn't a mistake," Daphne insisted. "She'll see that herself, when the scandal dies down and a more suitable gentleman presents himself."

"He won't be as handsome as Lord Deveraux."

Imagine calling things off with a man who looks like that . . .

A man who kisses *like that . . .*

"Looks aren't everything, Bell."

Her sister chuckled, rather disbelievingly, then sobered. "Are you going to quit writing for the magazine?"

Daphne squeezed their still-joined fingers. "No."

After a moment, Bell nodded again. "Good. Your column

is my new favorite item—after the Unfashionable Plates, naturally."

"You mean you—you've been reading—?"

"Of course, silly," she said with a shrug and a laugh. "*Everyone* is."

Behind them, the orchestra struck up a tune and strains of music filtered out into the night air. Bell sent a longing glance over her shoulder. "You should go dance," Daphne said.

"I can't leave you here alone."

"I'll come inside in another moment." Daphne tipped her chin to the night sky. "I haven't a partner waiting for me."

"If you're sure . . ." Though hesitant, Bell slipped her hand free and turned to go.

Daphne drew a deeper, steadier breath, luxuriating in the scent of wisteria blossoms. Not difficult, on such a night, to imagine the stars did hold the answers, some knowledge of the future, which they parsed out in mysterious patterns and sly winks.

The sound of footsteps dragged her gaze back to earth. A gentleman had entered the balcony from another set of doors. When he spied her, he started in surprise, paused as if weighing his options, then began to make his way toward her with a slow, easy stride. Not quite a prowl.

Daphne's stomach, which had at last begun to settle, performed an uneasy somersault. Of all the men to interrupt her solitary reflections.

"Lord Deveraux."

The name passed between her lips on the faintest breath. Even beneath the dimmer light of stars and torches, he glowed with vitality, the sort of animal spirits that made her palms sweat.

He reached the balcony and bowed, the same lazy, insolent gesture he'd made upon entering the ballroom. "Miss Burke, yes?"

His recognition surprised her. She managed a curtsy of acknowledgment, one hand along the rail for balance.

"Are you well?" he asked, studying her.

"Perfectly." She lifted her chin, determined not to squirm beneath his gaze. "I'll wish you good evening, my lord," she said, turning toward the house.

"Will you?" One hand shot out and she gasped, thinking he meant to catch her by the wrist.

Instead, Lord Deveraux curled his gloved hand around the iron railing, exactly where hers had been resting not a moment before. With his first finger, he rubbed absently at the metal's sharp edge. She wondered whether he could still feel the trace of warmth left behind by her touch.

"I must say, those are kinder words than any I expected to meet with tonight."

His tone was self-deprecating, the tilt of his head almost shy. There was something boyish about his charm—not at all what Daphne had been led to expect from a rake known far and wide as *that devil, Deveraux*.

"May I ask why you are out here," he asked, "rather than inside, enjoying the entertainment?"

He didn't care. Not really. But he had the ability to make it seem as if he did—another dangerous gift.

She took another step backward. "The ballroom is crowded, and I needed a breath of fresh air. Now, if you'll excuse me—"

"Do you dance this evening, Miss Burke?"

She started to shake her head. She certainly didn't want to dance with him.

Not that he was asking.

Although . . . he followed his question by holding out his hand, palm upward. Then his eyebrows rose in a hopeful arc, and he smiled another winning, boyish smile. Despite the buzz of scandal in the ballroom, he clearly did not expect to be rebuffed—again. He probably imagined someone like Daphne ought to be grateful for his notice.

"I have already declined one invitation to dance this evening, my lord," she lied. "The rules of the ballroom forbid me from accepting another."

He nodded his head in understanding, but he did not lower his hand.

"And do you always play by the rules, Miss Burke?"

A shocking speech . . . and yet, somehow not shocking at all from a man like him.

A man who looks like that . . .

A man who kisses *like that . . .*

She squeezed shut her eyes and called up the memory of Miss Grey's tear-stained face. If only there were some way to make Lord Deveraux feel the sting he so callously inflicted on others.

When she opened her eyes, she glanced over her shoulder, toward the French doors. Light and music and laughter spilled through them. Ordinarily, she accepted, perhaps even preferred, being an unknown, the overlooked wares on the marriage mart.

But the balcony was far too private to humiliate him thoroughly.

With another curtsy, she laid her hand on his palm and tried to ignore the welcome warmth of his fingers curling about hers as he led her toward the ballroom.

CHAPTER 4

Miles had never been a strong student. He'd muddled his way through school on a combination of luck, Alistair's patience, and his teachers' reluctance to risk the ire of Miles's grandmother.

But he'd always been good at reading people—especially women. The quickness of a breath, the lightness of a touch: they were a language, a poetry his mind unraveled with ease and delight.

Unlike, say, Greek, which he'd long suspected was not a language at all, but an elaborate swindle played on unsuspecting schoolboys. A jumble of signs he couldn't sort into meaning. Frustrating. Unreadable.

Daphne Burke was Greek.

Well, Irish, actually. The Dublin-born daughter of a solicitor. That much he knew, thanks to the list of every marginally eligible miss with which Alistair had supplied him earlier that afternoon.

She was not the sort of woman to whom Miles would ordinarily give a second glance. Neither the arrangement of her brown hair nor the white dress she wore suited her. She was a wallflower, and that was precisely why he'd asked her to dance, hoping to rub a bit of tarnish off his reputation.

But here, beneath the stars, her skin was soft, luminous.

And now that he was standing close enough to see the glitter in her eyes, the defiant tilt of her chin, he had the feeling she might have been deliberately disguising herself among those pallid blooms, a sort of camouflage to ward off potential suitors. Almost as if she had been trying to pass through the Season unnoticed. Almost as if there were something she hoped to hide. . . .

If that were true, it would explain why she obviously had not wanted to dance with him.

But what had made her change her mind?

His tumbling thoughts made his steps slow.

"If I didn't know better, my lord, I'd think you regretted your invitation," said Miss Burke on the edge of the ballroom. The roundness of her vowels only just softened the edges of an otherwise governess-y sort of voice.

"I only wished to give you another chance to refuse, ma'am. In case you'd thought better of being seen with me."

She freed her fingers from his grip—he'd kept his touch light on purpose.

What would she do next? What did he want her to do?

She slid her hand through the crook of his elbow and curled her fingers around his forearm.

Why in God's name did his pulse began to race?

He laid his hand over hers, securing her there. "Is it possible, Miss Burke, you are unaware of my reputation?"

"No, my lord." A blaze of light washed over her, and for the first time, he could see her eyes. Gray, with just a hint of blue. She looked up at him as if oblivious to the fact that a hundred people had turned to look at her. A hundred people who could not see the cold steel in her gaze. "But I'm quite sure you're unaware of mine."

Ah.

With a smile and a dip of his head, he led her to her place in a nearby set. He didn't yet know the strength of her blade, whether she meant merely to wound or to eviscerate him. He'd never dueled a lady before. At least, not while standing.

And God help him, he was . . . intrigued.

Heedless of the other dancers, he took his position opposite. The couple they'd displaced shifted lower in the line.

"Do—do people just make way for you, wherever you wish to go?" she demanded in an indignant whisper as she curtsied.

He bowed. "Generally, yes."

Oh, but her eyes sparked delightfully at that. She could not make up her mind whether she envied him that power or despised him for using it.

"I suppose that explains why you're here tonight. You assumed Miss Grey would stay at home rather than dare to threaten your enjoyment of the evening."

It was true that he hadn't expected to see Arabella Grey in attendance at the Clearwaters' ball. He supposed her damnable father had insisted upon it; the man wouldn't have wanted his daughter to waste a new gown, or a fresh opportunity.

When Miles had heard her cry of outrage upon his arrival, he had considered leaving, rather than cause her further embarrassment. After a moment, though, he'd thought better of it. The crowd had been prepared to see the worst in him. It was easier to give people what they wanted, what they expected, and Miles liked to keep things easy.

But something about the twinkle of defiance in Miss Burke's eyes inspired him.

"Tell me, if I had turned tail and run, what would have been the result?"

The figure of the dance divided them into separate foursomes, allowing her ample time to consider her answer. As soon as they were together again, however, he spoke before she could.

"Miss Grey alone would have borne the brunt of every

stare, every whispered speculation. By staying, I ensured all those sneers of contempt and narrow-eyed glares would be directed at me."

Practically a noble gesture, for him—and one Miss Burke clearly regarded with distrust.

"In fact, I'm given to understand that some gentlemen will no doubt find Miss Grey's conduct admirable," he went on. "Something about casting aside the devil to make way for a saintlier suitor, I think it was? In any case, I can assure you that her heart was not broken." He'd never seen the slightest sign of affection from his former betrothed. Releasing Miss Burke's hand, he laid his palm on his chest. "So, if anyone is suffering here tonight, it is I."

Under cover of the dance's next formation and the scalloped hems of her skirts, she stepped boldly toward him—and trod squarely on his foot. When he yelped, she smiled. "Fortunately for you, wounded pride is rarely fatal."

"You fancy me proud, do you?" Miles demanded after he'd shaken the feeling back into his toes.

She weighed either the question or her answer. "Arrogant, unquestionably. And vain, I suspect. Frankly, I'm surprised you were willing to partner me." And then, in another clearly calculated move, she spun in the wrong direction, disrupting the swirl of couples moving around them. "I might have embarrassed you by being a terrible dancer."

"I knew better," he gritted out as he wrangled her back into position, "or I should not have asked."

"How could you know any such thing?" she scoffed. "And I almost never dance at these sorts of affairs, so you needn't lie and claim to have been admiring me from afar."

"I know, Miss Burke, because there is music in your voice, and a certain something in your—" He paused to drag his gaze over her, head to toe, intending to provoke a blush.

But somehow, he found himself provoked instead. The stiffness of her spine and the quickness of her breath had thrust her bosom into prominence. His pulse, which he'd managed to steady, ratcheted up again, although a moment before he would have been willing to swear she was hardly even pretty.

"Something in your . . . figure," he finished, with more sincerity than he'd begun.

She did oblige him by blushing, at least. Though as a becoming shade of pink swept down her throat and spread across her decolletage, drawing his eye to the very edge of her bodice, a place it ought not linger, he questioned the wisdom of his efforts.

"I am not sure those are gentlemanly observations," she said primly.

"Whoever said I was a gentleman?"

"True. You are a rake." Her voice rose on the last word, as if she were testing to see whether those around them were still listening and if so, how they would react.

If she were hoping the neighboring couples would be scandalized by her declaration and turn to stare at him, she was destined to be disappointed. His rakish reputation was nothing new to anyone in the Clearwaters' ballroom.

Instead, she'd managed with her outrageous performance to draw the ballgoers' curious eyes to *her*. All along the two lines of dancers, people had been sending looks and pointing. At either side of the room, he spied ladies whispering behind fans.

Miss Burke did not yet seem to realize that her plan had gone awry, but he felt certain she was not the sort who would relish the attention.

"Yet in full awareness of that fact," he reminded her, steering her out of the set as smoothly as he'd led her into it, "you agreed to partner me."

And he still wasn't sure why. Had she thought to enact some revenge on behalf of poor Miss Grey? But surely no one was innocent enough to imagine squashed toes and a few snickers sufficient punishment for his sins.

Good manners dictated that he return her to her chaperone after a dance. But Miles had never been one to worry much about etiquette. And anyway, their dance wasn't done.

Determined to make sense of her behavior, he pointed their steps in the opposite direction.

"Do you wish to know what I think, Miss Burke?" he asked as they walked.

"Not in the slightest."

"I don't suppose you'd find it much to your liking," he conceded. "Shall I tell you what you're thinking instead?"

"Party tricks, Lord Deveraux?"

"You think you know me, my failings. You think I deserve to suffer a far greater indignity than a broken betrothal and a lost wager. You agreed to dance with me with the sole intention of humiliating me. If I'd let you carry on back there, you would have shouted about what a scoundrel I am for making a wager involving a lady—just in case someone in this ballroom hasn't yet seen the latest issue of *Goode's Guide to Misconduct*."

"Don't call it that."

"Why not? Does the truth sting?" he hissed.

To his surprise, she sucked in an alarmed breath through her nostrils and searched his face with narrowed eyes. "What a strange turn of phrase, my lord," she said when she'd recovered some of her aplomb. "It almost makes me wonder whether . . ." Then she broke off with a brisk toss of her head and a forced laugh. "No. Surely a gentleman would not waste his time reading a magazine for young ladies."

Try as she might, she could not firm her lips into a prim enough line to disguise their plumpness. When she spoke, he watched her mouth and caught himself wondering, in true rakehell fashion, what it would be like to kiss her.

"I believe we ascertained just moments ago that I'm no gentleman."

All at once, she seemed to realize where they now stood: on the dimly it balcony, alone.

"Oh, I see." She looked around, and then her chin jutted forward. "I ought to have been on my guard, given what I've heard about your penchant for darkness and . . . chess."

Chess?

Good God, had Alistair been serious? Was *playing chess* really the latest slang for seduction? Though it would surprise him if even Miss Burke was outspoken enough to use the kind of vulgarities favored by dandies and rogues.

No, her choice of words felt almost as mocking as her moves on the dance floor had done. As if she somehow knew . . .

But how could she? The magazine had omitted certain details about that night from its sordid tale, including that fateful game of chess. Had Miss Grey originally been more forthcoming? And had Miss Burke somehow seen that letter in its entirety? How could that be, though, unless she had some connection to the magazine . . . ?

Understanding dawned, uncharacteristically sharp and bright.

She spun to face him, and the timing of her movement made him half wonder whether there had been an audible click as the pieces came together in his mind.

Her steely eyes flashed. She stood closer now than she had earlier. Too close. "What is it you want, Lord Deveraux?"

"I think you already know the answer."

She shook her head, as if trying to deny it.

"I need a wife to win a wager. And you're going to find me one."

A sound grated in the back of her throat, something between a choking noise and a scoff. "Why would I do that?" she demanded, though some of the certainty had left her voice.

"I think you know the answer to that too." He tipped his head closer still, so that his lips brushed the shell of her ear as he whispered, "Don't you, Miss Busy B.?"

CHAPTER 5

The buzz in Daphne's ears was loud enough to drive away thought. When she managed to speak—"I haven't the faintest notion what you're talking about!"—the words sounded muffled and far away.

His warm laugh stirred her hair. "Oh, I think you do."

Quickly, she moved away from the door, where they might be overheard, and toward the railing, near where she'd been standing earlier. When she glanced back at him, he was wearing a smug expression.

"How did you—?" she demanded incoherently. "Were you eavesdropping on my conversation with my sister?"

"Eavesdropping?" As he'd done while they were dancing, he laid his hand over his heart in a gesture of mock sincerity. "Perish the thought. No, *you* told me who you are."

"*I* told you?"

"Oh, not in so many words," he acknowledged, stepping closer. The light from the torchieres made his golden hair gleam. "Well, one word. *Chess.*"

Daphne had never let herself dwell for long on what exactly Aggrieved in Grosvenor Square had witnessed between her betrothed and another woman, though she'd always suspected the game of chess was a euphemism for something salacious.

Now that she had realized the man involved was Lord Deveraux, she was sure of it.

"The only person who could have told you exactly what she saw that night in the library was Miss Grey," he said. "The details weren't included in the magazine, if you recall. I asked myself why she would have done that, how she happened to know Miss Burke. Burke with a *B*, you see. And then I asked myself why you seemed to have taken a personal interest in avenging her honor. Why you reacted so strangely when I suggested that the truth . . . *stings*."

With every revelation, her jaw tightened further, until by the end of his explanation, her teeth ached. A better writer would have been more careful with her words.

"Do you know," he added, with one of those lopsided, charming smiles, "if I'd realized when I was younger that my brain is capable of such perspicacity, I wouldn't have had to snap quite so many of my mathematics tutor's pencils, nor hide from lessons quite so often."

Of course he'd been a poor student too. She narrowly avoided rolling her eyes. "And now you expect me to find someone willing to marry a cad like you?"

"Yes, yes. *That devil, Deveraux.* The worst scoundrel in existence." He sounded bored. And vaguely . . . hurt? But no. That couldn't be. He hadn't even tried to deny Miss Grey's accusation. "I find it strangely reassuring, knowing I can't sink any lower in your estimation."

"Yet you seem determined to try."

"Oh, Miss Busy B." He laughed. "Well, at least you're going into the task with both eyes open."

"And if I refuse?"

His answer, though oblique, was chillingly clear: "I

suspect your good name means something to you, or you wouldn't trouble to shield it from your readers."

It would mean the end of her association with the *Magazine for Misses,* the loss of friendships she'd looked forward to developing, the freedoms she'd hoped to enjoy. . . .

Fists balled at her side, she began to pace along the balcony's edge. The moon had painted the garden below in a chiaroscuro of light and shadow that promised innumerable, though temporary, hiding places. Escape would require a treacherous vault and probably cost her a torn dress and twisted ankle, but at least it would give her a little time— time to gather her thoughts, time to plan a course of action.

"How exactly am I to manage to find you a bride, when every woman on this island knows about your ridiculous wager?"

"I fear you may have an exaggerated notion of your little magazine's circulation," he said, a sardonic smile twitching at his lips. Then he shrugged. "Figure something out. You're meant to be the clever one. 'Trust Miss Busy B. for good advice,' and all that."

All at once, Miss Grey's tear-stained face rose in her memory.

Such wretched advice . . .

Daphne's skirts whipped tight to her legs as she spun to face him. "I—perhaps I could use my column to explain. Say I answered too hastily and encourage Aggrieved in Grosvenor Square to reconsider."

"In the next issue of the magazine?"

Relieved, she nodded. "Yes, exactly." She despised the very thought of it, but if Miss Grey really did regret her decision . . .

"Haven't got a month," he replied, crossing his arms over his chest. "I need to be wed by end of June to win my bet."

Not even three weeks away. In such a short amount of

time, she couldn't possibly manage to fix the mess she—
he—had made.

"But it wouldn't have to be Miss Grey," he offered. "Any
accomplished young lady of good family, with an education
and upbringing suitable to the duties of a viscountess, will do."

"Oh, is that all?"

He lifted one shoulder and managed to look almost
sheepish.

"Don't you care about affection? Or—or passion?" She
had to push the last word past her lips, barely a whisper.

He laughed. "Fortunately for you, love is not one of the
terms and conditions of the wager."

She thought of the looks she'd seen in her elder siblings'
eyes on their wedding days and so frequently since, the glances
still exchanged between her parents. She knew, of course, that
not every marriage was a love match. But what could cause
someone to be willing to wave away even the possibility, as
if it were a matter of complete indifference . . . ?

No. She would *not* pity Lord Deveraux. Why, if anyone
deserved her pity, it was his future bride.

"So, it's really quite simple," he said, stepping close
enough to grasp the railing beside her, effectively blocking
her from returning to the ballroom. "All you must do is find
me a suitable wife in time."

She had to swallow hard before she could speak. "Or
you'll expose me."

"Cheer up," he urged, leaning forward to speak once
more into her ear. "You might find you quite enjoy being
ruined."

A shiver passed through her, and to her eternal shame, it
was not entirely the product of anger. Or fear.

In spite of everything, there was still something thrilling
about hearing those words from Lord Deveraux's lips.

 . . . *a man who looks like that* . . .
 . . . *a man who* kisses *like that* . . .

She drew back enough to glance from his face to his hand on the railing and back again. "It would seem I'm caught between a rake and a hard place."

"Ah, you see, Miss Burke." His low, wry laugh ghosted over her skin and made it tingle. "You *are* clever."

Perhaps. But I'm also an eejit.

"Daphne?"

Bell's voice, alive with both worry and wonder.

Daphne squeezed shut her eyelids and drew a steadying breath before turning to face her sister.

"Is everything all right?" Bell asked, glancing uncertainly between them.

"Perfectly," Daphne insisted, slipping free of the cage created by the railing and the viscount's arm. "You will excuse me, my lord."

"For now."

The words, spoken too low for Bell to hear, sent another frisson of awareness down Daphne's spine. Would there need to be more secret meetings, other whispered conversations in the dark?

Almost before she was within reach, Bell grabbed her by both hands and dragged her inside, toward respectability. Daphne had to blink against the light. "What happened?" her sister demanded.

"Lord Deveraux asked me to dance, and I accepted."

"I saw. *Everyone* saw."

So much for Daphne's faint hope that they'd gone relatively unnoticed in the crush of the ballroom.

"But afterward, you disappeared," Bell went on. "Cami sent me to search for you. Were you feeling unwell again? How did you end up out here?"

"It seemed as good a place as any to talk."

"Talk?" Bell's eyes flared. "With *him*?"

"Yes, well . . ." Daphne flicked one hand in a helpless gesture. A part of her longed to tell her sister what Lord

Deveraux had discovered, the price he'd demanded for keeping her secret—and ask what she ought to do.

But Miss Busy B. gave advice. She didn't seek it.

"Anyway, thank God no one else noticed," Bell went on. "Five more minutes out there, and you might have been ruined."

It was the familiar threat, marshaled to keep young women in line.

Being ruined meant attaining forbidden knowledge and experiences.

Being ruined meant no more society balls or expectations of a grand marriage.

Being ruined had always sounded to Daphne an awful lot like the kind of freedom called for and celebrated in the *Magazine for Misses*.

"And I might quite have enjoyed it," she quipped.

Bell gaped at her, eyes round as saucers.

"Come on," Daphne said, steering them toward their sister, where Daphne would see out the night surrounded by the dull safety of the matrons, while Bell returned to the dance floor and the favored gentlemen eager for her hand.

Lord Deveraux might not have been entirely wrong about her.

But if she was going to be ruined, she intended to find a way to make sure he was too.

Absorbed in watching the sway of Daphne's skirts as she walked away—she was, indeed, rather more attractive than he'd first thought, and somehow, her disdain for him only made her more so—Miles did not immediately realize someone else had entered the balcony through the other set of French doors.

"Are. You. Mad?"

For the second time that day, the disapproving voice of his best friend snatched Miles back from a dangerous precipice.

"Undoubtedly," he replied, shaking off his untoward thoughts about Miss Burke. "But after all these years, Alistair, you shouldn't sound so surprised. What did I do this time?"

"Were you not out here with a young lady, unchaperoned, practically in the dark?"

"I did tell you I was coming here tonight with the express intention of finding a wife," he reminded him. "Perhaps I was just doing a bit of wooing."

Alistair poorly disguised his laugh as a cough. "I beg your pardon. Did you say . . . *wooing*? Do you even know what that means?"

Miles humored him by appearing to give the matter some thought. Truth be told, he didn't often have to exert much effort where women were concerned. "Let's see," he teased. "If I recall correctly, it has something to do with ravishing, seducing, debauching . . ."

"No." Alistair shook his head, his lips curved in a half smile, half scold. "You're thinking of *ruining*."

I am.

"Wooing is respectful," Alistair went on. "Respectable. Involving activities that can be carried on in public, in broad daylight."

"Sounds dreadfully dull."

Daphne Burke wasn't, though. In those moments together on the dance floor, and then under the night sky, he'd glimpsed something vibrant inside her.

A pity he'd soon be married to someone else and wouldn't get to see more.

"In any case, you needn't worry," he went on, ushering Alistair back toward the ballroom. "As it happens, Miss Burke has just such a degree of acquaintance with Miss Grey that makes her believe she can persuade my former betrothed to give me another chance."

Alistair's left eyebrow shot up. "So, I'm to believe the two of you were out here scheming together . . ."

"Now, now. You know I never scheme." In truth, he was mostly too indifferent and usually too impulsive to bother. "Desirable opportunities just have a habit of falling into my lap."

"I suppose that's what happened with that charming actress last summer?"

"Exactly! And when opportunities fall into my lap, I make it a rule to seize them. So, you see—purely practical. A business arrangement. I certainly was not wooing Miss Burke."

Alistair still looked skeptical, but his posture relaxed. "Speaking as your friend, I'd say that's probably for the best. Knowing you, you'd likely find yourself at the business end of a dueling pistol before the week was out." At Miles's expression of confusion, he asked, "Didn't you read that list I gave you?"

"I, er, didn't have time to commit all the details to memory, I'm afraid."

"Well, just in case, even if you don't intend to woo her, you should know your Miss Burke is far from friendless, " Alistair explained. "She is a niece of the Earl of Merrick. She also has two elder brothers. Now, the younger of them is a poet, so a suitor might be safe there. The older one, though—Paris Burke—is an MP, and notoriously hot tempered. Rumor has it he fought with the United Irishmen in '98."

After just one conversation with the man's sister, Miles wasn't exactly surprised to learn that a member of the Burke family had a rebellious streak.

"But really, it's her brothers-in-law a fellow would have to watch out for," Alistair continued. "The Marquess of Ashborough may be a family man now, but I daresay he'd be willing to make an exception for the pleasure of running through a rogue."

He'd seen Ashborough at his club—*Lord Ash,* people still called him, though only when they were sure the man wouldn't overhear.

"And as for the Duke of Raynham . . ."

They'd never been introduced, but Miles knew the stern-faced man by reputation. "Military type, yes?"

Alistair nodded grimly. "I believe the word you're looking for is *spy.* I suspect he's more than capable of dealing a death blow without any warning at all."

Miles understood Alistair's point in telling him. But it wasn't the fierceness of her brother or brothers-in-law that ratcheted up Miles's pulse.

It was hers.

"You needn't worry about me," Miles said again, clapping a hand on Alistair's shoulder. "Miss Burke is—why, I suppose you could consider her something of a matchmaker. Nothing more."

By the light passing through the glass-paneled door, his oldest friend studied him, a crease notched into his brow. "I do, you realize. Worry."

"Why? You know I never lose."

Alistair sighed. "I wasn't thinking of your wager, Miles. Or, rather, I was wondering . . . Have you given any thought to what happens after you win?"

Don't you care about affection? she had asked.

He did, of course—though not in the way she'd meant it.

He knew what he wanted from this marriage. He'd agreed to the terms of the wager, hadn't he?

Or—or passion?

He paused on the threshold and scanned the ballroom, though he certainly was not looking for anyone in particular.

This was no time to be distracted. He had no reason to feel . . . disappointed.

Everything was going exactly to plan.

CHAPTER 6

L ong before any other member of the household arose, Daphne got dressed, grabbed a bonnet, and went downstairs. All was quiet, though the shadowy entry hall bore witness to several early-morning deliveries, bouquets and nosegays from the gentlemen who had danced with her sister last night.

Most of them included daisies, Bellis's namesake flower, though she'd never been particularly fond of it. Daphne reached out a hand to trace the edge of one delicate petal. Why were men so unimaginative when it came to sending tokens of their affection? One could only hope they were more invested in the lady's feelings when it came to bestowing the affections themselves.

Don't you care about affection?

She jerked away her hand, nearly toppling a vase of pink roses in the process.

Why the devil should she care about Lord Deveraux's heart?

From somewhere behind her came a weary groan. She turned to discover a black-and-fawn mastiff watching her expectantly.

"Walk?" she suggested to the dog, who perked up his ears at the word.

The *Magazine for Misses* staff meeting wasn't for another

hour. But Daphne needed to clear her head now. She had expected to have to persuade one of the footmen to accompany her. She could already foresee spending most of the wages she earned writing for the magazine on ensuring the silence of half a dozen servants, scattered throughout the British Isles, on the matter of her comings and goings as well as that of the post.

But this was better. Dogs couldn't talk.

"Walk?" she said again, and the giant canine lumbered to her side. Swiftly tying the ribbons of her bonnet, Daphne set out.

The clerk at Porter's expressed no surprise at her early arrival, though he did cast a chary glance at the dog.

"He wouldn't hurt a flea," she reassured the young man, who bobbed his head in a skeptical nod, then pretended to look the other way while Daphne fished for the key to the back room, which hung on a hook behind the counter. After that first meeting, Lady Stalbridge had told her where to find it and explained that the room was reserved for the exclusive use of the magazine's staff.

But someone else had already retrieved the key, and she found the door to the back room ajar.

The room was just as disorganized as it had been before, but someone had polished the window, and a complete run of the *Magazine for Misses* now lined the sill.

Constantia Cooper, the artist behind the monthly satirical cartoons, "What Miss C. Saw"—known among readers as the "Unfashionable Plates"—was seated at one end of the oval table, sketching. She wore a dress of drab green muslin and, as usual, all that had been done to tame her frizz of curls was insufficient to the task.

Once, Daphne had puzzled over Constantia's role at the magazine, but now she understood that Miss C.'s drawings were intended not to highlight the day's fashions but to skewer the fashionable.

Only after Constantia had completed the exaggerated outline of a figure did she lift her head. Pushing her spectacles up her nose, she favored the dog with an exasperated look and then shifted her gaze to Daphne.

"Are all the Burkes incapable of leaving the house without some sort of animal companion?"

Daphne had never confessed the matter of her sister's cat's misbehavior and its role in bringing her to the magazine.

"This is Zwolf." She patted the dog's broad head as she made the introduction. Given the dog's size, the movement hardly required her to extend her arm.

Constantia tapped the end of her pencil against her paper. "You have a dog named Twelve?"

"His mother was called Elf, you see," Daphne explained. "You wouldn't believe it to look at him now, but he was the runt of her last litter. Bell and I were studying German at the time and since zwölf follows elf . . ." Constantia's expression remained resignedly disapproving. "Well, I thought it was clever," Daphne finished weakly.

Lips pursed, Constantia glanced between them before returning her attention to her drawing. "Lady Stalbridge won't be here for half an hour, at least."

"Why are *you* here so early?"

"I came to work," she explained, her voice and her posture stiff. "Undisturbed."

"Oh, right. Yes. Well, pretend Zwolf and I aren't here. I'll just—I'll read," Daphne said, picking up a book that was lying nearby and motioning for the dog to lie down beneath the table.

She opened to the title page: *The Justification of a Sinner; Being the Maine Argument of the Epistle to the Galatians*.

In keeping with the rules of Latin, from which the dusty volume might have been translated a hundred and fifty years or so earlier, *Justification* had been spelled with an *I*. Thus it appeared at first glance as if the titular sinner was to be *lustified*. Daphne resolutely bit back a snicker. The book did not promise much in the way of entertainment, beyond that bit of unfortunate typography, but it might at least serve as a distraction.

Even deft feats of textual exegesis by "a Reverend and Learned Divine" were unable to engage her interest, however—or keep her thoughts from wandering back to last night.

If only she had never accepted Lord Deveraux's invitation to dance . . .

Though he *had* been quite the handsomest man she had ever danced with.

But what difference did his looks make? Why, it would be traitorous for her to find him attractive. He had knowledge that could put an end to her time here, even undercut the success of the magazine itself. He was a scoundrel who cared about nothing but winning that ridiculous bet.

"For pity's sake!" Constantia snapped her pencil flat on the table and sucked in a breath that threatened to pull all the air from the room. "*What* is in that book?"

"It's, uh . . ." Daphne glanced down at the open page, the one over which her eyes had been sliding for the past few minutes without taking in a single word. "It's a treatise on St. Paul's epistle to the Galatians. Why?"

"Because your sighs are ruffling my papers. I had no idea you felt so strongly about theology."

Daphne was spared from having to concoct an excuse for her behavior by the arrival of Lady Stalbridge. "Good news, ladies," the countess sang as she tugged off her gloves. "Every last copy of the latest issue of the *Magazine for Misses* has already been sold."

Constantia leaped to her feet and shook Lady Stalbridge's hand; Daphne too rose and expressed her excitement at the news. And while Lady Stalbridge removed her bonnet and explained her hopes for a larger printing next month,

Daphne and Constantia even shared a cool nod of mutual satisfaction.

Only after Lady Stalbridge had seated herself and withdrawn her notes for the meeting from a neat leather satchel did Daphne venture the question that had been weighing on her for hours.

"Did you know that Aggrieved in Grosvenor Square was Arabella Grey?"

Lady Stalbridge squared a stack of papers and gave a discreet cough. "Perhaps I . . . suspected. When the letter writer mentioned a wager, I happened to recall something Oliver had told me. . . ."

Oliver was Lord Manwaring, Lady Stalbridge's stepson; only those admitted to this room knew that he was also the mind behind the famous, but fictitious, Mrs. Goode.

"Once you had composed your exceptional reply, I realized it contained a message many of our readers needed to hear. So I said nothing more of my suspicions. Though in truth," she added sheepishly, "I did not think Miss Grey would act on your advice in quite such spectacular fashion."

"You did not think she would be *permitted* to act on it, you mean," corrected Constantia. "Miss Grey has a despotic and improvident father, just the sort of man who would be eager to claim Lord Deveraux for a son-in-law."

"Given the circumstances, then," Daphne ventured, "don't you think it's possible Miss Grey will be persuaded to marry Lord Deveraux after all?"

"Oh, I don't think so," said Theodosia Nelson, as she breezed into the room. A West Indian heiress, she penned newsy notes about current events—actually a column about politics, abolition, and the war, full of information generally deemed inappropriate for the audience of the magazine. Her secret ambition was to write for *The Times*.

"Haven't you heard the latest?" When Theodosia plucked off her bonnet, dark brown curls sprang free, perfectly framing her brown face and eyes. "Arabella Grey has eloped! Disappeared in the night with the son of a Welsh coal merchant. They're said to be desperately in love."

"Oh, won't her papa be fit to be tied," said Lady Stalbridge with unexpected glee.

Theodosia shrugged. "I daresay he'll bring himself to forgive his daughter. Her new husband is said to be terribly rich."

Their chatter washed over Daphne in waves. She was delighted for Miss Grey, of course. Impressed, too, by her feigned devastation the night before, at the ball—a ruse, she supposed, to divert her family from her plans. Why, her mother had probably insisted that she needed to retire early and rest without interruption, giving her the perfect opportunity to escape.

But now who was Daphne to find to satisfy Lord Deveraux's list of demands?

"Forgive me for interrupting," said Theodosia, laying her bonnet and gloves aside. "What were you discussing when I came in?"

Lady Stalbridge picked up a sheet of figures, the uppermost item in her stack of papers. "From what I can see, we have Lord Deveraux's broken engagement to thank for our success this month. As soon as rumors about the identity of the man in Aggrieved in Grosvenor Square's letter began to circulate, so did the *Magazine for Misses*. And I have an idea for how we can thank him," she finished, lowering the paper to look straight at Daphne.

"Th-th . . ." Daphne's mouth was dry, too dry to form the word without pausing to swallow. "Thank him?"

"Although, I doubt he'll appreciate the sort of gratitude I have in mind," Lady Stalbridge said with a humorless smile. "You see, since I read your answer to Miss Grey, I've been considering the need to speak to our readers in more pointed terms about the dangers posed by certain gentlemen of the *ton,* both those who wear their villainy like a badge of honor, and those who hide every appearance of it."

Lord Deveraux was the former sort, of course. But when Daphne looked back on his behavior of the evening before, she wondered whether he might be hiding something of himself, nonetheless.

"Is not the *Magazine for Misses* our *united* attempt to speak to our peers on such matters?" demanded Constantia, her chin tucked back toward her breastbone, like one affronted.

"Of course it is, Miss Cooper," Lady Stalbridge said in a mollifying tone. "But subtlety may be overlooked. Satire may be misread. Miss Busy B., however, has a knack for plain speaking, and clearly readers do listen. I had in mind an essay, or a series of essays, on rakes—"

Daphne's heart began to race. On one hand, she would like nothing better than another opportunity to shame Lord Deveraux. On the other, more exposure of his bad behavior would hardly improve her chances of finding him a suitable wife—which was to say, her chances of saving herself and the magazine.

"I want young women to be able to recognize them," continued Lady Stalbridge, "and thus avoid being ruined."

Beneath the table, Daphne twisted her fingers into a knot. She could have done without hearing that phrase again.

"Rakes and ruination?" Miss Julia Addison peered around the tall bookshelf that screened the room from the doorway. "We must be talking about Lord Deveraux again. Do tell us, Miss Burke, what was it like to dance with him?"

Lady Stalbridge's dark, delicate brows rose in a perfect arc. Constantia, who had been gesturing with her pencil for emphasis, lost her grip and flung it across the room. Zwolf obligingly lumbered out from beneath the table to fetch it.

"And who is this darling boy?" Julia crooned, stepping forward. Zwolf tilted his head at the sound of her voice.

Daphne took advantage of his momentary distraction to retrieve the slobbery pencil from the dog's jaws and return it to a nonplussed Constantia. "I didn't realize you were at the Clearwaters' ball, Miss Addison."

"I wasn't," Julia said, scratching the dog between the ears and favoring him with a scrunch-faced smile before taking her seat. "But Mrs. Hayes was—she and Lady Clearwater are old friends, you know."

Mrs. Mildred Hayes was the liberal-minded aunt of Julia's sister-in-law, Lady Sterling, and a devout lover of the theater, the more awful the farce, the better. Following the recent marriages of both Julia's brother and mother, Mrs. Hayes had invited Julia to move to Clapham as a sort of companion. Together, they attended all the plays and performances Julia reviewed in her column under the name Miss on Scene.

"She regaled me with the news over breakfast. Said that when you and Lord Deveraux danced together, the ballroom was . . . *abuzz*." That last word, a clear reference to Miss Busy B.'s column, was punctuated with a mischievous giggle.

Constantia and Theodosia were all astonishment. Lady Stalbridge looked thoughtful. "Tell me, my dear, did Lord Deveraux say—or do—anything of note in your presence last night? Anything particularly scandalous?"

Daphne gnawed at her lip. "Um, maybe?" She glanced around the table. "My goodness, shouldn't we wait for Lady Clarissa?"

"She won't be joining us this morning. She is preparing for her debut performance at the Estleys' musicale this evening," Lady Stalbridge said with an indulgent smile at Daphne's obvious attempt to change the subject. "She credits your marvelous advice for her ability to persuade her papa to allow it, even though she is not strictly speaking 'out' in society."

Daphne knew then that the countess had no intention of letting Miss Busy B. squirm her way out of the planned essay on rakes.

"She is to play a duet with her mother," Lady Stalbridge went on, "and they have been practicing three hours every morning. Lady Clarissa feared that to cry off on the day of the performance itself would raise suspicions and so she had to miss our meeting. Now, you were saying about Lord Deveraux . . ."

"I heard he tried to take you off somewhere—alone— after you danced," said Julia.

"Excellent," Lady Stalbridge purred.

"*Excellent?*" Constantia echoed, incredulous. "How so? Why, he's obviously only looking for some way to win his bet."

Slightly wounded by that harsh truth, Daphne nevertheless looked to Lady Stalbridge for an explanation.

"If Miss Burke is to speak with her usual authority on this matter, it will unfortunately require some first-hand experience with rakes. If Lord Deveraux has shown interest, I believe you should encourage it. That way, you will soon know his tricks well enough to be able to teach our readers to avoid them."

"It seems to me any plan for Miss Burke to associate further with the man runs the risk of damaging her own reputation," observed level-headed Theodosia.

"If there is any scandal—which I doubt," said Lady Stalbridge, "for our Miss Burke is far too clever to be ensnared—her family will help her to weather it. They strike me as a fiercely loyal clan."

"Anyway, those sorts of scandals never last long," Julia added, sounding vaguely disappointed. She was still scratching Zwolf behind the ears. A rope of saliva hung from the dog's jowls, and a puddle of drool had begun to form beneath the table, a sure sign of his contentment. "By next Season, everyone will have moved on to something else."

Daphne managed a nod. They weren't wrong; scandal swept through the *ton* like wildfire, and her family had proved itself strong enough to withstand those flames more than once. Still, spending more time in Lord Deveraux's company was not without risk.

More time . . .

"But this Season will be nearly over by the time the next issue is available," she pointed out. "I'm quite sure he expects to be married by then."

"We could publish the essay more quickly as a separate pamphlet, or a broadside." Two pink spots burned on Constantia's cheeks. "Illustrated, perhaps?"

"What a clever notion," said Lady Stalbridge, jotting notes on the sheet of figures. "We can reach more readers that way, too, and use the opportunity to promote our magazine. Now then, are we agreed?" She looked around the table at each of the contributors, marking their assent to the project on a tally. "Very well. Miss Burke, I recommend you continue your research tonight at the Estleys."

"Do you really think it likely Lord Deveraux will attend this evening, ma'am?"

Gentlemen found any number of excuses to avoid musicale evenings—ironic, given that young ladies usually acquired musical accomplishments because it was supposed to help them attract a husband. But, since most young ladies played insipidly and sang worse, Daphne couldn't exactly blame the men for suddenly remembering they had another engagement or even coming down with an otherwise inexplicable bout of dyspepsia.

"I think it more than likely, Miss Burke," was Lady Stalbridge's reply. "Unless and until he finds someone foolish enough to marry him, you'll find him everywhere respectable young ladies are gathered."

"As opposed to his general habit," proclaimed Constantia, "of associating only with the less-than-respectable ones."

General merriment greeted that witty remark.

Daphne leaped to her feet. "It's late. My, uh, my sister will be looking for me. Come, Zwolf." Still mesmerized by Miss Addison's attention, the dog ignored Daphne's command. She had to grab him by the collar to persuade him to accompany her from the room.

"Oh, Zwolf," she moaned softly when they were on the pavement in front of the shop. "Now I'm caught between an essay on rakes and a hard place. What am I going to do?"

The dog looked up at her with sorrowful eyes.

You're meant to be the clever one.

Well, yes. She *was* fairly clever, last night notwithstanding. But was she clever enough to figure her way out of this?

CHAPTER 7

That evening, as Daphne was climbing the steps of the Estleys' Grosvenor Square townhome, the solution to her dilemma came to her.

Not, to be sure, a perfect solution. It would almost certainly create new problems.

But it would answer both Lord Deveraux's and Lady Stalbridge's demands, and it would give Daphne ample opportunity to research a rake's ways.

A breath shuddered from her.

If she weren't careful, it could be more than ample opportunity.

From the doorway, Cami glanced over her shoulder. Concern wrinkled across her forehead at Daphne's hesitation. "Is everything all right?"

Daphne dragged up a smile and looped her arm through Bell's. "Of course."

They were greeted by the Marquess of Estley, a handsome gentleman of about forty, with pale blue eyes, dark blond hair that Daphne refused to compare to Lord Deveraux's, and a thin scar along one cheek. He had come into the title some two years earlier, on the death of his father.

He bowed. "Lady Ashborough, Miss Burke, Miss Bellis.

My wife hopes you will excuse her for not being here to welcome you."

"Of course," said Cami. "Her mind must be on her and her daughter's performance. We are honored to have an opportunity to hear them play."

Upstairs, the drawing room had been rearranged to accommodate rows of spindly chairs, all facing a Broadwood pianoforte. Daphne and her sisters found three seats near the front. In the row ahead sat Lady Stalbridge, accompanied by her stepson Lord Manwaring. She turned to speak briefly to Cami, offering little more than a polite nod to Daphne; after all, they were not meant to know one another well.

But when no one else was looking, young Lord Manwaring—the person behind the shadowy figurehead, Mrs. Goode—sent her a saucy wink. Lady Stalbridge must have told him of her plan.

What, Daphne wondered, would either of them make of *her* plan?

Well, she would know soon enough, for at that moment, the hum of voices, its pitch already reflective of an audience made up mostly of women, rose sharply. The cause? Lord Deveraux's athletic figure framed by the doorway.

Tonight he wore a coat of dark blue over a gold and ivory waistcoat, a combination of hues that set off his coloring perfectly. Instead of scanning the room in proud defiance, as he had at the Clearwaters' ball, he now exuded that boyish charm that had succeeded in disarming so many women.

When setting down the qualities and characteristics young women ought to be wary of, that crooked smile would be high on her list.

Lady Stalbridge turned her head, not enough to meet Daphne's eye, but enough that she could see the triumphant smile curling the countess's lips.

Daphne gnawed the inside of her cheek. Despite Lady

Stalbridge's insistence that he would come, Daphne had still dared to hope for one more night's reprieve.

She did not see where he took his seat, for just then a longcase clock struck eight. At that signal, a pair of liveried footmen stepped forward to douse most of the candles in the sconces along the room's walls, leaving only the candelabras nearest the pianoforte untouched, casting the audience into dimness and drawing the eye toward the performers.

Lady Estley entered first. She was a small, plain woman with mousy brown hair, a few years younger than her husband. After tipping her head to acknowledge the applause, she gestured for her daughter to join her. Lady Clarissa Sutliffe, all pink-cheeked nervousness and excitement, stepped to the pianoforte, seated herself, and began to play. The careful, precise notes of Bach and Mozart flowed from her fingertips with ease, and once she had finished several solo pieces, her mother joined her at the keyboard to play a haunting, lyrical duet that brought a lump to Daphne's throat. Whispers soon made it known that the piece had been composed by Lady Estley for the occasion of her daughter's musical debut.

Lady Clarissa Sutliffe had been blessed with her father's good looks and her mother's talent. Daphne had no difficulty imagining a packed concert hall, listening in awe as Clarissa played. She recalled the mission of the *Magazine for Misses,* the general agreement among the staff that young women must not be forced to squander their gifts simply on account of their sex.

"Daph," Bell said, under cover of thunderous applause, "are you all right?"

Daphne nodded and swallowed hard, twice, as the pressure in her throat threatened to find relief in tears. "Perfectly well."

The performance, the memory, the magazine's mission had only firmed her resolve about what must be done.

After curtsying to acknowledge the adulation, Lady Estley

held up a hand for silence. The footmen began to relight the candles that had been snuffed.

"Thank you," Lady Estley said. "We will now pause for some refreshment. Afterward, it is our hope that some of our guests will entertain us."

While almost everyone else moved toward the groaning tables at the back of the room, Daphne stepped to the front to congratulate Lady Estley and Lady Clarissa on their triumph. When they had moved on to speak with someone else, she paused to admire the beautiful instrument on which they had played, a far cry from the tinkling spinet on which she'd learned, so many years ago and so many miles away.

She was lost in thought, her fingertips trailing soundlessly over the keys, when a hand appeared at her elbow, proffering a cup of lemonade.

"Are you preparing to delight us next, Miss Burke?" asked Lord Deveraux.

"No." She accepted the cup only to have something else to do with her hands. "I did not expect to see you here tonight, my lord."

"Why not?" He tipped his head to the side and smiled one of those half smiles that could make a woman's breath catch—if she were susceptible to such nonsense. "I enjoy music."

"True enjoyment of music is often reason enough to avoid such entertainments," Daphne said. "Though admittedly this one has been an exception to the rule."

His smile grew to a laugh. "How severe you are, Miss Burke. And you have not taken a sip of your drink, so I cannot blame the lemonade for making your tongue so tart."

There was something suggestive in those words—in almost everything he said, and she despised the prickle of heat that rose to her cheeks as he spoke them.

Two young ladies approached the pianoforte, tittering as they sidled past the viscount to reach the credenza, where sheet music had been thoughtfully provided for potential performers to peruse. Whatever their parents might say to the matter, at least some of the young ladies of the *ton* were evidently willing to overlook the sins of that devil Deveraux.

Daphne had in her hands the power to put an end to all that.

With a flick of her wrist, she downed the dainty cup of lemonade in a single gulp, its sharp sweetness stinging the back of her throat. "My lord," she choked out, "we need to talk."

He was looking at the fair-haired and fashionably gowned young ladies near the window. When they had passed, his gaze had followed them automatically. Daphne would very much have liked to dismiss his behavior as ogling. But as he turned toward her, she glimpsed a sort of weariness in the fixed, though still charming, smile on his face, nothing of genuine interest in those two giggling girls.

His expression when he looked at Daphne, however, was . . . well, *intrigued.* One golden-brown brow arched. "Oh?"

"I have given your—my—this predicament a great deal of thought, and—"

Surprise flickered into his face. He lifted a finger to his lips, a call for quiet. "I'm not sure this is the time or the place, Miss Burke."

Perhaps not, but if she waited, she would lose her nerve.

"Very well." She glanced around at the milling company. Everyone seemed to be absorbed in food and conversation. The floor plan of this house was a mirror of Gabriel and Cami's house on the other side of the square. Which meant . . . "Directly above us will be a small room." At Finch House, Cami had claimed it as a place to do her writing. Whatever purpose it served in the Estley household, it was unlikely to be among the public spaces this evening.

"I'll go first, pretend to be looking for the ladies' retiring room, if anyone asks."

Now curiosity sparkled in his eyes. "And I will follow a few minutes later."

He reached to relieve her of her empty cup, and his fingertips brushed hers—deliberately, she felt sure. With a nod she'd meant to be crisp and businesslike, but which wobbled rather more than she'd hoped, she stepped away from the pianoforte and toward the door.

Upstairs, she found exactly what she had expected to find: a smallish square room with windows overlooking the street. From the dark, masculine furnishings—leather chairs, glass-fronted bookcases, a mahogany desk—she gathered it belonged to Lord Estley. With trembling fingers, she drew the draperies over the windows, busied herself with lighting candles, and prayed the marquess wouldn't have cause to venture into the room tonight.

She was still weighing whether to sit or stand, or whether perhaps it might be best simply to lean against the desk for support, when the door opened with almost preternatural slowness.

For once, Lord Deveraux had been true to his word.

The door closed behind him with a soft click. He turned, but did not immediately approach, as she had expected. Instead he leaned his shoulder against the paneled door and crossed his arms over his chest.

His eyes scanned the room and a wry laugh gusted from his lips. The gold threads of his waistcoat gleamed. "Eleven candles in four minutes. Impressive, Miss Burke."

"You forget, I'm familiar with the sort of tricks you get up to in darkened libraries."

A frown—part sardonic amusement, part something else—notched between his brows and then disappeared. "Are you perfectly certain you understand what happened at the Greys' that night?"

"I, er—"

Before she could muster a response, he pushed away from the door and took three loose-limbed strides toward her. "In any case, I'd call this more of a study. Now, what was it you wanted to discuss?"

Her resolve faltered with each of his steps. She slid her fingers into the grooves of the carved edge of the desktop behind her, trying to absorb some of its firmness.

"Y-you've heard the news about Miss Grey's elopement?"

His smile stretched, though more humorless than she had ever seen it. "Oh, yes."

"I spent most of the day racking my brain for a suitable substitute. I have a fairly large acquaintance among the sorts of young ladies whom I believe would fulfill the conditions of your wager. But I could not settle on a single one I thought likely to consent to such a match—or more to the point, whose parents would consent on her behalf."

He looked unsurprised by that declaration, and remarkably unperturbed. "Giving up so soon, Miss Busy B.?"

"N-no. I believe I have another solution, my lord." She swallowed hard, and the sharp edge of some ornate vine bit into the palm of her hand. In spite of the tautness of her muscles, a shiver slipped through her. "Marry m-me."

She'd expected him to laugh. Or worse yet, shudder in disgust.

Instead, he tipped his head to the side as he looked her up and down.

All at once, she wished she hadn't lit so many candles. Wished she hadn't worn her favorite gown, a blue-gray silk with a low-cut square neckline and skirts that fell straight until they reached her ankles, where they curled and swirled in an elaborately ruched hem. Wished she had refused the maid's offer to arrange her hair with Cami's pearl-headed pins.

He would think she had primped and preened just for him.

As if she cared one jot for his approval.

Although . . . at least it wasn't disapproval that streaked across his expression. More like disbelief. Confusion. Clearly the flash of brilliance his mind had mustered last night had deserted him.

"Marry you," he echoed. Though he put the stress on the first word, rather than the last. As if he'd been considering some other action entirely.

Strangle, perhaps.

"But before any announcement, I expect a proper courtship," she said, raising a hand to ward him off, though he'd made no move to come closer. "A fortnight, at least."

The courtship period was key to her plan. It was the one sure way she knew of to get close enough to discover the extent of Lord Deveraux's devilry. Not merely ill-conceived wagers and "playing chess." The sorts of behavior that would truly shock and scandalize the *ton*. She would write her essay, and shortly before their engagement was made public, she would show it to him and offer a deal: lose his wager or be driven from respectable society forever.

Now that he knew the *Magazine for Misses* had the capability to make his life miserable, she felt certain which he would choose.

Her words seemed to rouse him to himself. A slow, wicked smile curved his lips. "An improper courtship would be much more fun."

She willed herself not to blush. It was a stark reminder of the dangers of the situation. Spending any amount of time in his company would cause her reputation to suffer too.

When it was all over, Cami might throw up her hands and send her back to Dublin—if she were fortunate. There, Daphne could . . . why, she could spend her time writing a treatise on the education of girls, something that wasn't about accomplishments and angling for a husband.

Despite Miss Busy B.'s advice, Aggrieved in Grosvenor

Square hadn't chosen contented spinsterhood on the heels of her apparent ruin.

If all went to plan, Daphne still could.

She thrust out her hand. "Do we have a deal, my lord?"

Mischief twinkled in his eyes. He took her hand, but instead of shaking it, he used his leverage to tug her away from the desk. When she stumbled a bit, his arms were there to catch her.

"Given the nature of the bargain, my dear," he murmured, "I'd prefer to seal it with a kiss."

CHAPTER 8

M iles had always loved kissing. The anticipation. The first, tentative brush of lips. The melting sweetness that transformed one thing into something else entirely, like crystals of sugar dissolving in a cup of hot tea.

Sometimes he thought he might even prefer kisses to the things that usually followed them—though that position was hardly consistent with his status as a rake. And in truth, he rarely had to choose.

One hand at her waist, he raised the other to cup her face, careful not to dislodge her pretty hairpins. When he brushed the pad of his thumb over her cheek, tracing the contour of her heated blush, her pupils flared and her lips parted on a silent gasp. But she made no attempt to pull away.

And thank God for that. He lived by the motto that pleasures were only pleasurable when shared among the willing—but he wasn't sure he could stop himself from kissing Daphne Burke.

In the candlelight, her wide, unblinking eyes were the same steel-blue shade as her gown. *Her suit of armor,* he'd thought to himself when he'd first glimpsed her across the drawing room. But beneath his touch, the fabric was soft and warm, *she* was soft and warm. He closed his eyes and dipped his head lower.

She'd never been kissed before. Although he didn't make a habit of kissing innocents, that much was clear to him the moment his mouth found hers: puckered and tremulous and oh, so sweet.

Tart, too, of course. He could still taste a hint of lemonade on her lips.

Pushing aside every doubt, every question—*Why was she so ready to give up her search and marry a man she clearly despised? What sort of man would he be if he allowed her to go through with it?*—he concentrated instead on making her first kiss one to remember.

He knew how to shape his mouth to hers, the way to fit the sharp peaks and soft contours of their lips perfectly together. He knew how to nibble and coax, knew when firmness would give way to a gentle caress.

But every bit of his experience was suddenly rendered meaningless when, God help him, she began to kiss him back.

One tentative hand slipped between his coat and waistcoat to rest over his heart, an anchor as she rose up on the balls of her feet and sighed into his mouth. Artless, uncertain, she advanced and retreated—innate desire doing battle with her better judgment.

Flexing his fingertips against the edge of her skull, stroking his thumb along the hollow of her cheek, he urged her to relax her jaw, to savor each sensation, to relent.

The sounds of the pianoforte rose from the drawing room below as breath and lips and tongues came together in a sensual dance, erasing every memory of last night's ballroom disaster. He'd suspected all along she had put on a performance of awkwardness, though he hadn't been entirely sure why.

Never mind Miss Busy B., this—*this*—was the woman she'd been trying to hide. From him. But most especially from herself.

He had knowledge that could ruin her.

And some part of her wanted to be ruined.

At least on this occasion, however, the sensible part of her won out. After another moment, she sank back on her heels and, with a none-too-gentle shove from the palm still resting on his chest, wedged their bodies apart.

He'd been careful not to muss her soft brown curls. But she still looked thoroughly kissed, her lips pink and slightly swollen, her eyes heavy lidded and dazed.

"My lord!"

He thought she'd intended the words as a scold for him, but in her breathless state, they sounded more like blasphemy.

"Under the circumstances," he said, "I think we can dispense with the formalities. Call me Miles."

She drew the back of her hand over her mouth, as if the revelations of this moment could be so easily erased. "I most certainly will not."

"As you wish," he replied easily as he took a step backward and tugged his waistcoat smooth. "Though you will have to say it once. In front of the clergyman. I don't have a great deal of experience with weddings, but I'm quite sure that's a rule. And afterward, of course, you should be prepared that a continued insistence on addressing me as *my lord* will set a certain tone with respect to conjugal matters. Particularly in the marriage bed."

Her whole body twitched. A shudder of disgust? A shiver of longing?

She wanted to believe she was too controlled, too careful, for any such displays of passion.

Now, he knew better.

She reached up to inspect her hair, then brushed away the wrinkles in her skirt, where his hand had gripped her waist. "So, we have a deal?"

If he were any sort of gentleman, he would rescind his

threat about revealing her involvement with the *Magazine for Misses,* release her from this promise, and find someone new.

"Yes," he said with a single, crisp nod, "we do."

"But courtship first." She did not meet his eye.

He tried to recall what Alistair had said about wooing, but the only words that he could find rattling around in his mind were his friend's taunt: *You're thinking of ruining.*

"Of course."

She moved toward the door, giving him a wide berth. "I should go. Before I'm missed."

Without waiting for his reply, she slipped silently from the room.

If he had any lingering doubts, he pushed them away without trouble. She was perfectly eligible to be his viscountess: noble lineage on her mother's side, respectable brothers, sisters married to a marquess and a duke. Pretty enough, in her way. She met every condition of the wager, and he . . . well, he'd never doubted he would win in the end.

Have you given any thought to what happens after?

Alistair's question of the night before poked at Miles's conscience, prodding him into movement. He set about snuffing each of the candles Daphne had lit.

She certainly could not claim to be ignorant of his reputation. And if that fiery first kiss had been any indication, the fact that she reviled him wasn't *all* bad.

He wished now that he hadn't agreed to wait two weeks. The rituals of courtship were beyond his expertise; his skills lay in quite another direction.

He'd just have to find some way to use the time to his advantage.

And speaking of time, why was he hiding in a dark room, if he was meant to be making his intentions toward Daphne known? Although, being subjected to the shrill notes of an inexpertly played flute filtering up through the floor had given him an idea. . . .

He returned to the drawing room just in time to join in the smattering of applause for the unfortunate flautist. Then, he spoke a few words to Lady Estley, who, after she had quelled her surprise and spoken to a footman in turn, presented him with a folio of music bound in green leather.

"Much obliged, ma'am," he said with a bow. Then he tucked the book beneath his arm and made his way to where Daphne was seated with her sisters.

"Might I persuade you to accompany me, Miss Burke?"

She parted her lips—to refuse, almost certainly, though they still bore the signs of his kiss—but a murmur of encouragement began nearby, accentuated by the sharp thrust of her younger sister's elbow.

Daphne stood. "I would be honored, my l—"

Then, evidently remembering how he'd teased her upstairs, she bit off the honorific, her chin jutting forward in a gesture of defiance that was becoming increasingly familiar to him, and which he enjoyed more than was wise.

He offered his free arm to escort her to the pianoforte.

"What do you think you're doing?" she demanded through clenched teeth masquerading as a smile.

"Courting you."

"Here? Tonight?"

He was vaguely aware of the whispered conversation around them, rising now to a buzz as anyone who hadn't heard about their dance at the Clearwaters' ball learned the news and speculation began to grow.

"A fortnight isn't much time," he reminded her. "And as I understand it, a proper courtship generally involves certain public actions. Unless you've decided you'd prefer an improp—"

"Certainly not." She seated herself at the instrument, her spine impossibly rigid.

"You needn't be distressed that I'll embarrass you. I've been told I have a fair voice."

She rolled her eyes, the expression hidden from the room. "I daresay at one time or another, you've been told you have a fair everything."

She'd meant the remark to be cutting, but he only returned a wicked smile. "More than fair, my dear. Now"—he leaned over her shoulder to place the book on the rack—"which of these do you think will suit?"

The words *Hibernian Melodies* gleamed up at them in gilt letters.

Her poet brother's verse, set to music.

Rather than respond with enthusiasm, as he'd hoped, she dropped her shoulders and her fingers, which had been resting silently against the keys. The magnificent instrument gave up a discordant *plink*.

He had a sudden memory of the Clearwaters' ballroom, and his toes curled in his shoes.

"All right, then?" he asked, using the pretense of turning pages to speak into her ear.

"Certainly."

Nothing sounded amiss in her voice; perhaps he'd misread her reaction. Still . . .

"If you'd rather something el—"

She flipped to a page two-thirds of the way through the book, nearly pinching his fingers in the process. "I believe this will just do for you."

Without further preamble, she played the opening bars of "The Fae's Lament," a song styled after an old folk ballad, made popular once again by the fashion for all things rustic and simple. Quickly, he scanned the lyrics of the unfamiliar tune, so as not to fall behind.

Her brother's words told the story of an Englishman who had taken a notion to visit Ireland and, having been thoroughly charmed by a certain green hill, had claimed it for his own. The green was no ordinary shade, however, but a reflection of the local fairy's fluttering, iridescent wings. The moment the hill was no longer her home, she departed and the green began to fade. Disillusioned with his conquest, the Englishman left, though he still possessed the land, now brown and sere.

Even Miles, who had never been particularly adept at understanding poetry, understood Mr. Galen Burke's metaphor for England's cultural and political mistreatment of Ireland.

And as for what Daphne meant by it? Well, that was no more opaque.

She might have no choice but to marry him, but she still thought Miles an unprincipled, insensitive rogue.

At least she didn't change the key mid-song or play sour notes or try to drown him out as some sort of protest. In fact, he doubted whether another soul in the room—with the possible exception of her sisters—even knew she was unhappy. Bright-eyed, she glanced back and up at him from time to time, a seasoned accompanist watching for cues, the better to weave the pianoforte with his voice. And once she had begun, the stiffness melted from her figure. She gave herself to the music so thoroughly, he took up the rhythm as much from the fluid motion of her fingers as from the notes themselves.

On some level, the performance—much like their kiss—revealed an unexpected connection between them; their innate responsiveness to one another belied the tenuousness of their bond.

But the peculiar shade of pink in her cheeks when they finished—somewhere between mortification and apoplexy—made it clear she did not see it that way at all.

Or, if she did, she took no pleasure from the observation.

She curtsied, absorbing the applause reluctantly, like a series of small blows to her body. And she winced when an elderly grande dame in the front row whispered to her neighbor in a carrying voice, "What a well-matched couple."

At that, Daphne spoke to him in a low voice. "Please, I'd like to return to my seat."

"I sense I've done something to displease you." He offered his arm, then surreptitiously dropped it to his side when she ignored the gesture.

"On the contrary. You behaved exactly as I ought to have expected."

"You played beautifully," he tried to reassure her a moment later.

"Then I suppose you may check another item off your list," she replied—a reference, he gathered, to the qualifications of his bride as specified by the conditions of the wager. "How gratified you must be by everyone's approval of your singing. I had no notion a rake's reputation could be rehabilitated with one sentimental air."

He mustered a bitter laugh. "Not with that song, certainly. As I think you well understood when you chose it. But in any case, you know that was not my object tonight."

"No, I'd say you were far more determined to make a mockery of me and my family, by performing a *foine* Irish melody"—her ordinary speech transformed into a thick, exaggerated brogue—"with a *foine* Irish lass."

"I would never—"

Daphne spoke over him. "How refreshing for a man of your . . . experience. There must be very few things of which that can be said."

In fact, he'd chosen the music out of kindness, misguided though the act might have been. Because he'd felt certain it would be familiar to her. Because he'd thought it might invoke the comforts of playing at home, instead of before an audience of nearly a hundred curious onlookers.

All of whom were surely watching this exchange with interest.

Both he and Daphne were breathing hard, as if they'd run a footrace around Grosvenor Square. Contempt flashed in her gaze. Until last night, he had not realized that it was possible for someone to have irises of that precise steely shade, capable of making the phrase *looking daggers* something less than figurative.

And he—well, it was all he could do to keep himself from pulling her into his arms and reminding her of their private duet in Estley's study, not half an hour before. He did not know if he'd ever understand what she wanted from this "courtship" she had demanded.

But when he looked deeper into her eyes, he knew she had not forgotten their kiss.

Her sister, Lady Ashborough, stood. "Forgive us, Lord Deveraux, but it's late, and I believe we must go home."

The marchioness swiftly led her younger sisters from the drawing room, pausing only to make their excuses to their host and hostess. Miles sank into one of the chairs they'd abandoned and watched them leave.

In the row in front of him, Lord Manwaring, almost the only other gentleman of Miles's age in attendance, tipped his head to whisper something to his stepmother, Lady Stalbridge. Then the pair of them enjoyed a low laugh—undoubtably at Miles's expense.

When he thought of what might have happened if Daphne's sister hadn't stepped between them . . .

Good God. Had he been bewitched?

Daphne's proposal had made it certain he would win his wager.

But if he weren't more careful, he'd lose whatever wits he had.

CHAPTER 9

"Sooo." Miles stretched the word, the preface to a question to which he already knew the answer. "What's on your calendar for today?"

He and Alistair were seated in Alistair's library, so named because of the single bookcase behind the door. A shaft of morning sunlight revealed half-empty shelves in desperate need of being polished. It was not that Alistair did not care about books. In fact, he had an impressive collection in his house in Devonshire—almost the only impressive thing about the place, in fact. It was also not the case that Alistair was indifferent to cleanliness—the rest of this house was spotless, in keeping with his rather fastidious nature.

But he had seven sisters: two older, five younger. Even those who were already married had recourse to this house now and again. And so Alistair had declared this room—hardly a room; two comfortable chairs and a writing table almost overfilled it—off limits to feminine interference. Including housemaids. And since he did not employ a butler for his town house, and his sisters kept the only footman busy fetching, carrying, and escorting them to and fro, Alistair's sanctuary sometimes grew a little dusty. He considered it a small price to pay for his peace of mind.

Occasionally, Miles wondered whether his friend had ever considered forbidding him access to it as well.

At present, Miles was enjoying the pot of coffee he had fetched from the breakfast room himself; Alistair was absorbed in the newspaper. From behind a wall of close-packed black type came a grunt in answer to Miles's question. And then, a few moments later, the crisp rattle of a turned page. And finally, a sigh.

"I have to take Freddie, Georgie, and Harry to the Duchesses' Garden Party," Alistair said before turning another page. The garden party was a much-anticipated annual event sponsored by the Duchess of Raynham, a noted botanist, and her mother-in-law, the dowager duchess. "My nose will be stopped up for a week." Flowers did not agree with him.

Ladies Georgiana, Frederica, and Harriet Haythorne were Alistair's youngest sisters. Harriet, in fact, was still in the schoolroom but managed to finagle her way into more than a few outings simply because, after fifteen years of being nominally responsible for his sisters' behavior, Alistair was too worn-out to resist.

"Oh. Well, er . . . I suppose I could escort them on your behalf," Miles suggested.

The upper half of the sheet of newsprint sagged, revealing Alistair's skeptical expression, one brow sharpy arched. "That's an astonishingly generous offer. What gives?"

"Can't a fellow offer assistance to a friend?"

Alistair closed the paper and laid it, folded, upon his knee. Waiting.

Miles squirmed. "All right, all right. I suppose you've heard about Miss Grey?"

"Mrs. Evans by this time, I daresay," Alistair corrected, making almost no effort at all to suppress the amused twitch of his lips.

"Very likely," Miles conceded. "So, I got to thinking that maybe you had the right of it the other night. Maybe I ought to try for Miss Burke after all."

"*Maybe I had—? Maybe you ought—?*" Alistair spluttered, sitting forward and slapping one hand against the newspaper in a noisy bid to keep it from sliding to the floor. "Did you even hear a word I said? Her brothers—"

"Would sooner kill me than welcome me into the family. Yes, yes."

And if they didn't succeed, Daphne might.

"But I think," Miles continued, "that you underestimate my charms. Why, only last evening, Miss Burke accompanied me in a lovely duet at the Estleys' musicale."

"Willingly?" Alistair's expression was one of patent disbelief. "I don't believe it."

"Oh, yes. I did a little of that . . . what was it you called it? *Wooing?*" He made a show of struggling to pronounce the word.

"She might sing with you," Alistair conceded, "but she's far too sensible to do more."

Miles couldn't help himself. "Care to make it interesting, old friend?"

Alistair wisely ignored him, though his eyes narrowed. "What makes you so certain you'll succeed?"

Miles opened his mouth to tell what he knew. He'd never kept secrets from his friend, even when Alistair probably would have preferred he had.

But somehow, revealing Daphne's secret didn't seem right.

"I just know," he said instead. "You, her family, and all the chaps at White's will have to accustom yourselves to the fact that I'm going to win my wager in the end—by marrying Daphne Burke."

Alistair looked thoughtful, and only marginally less skeptical. He unfolded the newspaper with a snap and held it up between them again. "Peculiarly unfortunate, then, that your invitation to her sister's annual garden party seems to have got lost in the mail."

Miles picked up his coffee cup and took a sip. "I haven't the faintest notion what you— Oh, that's right. The Duchess of Raynham is Miss Burke's sister, isn't she?"

"Good God, Miles." The wall of newsprint collapsed once more to reveal a stern-faced Alistair—though at least he hadn't resorted to calling him *Deveraux*. Yet.

"I just thought that, since Her Grace is always so particular about extending a *family* invitation to the Earl of Ryland"—indeed, the Duchesses' Garden Party was one of the only grand events of the London Season at which even young children were welcome—"and since you have, on occasion, led me to believe you think of me as the brother you never had . . ."

Alistair favored him with one of those looks, the sort he'd been giving Miles for nigh on seventeen years. "You might be interested to learn that Charlie paid me a call first thing this morning." *Charlie* was Charlotte, the second eldest of Alistair's siblings, more commonly addressed as the Honorable Mrs. Jefferson Powell. Miles hadn't long to wait for an explanation for that apparent non sequitur. "She was at the Estleys' musicale last night. Didn't you see her?"

"I, er—I hadn't the pleasure, no."

"Which is to say, you were too distracted by trying to win a smile from Miss Burke—who, by all accounts, hadn't one to spare for you. I believe Charlie's exact expression was, 'she looked as if she'd liked to have snapped his neck, given half a chance.'"

"Nonsense." Miles waved away Alistair's sister's assessment, preferring to think of the look in Daphne's eyes after they'd kissed.

With a grimace, Alistair folded the newspaper again, laid it on the table, and stood. "You are constitutionally incapable of believing someone might dislike you."

The room was not of a size to permit pacing, but he stood with his hands behind his back, examining a rather muddy-looking oil painting of a landscape that was decidedly not England; Miles knew for a fact he'd been studying that same picture for a decade at least, whenever he had something unpleasant to chew over.

"I've known that for a long time, of course," he went on without turning to face Miles. "But from the moment Sinclair laid down that first wager, you seemed . . . *obsessed* is not too strong a word, I think, with the possibility that somewhere out there might be a young lady immune to your charms, Deveraux."

Alistair only used his title when things were serious. Miles sat up a little straighter in his chair. "I've always enjoyed a challenge," he agreed. What was so wrong with trying to prove he was an amiable fellow?

At that, Alistair's left hand gripped his right wrist more tightly. "I suppose there is nothing I can say that would persuade you to set your sights elsewhere."

Vaguely, Miles wondered whether it was Miss Burke or his own friend Alistair hoped to protect.

But naturally it must be the former—the Earl of Ryland was nothing if not a gentleman.

Miles tried to weigh Alistair's remark with the seriousness it deserved, undistracted by Daphne's proposal, her soft lips, or the imagined look on her face this morning when his gift arrived—he'd hit on just the thing to please her, this time; proof that he knew her better than she believed.

"So," he ventured after a moment, "that'd be a *no* on the garden party, then?"

Regardless of Alistair's answer, Miles didn't intend to squander an opportunity to see her again today. She was the one who had asked for a courtship, after all.

Alistair's shoulders rose and fell on a noisy breath, but when he turned to face Miles, he was wearing a smile, albeit a weary one. "The girls and I will meet you in Curzon Street at two o'clock. Don't be late."

Daphne had managed to avoid her sisters' interrogation after the musicale by claiming a headache.

But no excuse could keep the memories of the evening from flooding her mind.

Those moments in Lord Estley's study were exactly the sort of dangerous research Lady Stalbridge had warned her about. When she had made her scandalous proposal, a moment of panic had followed as she wondered whether Lord Deveraux might refuse to go along as a matter of principle.

But of course, she needn't have worried. As he'd told her at the Clearwaters' ball, he was no gentleman. And his insistence on kissing her was precisely the sort of behavior that she intended to expose in her essay on rakes.

You didn't have to kiss him back. . . .

As for that duet in the drawing room, how dare he expect her to perform her Irishness in front of an audience of English aristocrats, to perform at all, in front of any audience? She had never in her life been the center of attention, the focus of every eye.

Of course, she still hadn't, because he had not been perfectly honest about his abilities, either. He didn't have a *fair* voice. He sang beautifully, in a strong, bright tenor that had made her skin pebble and the fine hairs rise along her arms. She had chanced a glance or two toward the audience, to see if they were equally surprised by the discovery, and had found them mesmerized, despite the song of warning she'd chosen.

If his charms had such power, what chance did she—or her essay—have?

After passing a largely sleepless night, she had risen feeling no better than she had when she'd retreated to her room. Nevertheless, when she arrived in the breakfast parlor, it was clear that her sisters' concern for her health no longer outweighed their curiosity.

Before the footman had even offered to serve Daphne, Cami nodded to dismiss him.

"Where's Gabriel?" Daphne asked. She had hoped her brother-in-law's wry sense of humor and easygoing manner would make the meal bearable.

"Raynham called at an ungodly hour and dragged him to breakfast at his club," Cami explained. "Said his house has been made uninhabitable by preparations for the Duchesses' Garden Party this afternoon."

Daphne glanced toward the window and was relieved to see bright skies. She'd forgotten that Erica and Guin's annual event was today.

"Will Lord Deveraux be attending, do you suppose?" Bell asked sweetly.

Suddenly Daphne had to will her shoulders not to sag.

Of course that devil, Deveraux, would find some way to finagle an invitation.

Cami peered at Daphne over the top rim of her spectacles. "Yes, has he given you any indication of his intentions?"

Though Cami was twenty and more years their elder, it would have been an exaggeration to describe her behavior toward her youngest sisters as motherly. Despite having four children of her own, clucking and fussing had never really been in her nature. But since Daphne and Bell frequently spent more than half the year with her, moving in society far beyond that of their Dublin upbringing thanks to her own marriage, she still held herself responsible for them. She would always expect to exert a shaping force over their lives.

Daphne had hoped to have a bit more time to acclimate

her eldest sister—and herself—to the idea of Lord Deveraux's courtship.

"I haven't the faintest idea what you mean," she said, busying herself with selecting a slice of toast from the rack at the center of the table.

"Let's see. Last night's duet. A dance at the Clearwaters'." Bell ticked off each occasion on the fingers of one hand as she listed them. "And of course, we mustn't leave out that whispered conversation in the moonlight. . . ."

At that last item, Cami's teacup, which had been on its way to her lips, clattered back into its saucer. "I beg your pardon?"

"We exchanged a few words on the balcony," Daphne explained, "when I stepped out for a breath of fresh air. Nothing more."

Cami drew in a breath—rather too ragged to be calming—before she went on. "Bell also told me about a column in some magazine. . . ."

Bellis had revealed her secret to Cami? Daphne's pulse began to hammer so loudly it drowned out every other thought. A sputtering protest rose to her lips.

"The *anonymous* advice column," Bell explained, silencing her with a pointed stare. "*No one knows* who writes it."

"That is the usual meaning of anonymous, yes," said Cami, a quick frown of befuddlement notching the space between her dark brows. "But my concern is for our sister, not some gossip peddler. In any case, it seems this writer exposed Lord Deveraux's participation in a most ungentlemanly wager about his impending marriage, which caused the young lady in question to cry off."

"Don't you see?" Bell shook her head at Daphne, as if impatient with her obtuseness. "He's lost Miss Grey, but he still hopes to win that wager—with you!"

Cami shot their younger sister a look, as if they'd rehearsed a slightly different version of this conversation before Daphne's arrival. "If it's true that the viscount is desperate for a bride . . . ," she began gently.

Desperate.

"Are you insinuating that a handsome, titled, charming man could have no other reason for pursuing me than winning a bet?" Daphne demanded.

The two of them were quick to deny any such motive. Too quick.

"We just don't want to see you hurt," said Bell. "You aren't accustomed to being the object of a flirtation."

In other words, they feared Daphne—the poor, overlooked wallflower, teetering near the edge of the shelf—might be desperate too. Desperate enough to let Lord Deveraux take advantage of her.

Oh, it was intolerable to be treated this way, with pity masquerading as concern.

It would never occur to them that their sister could be clever enough to work things the other way 'round and best the rake herself.

The truth burned in her chest, like the heat beneath a kettle on the verge of screaming. Before coherent words could make their way to her lips, however, a footman entered bearing an unusual floral arrangement, with pale, spiky leaves. No, not leaves. Feathers. Quills. . . .

He laid the strange sort of bouquet on the table between Daphne and her elder sister.

"That's odd," Cami said, though she spared the bundle of quills no more than a glance. "I wasn't expecting anything today."

Gabriel, bursting with pride over his wife's novels, had a standing order for fresh writing supplies to be delivered monthly. *Quills to Cami* was very nearly as apt an aphorism for superfluity as *coals to Newcastle*.

"Well, take them to my study," she directed with a wave of her hand.

The footman gave a discreet cough. "Forgive me, milady. But these were addressed to Miss Burke."

Attached to the bundle of quills by a slender green ribbon was a note. With a catch in her breath, she unfolded the square of paper. *Miss Daphne Burke,* it read, in a bold scrawl. The shop clerk's hand, she supposed. Until she spied the tiny drawing of a bee in the corner.

She jerked away her hand, nearly toppling her teacup.

"Are they from him?" demanded Bell.

After mopping up a bit of spilled tea with her napkin, Daphne managed to nod.

Why would that devil, Deveraux, send her pens? Send her anything at all?

Because you told him to court you, you eejit.

When the servant had left them again, Cami pushed her plate aside and dragged her teacup closer by its delicate saucer. She was studying the quills, her head tilted to one side. "An interesting choice of gift. . . ."

"A practical one," Daphne countered. "I'm sure even he knows that many young ladies keep themselves busy with letters, or a diary."

"But given your family connections, perhaps he hoped to encourage you to something more! Poetry, or a novel. . . ."

Bell made a little choking sound, but passed it off as a crumb caught in her throat. "How thoughtful," she agreed after taking a sip of tea, a mischievous twinkle in her eye. "Just like last night. . . ."

Color flooded Daphne's face, though of course her sister was referring to the scene in the drawing room. She could have no notion of what had taken place in Lord Estley's study.

"You find that a thoughtful gesture? Being asked to play

something of my brother's? Perhaps next I can read aloud from one of Cami's books. . . ."

"It seemed clear he hoped you would approve of his choice of music," Cami pointed out. "And, well, don't you? I never realized you felt such animosity toward Galen's success as a writer. . . ." One finger traced the rim of her teacup. "Or mine, for that matter."

"I don't, of course," Daphne hurriedly tried to explain. "It's only that I—"

"And for two people who know each other so little," Bell said before Daphne could complete the thought, "you performed together remarkably well." A dreamy sigh whooshed from her lungs. "Imagine being serenaded on an ordinary evening by that voice, when no one else was around. . . ."

Nothing was going to plan. Daphne had never considered that her family was likely to push her *toward* Lord Deveraux— and all thanks to his mocking gift.

Their encouragement of the courtship at least had the advantage of making her research easier, but what would they say later, when she refused to wed him?

"But surely you disapprove of Lord Deveraux as a suitor," she ventured. "You would not want to see me married to such a man."

"If his conduct has been what is often claimed," Cami said, "I disapprove of it, certainly. Though there are often innocuous explanations for what appears to the world to be outrageous, unforgivable behavior." Daphne knew now she was thinking at least as much of the stories that had swirled about her own husband before they married. "As to whether I disapprove of *him* . . ." She paused to take a sip of tea— an uncharacteristic hesitation. "Well, I should want to know him better before making a judgment, either way." A faraway look settled over her eyes, and her lips quirked at some memory. "You know what they say about husbands and reformed rakes."

Daphne nodded. "I do indeed."

She laid a hand on the bundle of quills, and though one corner of the note pricked her palm warningly, she tightened her grip. The entire conversation only confirmed that she must write her essay and remind young women of the true danger such men presented.

And there was something particularly satisfying in the notion of Lord Deveraux being hoist with his own petard.

CHAPTER 10

From the street, Laurens House was comparatively unassuming: a double-front brownstone, rows of evenly spaced windows, and an engraved brass knocker. It might have been the home of any well-to-do gentleman; nothing about it in particular marked it out as the home of the Duke of Raynham.

What set Laurens House apart were the gardens, a rarity in Mayfair.

Alistair's sisters were chattering about them when Miles joined their party. They were still chattering as the five of them waited in the receiving line, which wound through an elegantly furnished drawing room from whose windows the gardens could be glimpsed. He heard talk of spectacular roses and a display of exotics brought back from far-flung travels.

For his own part, Miles was considerably more interested in the duke and duchess.

He'd seen them before, of course, but not since he'd met Daphne. And, well, Alistair's words and present circumstances had cast the whole family in rather a different light. As they paid their respects to the dowager duchess, the present duke's stepmama, Miles was almost too distracted to weigh in on Alistair's apologies for bringing an uninvited guest. Freddie had to kick the side of his foot twice before he realized that he ought to bow and beg the woman's pardon on his own behalf.

"Not at all," she said with a smile. Her blue eyes twinkled knowingly. "You are most welcome, Lord Deveraux."

The duke did not smile—in fact, Miles wondered whether such an expression might not cause the man's granite-hewn features to crack. He said, "Deveraux," in a convincing approximation of a greeting, however, and Miles, who was trying to forget everything he knew about Daphne's brothers-in-law and their proclivities for spilling blood, bowed his head in acknowledgment and hurried Freddie down the line.

He searched the duchess's face for some familiar feature, a reminder of why he'd come. But Daphne, who looked nothing like her sister, the Marchioness of Ashborough, looked even less like her sister, the Duchess of Raynham. Not in the eyes, which in the duchess's case were a warm hazel brown, almost golden in the afternoon light, and certainly not in the hair, which was a breathtaking, scandalous shade of red.

Miles bowed and apologized for himself this time, but the duchess waved away his concerns. "What's one more?" That lack of restraint, a willingness to defy the rules of so-called good society, was the first family trait he noted, and one he generally admired.

As a philosophy of entertaining, however, it meant the house was almost uncomfortably full of guests. The receiving line wound through the drawing room with all the alacrity of a river of molasses. And in the dining room, opposite, people crowded together, talking around mouthfuls of watercress sandwiches and lobster salad.

Miles began to despair of ever even spotting Daphne in this mass of humanity.

The gardens, when he and Lady Frederica eventually reached them, were a welcome respite. Though there were ladies and gentlemen everywhere, walking arm in arm, admiring the abundance of roses in every imaginable shade, at least a fellow could breathe.

Well, most fellows could, anyway. Turning Freddie loose to follow her brother's sneezes, Miles set off in the opposite direction, down a path of springy, close-cropped grass.

Outdoors, it was easier to ignore the other guests' snubs and cuts, easier to tell himself that they were turning away to inspect an unusual flower, and not because they refused to risk brushing shoulders with a man so low, he would make wagers involving ladies. He thought of Alistair's claim that he was incapable of believing himself disliked. But the truth of the matter was somehow more embarrassing yet.

He was incapable of being alone . . . and to ensure such a fate never befell him, he was willing to marry a woman who disliked him intensely.

And speak of the devil . . . was not that Daphne, seated on a bench in a rose-bordered bower, enjoying the attentions of not one but three lovelorn swains?

His heart began to thrum in a way that he would have surely called jealousy in anyone else. But really, why shouldn't Daphne attract gentlemen's notice? She was witty, with a winning smile when it could be coaxed to appear; she had lovely, expressive eyes, and soft, kissable lips. . . .

The woman in the bower was Bellis, however. Not Daphne. And the relief he experienced at that discovery was not something he cared to investigate too closely. In fact, he turned away rather than approach her and see the contempt in her eyes, which were no doubt a familiar shade of steely blue. Daphne might not look like her elder sisters, but the resemblance between the two youngest sisters was striking.

"Lord Deveraux?"

He could pretend not to have heard his name, pretend that the hum of conversation, the lush shrubbery and flowers, had absorbed the sound of her voice. He took three strides back toward the house, then paused and glanced over his shoulder. She had risen and was coming after him.

"You were looking for Daphne, I suppose?"

The question was not as hostile as he had expected. Still, he hesitated. "I, er . . ."

"She's upstairs. With Vivi and the boys."

He didn't understand a word she'd said, but he smiled his gratitude nonetheless and focused on the first detail. "Upstairs?" Above them was nothing but brilliant blue skies, hardly even a cloud.

She tipped her head toward the house. "The conservatory. On the roof."

"Oh, of course. Much obliged." And before he could ask her anything further, questions that could not be so easily answered, he bowed and moved to go back, in the direction from whence he'd come, aware of her watching him until he'd disappeared around a bend in the path.

As he made his way through the lower level of the house, toward the stairs, he understood how a salmon might feel, swimming upstream—particularly if all the other salmon had been traveling the opposite direction and had been determined to avoid him. But a floor above that, the crowds cleared. He passed the family apartments, the nursery and schoolroom, without laying eyes on another person. Had he misunderstood Miss Bellis's directions? Surely any minute someone would call out for him to stop and demand to know where he thought he was going.

He tried very hard not to think of what Alistair had said about the duke's ability to slip a knife between a man's ribs without ever making a sound.

At the top of a narrow staircase, he passed through a low door and emerged into another garden, built on the flat portion of the roof at the back of the house, with a small glasshouse that shone like a diamond in the sun.

Out of nowhere appeared a slight, copper-haired boy of

about six, who tilted his head, looked Miles up and down, and said, "Who're you?"

"Deveraux," he said, when blinking to clear his vision of sunspots didn't also make the elfin-looking child disappear.

"Oh. They've been talking about you," said the boy, who then scurried away without offering to introduce himself in turn.

Here, the garden was contained in pots and stone-bordered beds, and the only shade came from a simple wooden arbor, where Daphne and a dark-haired woman were seated on a bench. As he approached, another child leaped into his path, this one a little older, with brown hair, carrying a wooden sword. "Password," he demanded.

Miles considered his options. "Flowers?"

The boy shook his head.

"Shrubbery?"

The sword rose menacingly. "Last try."

"Rowan Arthur," scolded the dark-haired woman.

"Aw, Aunt Vivi, you've spoiled it," the boy cried, stepping aside, his weapon drooping at his side.

"I'm much obliged, ma'am," Miles said, approaching the bench. Both women stood. "I'm sure I would've been run through before I could work it out."

"It's password," Daphne said, sounding vaguely amused.

"The password is *password*?"

She nodded, a smile threatening to curve her lips. "Lady Viviane Laurens, I'm sure you know Lord Deveraux."

"By reputation." The duke's sister gave a shallow curtsy as Miles bowed.

"And this is my nephew," Daphne said, laying a hand on the boy's shoulder, "the Marquess of Hawes."

The lad tucked his weapon into his belt and thrust out a hand.

Miles shook hands with him. "An honor, my lord. And I suppose that was your brother I saw a moment ago?"

"Percy," the boy acknowledged with a grimace. "I might've known better than to let him guard the door. Sorry, Aunt Daphne."

"It's all right," Daphne said, still not meeting Miles's eye. "We knew our sanctuary would be breached eventually. Your mama's plants are the buried treasure of the garden party."

The boy gave a somber nod.

"Come," said Lady Viviane, laying a hand around her nephew's shoulders, "we should go down. I didn't realize guests had already begun to arrive."

"You'll find quite a crush below," Miles told her. "I can't imagine why more of them haven't sought refuge up here."

"They require sustenance before making the climb," explained the boy and then added in a confidential whisper, "That's a fancy way of saying they all come to drink my papa's wine cellar dry."

Daphne made a choked noise. "Rowan! Where did you hear that? Have you been eavesdropping again?"

"Downstairs," insisted Lady Viviane. "They're your guests, too, Lord Hawes. And yours, Lord Percival," she added in a slightly louder voice, but the other boy did not emerge from his hiding place.

"Isn't Aunt Daphne coming?" asked the elder boy.

Lady Viviane and Daphne exchanged what could only be described as a series of speaking glances, accompanied by furtive hand movements. Miles could not make heads or tails of what they were attempting to communicate, and perhaps Daphne faced a similar struggle, for in the end, Lady Viviane heaved a resigned sigh and said, "I'm sure she'll be down soon."

Daphne nodded. "In a few moments."

With only one backward, chiding glance for Daphne, Lady Viviane led young Lord Hawes away. Near the door, they were joined by his younger brother, whose red hair was now sticking up on end and whose cheeks appeared to be streaked with blood.

"That'll be the juice of some berry he's found. Cook hides the shrubs up here, hoping to protect them long enough to bake a tart," Daphne explained with a shake of her head, watching Lady Viviane shepherd them through the door. "I would say I hope that the child Erica is expecting is a girl, but given the sorts of things Bell and I got into at that age, I fear it wouldn't be much of a reprieve."

Miles chuckled. "Now, why am I not surprised to learn you were a mischief-maker?"

"At least *I* outgrew the habit."

He ushered her back to the shaded bench. "I'm not so sure."

"And just what is that remark supposed to mean?" she demanded, rounding on him.

"If you had sworn off mischief entirely, you wouldn't be the favorite aunt," he said, sitting down in defiance of good manners and patting the space beside him. "You wouldn't be involved with *Goode's Guide to Misconduct*. And you wouldn't have stayed up here with me."

Despite looking affronted, she did sit down, though farther away than he'd hoped.

When a long silent moment passed, he asked, "Are you afraid that if we converse, you might discover something likeable about me? That you might find me amiable, amusing, attractive?"

Her lips twitched. "Not in the slightest."

"Then I wonder why you insisted upon a courtship at all. If it distresses you, we could just go ahead and get married without it." He slid closer and lightly covered her hand with his. "I can have a special license in hand first thing tomorrow."

She jerked free of his touch. If it were not made of stone, the bench would have swayed with the force of her movement. "You needn't keep reminding me of your power over me, my lord."

Miles disguised his own uncertainty by gripping the edge of the bench.

"I suppose that's why you sent me those quills—to mock me, as you did with that song."

"Mock you?" he echoed, genuinely astonished. "Is it not a custom of proper courtship for a gentleman to send a token of his esteem?"

"Gentlemen send *flowers*." The governess-y tone was back, a sort of exaggerated patience, as if she were delivering a lesson in etiquette to an unruly boy. "Bellis gets them by the cartload. Daisies, usually."

If he hadn't been watching, he would have missed the slight wobble of her chin as she spoke those words.

He didn't think she begrudged her sister those gifts. Not exactly, anyway. But with every bouquet of flowers, every reminder of her talented and famous elder siblings, she swallowed a pang of something like jealousy. Often enough that it had become little more than a reflexive tickle in her throat.

And he had unwittingly made that irritation worse.

"I'm quite aware *gentlemen* send flowers." He forced a lightness into his tone. "And setting aside any debate over whether that dubious distinction applies to me, I did in fact speak with the clerk at the florist's shop, who explained to me the botanical meaning of your lovely name." It was a source of some amusement in certain circles that all the Burke siblings were named after plants. "But a few branches from a shrub laden with poisonous berries didn't seem quite the thing."

That made her snicker. Reluctantly, to be sure. Just the tiniest hint of a laugh.

Nevertheless, his chest swelled with pride; he always enjoyed pleasing women. "I thought quills would be at least as apt as Bellis's daisies. Something befitting the woman you really are. Sharp, yes, but soft too. Strong, but delicate."

Like most women, in one way or another, he supposed. But they'd seemed to him a particularly perfect gift for Daphne.

"I pictured you writing your column with them," he finished simply.

She would start out with a straight spine and a spotless page. But as she went on, warming toward her subject, her quill would fly. Gradually, as if pouring a bit of herself into her words, she would bend her head closer to the paper.

He'd imagined pressing his lips to the soft skin that peeked between the collar of her dress and the few stray wisps of hair that tickled the back of her neck.

After a moment, she asked in a whisper, "Does that mean you intend to permit me to keep writing?"

The question was so unexpected, it took him a moment to comprehend. "Once we're married, you mean?"

Her chin dipped, almost imperceptibly.

"I will *not* permit it, my dear," he said. At that, her head spun and her gaze snapped to his. "I will insist upon it. I for one am eager to read your retraction."

"My *retraction*?"

"Oh, yes." He lifted his brows suggestively. "It should be easy enough to pen. Once you've discovered just how enjoyable it can be, being married to a rake."

Was it his imagination, or was the spark in her eyes brighter now? Warmer?

Could it be that she enjoyed being teased?

Oh, but that was promising indeed.

"I assume you refer to that old saw about *reformed* rakes." She tilted her head toward him and favored him with a look he was fast coming to consider her "Miss Busy B. expression"—part disapproving governess, part insufferable know-all, part inquisitive young lady who couldn't quite make herself look away, though she knew she ought. "Tell me, my lord. Do you have any intention of reforming?"

He stretched out his legs and leaned back as much as the bench would allow. In a more comfortable chair, his posture would have been described as a sprawl—a blatant invitation for her gaze to travel his body, head to toe. "Which of my vices would you have me give up? My bootmaker? My tailor? Surely, you do not want a shabby bridegroom, ma'am."

Again, the quirk of lips that were determined not to betray a smile.

"Or perhaps you object to my French cologne?"

"Your French brandy, rather," she retorted. "Your gambling. Your . . ." Her voice dropped to a whisper, barely audible above the chatter rising from the garden below. ". . . *flirtations.*"

A little frippery of a hat sat perched high upon her head. Beneath it, her hair was more simply arranged today, the sort of coiffure that could be mussed by a man's careless fingers without anyone being the wiser. And her gown was pale, diaphanous muslin, embroidered with a green vine and the occasional pink rosebud. Perfect for a garden party. On this warm day, its skirts clung to her limbs most provocatively.

He raked his gaze over her, tipping his head to the side. "Must I stop flirting with you?"

Her lips parted and her breasts rose. A gasp, though he hadn't heard it.

A gasp of pleasure.

Was it possible no one had ever flirted with her before? Or perhaps Daphne, so suspicious, so quick to take offense, had never understood?

Either way, he intended to use this moment to his advantage. *This* was the sort of courtship he understood.

"You blush most prettily," he said, reaching up to whisk a knuckle over one soft cheek.

She caught her plump lower lip between her teeth, rather than betray herself with another gasp. "Do I?"

God, but she was such an innocent—just the sort of sweet, simple perfection to tempt a man whose palate had grown jaded.

He leaned toward her, ready to capture her mouth in a kiss, when the rasp of hinges shattered the illusion of privacy. "The door," she explained. Voices began to float over the rooftop garden.

He started to sit up straighter, to put some distance between them.

She reached out a hand, tangled her fingers with his, and stood, tugging him to his feet. "Come on."

"Where are you taking me?"

"The glasshouse."

CHAPTER 11

When Daphne had retreated to the rooftop garden earlier that afternoon, she hadn't done so with any sort of plan in mind. Yet somehow, things had gone awry anyway.

She hadn't expected his answer about the quills and her writing. Certainly hadn't anticipated his evident intention of flirting with her—though of course that was how a man like Deveraux would think of courtship.

But most unlooked for of all had been her reaction. Her awareness of his attention, the way it made her pulse leap and her blood rush to places it shouldn't.

She had long since decided that the fact she found him attractive was nothing more than that—a fact. Nothing that required any alteration in her behavior. Just as a sunny day, though beautiful, did not *require* a person to go outside and tip her face to the sky. A lady could admire its golden warmth through the window and then go on about her tasks without risking pink cheeks and freckles.

But when he sat so close, and looked so perfectly, impossibly handsome, and acted so attentive, it was almost more than she could do to walk away. She'd tried to remind herself it was an act, the courtship she'd demanded. But when no one else was around, it seemed almost real.

He'd been going to kiss her. Again.

And she'd been going to let him. Again.

Then the door had opened and she'd imagined, just for a moment, the scandal that would erupt if they were seen alone, under the arbor, in an embrace. It would confirm him as a rake in the eyes of society and give her the last details she needed for her essay.

It might also make it necessary for her to marry him after all.

Cami would insist, which meant Gabriel would agree with his wife—conveniently forgetting his own rakish past. Tristan, Erica's husband, would look stern and say something about duty, and Erica would ignore all of it, but would not disagree with her husband either. Bell would express wide-eyed concern, while worrying not-so-secretly about what Daphne's disgrace would do to her own chances. And if her brother Paris, who still thought of her as a child, ever caught wind of it . . .

She shivered at the thought.

"Are you chilled?" Lord Deveraux spoke low behind her, a teasing note in his voice.

Sweat prickled along Daphne's spine and under her arms, but she couldn't entirely blame the steamy air of the glasshouse for that either. With swift, discreet movements of her fingers, she unbuttoned the top button of her dark green spencer.

"What is all this, anyway?" he asked.

"Exotics, mostly. Specimens Erica brought back from her West Indian voyage."

He gave a knowing nod as he inspected the nearest plants, though Daphne felt certain he couldn't identify one from another.

"Just don't . . . touch anything, all right?" she said. "They may look pretty and delicate, but some of them are deadly."

A smile tugged at his mouth. "I'm familiar with the type. So why did you bring us in here?" He glanced once more around the glass-walled room. "Not much in the way of privacy."

Had he been expecting her to take him to a place where he could kiss her senseless without anyone knowing?

What lay beyond the conservatory was vaguely distorted in places, by condensation or a rippled pane of glass, but on the whole, the view was clear enough. They could easily see and be seen. "These plants are what draw people to the Duchesses' Garden Party—well, the sort of people who care about botany, anyway. In here, I can claim to be showing you some of my sister's prize specimens, and it's obvious we aren't trying to hide anything. Whereas if we'd been spotted together in the shade beneath the arbor, people would have assumed . . ."

He tilted his head and his brows rose. "And would that be such a terrible thing? For people to assume? After all, we are to be wed."

The word made her heart stutter. "They will tell themselves, and others, that you are merely desperate to win your bet," she said, thinking of the conversation that morning over breakfast. "And that the poor, pathetic wallflower must be so desperate to get married, she's willing to go along with it."

"Well"—his nose wrinkled as he sniffed the purple and orange flower in front of him—"that doesn't paint either of us in a flattering light, does it?" She reached out and touched his shoulder, to discourage him from leaning any closer to the plant. He glanced first at her hand and then up at her. "Though I suppose it's no worse than the truth."

Was he having second thoughts? Actually feeling some regret over the position he'd put her in?

No, she doubted Lord Deveraux was capable of that sort of reflection.

She had gotten herself into this mess, with a few poorly chosen words and a hasty solution.

He shrugged and stepped to the next table of plants. She

dropped her hand to her side again. "I say, that's a strange looking fellow. '*Dionaea muscipula* (Venus's-flytrap). Carolina,'" he read slowly off the printed label, the Latin awkward on his tongue.

"The boys' favorite. It eats bugs."

"Eats?" he echoed, incredulous.

She picked up a nearby pencil and pointed to a pair of pink half-moon-shaped leaves, fringed with spikes. "An insect stumbles along, or is lured, perhaps by the color, and then—" At the slightest brush back and forth of the pencil tip, the leaves snapped shut like a mouth with teeth.

His eyes flared. "A carnivorous plant." He shook his head in disbelief. "These New World species are a bit alarming. I think I prefer our English roses."

"Well, they don't lure the bees to their doom, it's true, but those thorns aren't exactly sweet and gentle. And we've any number of poisonous plants that seem innocent. Mistletoe, for example."

"I'm not sure I would classify mistletoe as innocent."

Innocent didn't begin to describe the expression on his face, either, the suggestive movement of his mouth, the knowing lift of his brows.

It was an expression that made her . . . well, hot inside. Or it would, if she weren't already flushed from the temperature in the glasshouse.

"I don't think you can blame your Christmas party misdeeds on a plant," she said stiffly.

He laughed. "How right you are. Too many games of snapdragon must have been the culprit, then. All those brandy-soaked raisins."

She sent him a chiding glance. "You are incorrigible."

"And you are delightfully easy to provoke." He reached for her hand and threaded it through his arm, so that they had to walk side by side, though the space between the plant-laden tables and various large stone urns was almost too narrow. She was aware every time his thigh brushed hers. "This courtship scheme of yours has been most enlightening."

"That is the goal of courtship, is it not? To learn something of the character of the person to whom you propose to tie yourself for the rest of your life?"

"Is it?" The question sounded almost genuine. "I confess I do not have any prior experience."

"But you and Miss Grey—"

"I had neither opportunity nor need to court her. Her father sought the match and Miss Grey, being a dutiful daughter, agreed. I saw her out of company only once prior to that fateful encounter in the library—though I suppose I cannot really say that incident was 'out of company,' can I?" He laughed, but the sound was rueful. "In any case, we had not enjoyed more than five minutes of private conversation, all the time it took for me to request the honor of her hand and her to give it—reluctantly, as it turned out." He paused, as if wrestling with the implication of those words. "I did not know she fancied someone else."

"Nor did I," said Daphne. "If she had explained as much in her letter, I might have counseled her differently."

"Oh?" The brightness returned to his voice, but any hint of sincerity had gone. "Would you have advised her to go through with the marriage instead? Wait until she could style herself as a viscountess before cuckolding me with her coal merchant?"

An instinctive stiffness spread down Daphne's spine. "I beg your pardon?"

She would have withdrawn her hand from his arm, but he tightened his grip. "Forgive me." His voice was quieter again, but intense. She was almost glad they were side by side and she couldn't look directly at his face. "I didn't mean that. I only wish she would have been honest with me—but what right had I to expect any such thing? Was I honest with her?"

"About the wager, you mean?"

The shoulder nearest her hitched in a sort of shrug. She glanced up at him again, but he was deliberately avoiding her gaze now, his eyes tracing the path of a bougainvillea vine being trained to climb the building's frame to the ceiling.

Her head was spinning. She'd thought she understood the situation, understood him. Nothing about Lord Deveraux gave the impression of depth and complexity.

Was it possible his affable façade was the most complex thing about the man?

"Do you mean—? Was there—*is* there—someone you wish to marry?" She thought of what he'd told her, the night of the Clearwaters' ball. "Someone, perhaps, who does not fulfill the terms of the wager?"

"*Is there someone I wish to . . .* ?" A sort of laugh gusted from his chest. "What questions are these, my dear? And from you? How is a gentleman to answer them?"

"But you said—" She would have reminded him that he'd told her, twice at least, that he was no gentleman.

He spoke over her, clearly anticipating what she had been about to say. "I know my duty. I struck a bargain with you, Miss Burke. One I have every intention of fulfilling."

Those words gave her something like a twinge of conscience. She was the one who had made that pact, fully intending to break it. "If you were to lose the wager, would you be . . . ? That is, if very large sums are involved, I suppose you might be left necessitous."

"A gentleman's debts of honor are not really about the money, as I suspect you already know. But rest assured," he added, patting her hand, "your future husband is not poor."

Nevertheless, she had clearly struck a nerve. Beneath her palm, a fresh tension had spread into his forearm.

"Forgive me," she said. "I did not mean to be impertinent."

How on earth had the conversation worked its way to this point? Was she really begging his forgiveness?

"Not at all," he insisted. "As you said, a more open understanding of one another is the goal of courtship."

"But you've just said you weren't honest with Miss Grey. How do I know you are telling the truth now?"

His mouth pulled to one side as he considered the question. "I suppose you don't. However"—with a nod of his head, he directed her attention to the people milling about the rooftop garden; there was little chance he and Daphne had gone unobserved—"I'd say we're nearing the point in our courtship at which speculations give way to intentions, and your eldest brother, your sisters' husbands, perhaps even your father, will soon be making some inquiries about mine."

She squeezed shut her eyes, trying unsuccessfully to prevent a mental image of how that conversation would go. The distance between Dublin and London was an advantage, at least—though she'd never considered it one before. Papa would know nothing of it until it was too late. And Paris, normally so devoted to his business in the House of Commons, had stayed at his home in Berkshire this spring because of his wife Rosamund's imminent confinement for the birth of their third child. But such a meeting, even if only with Gabriel and Tristan—she almost laughed aloud at the thought; it was like saying "being locked in a room with *only* a tiger and a bear"—would surely be bad enough.

"And if they are not satisfied with the answers?" she ventured, reluctantly opening her eyes.

He was looking down at her. "How old are you, Daphne?"

"One and twenty."

The way he'd asked the question made her suspect he already knew the answer, and his crisp nod when she told him only confirmed it. "Old enough to decide for yourself, then."

What exactly was she meant to be choosing between?

She'd thought she knew, but now, she was not quite so sure.

On the surface, he seemed to expect her to defy her family if they forbade the match—naturally, since that was the only way to keep her secret from being revealed. But beneath that, somewhere in that hidden layer she had only begun to explore, was he preparing himself to be rejected—again?

As if to confirm her suspicions, he turned, letting her arm slip free of his, so they were no longer touching, though they stood face-to-face and still closer than was proper.

"I *am* sorry if the quills weren't quite the thing," he said, with something like sincerity in his warm brown eyes as he looked down at her. "It seemed to me to be the sort of gift a writer would like."

He thought of her as a writer. He wanted her to keep writing—though probably he would balk at an essay on rakes, if he ever learned of it. But still. She hadn't even begun to think of herself as a writer. She'd certainly never expected it of Lord Deveraux . . . Miles. . . .

Without conscious thought, she'd risen onto the balls of her feet, bringing them closer, almost close enough for a kiss. Just a swift, meaningless peck, perhaps on the cheek. Well, not *meaningless*. She wanted to express her gratitude for the gift. But not a kiss like the one in Lord Estley's study. Nothing to leave a body breathless and yearning. . . .

"Why, Miss Burke." The woman's voice came from behind her, near the doorway to the glasshouse, the hinge of which evidently had been oiled more recently than that of the entrance to the rooftop garden. "Fancy it being you."

Daphne turned awkwardly, her lips still slightly puckered, to discover Lady Stalbridge standing in the entry, gripping the hand of her niece, Isabella. Both of them were wide-eyed, though Isabella's attention was thankfully focused on the greenery and colorful blooms.

Out of the corner of her eye, Daphne saw Miles's arms drop to his sides, as if he'd raised them, intending to put them around her.

Lady Stalbridge's eyes flickered to the movement and back again. "As I just was saying to Mrs. Howard, between the reflection of the sun against the glass, and of course the steam"—she flicked open her fan and began to ply it against the humid air—"one can see figures moving in the conservatory, but it's impossible to identify them to a certainty."

Her meaning was clear: She considered herself as having saved Daphne from a near disaster of exposure.

Miles stepped sideways as far as the tight space would allow, managing to put almost a foot between them. "Miss Burke was just telling me about her sister's travels to acquire some of these strange specimens."

Lady Stalbridge looked around with a rather dubious expression before bringing her niece forward. "The duchess promised Isabella the sight of something frightful up here." Isabella gave an eager nod.

"Oh," exclaimed Miles, his face beaming with what could only be called pride. "I know what that is. If I may?" He held out a hand for Isabella's, and the girl stepped forward and took it without hesitation.

"Lord Stalbridge is below, with Luca," Lady Stalbridge explained. Luca was his nephew, Isabella's younger brother. "The pair of them are vying in a three-legged race, with the duke and his younger son, and some of the others. I must say, the dowager duchess is surprisingly cavalier about the fate of her roses, given that half of the teams are sure to veer off track at one point or another."

"The roses will fight back if they do," Miles pointed out, with a wry smile and a glance toward Daphne that made her heart expand uncomfortably in her chest. "Now, let's see . . . Where . . . ? Ah, yes." He led Isabella unerringly to the Venus's-flytrap. "A grown girl such as you needn't worry about being eaten up by this monster," he reassured Isabella, a dark-haired and quiet child of perhaps six, who giggled when he pointed to a plant only a few inches high. Miles picked up the pencil Daphne had used in her earlier demonstration and lowered himself to Isabella's level, heedless of the dirt on the floor. "But as you'll soon see, I think it's for the best that you left your little brother below. . . ."

A smile crept across Daphne's lips before she could stop it—but not before Lady Stalbridge had noticed. "Perhaps, Miss Burke," she said, stepping close enough to link her arm with Daphne's, a chiding look in her eyes, "you could show me something less bloodthirsty?"

A true rake would never sacrifice his dignity to please a child. That's what Daphne had told herself, the night of the Clearwaters' ball.

Did his willingness to amuse Isabella mean Miles wasn't the rake everyone believed him to be?

Or did Daphne understand so little about rakes?

"I never meant for you to take your research quite so seriously, my dear," said Lady Stalbridge, dropping her voice low enough that only Daphne could hear. "You must be careful not to be waylaid by his charms yourself. In fact, the sooner you're done with this business, the better. Have the essay to me by the end of next week."

Daphne nodded her agreement, her muscles taut with the effort of restraining herself from glancing over her shoulder.

She feared the countess's warning had come too late.

CHAPTER 12

Miles wasn't surprised to be denied admittance to Alistair's sanctuary. In truth, he could only be surprised it hadn't happened before.

The housemaid delivered the refusal with serious eyes and a sorrowful shake of her head. "No, my lord. He said he wasn't to be disturbed for *nobody*." And then, in a rushed whisper, she added, "His lordship's still abed." She clapped a hand over her mouth as soon as the words were out, as if she could call back her indiscretion.

Miles made no effort to hide his surprise. Alistair had never been one to laze about. "Is he unwell?"

The maid's fingertips slid low enough to permit a few more sentences to slip out. "It were the roses, sir. And maybe Lady Frederica, a bit."

It was Miles's turn to rub a hand over his mouth and down his chin, to disguise an incipient laugh. "Oh, I see. Well, then, perhaps I'll just—" He sidled past her, into the entry hall, and was halfway to the stairs before she seemed to have realized her lapse. "I'll just make sure he's all right."

The Earl of Ryland's bedchamber was cleaner than his hideaway downstairs, but only marginally less austere. Just a bed with no bed hangings. A chair and a spindly-legged table before the empty fireplace, on the mantel of which were piled nearly as many volumes as on the bookcase in his so-called library. And a pair of tall windows, over which had been drawn silk draperies that might once have been scarlet or burgundy, but which had faded over time to a shade that Miles was tempted to call pink.

In any case, they now served to do little more than filter the light, though it was such a gloomy, damp morning that the room was still comparatively dim. Not so dim, however, that Miles had any trouble picking out the figure of his friend, propped up in bed with a tray across his lap, his eyes puffy and his nose redder than the draperies.

He looked as if he'd gone several rounds with a prize-fighter and come out the loser—which only served to remind Miles of yesterday's exchange about plants' remarkable defensive abilities.

"Out," Alistair rasped. "And tell that chit of a housemaid who answered the door she'll need to look for a new place."

Or at least, that's what Miles thought he said. Owing to his congestion, some of the words were less than intelligible.

"Now, now." Miles approached the bed. "You mustn't blame her. You know how incorrigible I can be," he said, again recalling what Daphne had said.

"Incorrigible," Alistair agreed, though it sounded more like *incorithabuh* when he said it.

Miles managed not to smile. "It's positively unpatriotic for an Englishman to have such a reaction to roses. I think you must be exaggerating your symptoms—the maid said Freddie got up to some mischief after she got away from me yesterday. I suspect you're fancying yourself ill so you don't have to face her."

"Got away from you?" Alistair pushed himself higher on the pillows, the movement threatening to overset the tray. "Is that what you call it? Not 'abandoning my sister to go chase after Miss Burke, right under the Duke of Raynham's nose'? Freddie said you practically shoved her into Lord Cowell's arms."

"More of a gentle nudge really. Only there happened to be an uneven patch of ground just there. . . ."

"Enough." He rummaged around the linens for his handkerchief and blew his nose like a trumpet blast—for dramatic effect, clearly. "My head aches too much for this conversation. I'll have to kill you tomorrow."

Miles nodded his understanding. "The thing is, by tomorrow there may be a bit of a queue." He patted his breast pocket. "I've had another invitation, you see. From the Marquess of Ashborough."

Some of the bleariness fled his friend's face as he blinked. "An invitation. To a dawn appointment, you mean?"

Miles managed a laugh, but wished after the fact that he'd put in a bit more effort, made it somewhat more convincing. "Certainly not. A *dinner* invitation. A meal, I should add, at which we are to be joined by the Duke of Raynham and possibly Mr. Paris Burke." In other words, the three most powerful and important men in Daphne's life, excepting her father. "Tomorrow evening."

What followed were a series of deliberate, careful movements. Alistair folded his handkerchief, set aside the tray, swung his legs out of bed, padded barefoot across the room, and drew back the drapery, though he was clad only in his nightshirt and his windows overlooked the street. At no point did he look Miles in the eye. "So, what you're saying is, it would be a kindness if I were to kill you today instead."

"Just so, old friend."

Alistair nodded, his gaze still focused on the gray skies. "Over dinner last night, Georgie was full of some tale about you and a lady spotted together in the glasshouse, but I felt certain she'd made it up to deflect attention away from her sister's misbehavior. Surely, I thought, surely even Miles would not be so careless, so indifferent to decorum, so much a prisoner of his—"

"Cock?" Miles suggested harshly. The *even Miles* bit had stung more than he liked to admit. He'd never expected it of Alistair.

Alistair spun. "I was going to say *desires*. We're not schoolboys anymore, Miles."

"No, clearly not."

"I take it you're not going to try to defend your behavior?"

"Would it matter? If I told you that Miss Burke showed me her sister's collection of tropical specimens, under full view of anyone who cared to look, and that I acted the gentleman all the while, even when it seemed for a moment that she wanted to—well." He broke off, trying not to think of her upturned face, her body pressed close to his. "Would you believe me?"

Alistair folded his arms over his chest and looked Miles up and down, all sternness. Then he heaved a sigh. "Of course I would. Good God—this is serious, isn't it? If you were willing to listen to a lecture about plants . . ."

Out of habit, Miles chuckled, but he couldn't laugh off the question quite as easily as he would've liked. "Do you know, I think it might be," he confessed after a moment. "Serious, that is."

Breath wheezed into and out of Alistair's lungs, the only sound in the room for a long moment. "I see," he said finally. "So, you can't very well refuse Ashborough's invitation."

"No, I can't."

After a fit of coughing, Alistair made his way to the room's only chair and sat down. "All right, then. Since I haven't any dueling pistols, and I haven't the strength this morning to run you through—merciful though the gesture might be—I suppose we'd better discuss what you're going to do, or rather, *not* going to do, to avoid another betrothal dinner fiasco."

Miles nodded and propped one shoulder against the mantel, settling in for a conversation that promised none of the diversions of Daphne's impromptu botany lesson.

The realization that he liked her was both unexpected and more than a little unwelcome. Of course, he certainly might do worse than a woman who brought a smile to his lips, who kept him on his toes, who made him want to kiss her until she was too breathless to argue anymore.

But liking her made it deuced uncomfortable to be thinking of, well, blackmailing her. He'd threatened to use his knowledge of her work at the magazine to force her to help him win his wager. It was one of the—no, *the* most despicable thing he'd ever done, one of the most despicable things he'd ever heard of anyone doing.

If he liked her, he should let her go.

Because he liked her, the solution wasn't quite so simple.

She'd proposed marriage. She was willing to sacrifice herself rather than lure some other woman into a match with a profligate like him. In a matter of days, she could be his.

But only a fool would imagine he would ever be hers in return.

CHARM is the rake's principle means of attracting the notice of respectable young ladies. (What methods he may use to attract other sorts of women lies not within this author's expertise nor the purview of this publication.) A young lady has trained herself to accept the attentions only of those who speak intelligently and behave in a gentlemanly manner. She may therefore imagine it will be an easy matter to guard against a rake's charms—she will be on the watch for a too-handsome face, dandified dress, and a disagreeable demeanor.

Charm, however, is that which makes foolish nonsense seem like rational speech. The rake may flatter, cajole, tease, and even insult! The young lady, to whom these sorts of words have never been addressed, will naturally intend to make clear that such talk is unwelcome and offensive to her. She will have been taught to turn away from such prattle, or ignore it if it cannot be altogether avoided.

She is in danger of discounting the transformative effect of charm, which has the extraordinary power to make his flattery ^seem welcome and turn sharp words into sweet. ~~She may discover that to be teased is in fact delightful, heightening the anticipation and making her feel clever in turn.~~

Charm affects not only the ear, but also the eye. A young lady must guard against allowing the rake's ~~handsome~~ ^despicable visage ~~to appear in her dreams~~ to take up residence in her thoughts. Otherwise, she may find herself at most inconvenient times in a ~~flutter~~ dreadful disarray of spirits, with racing heart, quickened breath, and

"Daph? You'll never guess what!" Bell burst into the bedchamber the sisters shared, her cheeks pink and her hair disordered by the speed with which she must have flown up the stairs to deliver her news.

Instinctively, Daphne laid her forearm over her work, smearing the word *despicable*—her most recent addition to the page. Ordinarily, she wrote a neat hand, with no blots and few cross-outs. But the essay on rakes had bedeviled her. She'd consigned three drafts to the fire already and hadn't high hopes for the fourth. Every time she dipped her pen, she saw one of two faces: Lady Stalbridge, a slight frown creasing her brow, clearly disappointed by Daphne's slowness; or Lord Deveraux, smiling in that way of his, the effects of which expression Daphne had unwisely been trying to commit to paper when her sister entered the room.

She ought to have guessed that the movement of her arm would only draw Bell's notice and pique her curiosity.

"Ohhh." Bell stretched out the word, craning her neck as she approached the dressing table, atop which rested Daphne's writing desk.

To encourage regular correspondence, their parents had given each of them a writing desk—a wooden box, inside which could be stored quills, ink, and paper, with a slanted lid that served as a convenient surface for composing letters of all sorts—when the sisters had first left Dublin.

Well, not the *first* time they'd left Dublin. More accurately, the first time they'd traveled from home with permission.

In any case, the boxes had journeyed with them around the British Isles, ferried from Dublin to London and back again, and carted among Tavisham Manor in Berkshire, Hawesdale Chase in Westmorland, and Stoke Abbey in Shropshire, the various English country homes of their eldest siblings. Daphne's had grown battered and worn over the years, stained with ink inside and out. Bell's, still pristine in appearance, was at present stowed under her bed.

"Are you working on Miss Busy B.'s next column?" Bell spoke in something like a whisper. "What's this month's crisis?"

Daphne folded the still-damp pages of the essay together, lifted the writing desk's hinged top a scant half inch, and slipped her papers inside. "I'm not at liberty to say. But you had something you wished to tell me, I take it?"

Bell gasped, remembering her mission. "You will *never* guess!" she repeated.

"I don't intend to try."

Despite a huff of annoyance, Bell couldn't keep her tongue for long. "Gabriel invited Lord Deveraux to dinner."

Daphne, who had still been twirling her pen in her fingers, felt the quill snap without having been conscious of closing her hand. "Wha—why? Why would he do such a thing?"

"To test his mettle, Cami says. It's quite clear the man means to court you, and they intend to rake him over the coals before deciding whether to give him their blessing."

"*They*. Cami and Gabriel, you mean?"

Bell nodded. "And Tristan, of course. Erica too. Oh, and Paris, if Rosamund can spare him. It's a pity Galen is on that pedestrian tour of the west of Ireland. Your impending engagement to a scoundrel might have been the means of bringing all of us together again."

Daphne closed her eyes, suddenly grateful for the focusing pain of the quill's broken ends jabbing the tender heart of her palm. "Are Mama and Papa expected too?"

"Well, no, silly. They can't come all the way from Dublin in a day. But you know Papa gave Paris the authority to sign marriage settlements on our behalf. And failing that, I'm sure Gabriel or Tris would—"

"Has Lord Deveraux accepted this invitation?" She opened her hand just enough to let the pieces of the quill, one of the bundle he'd sent her, fall onto the dressing table. And then she looked at Bell to see the answer written across her sister's face.

"Delivered by messenger, not five minutes ago," she replied smugly. "Would be very pleased, et cetera, et cetera."

Daphne had seen enough gentlemen's correspondence— more letters of complaint had been sent to the *Magazine for Misses* than letters seeking advice—to know that the *et ceteras* might not be Bell's invention. She would not be surprised to learn that Lord Deveraux wrote in that immoderate style. "You read it, then?"

"I heard Cami telling Gabriel."

"*Over*heard?" She spun in her chair. "Have you been eavesdropping, Bell?"

She could not very well claim enough moral high ground from which to chide her younger sister for such a thing. But it did increase the possibility that Bell had misheard or misunderstood. Perhaps things were not quite as dire as they seemed.

Bell looked affronted by the accusation. Excessively so, to Daphne's way of thinking. "I have *not*!"

Daphne tried to hide her disappointment. She'd hoped to have another week, at least, time to finish her essay and refine her plan for ending her secret engagement without revealing *everything*. Now, thanks to her family's interference, her hand was about to be forced.

Provided, of course, that Miles survived the after-dinner port with Paris, Gabriel, and Tristan.

"When the Season began," Bell said, flopping onto her bed, arms spread across the coverlet, her gaze focused on the ceiling, "I didn't even think you wanted anything to do with the marriage mart. You made such a fuss about having to shop or dance or pay calls—it was unsettling, really. I'd never known you to hide before."

"I wasn't—"

Daphne cut short her own protest. She *had* been hiding, at least in a sense. She had carved out her own narrow corner—her place in her family, in the world—and told herself she did not mind being otherwise overlooked and ignored. She delighted in the prospect of working on the *Magazine for Misses,* but everyone knew, especially she, that Daphne was not as clever with her pen as Cami and Galen, nor as passionate about subjects as Erica or Paris, nor as pretty and perfect as Bell.

But the truth was, some part of her had always hoped to be seen and appreciated for who she was.

Miles *had* seen—at least enough to know the best ways to court her, with Irish airs and fresh quills and a playful spirit.

None of that was real, however. It was a sham courtship, at her request, and if she wasn't careful, it was about to become a sham marriage, without openness or understanding. Without love.

With a sigh, she collapsed on the bed beside Bell. "Well, it wouldn't have been very nice of me to outshine my little sister."

Bell laughed, though not with her customary giggle. And when she propped herself on one elbow to look down at Daphne, Daphne saw for the first time an unexpected maturity in her face. At nineteen, Bell was a woman grown, not the baby anymore.

Perhaps Daphne hadn't been seeing things as clearly as she ought either.

"I'm sorry," she began, though she hardly knew how to apologize for a lifetime of certainty that she knew best, when the truth was, she didn't know anything at all.

Bell only shook her head. "Eejit."

And then they were laughing together, in a way they hadn't for years, the sort of laughter that made Daphne's sides ache and tears leak from the corners of Bell's eyes. Eileen the cat, who had been sleeping curled in her customary cozy spot between the pillows, puffed up her tail and jumped down from the bed with a disgruntled "*merow!*" that only made the sisters laugh harder.

Finally, breathless, Daphne dropped her head back against the mattress. "Oh, Bell. What am I going to do?"

"Do?" Bell turned onto her side, facing Daphne. "What do you mean? I had the impression you rather liked Lord

Deveraux. And he doesn't seem a bad sort, despite what people say."

What people say . . .

What *she*—Miss Busy B.—had said, in other words.

It was on the tip of her tongue to tell Bell everything, what Miles had demanded to keep her secret, and the supposed—and temporary—"solution" she'd contrived, the one her loving family now seemed determined to make both real and permanent.

But if she told Bell the truth today, it would only highlight her reluctance to do so before. Bell would be hurt by her lack of trust, and Daphne could end up more isolated yet.

She managed a self-deprecating laugh. "I mean to say, what am I going to *wear*?"

"Oh, let me choose," Bell exclaimed, sliding down from the bed and hurrying to the dressing room. From there, she called out various suggestions, rejecting each of them before Daphne could offer an opinion.

Eileen leaped back onto the mattress to return to her usual safe and cozy nook. Momentarily startled by Daphne's continued presence on what she appeared to consider *her* bed, the cat prowled around her body, conducting a careful inspection before settling in to knead Daphne's belly.

It was uncomfortable. Her claws snagged the fabric of Daphne's dress, fortunately only a simply cotton day dress that now had an ink stain on the sleeve. But it was also so clearly intended as a gesture of affection, that Daphne couldn't bear to push her away. And Eileen, blissfully unaware of any dilemma, didn't even budge when Daphne's abdomen rose and fell on a wry laugh.

The cat, like her family, was only doing what came instinctively, even if it caused pain.

The true writers of the family, Cami and Galen, surely

would have rejected such a shoddy metaphor for Daphne's present circumstances. But it was no less true, for all that.

Her siblings had arranged tomorrow's dinner for her benefit. They wanted to protect her—and perhaps, at least a little, their own reputations. She supposed she oughtn't to blame them for not considering her feelings or asking her what she wanted.

After all, what would she have answered if they had?

CHAPTER 13

Miles enjoyed good food with much the same relish he enjoyed many of the various other fleshly pleasures life afforded. But he could not recall a well-prepared meal he had enjoyed less than the one through which he was presently suffering. And that included the wretched betrothal dinner at the Greys'.

Everyone else in attendance was either a Burke or married to one. The lack of other guests was in itself no surprise, first because the family was large enough to make up its own dinner party, and second because the mood was anything but celebratory, despite occasional sallies of wit and bursts of laughter. Miles was reasonably certain he'd attended more cheerful funeral repasts.

In fact, given the occasional hard-eyed stares coming from both Mr. Paris Burke and the Duke of Raynham, he wondered whether he wasn't attending one at present—just with the meal at the start, rather than the end.

And none of it would have mattered one whit to him, if he were the only victim.

The table had been arranged so that he and Daphne were in the middle, on opposite sides. On either side of her were the duke and her eldest brother. To Miles's left sat the duchess, and to his right, Bellis. Lord and Lady Ashborough were in their customary places at the head and foot. It made it easy for Raynham and Burke to skewer Miles with occasional dark glances, and impossible for Miles to converse with Daphne through either word or look without drawing the notice of the entire party. For the last quarter of an hour, in fact, Daphne's eyes had been steadily focused on her plate, though he hadn't seen her take a bite.

No one had spoken an untoward word, however. The meal proceeded as if they had agreed in advance not to ask what Miles hoped to gain from his attentions to Daphne, nor point out what their sister stood to lose. Well, they probably had—agreed in advance, that was. Neither Lady Ashborough nor the Duke of Raynham struck him as the sort who acted without a plan.

No, everything seemed to be proceeding as someone had laid out: both the topics of discussion and the courses changed with meticulous regularity. Burke asked after the success of the Duchesses' Garden Party. Someone enquired after Mrs. Paris Burke's health and received a good report. Miles gathered from the exchange that the lady in question was expecting a child, which made Burke's presence here tonight all the more noteworthy.

Was Daphne always so silent amid her boisterous family? It seemed unlikely. He knew she could hold her own when it came to conversation, after all, and watching them together, it was easy enough to imagine how such a skill would be honed.

That only made her present silence more unsettling. They spoke over and past one another, even occasionally making a point to include Miles. But they let Daphne disappear. Oh, not literally—she hadn't yet resorted to sinking low in her chair and sliding beneath the table.

The mental image gave him an idea, however. Stretching out one leg, he prodded her foot with his toe. At least, he hoped it was her foot. If it was Raynham's, Miles doubted the duke would take kindly to the gesture.

He knew he had hit the mark for which he'd aimed when she started, shifted on her seat, and withdrew her foot. So much for his attempt at surreptitious communication. He started to pull back his own leg when he felt a tentative tap against the side of his toes. Then, though she didn't lift her gaze to him, she pressed her foot lightly against his, twice, like the reassuring squeeze of fingers.

Was she worried? Nervous? For herself? For him?

She looked pretty enough, in a gown of primrose yellow overlaid with white lace, and great care had obviously been taken with the arrangement of her glossy brown hair. For his part, however, he preferred the blue dress she'd worn to the Estleys' musicale, the way its steely shade had seemed to imbue her with strength.

Bellis leaned closer to him. "Doesn't she look lovely?"

"Always," he said, and surprised himself by meaning it.

At last, Daphne glanced up, though not at him. "It's her dress," she explained, with a pointed look at her sister. "She's fishing for a compliment for herself, not for me."

And what was he to say to that?

"Well, you each may have one. I see no need to be stinting with my praise. Miss Burke looks lovely indeed, and Miss Bellis has excellent taste."

That earned him a simpering blush from the youngest Burke, a disapproving scowl from her brother, and the loss of Daphne's touch beneath the table.

"I heard," said the Duchess of Raynham, reluctantly drawing his gaze in the opposite direction, "that you know something of plants, Lord Deveraux."

The duchess was an unusual personality: warm and friendly, most times, but with a perpetual air of vague distraction. She was the least duchess-like lady he'd ever met and, if he dared to make such a claim, the least Burke-like

of the Burkes. Or at least, she didn't vibrate with the same
intensity as her two eldest siblings, Lady Ashborough and
Mr. Paris Burke, despite her singular red hair. Not having
met the other brother, the poet, Miles supposed he should
not claim more than that.

"Not a thing, Your Grace," he replied to her with an
uncertain smile. "I can't think who would so deliberately
and woefully mislead you."

"Miss Isabella Killigrew. Lord Stalbridge's niece."

Understanding began to dawn. "Oh. Well, I only repeated
to her what your sister"—he shot a quick glance at Daphne,
who had resumed her study of her untouched plate—"told
me about the, er, what was it again?"

"Venus's-flytrap," Daphne supplied automatically, and
then clamped her mouth shut as firmly as the plant's leaves.

"Yes, that," said Miles. "Then we had a look around at a
few other interesting-looking things. I, um, I might have
manufactured some scientific-sounding details about them.
Also, I, uh . . ." A peculiar warmth spread up the back of his
neck, toward his ears. Good God, was he blushing? Well, the
embarrassment was no more than he deserved. "I told her
something about the bees in warmer climates being helped
along in their work by fairies."

Lady Ashborough peered disapprovingly over her spectacles, an expression that nearly rendered him an awkward
schoolboy again.

"Tiny, winged creatures called hummingbirds, actually,"
Raynham said, as he leaned back in his chair and twisted the
stem of his goblet between the fingers of one hand. "You
weren't far off."

Even in what ought to have been a relaxed posture,
Raynham maintained a reserve, a stiffness, that seemed to
owe as much to his days as an army officer as to his present
rank. Either way, it seemed incongruous with a gesture of . . .
well, Miles wasn't sure what to call it. Friendliness? Not

quite, but at least the man hadn't left him to twist beneath Lady Ashborough's cold stare.

"How sweet," declared Bellis. "Doesn't it remind you, Daph, of how Gabriel used to pretend to drink tea with us? When Cami first brought him to Dublin?"

Daphne replied with another quelling look, but that was nothing to the exchange of glances between Lord and Lady Ashborough, a curious mixture of nostalgia and alarm.

These flashes of family history were too brief and too opaque to him to illuminate much. But they still offered some insight into family dynamics, which—for a man without siblings and with no memory of his parents—were something of a mystery. So, Daphne and Bell must have been about the age Isabella Killigrew was now when Ashborough, a gambler so notorious people still whispered about him more than a decade later, had wooed and married their eldest sister, a woman far beneath his touch, at least the way most of society measured such things. There was a story there, almost certainly. And he suspected it had at least some bearing on how the family thought about Miles's courtship of Daphne.

Whatever Ashborough had meant to convey with that look at his wife, Lady Ashborough interpreted it as a sign to put an end to the meal. Rising, she said, "Come, ladies. Let us leave the gentlemen to their port."

The men stood, too, and bowed the ladies out. Miles would have been glad of a backward glance from Daphne, but whether she sent him one or not was entirely obscured by the phalanx of Burke sisters who surrounded her and escorted her from the room.

With an elegant wave of one hand, Ashborough dismissed the footmen. Stepping to a sideboard, he retrieved four small footed glasses and two decanters, one of port and one of some amber-colored liquor, which he placed in front of Burke with a knowing smile. "I presume you'd prefer whiskey?"

Burke looked up at his host with those black eyes of his. Another set of glances, another exchange of meanings Miles hadn't a prayer of understanding.

Then Burke's sharp, handsome features eased into a smile for the first time that evening. "This had better not be some Scots-brewed swill you're trying to pass off as the true water of life, Ashborough."

"Would I dare?" asked the marquess as he returned to his seat, a mischievous glint in his own brown eyes.

From farther down the table came a *chink* as Raynham unstoppered the decanter of port. "I think we all know the answer is yes."

The three men laughed.

They were all at least ten years older than Miles, which was to say, somewhere around forty. Men of power and privilege, in the prime of their lives. All devoted husbands and fathers. And yet remarkably different too, linked by marriage to sisters who themselves seemed to have little in common.

Miles, who until recently had believed himself generally well liked, had always felt at home in the world of men—the clubs, the cricket pitch, the conversations about horse-flesh and women. But his usual qualifications might make him ineligible to join this particular fraternity. And he was no longer entirely certain who got a membership vote. He thought of Daphne's downcast eyes.

Perhaps it would be wiser simply to withdraw his application now.

"Nervous, Deveraux?" Raynham poured a glass of port and handed it to him.

"Should I be?"

"From all appearances," drawled Ashborough, "you're

thinking of marrying into the Burke clan. So, speaking from years of experience, I'd say *definitely*."

"I knew I should've killed you the first time I laid eyes on you." Burke was still eyeing his drink with deep skepticism, though the remark was made without heat.

Ashborough leaned down the table to accept a glass from Raynham. "I daresay Camellia might be inclined to agree, some days. But I do my best to prove to her that I'm worth the trouble." There was something lazy and suggestive in the words.

"Christ, Ash." Burke, who had at last dared a sip, sputtered into his glass and sent him a glare as he wiped the back of his hand across his mouth. Except for the colors of their eyes, he and Lady Ashborough might have been twins, with the same angular features and blue-black hair that as of yet showed no sign of turning. They appeared to be closer in age than even Daphne and Bellis. "I'm going to pretend that's a reference to all the paper and ink you shower my sister with, and leave it at that."

Raynham made a low noise that might, or might not, have been a chuckle. "Gentlemen, with full awareness that more than a decade of animosity toward one another cannot be easily set aside, may I suggest you focus your energy and attention elsewhere this evening?"

And with that, three pairs of eyes came to rest on Miles.

Determined not to squirm, he lifted his glass in a sort of toast and then took a deep swallow, though in truth he would have preferred some of Burke's whiskey to the sweet, heavy port.

"I presume you have questions for me, gentlemen," he said, as he returned the glass to the table.

"Observations," corrected Burke. "The first of which is that I've never seen Daphne look more miserable than she did tonight."

Miles reflected on the remark for a long moment. Burke was a barrister, quick-thinking and sharp-spoken—not traits for which Miles was particularly well known. Discretion was the better part of valor, so they said. But in the end, he knew what his answer must be.

"You're quite certain I'm to blame for that?"

Miles's meaning was clear. Burke glowered and tossed half the contents of his glass down his throat. "I fail to see how our family's determination to stand up for Daphne could be the cause of her low spirits tonight."

"Perhaps," Miles suggested, "she'd prefer to stand up for herself. She's a grown woman. I've noticed—if none of the rest of you have."

Something glittered in Ashborough's eyes. "Stand up for herself . . . against a man of your reputation? And just how do you think that's likely to turn out?"

A strange question, Miles thought, from a man whose own reputation had been far blacker than Miles's, a man who had married a woman who seemed, even on brief acquaintance, to be more than capable of squaring off with the devil himself.

Were the marquess's words meant to be a warning or encouragement?

"That's right," agreed Burke, pushing past any deeper implications of his brother-in-law's question. "Even in the country, I heard about your wager—and that was before Cami wrote and told me you'd turned your sights to our sister. Dancing with her, singing to her, and then the incident in the glasshouse. You seem determined to make a spectacle of her."

"On the day of the garden party, she seemed more unhappy *before* the incident in the glasshouse, as you call it, than she did after," Raynham interjected.

Burke turned toward his other brother-in-law, and so did

Miles, trying to interpret the duke's words. Perhaps he hadn't imagined Daphne's reaction to him on that rooftop, after all.

"According to Erica?" Burke suggested, referring presumably to the duchess. He sounded skeptical.

"According to *my* sister, actually. Not yours," the duke replied.

Miles recalled the wordless exchange between Lady Viviane Laurens and Daphne and realized that the substance of it must have made its way back to the duke.

Raynham pushed away from the table to give himself room to cross his legs. Somehow, the pose made him look even more imposing. "Vivi and Daphne have grown to be good friends over the years. And I would venture to say she is less prone to romantic exaggeration than some young ladies—Bellis, for example, from whom Lady Ashborough is likely to have had the report she passed along to you."

"Forgive me," Miles ventured, "but did none of you think to ask Miss Burke herself?"

The three men exchanged a look. By silent agreement, Ashborough volunteered to speak. "Daphne has not been terribly forthcoming on the matter."

"Daph has always been the quiet one—comparatively speaking," explained Burke, with the familiar weariness of a man with several sisters. Miles had heard that tone in Alistair's voice many times.

"Though all of you can be taciturn, from time to time," added Raynham, to which Burke agreed with a reluctant nod.

"So after some discussion," continued Ashborough, "we decided that it behooved us to see where matters stood on your end. I've seen the betting books in White's for myself, so I know you must be eager to avoid a loss."

"Why did you ever agree—?" began Raynham, then shook his head.

"Why does any man make a wager?" countered Ashborough. "Because he does not believe he can lose."

At that, Burke looked Miles up and down and made a harumphing noise in his throat.

"We also know about the broken engagement with Miss Grey," said Raynham, "and that your attentions to Daphne began shortly thereafter. Rather conveniently, I might add."

As he picked up the expected refrain, Burke stood and paced in front of the sideboard. "In the span of a week those attentions have grown pointed enough that my sister risks becoming the subject of gossip if things are not brought to their logical conclusion soon—though it pains me to say it."

Miles got to his feet, realizing that this meeting, too, had reached its final point. "A proposal of marriage."

What would these men say if they knew Daphne had already made one?

"We may not always like one another," acknowledged Raynham, with a glance around the table, "but this is a family built on love. Your only concern may be winning your wager, but understand—it is not ours. We want Daphne's happiness."

"So if she refuses," added Ashborough, "set your sights elsewhere. Don't gamble on a second chance."

"With Daphne?"

"With any of us."

There was something remarkable about their protectiveness. Miles found it both admirable and unsettling. No wonder Daphne wrote in secret and yearned for a place in which she was both appreciated for herself and allowed to stretch her wings.

But what chance had he, really, to be the sort of man such a clever woman needed?

"Understood. I'll speak with her tonight, with your permission."

Both Raynham and Ashborough deferred to Burke, whose face was set in hard lines as he gave a grudging nod. "Come," he said, and the other two rose. "We'll take you to her now."

CHAPTER 14

In the drawing room, Daphne sat with a book on her lap, pretending to read. She could not have said what it was about, but it served as a useful deflection for the others' attention. Her plan had seemed simple enough at the start, if hardly foolproof. She would write an essay on rakes—which was to say, an essay on *that devil, Deveraux*. Shocked by the essay's revelations, society would turn its back on him for good. He would have no power over her or the magazine then, which would render the proposal of marriage he'd extorted from her moot. She would be free.

She had not considered what might happen if Paris, Gabriel, and Tristan refused to let Miles continue his courtship—either by demanding that he marry her immediately, or by refusing to give their blessing to the match. Then, as Miles himself had said, she would be left to choose her fate: marry him against her family's wishes, her own inclination, or both; or be exposed as Miss Busy B. and face the consequences.

Whatever the nature of the conversation presently taking place among the four men, her courtship period was rapidly coming to a close, and so far her research had not turned up anything nearly scandalous enough to achieve the ends she desired.

While Daphne ruminated over her plans, she gave an occasional ear to Bell, who was amusing herself by playing the pianoforte—though not particularly well, because she rarely practiced. Pity the gentleman who sought an accomplished bride and set his sights on Bellis Burke.

Cami and Erica sat a few feet away, together on the same sofa, discussing babies: the much-anticipated births of both Paris and Rosamund's and Erica and Tristan's third child, any day for Rosamund and in the autumn for Erica. From the snippets Daphne had overheard, Erica would have preferred to return to the country, but because Percy's birth had been difficult, her husband was determined to stay in London for the rest of the year, where there were more and better physicians to care for her. Tristan was not an open or sentimental man, but no one could doubt how much he loved his wife.

With her eyes fixed unseeing on the page, Daphne struggled to remember word for word everything Miles had said over dinner—for the essay, of course. Except that nothing had struck her as particularly dangerous, or even all that rakish. Just that bit of nonsense about her dress, and Bell had practically forced that out of him. Otherwise, he'd been unusually quiet.

Was he still? Were Paris and Gabriel talking circles around him?

Or would they provoke him to say more than he should?

Both too soon and an eternity later, the doors to the drawing room opened to admit the gentlemen. All four of them—and none the worse for wear, though Paris looked tired, like a man who'd left Berkshire early that morning and would return in a few hours, at first light. He went and spoke to Bell at the piano.

Daphne had half expected fisticuffs to break out in the dining room after she and her sisters had left, and she didn't know whether to be relieved that they obviously hadn't.

Gentlemen had other, more dangerous ways of settling disputes.

Gabriel crossed the room to Cami, who rose and asked, "Shall I ring for tea?"

"In the family parlor, if you would, my dear," Gabriel answered with a smile that revealed nothing. "Lord Deveraux has something he wishes to say to Daphne, and I'm sure he would rather speak without an audience."

Cami's answering nod was so brusque, Daphne saw no more than the flash of light against her spectacles. The six of them left more quickly and quietly than Daphne would have imagined possible, leaving Miles gazing up at an enormous painting of a wooded valley in Shropshire, in which Stoke Abbey was nestled, if one knew where to look.

He did not turn until Daphne snapped shut her book.

When he walked toward her, he moved with an athletic grace that made it difficult not to watch, though she tried. She had considered whether the essay ought to include discussion of such matters. Young ladies were kept in woeful ignorance about bodies, their own and those of men. To her mind, and in the opinions of everyone at the *Magazine for Misses,* that lack of knowledge left them vulnerable.

But could she really put into print her recent discoveries about the appeal of the masculine form, and its consequent ability to distract a woman from her higher goals?

"Daphne?" He sounded both puzzled and vaguely pleased; she wondered how much of her thoughts her expression had given away.

Wrenching her wayward mind to heel, she laid the unread book aside. With a mild smile, she gestured to the chair nearest hers. He sat down on the edge of the seat, his legs angled beneath him as if he expected to have to spring to his feet on a moment's notice. Their knees nearly touched.

"Were they awful?" she asked at last, when he did not speak.

The question seemed to require more reflection than expected. Finally, he said, "Not to me, no. Your family is—"

"Extraordinary? Exceptional?" she suggested automatically.

One shoulder lifted. "I suppose. But I was going to say overwhelming. I find myself wondering whether they pushed you into their shadows, or whether you went willingly."

What a strange reply. "They never—" she began, then bit off the denial. What did her family's treatment of her have to do with the present moment? Except, of course . . . "They insisted on your proposing, I presume?"

"Not in so many words. But that was the general drift of the conversation." He hesitated. "Though I gather some of them, at least, would be just as happy if I'd take myself off tonight and never speak to you again, let the stench of associating with me be wafted away by the winds of time."

"That was Paris, I suppose." She had guessed her brother would be the one to want to put an end to this. "Or—or Gabriel? He has such a wry sense of humor."

"Indeed."

Another pause ensued, Daphne bracing herself for the inevitable, Miles uncharacteristically reluctant to speak. "Well?" she finally asked, when the ticking of the mantel clock had begun to grate her nerves raw.

"Well, what?"

"Are you going to ask me?"

A flicker of surprise crossed his face. "Hasn't the decision already been made?"

"But clearly you didn't tell them that." She hesitated. "Have you, perhaps, changed your mind after all about marrying me?"

An odd feeling fluttered in her chest as she spoke; it ought to have been excitement at the prospect of freedom, but it rattled against her ribs more like uncertainty.

"Aren't you really asking whether I've had a change of heart about revealing the identity of Miss Busy B.?" he demanded with a skeptical lift to one brow.

"Well, I suppose it's only natural to hope—"

"Hope what?" He leaned forward, closer still. "That I'll release you from your end of our bargain?"

"That's all that concerns you, isn't it?" she snapped. "Bargains and bets."

A muscle leaped in his jaw. "No. It isn't."

"What, then?"

He was looking at her but not seeing her. His thoughts, whatever they might be, were elsewhere. "I don't see that we have anything more to discuss tonight—other than the details of the wedding. Shall we rejoin the others?" he asked, rising.

Miles was neither as heartless nor as witless as she'd expected—or been led to expect. She'd learned that much at least over the last few days. But at the moment, he was as cold and unyielding as a block of ice.

She was beginning to have her doubts that anything she could write and threaten to publish would persuade him to alter his plan to wed her. His motives for marrying, whatever they were, must extend beyond a silly wager.

Rather than less research, as Lady Stalbridge had urged, Daphne was going to need to do much more if she had any chance of unraveling the knot by which she'd bound herself to him.

"Not yet," she said, though she, too, came to her feet. "If you give my sister an opening, she will organize our wedding down to the last detail."

A smile flickered into his eyes. "Which sister?"

"I was referring to Cami. But take your pick."

He tapped a finger against his lips, considering his options. "Not an easy choice. The Duchess of Raynham would arrange the prettiest flowers, I suppose."

"Erica doesn't really concern herself much with flowers' *prettiness,*" Daphne cautioned. "Perhaps we ought to talk things over just between ourselves, first."

Anything to get him to say something about himself. Something more than nonsense and flirtation. Something real. Something true.

"Does it bother you that all of your family likely won't be in attendance?" he asked. "Your parents, in particular? They can't possibly get here before the end of June."

She pretended to consider the matter, tried to imagine how she would feel if she really were going to marry within a few days.

"Somewhat, yes," she conceded. "Though they weren't at Cami's or Erica's weddings either. All of us were together only when Paris got married, and then it was quite the ordeal to find places for everyone—I remember Paris and Galen had to sleep in the village inn!" Images of that golden day flooded her memory, everyone laughing, Elf the mastiff and Eileen the kitten causing no end of trouble. "I remember worrying that Rosamund might only be marrying Paris because I tattled on them."

"Tattled?" Scandalized amusement curled the edges of Miles's mouth and glittered in his eyes. "About what?"

"I—" Heat swept into her cheeks, which was absurd. "I saw them kiss."

"Shocking," he teased. They were standing too close together for comfort.

Though what she felt when he was near wasn't exactly *dis*comfort either.

"And what was the story about you and Bellis having tea with Ashborough?" he asked.

"Oh, that." Her laugh was tinged with nostalgia. "He

came to Dublin with Cami. In the spring of '98, Galen had been badly hurt at the start of the uprising, and the house was in an uproar. Paris was—" she began, then caught herself with a little shake. Though more than a decade had passed, there was still no call for her to confirm the rumors about her brother's involvement with the rebels. "Gabriel took it upon himself to amuse us while Cami set everything to rights again, as she always did. I'll never forget his kindness to two frightened little girls."

"You must have been pleased, and perhaps rather surprised, by your sister's choice of husband."

"Oh, they weren't mar—" Heat prickled her cheeks. Eight-year-old Daphne hadn't given much thought to the fact that Cami and Gabriel had traveled from London to Dublin, unwed and unchaperoned, and none at all to what might have transpired on the journey. Now, however, she understood things differently. "That is to say, I think that visit might be why she decided to marry him."

Surprise flared in Miles's eyes. He clearly understood the more scandalous implications of her tale.

How had she been so easily led to speak of her past, when she had intended to get him to reveal something of himself?

"What of your family?" she asked. "Would they—*will* they be at your wedding?"

"All that I have, yes," was his cryptic answer. "Including the Earl of Ryland, I hope—he has been like a brother to me, since we began at school together. But beyond that . . ." His shoulders rose and fell in a shrug of acceptance, if not quite indifference. "Much of a bachelor's acquaintance does not accompany him into married life."

She had forgotten, for just a moment, the sort of world in which men such as he moved—and would continue to move. He might not introduce his friends to his wife, but neither would he abandon them. He would settle the new

Lady Deveraux somewhere in the country and return to his Town pursuits as soon as she was with child, if not before.

She made a mental note to include that warning in her essay.

"I suppose," she said, suddenly eager to change the subject, "this cannot be a topic of great interest to you. Young women spend more time thinking about weddings."

"While men think only of wedding nights, I suppose?"

How could his tone be both seductive and self-deprecating?

"No," she said, without stopping to consider how it would sound. "Women think about those too." Impossible not to be at least a little curious, or to wonder at the meaning of some of the more ribald whispers exchanged among the matrons.

"Do they?"

Without her having been aware of any movement, the distance between their bodies evaporated. He had dipped his head lower, and his whisper at her ear made her feel shivery and weak all at once. He wasn't touching her, and yet she could not work up the will to step away.

"This is a drawing room," she reminded him, determined to regain some measure of control over the situation, even if she couldn't seem to control herself. "Not a darkened library. No chess game tonight."

Her scalp prickled as his warm laugh ghosted over her. "For a young lady who insisted upon a proper courtship, you have a remarkable curiosity about impropriety. Would you like me to show you exactly what went on in the library that night?"

She lifted her chin to face him. "Is that some sort of threat?"

"A promise," he murmured. She felt the words as much as heard them; her movement had brought her mouth within an inch of his.

Perhaps it didn't matter who initiated the kiss, though she

rather feared she had been the one to close the remaining gap between their lips. Without any conscious effort, she found herself on the balls of her feet, with her fingers curled around the lapels of his coat, urging their bodies closer yet.

Until a few nights ago, she hadn't understood all the fuss about kisses. Hadn't known the delicious pleasure of it all, how a man's mouth could be soft and hungry all at once.

But of course, that's why such knowledge was kept from young women.

Or perhaps kisses *weren't* always like this? Perhaps it was simply his kisses—*their* kisses. . . .

No, she couldn't think like that . . . couldn't think . . .

His lips moved over hers with slow deliberation, savoring. He seemed to be intent on discovering and devouring every curve of her mouth, learning her taste.

A man who looks like that. . . . A man who kisses *like that. . . .*

The tip of his tongue touched the center of her bottom lip. And when her lips parted on a sigh, his tongue ventured farther still, sweeping right into her mouth. Surely such a sensation ought to be appalling to a gently bred young lady. So why did she tilt her head, open wider, moan with pleasure as his tongue tangled with hers?

He was a rake, practiced at the arts of seduction. Nothing more, nothing less.

His hands, which had bracketed her ribs, slid slowly higher, beneath her bosom. He must feel how her heart raced, how her breath had quickened. And when he swept one thumb over the curve her breast, then higher, over her nipple, her borrowed dress suddenly felt much too tight.

He dragged his mouth along her jaw and down her neck, peppering the thin skin there with sharper kisses that made her pulse threaten to leap from her throat. "Checkmate?" she managed to whisper in his ear, a plea for mercy, a surrender. She had neither the strength nor the desire to push him away.

He chuckled softly. "My dear, that was only the first move."

You might find you quite enjoy being ruined.

But he did take half a step back, and his hands slid to her waist. Hardly enough space for her to catch her breath, to say nothing of gather her thoughts, which had scattered to the four corners of the earth.

He was studying her face, and she hardly knew how to describe his expression: surprised but triumphant was the closest she could come. "I am glad to know that your siblings weren't perfect saints in their own courtships. They won't have much room to complain when they see you looking so thoroughly kissed."

She released his lapels with the intent to reach up and smooth her hair. But she found herself smoothing the fabric of his coat instead, her palms sweeping over his firm chest.

And when she at last dragged one hand away, he caught it before she could cover her mouth with it. "It's not your lips that give you away," he insisted, kissing her fingertips. "It's your eyes."

Even his own pupils were flared—and she couldn't imagine how many women he'd kissed. What could be new and exciting about the experience to him? But if he looked like that, then she—why, she must look like Eve in the Garden, after her first taste from the Tree of Knowledge.

Hungry for more.

No matter how many cross-outs and crumpled sheets of paper it took, she was going to have to find the words to explain everything that a rake had the power to make a young lady feel. Ruination, she was discovering, did not exactly come in the form young ladies were taught to guard against.

Her body was far more prone to betrayal than she had been led to expect.

Her mind had turned out to be no firmer or more dependable than a bowl of porridge.

Thank God her heart remained her own. At least, for now.

Attached as it was to the rest of her, she no longer felt certain even of that.

"Come," he said, letting go of her, tugging his coat into place, and holding out an arm. His wry expression told her that he had guessed at least a fraction of her thoughts. "It's best if we rejoin the others before someone comes looking for us."

She nodded and slipped a hand around his elbow. Rather different from their furtive, separate departure from Lord Estley's study. Now everyone was meant to know. . . .

Upstairs, in the family parlor, there was no pretense of distraction, no books or cards or tinkling pianoforte. The men were all still on their feet, and every head swiveled to face the doorway the moment she and Miles crossed the threshold. Even Zwolf, who had been lounging in front of the fire, rose and ambled toward them.

"Well?" Paris demanded.

Ignoring the question, Miles released her arm, crouched, and rubbed the dog's ears. "And who is this good boy?"

"Zwolf," Daphne whispered, moving her mouth as little as possible. She laid a hand on Miles's shoulder, to urge him to rise, and darted a quick glance around the room at her siblings' astonished stares. Only Gabriel looked amused by his attention to the dog—perhaps even approving.

"Oh, right," Miles said, as if suddenly aware of the pressure of Daphne's fingers. "Sorry." He straightened, dusted off his hands, and nodded toward Paris. "Your sister has agreed to make me the happiest of men."

She wasn't exactly surprised to see something other than relief in her family's faces as they took in Miles's perfunctory announcement. (He had resumed scratching the dog's broad head.) Only Bell clasped her hands in excitement and started forward, but she stopped herself even before Cami could raise a staying eyebrow.

"Allow me to extend an invitation to my home, Lyneham Park, in Hertfordshire. I know you are not all at liberty to travel, particularly on such short notice," Miles acknowledged, with a slight dip of his head toward Erica, whose condition was just beginning to be evident beneath her fashionable high-waisted gown, "and this is not the usual season for a house party. But I'm sure Daphne will wish to see the estate of which she is soon to become mistress. And I—well, I confess it has always been my fondest wish to marry in my village church."

His fondest wish?

Was that a teasing reference to Daphne's claim that only young ladies thought about weddings? Or merely a satirical reflection on the fact that he'd planned one wedding already this spring?

"Before the end of the month, I take it," said Tristan—merely to keep Paris from doing so, she thought. Away from Rosamund's softening influence, her brother's features were hard as granite.

"Just so, Your Grace," Miles replied, with a smile that revealed yet another reason why he was called *that devil, Deveraux*. "Now, allow me to thank you for your hospitality, Lady Ashborough, and wish you all good night." He snatched Daphne's limp hand and lifted it almost to his mouth. Even without the brush of his lips, her fingertips tingled. "Hurry to your packing, my dear."

And with that, he was gone.

Hardly had the door closed behind him when her family's voices rose, surrounding her, speaking to one another, rather than to her. *"The nerve!"* and *"We certainly cannot allow . . ."* and *"Hertfordshire?"* buffeted her like so many waves.

And then, worst of all, Cami's voice, in a terrible whisper:

"If it weren't for that ridiculous Misbehavior Magazine, or whatever it is, he'd still be marrying Miss Grey and we would be well out of it."

Daphne sank beneath the weight of those words and rested her forehead on Zwolf's warm flank.

She could only pray that she would find what she needed—the truth about Miles—at Lyneham Park.

CHAPTER 15

"Feeling better, old chap?" Miles called out as the door of Alistair's library swung open. "When Mrs. Swetley answered my knock, she told me she had brewed up a pot of her special tea, just for you." Alistair's housekeeper had always treated Miles as one of the family.

Alistair was seated at the table, bathed in a narrow circle of lamplight. Pen poised above the letter he'd been writing, he turned and grimaced at Miles. "Mrs. Swetley's special tea may be special. But it is decidedly not tea. I poured it out, as usual." He nodded toward a half-dead plant in the corner of the room. His eyes were still bloodshot and his nose was red, but he sounded considerably more like himself. "What improved matters was last night's rain. Cleared the air."

"Excellent." Miles threw himself into a chair. "Then you'll be fit to travel day after tomorrow." The trick always, with Alistair, was to deliver news as if it were a foregone conclusion.

With a sharp sigh, Alistair laid his pen in the tray and corked the ink bottle. "Where exactly am I going?"

"Lyneham Park. With me."

"Why?"

"Because I'm getting married, of course. Congratulate me?"

Alistair tipped back slightly in his chair, the better to bring Miles directly in his line of sight. "To Miss Burke?"

"Who else?"

"I can think of—very well," he broke off when Miles hefted a nearby book and threatened to lob it at his head. "You have my heartiest congratulations. I can see that you've come through your dinner at Finch House unscathed, and I take it from your jovial mood you managed to secure both Miss Burke's and her family's approval—"

"Well, *approval* might be a bit strong," Miles conceded, thumbing through the book—a surprisingly weighty tome on the care of sheep. "But the matter's all settled. We're to be wed in Lyneham in a few days. You'll come?"

Alistair appeared to consider the matter. "Do I get to give you away?"

"You know you'd miss me if you did," Miles retorted with a laugh.

He was feeling more chipper than he had any right to be, given the death glares that had been cast at him by the extended Burke family this evening, and given that Daphne had all but told him that she didn't want to marry him.

Ah, but she *had* kissed him. And with none of the reticence he'd sensed in her the night of the Estleys' musicale. She was not indifferent to him, not cold or prudish. She had indeed looked lovely in that yellow dress, and her bosom nestled perfectly in his palm, just as he'd predicted.

It was not a great deal to be getting on with, but he could think of several marriages among his acquaintances that had been contracted on less.

"What am I to do with my sisters if I go hying off to the country?" demanded Alistair. "I suppose they could tag along, but you know they'd sooner die than leave Town during the Season."

"Bernie has agreed to come and stay with them," Miles explained, "until you return." Bernie—Bernadette—was Alistair's eldest sister.

"You understand that Bernie prefers you to address her as Lady Brinks," Alistair pointed out with a chiding look.

"Yes, well." Miles tossed the book aside. He knew Alistair was more enthused at the prospect of a week or more's freedom from the responsibility of squiring Freddie, Georgie, and Harry about than he let on. "Lady Brinks forgets that I once saw her run shrieking down a corridor in nothing but curlers and a nightdress."

"Ah, yes." Alistair chuckled. "The great toad incident of '95. You're fortunate she's pushed the memory of that morning from her mind, or else she never would have been willing to lift a finger to help either of us." He picked up his quill and twirled it absently. "Day after tomorrow, you say?"

"First light," Miles vowed.

"Which means ten o'clock at the earliest." He uncorked the ink, added a line to his letter, then signed with a flourish before tossing the pen back on the silver tray, where it landed with a quiet clatter. He did not, however, turn back to face Miles. "You're certain about this?"

"I am," Miles vowed, with more confidence than he felt.

"Merely to avoid losing a bet?"

"You know I never liked to lose," he pointed out, not for the first time. "But rest assured, this isn't just about the wager. Or at least, not about the one laid down at White's."

Alister twisted on the chair and fixed him with a wrinkled brow. "How's that? *Another* wager?"

"Not exactly. More a vow I made to myself. I'll explain when we get to Lyneham Park," he said, rising. "I'll be back tomorrow to help you pack." Alistair didn't keep a valet—if he did, his clothes surely wouldn't be permitted to hang on him in that stiff, ill-fitting way.

"Haven't you your own affairs to put in order?" Alistair asked.

"I took care of all that before dinner."

"You were that confident of the outcome?" Alistair marveled, shaking his head.

Miles shrugged. "I needed to do something to take my mind off all the possible ways to be murdered by a duke, a marquess, and an Irishman."

Or eviscerated by an Irishwoman with a glare like a blade and the mouth of his dreams.

Alistair laughed, though Miles hadn't entirely been joking.

"All that pacing might give a person the impression you were eager to get to Hertfordshire."

Gabriel's words brought Daphne's latest trip across the library floor to an abrupt halt. It had always been her favorite room in Finch House, with its warm wood paneling, well-stocked bookshelves that stretched from floor to ceiling, and tall windows framed by dark green draperies.

Windows that just happened to face the street.

Where the traveling coach was being loaded.

Turning her back on the bustle outside, she smiled—perhaps a shade too brightly—at Gabriel instead. "Shouldn't I be?"

He'd been working at his desk for the last half an hour on some matters of estate business. His study could be closed off from the adjoining library, but he generally preferred to leave the door open. It was a larger, grander version of the arrangement at the Dublin town house in which she'd grown up, where her father's desk sat at one end of the drawing room, and his—and later Paris's—law work had always simply been part of the family's daily living, conducted alongside schoolwork and sibling squabbles and the sounds of a tinkling spinet.

Gabriel pushed aside the account ledger he'd been studying, got to his feet, and came to lean in the doorway. "I've been asking myself the same question," he said, crossing his arms over his chest and studying Daphne with a curious expression, "but I can't quite make out the answer. On paper, it's an excellent match for any young lady. But *should* you be eager to marry a man of Deveraux's reputation? Under these circumstances—any circumstances, really?"

"What nonsense," she answered with an impatient wave of her hand. "And from you, of all people. Why, you're the closest thing to a romantic this family has. Well, except for Galen."

Gabriel chuckled. "No, whenever I get the urge to give vent to my feelings in poetry, I sit down until it passes." He tilted his head toward the sound of another trunk being brought down—surely Bellis's last. "Reputation and rumors aren't everything," he reminded her, a reference to his own checkered past. "Follow your heart, Daphne. Just know that if we get to Hertfordshire and you change your mind—"

"What a scandal that would be," she said, trying to sound dismissive of the very notion.

"Wouldn't even crack the top five scandals this family has weathered." He pushed away from the door and turned back toward his desk. "I should finish reviewing this report. Try not to wear a hole in the carpet, all right? Zwolf has done enough damage already," he added with a nod toward a frayed edge. Then he paused. "Speaking of Zwolf . . . and Deveraux . . ."

"If you're going to make some ridiculous claim about how you can judge a man's character by whether or not a dog likes him—"

"It's not ridiculous. And the night before last—"

"Zwolf went right to him. Yes, I saw. We *all* saw,"

Daphne said, trying hard to dispel the mental image of Cami's expression at the sight of Miles addressing the dog first when they came into the room. "But that dog would pledge his undying loyalty to anyone who scratched behind his ears."

"I'm well aware," Gabriel said with a bemused smile. "But Deveraux wasn't. He might have been alarmed, or annoyed, or any number of things. It's not every man who'd stoop to pet the dog—especially one so big it hardly requires stooping."

She knit her brows together. "Are you saying that you think Lord Deveraux's willingness to scratch Zwolf's head—in defiance of good manners to the company, I might add—is reason enough to reevaluate his character? That, in fact, I *should* be eager to marry such a man?"

It couldn't be eagerness, this fluttering, anxious feeling in her chest and her stomach.

Could it?

No, of course not. She wasn't *eager* to marry Miles. She wasn't going to marry him at all.

She liked kissing him, it was true—but that fact alone really ought to be enough to dissuade her, or any sensible young lady, from thinking of such a man as husband material. He kissed like that because he was a rake.

A rake who was the subject of the half-written essay locked in her writing desk. The writing desk she'd watched a footman load into the traveling coach with her own two eyes. She'd been pleased to see how he handled it with care, almost as if he knew its incendiary contents.

If she *was* eager to get underway, it was the sort of eagerness one felt at the prospect of finishing an unpleasant task once and for all.

"More and more, I see these flashes of Camellia in you," Gabriel said with a wry laugh. "What I'm saying is—"

His explanation remained unspoken, for at that moment

a maid appeared in the doorway, looking nervous. "My lord?"

"Yes?" Gabriel waved her into the room.

The girl bobbed an uncertain curtsy and approached. "Do you remember, my lord, a few days ago, when the children all had a touch of fever—?"

"And that nasty rash? How could anyone forget?" The physician had assured them that it wasn't anything to worry about, and it hadn't been, for they'd recovered without incident in a day or two, though it had caused them all to miss the Duchesses' Garden Party. Gabriel's nose wrinkled now as if he were still smelling the ointment the apothecary had sent over to alleviate the itching.

"Well, my lord, it, er—it would appear that Lady Ashborough has succumbed to the same malady."

His face blanched. "Is she—? Have you sent for the physician?"

"Yes, my lord. And Lady Ashborough asked me to tell you she's perfectly fine—other than a bit of scratchin', beggin' your pardon. But she did wonder, my lord, whether you—"

Gabriel was already digging a finger beneath his collar—out of sympathy, Daphne hoped, or the power of suggestion, rather than any sudden onset of symptoms.

Just to be safe, both she and the housemaid took a step away from him.

"She also says the journey to Hertfordshire will have to be put off a few days," the maid added, with an apologetic glance at Daphne.

All the air rushed from Daphne's lungs. It was the last week of the month. Miles didn't have a few days. Which meant *she* didn't have a few days. How was she going to—?

"Perhaps I could be of assistance?"

Daphne jerked her gaze toward the doorway again to find Lady Stalbridge framed there, wearing a china-blue pelisse and clutching something to her chest. "My apologies for intruding, and at such an early hour. I wanted to return this book I borrowed from Lady Ashborough before we left Town," she explained, holding it out in one hand. "No one answered my knock, and the front door was open. . . . Did I hear you say that she is ill?"

"Merely the sort of trivial complaint one is prone to when there are children in the household," Gabriel answered with a weak smile, before squirming slightly to reach for a spot between his shoulders.

"Oh, dear. And I saw the coach waiting in the street. You were to travel today?"

"Yes, ma'am," Daphne said, turning slightly so that no one but Lady Stalbridge could see her expression. "To Hertfordshire. Lord Deveraux and I are to be wed there in a few days' time. Or *were* to be. . . ."

"My felicitations, Miss Burke," she said, masterfully hiding her own surprise and appearing to ignore the panicked look Daphne sent her. "But what an unfortunate circumstance! To have to delay your wedding . . ." She trailed off with a sorrowful shake of her head.

"I'm certain Lady Ashborough will be right as rain in time for the happy day," Gabriel reassured her. "But Lord Deveraux *had* expressed his hope we all might arrive as soon as possible, so that Daphne could become acquainted with her new home."

"Lyneham Park, yes. But, my heavens! I've just realized—we are to be neighbors, Miss Burke," Lady Stalbridge exclaimed. "How delightful! In fact, I wonder . . ." A thoughtful expression settled over her face.

"Ma'am?" Gabriel prompted after a moment. He was clearly anxious to check on Cami. Or to find some private place in which he could indulge in a thorough scratch.

"Well, Lord Stalbridge had word from his steward late

last night and must hurry to Ferncliffe this morning. If we could be of help to you . . ." She sent Daphne a pointed look.

"Do you mean that you would be willing to take me to Lyneham Park, ma'am? But what of your niece and nephew?"

"Oh, they shall enjoy romping about with their uncle Oliver—my stepson, Lord Manwaring," she added, by way of explanation to Gabriel.

"And would it be any trouble if my younger sister, Bellis, were to join us? I should like to have her with me."

"Of course, my dear," she said with an indulgent smile. "No trouble at all."

"An excellent solution, ma'am," declared Gabriel. "I'm much obliged. Lady Ashborough and I will surely be fit to join you in the country in a day or two." His whole body twitched. "Three at the most. Now if you'll excuse me, I really must check on my wife."

The maid reluctantly stepped between him and the door. She held up a hand, palm outward, her body leaning away. "I'm sorry, my lord, but her ladyship did insist that you stay away, at least until the physician has paid his call."

"Right. Of course. I'll just—" He stepped nimbly around the girl and headed for the door. "When he's finished with Lady Ashborough, send him straight to me."

The maid darted a wide-eyed glance between his escaping form and Daphne, sketched a curtsy, and hurried after him.

An impish smile twitched about Lady Stalbridge's mouth, as she tucked the book once more against her breast. "I'd say that couldn't have worked out better."

"That isn't my sister's book, is it?"

"No, dear."

"And *does* Lord Stalbridge have business to attend to in Hertfordshire?"

Her smile deepened. "He does now."

"But—Lord Manwaring and the children! He'll be fit to be tied when you tell him."

"Oh," she dismissed the concern with a wave of her hand, "he'll have Mrs. Goode's invaluable guidance, as you know. Besides, it's only a few days. Just until you finish your essay, I presume."

Daphne nodded to disguise a nervous swallow. "Yes, ma'am. I'll go and tell Bellis about the change in plans, shall I?"

"And I shall order our coach 'round and have your things transferred into it. We will leave in an hour."

"So soon, ma'am?"

Lady Stalbridge tilted her head to one side and pinned Daphne with an assessing look. "Is not Lord Deveraux expecting an eager bride?"

Eager.

The great winged creature in Daphne's chest, briefly pinioned by the news of Cami's illness, resumed its flapping. "He is."

"Well, then." She turned and strode toward the door. "I'll see you in an hour."

CHAPTER 16

Though Miles never let many weeks pass between visits to Lyneham Park, every time it came in view, he found himself wondering why he had stayed away so long.

The house itself, constructed of red brick, had been some four hundred years in the making, though the oldest portions of it had been relegated to offices and storerooms in Miles's great-grandfather's day, in favor of what had then been newly built in the Palladian style. Its position on rising ground, backed by lush woodland, made it appear even larger than it was, impressive, but not imposing.

It looked . . . well, it looked like home.

Which was a rather silly way of phrasing things. Lyneham Park *was* his home, after all—one of them, anyway.

He'd been born here, twenty-eight years ago, to parents who had doted on him—or so he'd been told. They had been killed in a carriage accident when he was two. As far as he could remember, he had been Viscount Deveraux all his life. Had they lived, he surely would have shared this home with siblings, as many or more than Daphne's, he supposed. Instead, he knew his mother and father's faces only in portraits.

Lyneham Park was full of portraits.

"Do you think they'll come?" he asked Alistair, turning away from the carriage window.

Alistair looked up from his book. "Hm?"

How the man could read in a jostling coach had always been a mystery to Miles. Then again, Miles didn't particularly enjoy reading even when he was still—or didn't enjoy being still long enough to resort to cracking a book.

"The Burkes," he explained. "Do you think they'll come?" He wanted, suddenly, to show off his home, not as some ostentatious display of wealth, but because . . . well, he hardly knew why.

Alistair closed his book around his finger to mark his place. "All of them?"

"Any of them." His mouth felt suddenly dry, the words difficult to speak.

With a laugh, Alistair whacked his book against Miles's knee. "I suspect at least one will. Whether it's the one you're hoping for remains to be seen, old chap."

The coach rattled along the gravel drive as it curved between the house and a terraced garden that sloped down to a close-cropped green lawn. The garden was full of roses, a profusion of varieties that would have done the Duchess of Raynham proud. *Or perhaps the dowager duchess,* he corrected himself, thinking of what Daphne had said about her sister Erica, who was probably not interested in such mundane matters as a flower's color or scent. Even just passing by with the carriage windows closed, he could catch the roses' perfume on the air.

Miles leaned forward and reached behind Alistair to slide open the panel that permitted communication with the driver. "Straight to the carriage house, John. We'll sneak in," he added with a wink to Alistair.

"Very good, my lord."

Alistair mouthed the words *thank you*. Entering the house through the front, where more roses had been trained to grow up the columns supporting the pediment, would have left him in stuffy-nosed, red-eyed agony.

So they entered instead through the oldest part of the house, past the gun room, the still room, the steward's office. It meant risking seeing the occasional footman out of livery, but it was, after all, Miles's house, and Alistair was such an old friend he was almost as much at home here as Miles himself.

After a bit of wending and winding, a detour through the kitchen where Cook pretended to squawk when they stole a couple of hand pies, and finally startling a parlor maid who dropped a tin of beeswax on the floor in an awful clatter, they found themselves in the entry hall.

Out of habit, Miles looked up. The high ceilings were adorned with scenes from the twelve labors of Hercules, and he'd always been fascinated by them. Was it vulgar to be enamored of one's own house? Alistair was watching him with an odd expression.

Miles didn't really care what anyone else thought. Well, perhaps one person.

"At least I didn't sing," he reminded his friend. "Yet."

The acoustics in the space were magnificent, as he'd proven many times, most infamously by bellowing out a naughty ditty he'd learned in the village pub at sixteen and rousing his grandmother from a sound sleep.

"My lord," cried the butler, approaching at a brisk pace. "How delightful to see you at Lyneham again—though a bit earlier than expected." He and Alistair shared a knowing glance.

"We made surprisingly good time, Frost," explained Alistair, who had still been at his coffee and toast when Miles's coach had drawn up—for once, just when he'd said he would arrive.

"I'm pleased to hear it, sir. Shall I see to your things?"

"Thank you, Frost," said Miles. "Put Lord Ryland's in the

usual place, if you please"—which was to say, the nicest bedchamber *not* overlooking the rose garden. "And as I said in my message, I'm expecting a few more guests. Still can't say how many, I'm afraid. Or just when they'll arrive."

Frost took the news in stride. "We'll be ready whenever they do, my lord."

"The very best rooms," he insisted, then winced at his own eagerness.

"Of course, sir."

Before Frost could turn to leave, Miles lifted an enquiring brow.

"She's in the winter parlor, my lord."

"Naturally," Miles said with a nod. "The light, I suppose?"

"Just so, my lord."

"Off you go, then." He dismissed the butler with a wave of his hand as he turned toward the staircase.

Alistair hung back a step. "If you'd rather, I could—"

"Nonsense. She'll be thrilled to see you."

They ascended the stairs together, without further conversation. That was one of the advantages of old friends, those who understood things with no need for words—and just as well, because the thoughts tumbling through Miles's head frequently seemed reluctant to be formed into sentences.

The winter parlor was a small sitting room on the second floor, with southerly facing windows designed to catch the light during the bleakest months of the year. On a midsummer day, with no heavy draperies to obscure the wall of glass overlooking the rose garden, it was almost too bright, and stuffy to the point of being too warm.

A maidservant sat unobtrusively in a straight-backed chair near the door and would have risen when Miles entered, but he gestured her back to her seat.

He had no difficulty finding what he sought, the frail, black-garbed figure positioned in a softer chair, a blanket over her lap, her chin on her chest, her back to the view. Still, he hesitated for a moment, reluctant to disturb her rest.

Alistair broke the silence by sneezing. Belatedly, Miles realized there were at least three large vases of flowers scattered about the room.

Her head jerked up at the sound. "Who's there?"

"It's Miles, Grandmama," he said, approaching with outstretched hands. "And I've brought Lord Ryland with me."

She turned cloudy eyes, once the mirror of Miles's own, in his general direction. She looked more fragile each time he saw her, and the skin of her cheek was as cool and dry as paper as he brushed his lips across it in a kiss of greeting.

"About damn time, boy," she scolded, then chuckled. "Though I might have known you wouldn't forget an old lady on her birthday."

"Is it your birthday, ma'am?" asked Alistair, approaching.

She freed one gnarled hand from the tangle of yarn on her lap—she'd not been resting, Miles saw now, but crocheting, the stitches so familiar to her fingers, they had no need of help from her eyes—and offered it to Alistair for a kiss.

"It is indeed. On Sunday."

Alistair sent Miles a sidelong glance from his position bowed over her hand. "Sunday," he repeated, releasing her and rising. "The first of July."

"That's right," she said. "And how old do you think I'll be?"

"Oh, I couldn't possibly guess," Alistair demurred—or pretended to. "Surely not as old as . . ." His voice dropped to a dramatic stage whisper. "Seventy?"

"Eighty!" she crowed, clapping her hands in delight at having fooled him.

Miles's father had been the youngest of her four children, and she had outlived them all.

"Impossible," Alistair declared, which made her beam.

"Well, now, that's not likely to be the sort of thing a lady would fib about, is it?" she retorted, before tilting her head slyly at Miles. "One might even say such an occasion called for a party."

Alistair's stare grew more pointed still. "Indeed, one might," he said, as much to Miles as to his grandmother.

"As luck would have it," Miles told her, ignoring him, "you can expect a few more guests shortly. Perhaps as soon as later today."

"Oh? That will be lovely."

"And if all goes to plan, I've a special celebration planned for the end of the week."

A choked sound escaped from Alistair's throat, and Miles was fairly certain that this time, it had nothing to do with roses.

"I do hope it will include dancing," said his grandmother, her toes beginning to tap beneath her blanket.

"Of course," he assured her. "Now, I'm certain Lord Ryland would like to freshen up after our journey. Will you excuse me for a few minutes, Grandmama, while I show him to his room?"

"Show him to his room?" she echoed. "What nonsense is that? Hasn't he the same room as always?" But she tipped her chin up for another kiss from Miles and resumed her needlework, humming a little tune beneath her breath, in time with the tapping of her toes.

"What the devil?" Alistair exclaimed as soon as they were alone in the corridor, and the door to the winter parlor had shut behind them. It was the closest Miles had ever heard Alistair come to uttering an oath.

"Just—" Impatient himself, he gestured his friend toward the stairs, and eventually to a familiar suite of rooms on the back side of the house, comparatively dim and entirely free of flowers. Once inside, Miles sank into a chair and waited for the barrage of questions.

But Alistair, clever Alistair, had worked it all out on his own.

"You promised yourself you'd get married by the end of the month as a birthday gift to your grandmother," he said, incredulous. "That was the *other wager* you referred to last night."

Miles, who had been poised to explain and make an excuse, found himself with parted lips and nothing to say. Snapping shut his mouth, he simply nodded.

Grandmama worried when he was "alone." That was how she phrased it, always. He might have corrected her: away from Lyneham Park, he was almost never alone. He made a point of surrounding himself with companions, male and female, though rarely the sort one could discuss with— to say nothing of introduce to—one's grandmother.

He had understood, without either of them saying it, that what concerned her most was what would become of him after her death. Would he let himself go, too, content to be only the man he was away from this place? Would this place, which was everything to him because she had made it so, cease to be his comfortable home?

And so, he'd gone to Town in May with the vaguest notion rattling around in his head: wouldn't it make Grandmama pleased if he found himself a wife, so he wouldn't be alone when she was gone?

He hadn't given his own happiness much thought. Nor had he thought about love—well, other than his grandmother's love for him, and in turn, his for her. Excepting, perhaps, Alistair's sisters, he had never spent much time with the sort of women a man like him was expected to marry. He had fully expected—accepted—that the woman he married would be accomplished and proper, which was to say dull and passionless.

All that mattered was that she be the sort of woman with

whom Grandmama wouldn't object to sharing the name Lady Deveraux.

He hadn't expected to have any trouble finding such a woman. He was titled, good looking, and rich, after all. He'd spoken rashly, as he often did, and taken the wagers against him in good fun.

He certainly hadn't expected Daphne.

"Do you think she'll like her?"

Alistair, who knew him better than he knew himself, understood the question, despite its ambiguities. Miles could see it on his face. But being Alistair—which was to say, cautious, thoughtful, and just a little bit sanctimonious—he had to spell it out.

"Do I think . . . ?"

He was pacing in front of a tall decorative screen that divided the bedchamber from the dressing room. It was covered with pictures of naked cherubs, cavorting across a blue sky dotted with fluffy clouds. It had been standing in that spot the first time Alistair visited Lyneham Park, at an age when cavorting, naked *anything* had been of interest— perhaps too much interest—to both of them. In more recent years, Miles had offered to replace it, but Alistair had laughed and said he wouldn't recognize his room without it.

"Do I think that your grandmother will like the woman with whom you are about to take the vows of holy matrimony, a young lady you hardly know—one who seems, forgive me, less than enthusiastic about the prospect of marrying you—and to whom you only proposed to avoid losing a foolish bet you made to find a wife by her birthday? Is that—is that really what you're asking?"

"Christ," Miles muttered, running a hand through his hair. "When you put it that way . . ."

Alistair dropped into the chair opposite Miles and tipped his head against its tall back. "How else am I to put it?"

"Well, you could start by leaving out anything to do with the wager. Grandmama must never know I've been gambling."

Alistair's chin dropped forward far enough that he could fix Miles with a dark, level stare. "It's been in all the papers, old chap. Newspapers from which I've heard Lady Deveraux's companion read aloud to her on more than one occasion."

"Oh, that." Miles dismissed the concern with a flick of his wrist. "I instructed the servants a decade ago to skip over any item that makes mention of me."

"Must make the news rather thin, some days. More of a leaflet, really." To emphasize the point, he drew a small rectangle in the air with his fingertips.

"And," Miles continued, ignoring him, "I don't see any reason to mention how well Miss Burke and I do, or do not, know one another. People marry on short acquaintance all the time."

"They do." He managed, somehow, with two short words, to make clear he thought it an ill-advised practice.

"So then, it's really just a matter of Miss Burke's supposed reluctance. *Is* she reluctant, do you think?"

"You tell me."

The truth was a leaden weight in Miles's chest. How good it would feel to relieve himself of the burden, to tell Alistair about Miss Busy B., his damnable insistence that Daphne owed him a bride, the wobble in her lip and the fire in her eye when she'd offered herself instead.

"Though I suppose we'll know soon enough," Alistair said, pushing to his feet again, "when the Burke clan descends on Lyneham Park." He made his way across the room, this time to the window. "Or doesn't."

"She'll come," Miles vowed harshly. What choice did she have?

And when she did, she would see why he'd done it. He would show her his home, show her this part of himself that almost no one had ever seen.

He would prove to her that he was more than *that devil, Deveraux.*

CHAPTER 17

At least the presence of Bellis and Lord Stalbridge in the traveling coach had made it impossible for Lady Stalbridge to press Daphne for details about the essay on rakes—or anything else.

Daphne had never been able to determine how much, or even if, Lord Stalbridge knew about the magazine. He seemed a fair-minded, easygoing sort, and clearly head over ears in love with his wife. But none of that meant he would be pleased to discover she was the leader of a secret cabal of young ladies writing to encourage others of their sex to rebel against authority and throw off the burdensome yoke of society's expectations.

"This is a pretty part of the county," he declared, inspecting from the window as the carriage rolled past green fields. "I think we must be almost there."

At those words, the lid of the basket on her sister's lap popped up and Eileen stuck her head out, as if the cat were determined to see for herself whether it was true. Though never particularly happy about being confined to her basket, she was a seasoned traveler, having made her first lengthy voyage, including a trip across the Irish Sea, as a kitten.

With a sideways glance at Daphne to see if she had noticed, Bell poked the cat's pink nose back into the basket and held the lid shut more securely. Daphne had urged her to leave the cat at Finch House, but Bell had insisted Lord Deveraux wouldn't mind. "He likes animals, remember?" she had said, a clear reference to his behavior the night before last, after dinner.

Which had in turn made Daphne doubly determined to prevail, first because Bell never listened to her, and second because she was sure her sister was right. Daphne didn't need another opportunity to confirm Gabriel's claim that you could judge a man's character by whether animals liked him.

As always, however, Bell had her way.

Within the hour, Lord Stalbridge's surmise was proved correct as a redbrick manor house appeared in the distance, at the end of a winding tree-lined road. Daphne glanced out the window from time to time, hoping to catch glimpses through the branches, but reluctant to appear too curious.

"Aren't you dying to see it?" Bell asked, leaning forward to better her own view.

Daphne folded her hands in her lap and deliberately settled her shoulders against the squabs. "Dying? I should hope not."

Soon, though, even tucked well back in the seat as she was, she could not avoid the sight of it: its neat, regular appearance; sunlight glinting off tall windows; lighter stone accenting the darker brick in fanciful designs.

But of course the man had a *charming* house—what else would he have?

"Everything appears to be well-maintained," Lady Stalbridge said approvingly, with a nod toward a rose garden, bordered with perfectly manicured shrubbery on three sides, and a stone wall closest to the house.

"The farmland and cottages too," added Lord Stalbridge, who, when he had unexpectedly inherited his title a few years ago, had foregone repairs to his own house in favor of improving living and working conditions for his tenants. "I couldn't help but notice as we passed."

As they descended from the carriage and approached the house a few steps behind the Stalbridges, Bell touched Daphne's elbow. "How does it feel to know you'll soon be mistress here?" she whispered.

At first, Daphne suspected her of taunting and parted her lips for a sharp retort. But there was openness in her sister's face, a mixture of both awe and encouragement, and Daphne could only answer honestly: "I'm not sure." She was beginning to think that coming here had been a mistake.

The door swung open, and they were bowed inside by the butler, a stately man of about fifty years of age. "Good afternoon. Welcome to Lyneham Park. We've been expecting you."

The central hall was not especially wide, but high ceilings made it feel larger than it was. A curved staircase led to the second floor, while on either side of the hall, double doors stood open to reveal a series of tastefully appointed rooms for dining and other formal entertainments. All was elegant without being showy—choices reflecting the tastes of a previous Lord Deveraux, she felt sure, and not the young man who was currently wasting away his life in Town.

"You are Miss Burke, I take it?" the butler said, showing no hesitation in choosing which of the sisters to address, to Daphne's surprise. Someone must have prepared him for the task.

"I am," Daphne said. "And this is my sister, Miss Bellis Burke, and our traveling companions, Lord and Lady Stalbridge."

The butler bowed to acknowledge all that information. "Very good, ma'am. I am Frost, if you need anything at all. Lord Deveraux was not certain when you would arrive, and so has given me instructions to welcome you and show you to your rooms."

"And where is he?" asked Lady Stalbridge.

"He and Lord Ryland are riding about the park, my lady."

She rolled her eyes at Daphne: *always in pursuit of pleasure,* the look communicated, as clearly as words.

Then Frost continued. "Whenever he returns to Lyneham Park, Lord Deveraux always goes out first thing, to see for himself what is happening on the estate, and to determine whether there are any matters his steward might have overlooked or which require his personal attention."

Without further explanation, he led them up the stairs. Bellis was craning her neck, trying to take in as much as possible, while Lord Stalbridge made some inquiry of the butler Daphne couldn't quite catch. Lady Stalbridge looped her arm through Daphne's and spoke low.

"Matters which require his lordship's personal attention," she echoed. "What a remarkably discreet way of referring to the local farmers' daughters."

Was that the sort of thing Lord Deveraux was hiding?

Daphne forced a wry smile to her lips. "I suppose a rake must have his country amusements, as well as his Town pursuits."

"And here we are," said Frost, pausing before a door. "I hope this will be to your liking, Lord and Lady Stalbridge." The large and lovely room overlooked the grove at the back of the house. "And across the corridor, I've placed Miss Burke." This room, larger yet, was filled with light and provided a lovely view of the rose garden. The furniture was elegant and feminine, the walls painted a soft blue, with coverlet and draperies to match. "Your sister's chamber is adjoining," he added, indicating a connecting door through which a slightly smaller room could be seen.

Her own room! Daphne had to battle the temptation to twirl through the space with open arms. She had never minded sharing with her sister, but what luxury to have all this, all for herself. Had Lord Deveraux realized—? But no, of course not. He'd doubtless left the assignment of the rooms to the housekeeper.

Daphne realized her thoughts were wandering when Frost cleared his throat. "If I may, ma'am? Lord Deveraux did mention something about a rather large dog."

Bell giggled and answered for her. "No dog."

Yet, Daphne added silently.

"Just a cat," Bell finished, holding up her basket. Eileen gave a rather pitiful mewl.

Frost dipped his head, revealing nothing about whether the news surprised or dismayed him, as was only fitting. "Very good, ma'am. I'll see to it that your things are sent up—including a dish of milk. Will there be anything else?"

"Hot water?"

"Already ordered, ma'am. Dinner will be at six o'clock. In the meantime, shall I send some up refreshments, or would you prefer to take tea in the winter parlor, with Lady Deveraux?"

Those two words drove the air from her lungs. *Lady Deveraux.* He was already married? Then what sort of game had he been playing—the wager, Miss Grey, all of it?

It's probably his mother, her brain interjected rationally, trying to calm her racing pulse.

But he's an orphan, some other part of her countered. *Everyone knows that. It's said to be why he's so wild.*

"Who is—?" Bell began. Leave it to her to cut right to the heart of the matter, even if it required interrogating servants.

Lady Stalbridge, who was still standing in the doorway to her own chamber, cut across Bell's question. "Tea in the winter parlor sounds lovely," she said, in a perfectly cool and collected manner. "In half an hour? Will that suit her ladyship?"

"Of course, my lady." Frost explained where the winter parlor was to be found. "I'll see to your things," he finished, though he waited for Daphne's nod of dismissal, which required a nudge from Bell.

"But who is Lady Deveraux?" Bell demanded to know as soon as the butler was out of earshot.

"Lord Deveraux's grandmother," said Lady Stalbridge, with an indulgent though slightly annoyed glance toward her husband. "Apparently."

"I met her," said Lord Stalbridge, "several years ago. When I first inherited the earldom, I took a notion to introduce myself to all my new neighbors—Ferncliffe is only seventeen miles from here. When I called at Lyneham Park, Lord Deveraux was away from home. I had the pleasure of making Lady Deveraux's acquaintance instead. I would have mentioned her, but I assumed you already knew, Miss Burke—and of course, there was always the possibility that she was no longer . . ." He made a circle in the air with one hand, rather than speak the morbid words aloud. "She was elderly and frail, even then. But an extraordinary woman. She raised him, you know. Your betrothed."

Daphne could only shake her head. Being brought up in the country by one's grandmother was not the sort of life experience one bragged about to cement one's status as a rake.

"She must be so proud of the man he's become," said Lady Stalbridge. Her tone of voice made it impossible to determine whether she meant the words to be sincere or cutting.

And on that note, they all retreated into their separate chambers to freshen up before tea.

"His grandmother," Bell repeated with a soft, incredulous laugh, shaking her head as she unhooked the catch on Eileen's basket and set the cat free to roam. "Do you know, for a moment I thought—"

"You've been reading too many novels," Daphne chided, rather than reveal her own alarm. Her heart was still racing, though now the speed of her pulse was driven as much by guilt as surprise. Had she really imagined he'd lured her here, like the villain in some gothic romance, even extended an invitation to the most powerful and protective members of her family, all the while plotting to commit bigamy under his wife's nose?

She was in danger of putting too much stock in her own essay.

In a matter of moments, trunks, bags, and cannisters of hot water began to arrive. Daphne washed her face and, with a maid's assistance, changed into a dress of sprigged muslin that Cami's lady's maid had packed with special care to avoid it becoming wrinkled on the journey. "You will want to look nice from the start," she had insisted, "without waiting for some poor girl to heat an iron."

While the same maid assisted Bell in changing her gown, Daphne strolled to the window and looked down. She wasn't quite sure what she had expected of Lyneham Park, but a garden that put the Dowager Duchess of Raynham's to shame hadn't been a part of it. It was a large house, but not so big that one could never really feel comfortable. Impressive without any sign of showiness—unless one counted the riot of roses below. Even then, the flowers were restrained by borders of carefully trimmed shrubbery.

This sort of home and estate weren't maintained through absence and indifference. Someone cared a great deal. And even if that someone was the steward, he still would be acting on the wishes of—

She snapped off the thought—or tried to. Rather like a green twig, it bent instead of breaking.

She did not know how to reconcile this place with the Miles she knew.

Or, more accurately, with the Miles Miss Busy B. had created.

Perhaps the answer lay in Lady Deveraux's character. Perhaps she was a dragon who demanded everything here be kept in perfect order and who had the servants trembling to fulfill her every unreasonable wish. Perhaps she had exerted such terrible authority that Miles had been driven to escape as soon as he could, been driven to rebel against the rules, to sample every pleasure that had been forbidden to him. . . .

"Are you ready?" Daphne called out impatiently to Bell, eager to test her hypothesis.

"Not quite. Go along without me," Bell urged. "I don't wish to keep Lord and Lady Stalbridge waiting, and I'm sure I can find my way."

With a nod of understanding and agreement, Daphne stepped across the corridor to discover that Lord and Lady Stalbridge's trunks had only just been brought up— precedence had been given, quite unaccountably, to fetching and unpacking Daphne's things.

"There must have been some misunderstanding," she began.

But Lady Stalbridge waved away her explanation. "It's quite natural that you be the guest of honor," she said. "Go along. We shan't be a moment."

So Daphne made her way alone to the far end of the corridor, where Frost had told her she would find the winter parlor. Contrary to its cold, gloomy name, it was a bright, window-filled room that had clearly been fitted up for a lady's enjoyment, with delicate furniture and walls papered in wide, cheerful stripes of butter yellow and apple green, the least wintry shades imaginable.

Two women were seated near one another in a pair of chairs facing a window and the garden below. When Daphne entered, the woman on the left rose quickly and turned. She was plump, with light brown hair and a merry smile. Her hands, which she was holding up a few inches apart, were wrapped in purple yarn. "Ma'am," she said to the other lady in an enthusiastic tone, "it seems Lord Deveraux's guests have begun to arrive."

"'Bout time," said the older lady gruffly, without looking up from her needlework. And then she laughed. "Well, come and introduce yourself, since my grandson isn't here to do it."

Hesitantly, Daphne approached and circled around in front of the two women to drop a curtsy. "Pleased to meet you, my lady. I'm Daphne Burke."

Lady Deveraux had probably always been a small woman, but the frailties of age had shrunken her further. Her presence, however, was considerably greater than her stature. As she spoke, she went on crocheting, though never glancing toward her needle. "I was not expecting a young lady among the guests," she said. "And unmarried?"

"Yes, ma'am," said Daphne, somewhat taken aback by the question.

"Interesting." She tilted her head to the side, and when the light struck full in her face, Daphne realized suddenly that Lady Deveraux was blind, or nearly so. A lack of sight did not seem to have diminished her perceptiveness in any other area, however. "Irish, yes? I can tell from your voice."

"Yes, ma'am," she answered again, bracing herself for some cutting remark. "From Dublin."

The needle flashed, and the other woman, evidently Lady Deveraux's companion, sat down in order to relieve some of the tension on the yarn. "I assume you did not travel all this way alone," Lady Deveraux said after a moment.

"I came from London with my younger sister, Bellis, under the chaperonage of Lord and Lady Stalbridge."

"Stalbridge," she echoed, pausing. "Ah, yes. Of Ferncliffe. I met him once."

Daphne, uncertain how else to respond, once more said, "Yes, ma'am," and then added, "They'll be joining us any moment. I was ready first and came ahead to the winter parlor, as your butler instructed."

"Eager," she said with a sort of chuckle that made the word less alarming to Daphne than it had been earlier that day. "I like that. Well, ring for tea, Palmer."

Miss Palmer glanced at her yarn-encased hands, and then over her shoulder, at the bell pull near the door.

"May I—?" Daphne began.

Before she could finish her offer to go the bell, Miss Palmer smiled her gratitude and handed off the yarn, sliding it around Daphne's hands. With a slight flicker of uncertainty, Daphne took her place in the chair beside Lady Deveraux.

"Now, tell me," the viscountess began in a lower voice, "how did my scoundrel of a grandson lure you here for an old lady's birthday celebration? Mind the yarn, child—not too taut—there's a dear."

Birthday celebration? Not a wedding?

Daphne felt suddenly if she'd walked onstage in the middle of a theatrical performance and taken up a part without knowing any of the lines. "Wh—I, er—"

"One presumes he lured Miss Burke with much the same bait he lures me, time after time," declared Lord Ryland from the doorway. "Good company and fresh country air." He was still clad in his riding clothes, looking more comfortable than she had ever seen him, though from his reddened eyes, she could guess the much-lauded country air didn't entirely agree with him.

Lady Deveraux seemed content with his explanation and accepted a kiss on the cheek from him. "Did you find ought amiss at Lyneham?" she demanded.

"Never. You have been singularly blessed in your choice of steward, ma'am."

Daphne was prepared to believe this formidable old lady ran the estate with a mere snap of her fingers, but

Lady Deveraux demurred. "Deveraux's choice, as you well know."

A reference to Miles's father, perhaps?

"And for what am I being slandered in my absence?" Miles called out as he sauntered into the room—then stopped the moment he laid eyes on Daphne. He snapped into a bow. "Miss Burke."

She had considered him handsome when dressed for the ballroom, but this was a version of him she had never even thought to imagine, and would never have imagined could be so appealing, clad in worn buckskin breeches and a drab duster with mud on the hem and a tear on one sleeve. He gathered his gloves, crop, and hat in one hand and dragged the other through his sweat-dampened hair.

"You are . . . here. And"—his brown eyes darted between her and his grandmother—"*here*. And . . . alone?"

"Very astute," chided his grandmother, who had handed off her needlework to Daphne and was struggling to rise with the assistance of a cane and Lord Ryland's hand.

Miss Palmer scurried over to collect the yarn and needle from Daphne and laid them in a nearby basket.

Daphne stood and turned to face Miles. "Lord and Lady Stalbridge had planned to travel into Hertfordshire already and were good enough to bring me and Bellis."

Miles's voice was flat when he spoke. "Lord and Lady Ashborough would not come, then." Some of the pleasure leached from his expression, giving way to what looked for all the world like anger.

"*Could* not come," corrected Lady Stalbridge as she sailed into the room behind him, her arm linked with Bell's. "Young children have an inordinate capacity to disrupt plans, as you yourself may discover one day."

Lady Deveraux chortled. "You must be Lady Stalbridge. And the younger Miss Burke is with you?"

Daphne wondered whether she had made out Bell's shape or heard the extra footsteps.

"Yes, ma'am," Bell said, and curtsied. "Pleased to make your acquaintance."

"And where is Lord Stalbridge?"

"Begging your pardon, ma'am," answered Lady Stalbridge, "but after all those hours confined in the carriage, he could not resist taking a stroll."

"An excellent notion," Miles declared, still looking rather agitated. "Shall we join him?"

"Palmer has just rung for tea," said his grandmother.

"I will stay with Lady Deveraux, if you please," said Lord Ryland, patting her hand, which now lay along his arm.

"As will I," said Lady Stalbridge.

Her wrinkled face creased into a smile. "Excellent. Be warned, we shall not promise to save any jam cake for those who abandon us."

"I never pass up jam cake," said Bell. She sent Daphne a sly glance. "But I do believe my sister would prefer a walk in the flower garden."

"Is that so, Miss Burke?" Though there was still some strain lingering about his mouth, Miles mustered a boyish grin as he approached and held out his arm.

If she had dared to glance toward Lady Stalbridge for permission to walk with him, she would have seen an encouraging glint in her eyes.

Research, Daphne tried to tell herself. An opportunity to observe the man in—well, perhaps not quite his natural habitat, which was more likely to be a gaming hell or a brothel. But at Lyneham Park she had a unique opportunity to discover what, if anything, lay behind his mask of rakish charm.

Drawing a deep breath, she laid a hand along his forearm, instantly aware of his strength yet determinedly ignoring the way her fingertips tingled. "Indeed it is."

CHAPTER 18

How could something be so wonderful and so terrible at the same time?

Seeing Daphne at Lyneham Park, the window behind her framing her in a lovely view of the rose garden, Grandmama's yarn encasing her hands, a smile on both women's faces—it was better than he had imagined.

And a potent reminder of how low he had sunk to make it reality.

Perhaps Daphne, like Alistair, would understand why he'd done it without him having to explain. She was clever, after all.

But she *deserved* an explanation, whether she required one or not. Then, an apology.

And finally her freedom.

Unless . . . Unless, in one-two-three-four—oh, God, only *four?*—days, he could convince her she wanted to stay. At Lyneham. With him.

With his fingers resting on the carved finial at the top of the stairs, he tapped out the remaining days of the week—twice, to make sure he hadn't miscounted—feeling the time slip away. Even these few minutes, waiting for Daphne to retrieve her bonnet and pelisse, were too precious to lose.

At last, she emerged from her chamber and approached him, her hands folded in front of her. He did not offer his arm.

"The room is to your liking? It's the nicest of the guest rooms—but you may have any you choose." No sooner had the offer passed his lips than he wished he could take it back. She would suspect him of mocking her again, would doubt the sincerity of his desire to please.

"Shouldn't that room go to Lord Ryland?"

"He abhors the view. He would prefer to forget the existence of roses entirely."

The brim of her bonnet shielded her expression from him; he felt certain she'd chosen it for just that reason. But it could not hide her soft laugh. "Well, *I* think it's lovely. And quite an indulgence not to have to share with Bell and her cat. Please thank your housekeeper for me."

I chose it, he wanted to correct her.

But that would only make matters worse.

In the entry hall, a footman swung open the front door and bowed them from the house. Even with the broad gravel drive separating them from the roses, the flowers' scent was heavy on the air, and he would have been willing to swear he could hear the low murmur of bees at work among the blossoms.

"What a lovely afternoon," she said, pausing to tip her face to the fair sky.

"Isn't it?"

He was jealous—jealous of the sunshine caressing her cheek, being rewarded with her lovely smile.

Could a fellow be more pathetic?

He was willing to admit, even to himself, that he liked her—but such thoughts hinted at more than mere liking.

"The garden was my grandmother's plan," he explained, bending to unlatch the wrought iron gate in the low stone wall that divided the garden from the drive. "Her pride and joy."

"She has not always been—?"

She bit off the rest of her question, but he could guess what she had been about to say. "Blind? No, that affliction has befallen her gradually over the last few years. She manages remarkably well, however, with the assistance of her companion, Miss Palmer."

The brim of the bonnet dipped, not quite a nod. "She seems happy to have you here. Do you visit often?"

"I fear the only proper answer that can be given, even by a dutiful grandson, is 'not often enough,'" he answered, waving her into the garden with a sweep of his arm. "I spend every autumn and part of every winter here, and during the rest of the year, I visit on occasion."

"Occasions such as her birthday."

Had she worked it out already, his ridiculous plan? Not trusting his voice, he made no answer.

They strolled along one of several winding gravel paths, which, despite meticulous raking by a veritable army of gardeners, was still uneven in places. He longed to offer his arm again, but she gave no sign of wanting it.

"Your journey was not unpleasant, I hope?" he ventured after a stretch of silence, filled only by the buzzing of insects and Daphne's occasional deeply drawn breath. "If I may, how did it happen that the Stalbridges—?"

"My sister is indisposed—nothing too serious," she hastily added. "Lord and Lady Stalbridge were on their way to Ferncliffe, and as Cami and Lady Stalbridge are friends, the Stalbridges were kind enough to bring me and Bell, and to offer their chaperonage until Cami and Gabriel are able to travel."

"Lord and Lady Ashborough will come, then?"

"Yes, in a day or two."

"You might have waited," he pointed out, though he was glad she hadn't. His four precious days might have been cut down to two, or only one.

At last she turned and looked him full in the face, her eyes a true blue in the sunlight, her expression wary. "Might I? You would not have objected? Threa—?"

"No!" He spoke more sharply than he had intended, desperate to cut across that terrible word. "No," he repeated in a softer voice. "I assure you I have had ample practice in mastering my disappointment."

She made a small noise—skeptical, dismissive—and turned back to the flowers.

"You don't believe me?"

"I am hard-pressed to imagine you have even *experienced* disappointment," she said, with a wave of her arm intended to encompass the glorious garden, the manor house, and the park beyond, "to say nothing of having suffered through enough of it to call yourself its master. Though perhaps it is simply your nature, to lord your power over everything, and everyone, around you."

An instinctive protest rose to his lips. He loved her wit, her ready retorts, the spark of defiance in her eyes. But now was not the time to encourage such a display. His devilishness was hardly up for debate.

He had caroused when he should have been sober, rattled when he should have listened, shouted when a quiet word would have better served the purpose. He had often been selfish—was being selfish now, he supposed, though that hadn't been his intent.

"Perhaps you're right," he conceded.

Slowly, she twisted to look up at him with slack-jawed astonishment.

"But what boy, or even young man," he went on, "born to such immense privilege, with none but an elderly grandmother to check him, would not have tested the limits of his authority from time to time? Purely a rhetorical question," he assured her, raising a staying hand. "No need to reply."

He glanced up at the windows of the winter parlor, wondering whether their little tête-à-tête was being held under the watchful eye of Lady Stalbridge. But the sun glanced off the panes of glass, transforming them into sheets of hammered gold.

"The correct answer, by the way, is obviously Lord Ryland." He led Daphne toward a stone bench nestled into an alcove in the shrubbery, the only spot in the garden not in full view of the house. "He has shouldered his own inheritance—a crumbling estate and the care of seven sisters—with grace and generosity of spirit. If, in the last sixteen years, he has ever stepped a toe out of line, I'm sure I was behind him, giving him a nudge."

"A pity he could not have been a better influence on you," she said, as she sat down and arranged her skirts.

She was teasing him, or so he thought from her voice.

"Ah, Miss Burke," he countered. "You fail to consider: without him, I might have been worse."

Before he sat down, he broke off a single blossom from a nearby rosebush, a deep, vivid pink, almost red. When he held it out, she took it from him without meeting his eye, twisting the stem between her first finger and thumb. "What a vibrant shade."

The stone was cool beneath his palms as he eased himself onto the seat beside her. "Almost as vibrant as you."

She twirled the blossom again, lazily back and forth, then brought it up to her nose, inhaling its sweet scent and brushing its velvet petals over her upper lip. "Why do you do that?"

"Do what?"

"Pay me such outlandish compliments. Flirt even when no one else is by to overhear."

He considered the possible answers—and coy non-answers—he might offer. Then he remembered his wish, halfhearted though it might have been, that there had been some honesty between himself and Arabella Grey.

"Habit, I suppose," he told her with a weary sigh, curving his hand around the front edge of the stone bench. They'd been in this position once before, in the Duchess of Raynham's garden. He wasn't sure yet how to measure that day in the progress of their strange not-quite-a-sham courtship. "Because, in my experience, those are the sorts of things women like to hear." Out of the corner of his eye, he caught the movement of her hand as she laid aside the flower, and her head, bobbing in agreement, her worst suspicions about him confirmed.

So, he cast his gaze out over the rose garden instead, thinking about the curious mixture of wildness and careful cultivation, the juxtaposition of sweetness and thorns. "And also because it is the truth, though I did not recognize it at first. You *are* beautiful and sweet and lively and sharp—whether you see those things in yourself or not. Whether you want them to be seen, by me or anyone else."

The hum of insects filled the silence that followed, punctuated by the trills of a lark somewhere beyond the hedge wall. Daphne crossed and uncrossed her feet at the ankles. Her hands, which had been folded in her lap, slid to the bench, one on either side of her hips, as if she were preparing to rise and leave him there.

Then the little finger of her left hand brushed—accidentally, surely—against the little finger of his right hand. Hers gloved, his bare. He thought again of that moment beneath her sister's rooftop arbor.

This time, however, she didn't pull away.

"Does she know? About our . . ." She swallowed before speaking the word. "Betrothal?"

"My grandmother? No. Though I'm sure she senses something unusual in the air. I've never invited a young lady to Lyneham Park before."

"Oh." Her knuckles poked sharply against the soft leather

of her glove as she curled her fingers against the stone. "Then I . . . I'm honored you wish to show it to me."

"Even under the circumstances?" he dared to ask after a moment.

"Even then." The tremor of a nervous laugh passed through her. "I think. That is to say—"

"I understand. We each of us had in mind a list of attributes that were wanted in the person we married. I have undoubtedly been more fortunate than I deserve, and you"—he turned toward her and winked—"you are mastering—mistressing?—your disappointment."

She laughed, very clearly in spite of herself. "It's not *that*—not exactly, anyway. It's . . . well, I suppose it does come down to knowledge: the things I know, wish to know, may never know about you. But to be willing to share your home, your family, with me . . . Why, it's as if I had dragged you to Merrion Square and offered to show you the box in which I kept all my childhood treasures. Are you not afraid you may reveal too much?"

"Afraid *I* may reveal too much? Ryland and my grandmama are the real dangers there, I should think."

She shook her head, but reluctant amusement still danced across her features. "Aren't you afraid *this place* may reveal too much, then?" she corrected herself.

He tested the notion. Ought he to be frighted by what she might discover about him here? Probably.

But for better or worse, he wasn't.

"No."

That single word sent her springing to her feet, startling into flight the bird that had been hidden in the shrubbery behind them. Almost as if Daphne were the one who was frightened—as if, as he'd once accused her, she feared liking him too well.

"Because you're not worried about what I might find?" She twisted her fingers before her. "Or because, whatever I find, nothing will change? I'll still be expected to marry you at the end of the week, or have my own secrets revealed."

He stood, too, and crossed his arms behind his back, but did not speak. Whatever reassurance he could make would sound hollow. He had to concentrate his efforts on proving to her that his winning a wager did not mean she had lost everything.

"Do you wish to explore more of the garden? Or return to the house?" He tipped his head, the better to see beneath the shadow of her bonnet's brim. "Grandmama wasn't joking about the jam cake. We'll be reduced to bread and butter if we wait much longer."

She didn't smile again, but some of the panic left her eyes. "I don't mind. I prefer bread and butter, to be honest. But I . . . I'm not really hungry right now. I think I'd rather walk a bit longer."

"Alone?"

Strange how one person's greatest fear could be another's deepest craving. Time to herself was a concession he could hardly afford to make, a precious half hour carved from the few days he had left to make things right.

But if she needed it, he would give it to her.

She lifted one shoulder, her lack of certainty both genuine and reassuring—he'd half expected her to shout *Of course, you dolt!* and order him from the garden like a petite Irish archangel, minus the flaming sword.

Instead, she turned toward a path they had not yet wandered, casting an uncertain glance over her shoulder. He took it for an invitation to follow.

"What are you most eager for me to see?" she asked after a moment.

He answered with a question of his own. "What do you most want to know?"

"Your favorite spot at Lyneham Park."

"Oh, that's very tricky. It changes, you see, depending

on the season and the weather and . . . well, my mood, I suppose."

That wasn't quite true. There was a spot . . . one spot. But surely Daphne had meant something a bit more . . . ? Or perhaps a bit less . . . ? Well.

Nothing ventured, nothing gained.

"Can you ride?" he asked.

"A little. Tristan insisted that if we were going to spend any time at Hawesdale Chase, both Bell and I had to learn how. It's very remote. But I think . . ." She gave a self-deprecating laugh. "I think I prefer walking. Or rather, I think every horse I've ever ridden would rather I had chosen to walk instead." They strode a few steps farther, side by side. "I suppose—" She glanced up at him. "I suppose you're a smashing rider?"

He was.

"We'll manage," he assured her. Humble though it might be, he found he genuinely wanted to share with her the spot he'd never shown another soul, not even Alistair. "There's always the dog cart."

That earned him the Miss Busy B. expression that amused him so.

She had paused in front of a statue of a winged cherub—thankfully more clothed than those in Ryland's room. Cupid, he supposed, given the bow clutched in the figure's dimpled hands. The arrows were still in the quiver; Miles tried not to see it as an omen.

"What about your least favorite spot?"

"The schoolroom," he answered without hesitation.

He heard her gasp of dismay, though she'd tried to contain it. "I used to dream of being a teacher."

Of course she had.

"We never had a proper schoolroom, though," she went on. "And I daresay the lessons weren't all that conventional either. Entertaining, to be sure—and we still seem to have learned a lot, in spite of the messes and the laughter."

"I might have enjoyed school with a bit more of either," he said with a rueful chuckle, rubbing his hands together at the memory. "It's a wonder I'm not arthritic from all the rapped knuckles."

"How awful. We won't go there, then," she declared.

"I imagine it's in a dreadful, dusty state. But I shouldn't mind seeing it again," he insisted. "Not after all these years. Not with you beside me."

"More flirtation?" The words were clearly meant as a scold, albeit a gentler one than he deserved.

"Yes," he confessed. "Is it working?"

One brow arched higher yet, and she did not answer. But she did match her steps to his as they continued on the path, and a few moments later, she slipped a hand around his elbow.

"What happened here?" She plucked at the frayed threads along the split in his sleeve.

"Foolishness," he answered dismissively. He hadn't yet examined whether the tear had gone through to his coat beneath. And he'd be lucky his valet didn't succumb to the vapors when he saw the state of his boots. He laid his hand over hers to stay her worrying fingers—and to keep her by his side.

"Foolishness and flirtation," she repeated. "I believe I could've seen that without coming all this way."

He let the gentle pressure of her hand on his arm steer them back toward the house. A retreat, of sorts. He supposed he couldn't blame her.

"If you're expecting to uncover a great depth of character," he warned, "I fear you're bound to be disappointed."

She tilted her head slightly, as if she were looking him up and down. What, he wondered, did she see? The brim of her bonnet, combined with the disparity in their heights, meant he could glimpse nothing more of her expression than the upturned corner of her mouth.

"Am I?"

Good God. He couldn't make up his mind whether she liked him or despised him.

Perhaps she couldn't make up her mind either.

Her confusion was understandable. Probably the best he could hope for, under the circumstances. But it left his thoughts as convoluted as the maze of garden paths beneath their feet.

CHAPTER 19

Daphne flopped onto her back, her head striking the pile of down-filled pillows with a soft *whump,* then flailed about trying to free her limbs from the tangle of linens.

As it turned out, it was not as easy to sleep without Bell nearby as she had thought it would be.

But really . . . how long could she possibly lie there, staring into the dark, recounting snippets of dinner conversation in her mind?

One snippet, in particular.

It had been a pleasant meal shared among pleasant company, and no one, not even Bell, had been inclined to tease Miles about missing tea or remark on Daphne's sudden propensity toward woolgathering.

They had been joined at the table by Lady Deveraux's companion, Miss Palmer, and by Mr. Palmer, her brother and Lyneham Park's steward. He was a man of at most thirty-five, clearly too young to have been hired by the late Lord Deveraux, as Daphne had at first imagined. A pleasant, gentlemanlike fellow, he had spent most of the evening discussing matters of estate management with Lord Stalbridge, who took an acute interest in such things.

The problem—and it was, to be clear, a problem only in Daphne's mind—was when Lord Stalbridge had asked some benign question about livestock. Mr. Palmer, whose smile was almost as merry as his sister's, had suggested that Lord Deveraux's opinion be consulted on the matter. Upon having the question repeated, Miles, who had been talking about something else entirely with Lady Stalbridge, blushed.

And that was how it had come to pass that Lord Ryland regaled the whole table with the story of Miles's assistance to the farmer whose ram had got his horns tangled in a hedgerow and couldn't work himself free.

In Lord Ryland's telling, the encounter had been amusing, rather than alarming, with considerable suspense in the outcome—whose stubbornness would win out in the end, Miles's or the ram's?

It also perfectly explained Miles's muddy, disheveled state when he'd returned to the house.

Though it had produced much laughter—and a striking mental image—none of it would have been the sort of thing that kept Daphne lying awake, restless in her bed. No, the problem was Mr. Palmer's quiet words to Lord Stalbridge, when the general conversation had moved on to another topic: "Lord Deveraux has never been a man for numbers, but he's right good with his hands."

The steward had clearly intended the remark as praise, though Daphne could think of few gentlemen who would regard it as such. During the rest of dinner, she had considered what it said of Miles that he was willing to get involved, to help his tenants, in such a personal, physical manner. She had thought first of what the butler had said that afternoon, about how a tour of the estate was always one of Miles's first acts whenever he returned, to see for himself how things were. Such details spoke surprisingly well of him as a landowner.

In the drawing room afterward, while Miss Palmer played and Miles and occasionally Lord Ryland and Bellis sang, she had begun to reflect more on Mr. Palmer's claim that Miles wasn't good with numbers. In the garden, Miles had named the schoolroom as his least favorite spot at Lyneham. It was of a piece, she supposed. In her own family, learning had been highly valued for both boys and girls, but she understood that in the world at large, girls were often forbidden from acquiring much education, and many boys like Miles spent much of their time at school on things other than books.

Still, something about the exchange niggled at her.

By the time she was alone in her bed, her wayward thoughts had begun to dwell on the latter part of Mr. Palmer's observation. And now, she couldn't stop thinking about Miles's strong, long-fingered, and surprisingly tanned hands.

Or perhaps not so surprisingly. He'd tossed aside his ruined gloves before going out to the garden and not bothered to don another pair. Which made the succession of pictures in her mind's eye distressingly clear: his hand proffering a rose, his hand resting beside hers on the rough stone bench, his hand lightly pinning hers to his corded forearm.

Good with his hands . . .

It was a short jaunt from those mental images to the memory of his touch, the heat of those strong hands on her nape, her waist, her breast.

Good with his hands . . .

She swept a sweat-dampened palm down the front of her nightgown to quell a shudder of longing. Of *course* he was good with his hands. He was a rake, after all. She should be writing all this down, recording his own damning words about flirtation and the sorts of silly things he believed women liked to hear. Nonsense about being as beautiful and vibrant and sweet as a flower . . .

Where *was* her writing desk? She hadn't seen it since their arrival. Probably, in the flurry of unpacking, someone had taken it to Bell's or Lady Stalbridge's room by mistake.

No matter. She could retrieve it in the morning. But in the meantime . . .

She swung her legs out of bed and reached for her dressing gown. Through a partly opened door, she'd glimpsed a library on the far side of the drawing room. Surely she would find paper and ink there. Perhaps even something more useful for her essay, letters or a diary or a record of his gambling debts. And barring that, she could at least find a book, anything to quiet this strange restlessness that had suffused her spirit.

On bare feet and by the light of a single candle, she padded along the corridor and down the stairs, stepping with comic quickness over the cold marble tile of the entry hall and more slowly over the drawing room's plush wool carpet.

The door to the library had been designed to disappear when it was fully closed, as it was now, painted and trimmed so that it blended seamlessly with the wall around it. It took several moments for her to find the latch, and when she did, she wondered whether she mightn't find it locked.

But it sprang open at her touch. Moonlight joined with her candle to reveal a modest-sized room, warmly furnished in darker, heavier pieces than the rest of the house. Two tall bookcases, filled with leather-bound volumes, stood opposite the door, with a window between them and a stately desk in front of it, facing into the room.

Ignoring everything else, she approached the bookshelves, intending to survey the titles. But when she reached the desk, she could not help but caress the cool, highly polished wood. The only items on its top were a silver tray containing pens and sealing wax, and a blotter that bore no mark of use, not a single scratch or drop of ink. Perhaps everything of any significance was tucked away from prying eyes. Perhaps he did his real work elsewhere, and the desk in the library was merely for show. Or perhaps he avoided the sort of work that required a desk entirely.

She slipped around the corner of the desk, set the candlestick on its top, and eased silently into the chair. If she was careful, she could explore without anyone being the wiser. With one trembling fingertip, she traced the brass fixtures, ornate scrolled faceplates and knobs and tiny keyholes. She might find any number of intriguing items in the desk's myriad drawers and cubbyholes, things that would reveal much about the master of Lyneham Park. Things that would prove beyond a shadow of a doubt the thesis of her essay on rakes.

Things she was no longer certain she wanted to find.

What had happened to her over the last few days? She folded her arms on the desktop and dropped her forehead to them, resisting the impulse to *thunk* it down on the unforgiving wood instead.

Had Miss Busy B. lost her sting?

"Daphne?"

Popping up her head, she discovered Miles watching her from across the room, lounging against the doorframe, arms crossed over his chest.

She jumped to her feet with such rapidity, she had to spin around to catch the chair before it fell and nearly knocked over her candlestick in the process.

"All right, then?" he asked, unfolding his arms and taking a step closer.

"Perfectly. That is, I . . . I couldn't sleep."

His eyes grazed over her, seeming to take in every detail of her dishabille, most particularly the rapid rise and fall of her breasts as she tried to rein in her racing heart.

"Nor I," he confessed with a boyish, self-deprecating smile that did nothing to aid her efforts. "I saw your light."

She sidled around the corner of the desk and came to stand beside it, closer to one of the bookcases. "Were you also looking for something to read?"

"No." Three steps closer, then he paused. "I fancied a walk."

He was still dressed, she realized. Or mostly. His shirt was open at the collar, his cravat missing entirely. He was once more clad in the buckskin breeches, soft with wear, now paired with scuffed, slouching boots that would not require his valet's assistance to doff. His only coat was his drab duster; someone had brushed the mud from the hem and carefully mended the torn sleeve.

"I would invite you to join me, but . . ." His gaze had fallen to her feet.

She crossed the ball of one foot over the toes of the other, though there was no disguising that they were bare. "Anyway, I'm not sure that would be wise."

He shook his head in agreement, and the candlelight picked out glimmers of gold in his hair. "I wouldn't want you to catch a chill."

Though she hadn't felt cold, at his words, a shiver chased up her spine, betraying her.

Shrugging out of the duster, he came forward to drape it around her shoulders. "Better?"

Worse. So much worse. His scent rose from the fabric, so wonderfully, provocatively male.

Even after the coat was in place, he still gripped it by the placket, holding it closed at the base of her throat, his knuckles resting lightly against her collarbones. Surely, he felt how she had to swallow before she could manage even three hoarse words: "Yes, thank you." She didn't dare look up to meet his eyes.

But looking straight ahead was dangerous too: the wedge of bare skin revealed by his open collar. That intriguing hollow at the base of his throat. A dusting of light brown hair below it, disappearing into his shirt.

She wanted, quite desperately, to lay her palm—her cheek—against his chest, to feel the heat of his skin, the contour of his muscles, the beating of his heart. But to cross such an intimate line?

After such a bold advance, there could be no retreat.

"Close your eyes," he ordered.

"What?"

Startled, she managed to drag her gaze upward, over his stubbled jaw, to his mouth. She watched as his lips curved into a sardonic smile.

"I've just remembered. We're in the library, and I'd say this is dimly lit, wouldn't you? I promised I'd show you—"

Blood rushed into unexpected places. The tips of her ears. The secret spot between her legs. "That's really not—I should go back to—"

"Shh." Forming that sound pushed his lips into the most kissable shape. "Close your eyes, my dear. That's it."

To her utter astonishment, once she had complied, he released his hold on his coat and stepped away from her. Before she could form a question, she felt him behind her. His right arm passed around her body and his hand came to rest lightly over her closed eyes. "No peeking." She could hear the smile in his voice. He slid his other hand down her left arm to her wrist, her hand. "Now walk," he murmured into her ear, guiding her steps with their joined hands and the gentle pressure of his body at her back.

Absent her sight, her other senses seemed painfully acute: her awareness of everywhere they touched, his warmth, his scent, made her feel weak at the knees.

"I won't let you stumble into anything," he said. "You can trust me."

Had there ever been a more outrageous claim?

But she did as he asked, nonetheless. Let him lead her across the room. From behind closed eyes, she tried to recall the rest of the room's furniture, tried to picture where he might be taking her. She hadn't paid much attention, her focus solely on the desk, but hadn't there been a sofa to the left, by the window that faced the front of the house? Except he seemed to be steering her toward the right. . . .

"Stop. That's far enough." He lowered his right arm to uncover her eyes but did not release her hand. "Now, open."

She blinked several times, but even when she could focus clearly, she couldn't make sense of what she saw. In the corner of the room to which he'd led her sat a small, round, pedestal table, its top inlaid with a checkered design. And on that pattern sat a marble chess set, the pieces arrayed for play.

"I . . . I don't understand."

"That night, in the Greys' library," he prompted. "What Arabella saw me doing with Mrs. Wellcroft . . ."

"You and she were . . . playing chess?"

"I'm not very good. Ryland tried for years to teach me, but . . ." Her own arm lifted slightly with his sheepish shrug. "I'm something of a hopeless case."

Unbidden, Daphne squeezed shut her eyes again, trying to call up the details of Aggrieved in Grosvenor Square's letter, the specific accusation it had leveled. The detail she had assumed was a euphemism, unfit for print.

"You were playing chess," she repeated flatly.

His soft laugh stirred her hair, the sound of a man pleased by his own cleverness, and he brushed the pad of his thumb across the back of the hand he still held, in what she supposed was intended to be a soothing gesture. "You see? I'm not the rakish villain everyone's made me out to be." He chuckled again, more rueful this time. "Not entirely, anyway."

No, he wasn't the man Miss Busy B. had imagined when she'd set out along this path to avenge Miss Grey and to warn the innocent readers of the *Magazine for Misses*. And the more time Daphne spent with *this* Miles, the more her desire for him grew.

Slowly, she opened her eyes again. So far from the candle,

with their shadows falling over the chessboard, it was difficult even to distinguish the light pieces from the dark.

But someone had to make the next move.

She drew in a breath, the ragged sound loud in the stillness surrounding them. "What if . . . what if I wanted you to be? Rakish, that is. Just a little."

She'd shocked him. His thumb, which had been sweeping lazily over her knuckles, paused, as if every part of him were involved in considering what his answer ought to be.

Mortification consumed her like a flame when he released her hand and took a step backward. Of course he didn't want her—he wanted to win his wager. Their courtship was nothing but a show for others. Just flirtation and foolishness, as she'd said in the garden.

Well, it didn't matter anyway. She didn't really want him either. She'd only been hoping to trick him into revealing the side of himself she needed to see for that blasted essay. It was fine. All fine. She could still use tonight's encounter to—

His hands rose to her shoulders, plucking off his duster and tossing it onto a nearby chair. Then his lips found the side of her neck, below her ear. Three kisses whose very softness hinted at something barely leashed. And when he spoke, the strain in his voice made her shiver with delight.

"Just a little," he vowed, his breath hot against her skin.

CHAPTER 20

Just a little. Had more foolish words ever been spoken? As if he were known for moderation and restraint—especially with a half-dressed, beautiful woman in his arms. As if his rakish thoughts about Daphne hadn't driven him from his bed to seek a measure of . . . solace, self-restraint, anyway . . . in the cool night air.

If necessary, he had known where to find an icy spring.

Now, here he was, with his arms around her—

Good God. When had he put his arms around her? It was as if his body had a mind of its own, one forearm banding her waist, snugging their hips together, the other across her chest, pillowed on her breasts.

He wanted to mark her pale skin with his kisses, to claim her for all to see. To nudge forward with his pelvis so she could feel his growing arousal. To gather her nightclothes in his fist and inch them higher, higher . . .

It was like some horrible test of his character, his will.

And he'd never done well on tests.

He slackened his hold, just a little, and managed to put a scant inch between his rapidly thickening cock and the lush curve of her bottom. "Daphne, love," he whispered against her ear, "when you said you wanted me to be *just a little* rakish, what did you have in mind?"

Her chest rose and fell on an unsteady breath as she considered. "I don't know," she said after a moment, her voice fretful, almost at the edge of desperation already.

"Hush," he sighed soothingly against her cheek.

Not that he knew the answer either. He tried to imagine what she might be thinking. But he'd never taken an innocent to his bed.

"Kisses?" he suggested.

Some of the tension eased from her frame, the relief of encountering something familiar on a journey that had the potential to be perilous. Her head dipped up and down. "Yes, please," she said, moving as if to turn in his arms.

He tightened his grip to keep her in place. He wanted that bit of skin her nod had revealed, the back of her neck, where a few soft curls had escaped her braid and beckoned to him now.

Shifting slightly, he bent his head to that precious spot, freeing one hand just long enough to peel away the collar of her dressing gown and expose a wider swath of skin to his lips.

Ah, how sweet she was, tipping her head forward to give him greater access, sighing as he explored her with kisses, gentle to start, then firmer, gasping when he grazed her with his teeth and followed with a soothing sweep of his tongue. Slowly, he moved to the top of her shoulder, the side of her throat, the sensitive hollow beneath her ear, noting what pleased her, drawing in the soft scent of her soap, relishing the salty tang of her skin. Her body seemed to melt in his arms, though the cords of her neck were taut as she strained to offer him more of herself.

Brushing aside her heavy braid, he lavished equal attention on the other side before allowing her to turn just enough that he could capture her mouth. This time, she didn't hesitate to open to him, welcoming the slick invasion of his tongue before tentatively reaching out to taste him. With a groan of encouragement, he let her explore the sensitive skin behind his lips, the sharp edges of his teeth, the roof of his mouth. So eager, his Daphne. So hungry.

Just a little, his conscience cautioned as he put a hand on her hip and spun her to face him, relishing in the press of her breasts against his chest. With fumbling fingers, he reached between them to untie the sash of her dressing gown. Once undone, the silk glided over her shoulders of its own volition, revealing a demure cotton nightdress, the curve of its neckline hardly low enough to show the tops of her collarbones. It fastened just below the base of her throat with a half-dozen buttons that ran between her breasts, and the fabric was too sturdy, the fit too loose even to hint at the taut peaks of her nipples, let alone their dusky shade.

He'd never seen a garment more erotic.

His trembling hands were too clumsy to bother with undoing the tiny pearl buttons. He could hardly trust himself to be gentle when he reached up to cup her breast through the cloth. He felt as much as heard her sharp intake of breath as he lowered his head and pressed his lips to her chest, just at the point where it began to swell. Her hands, still tangled in the sleeves of her dressing gown, scrambled behind her to grasp the edge of the table for support, but she did not pull away.

With hot breath, teasing lips, and infinite patience, he traced the generous curve of her breast, the pebbled edge of her areola, the firm jut of her nipple. When she rewarded his efforts with a needy whimper, he captured that sweet point in his mouth and sucked until the cotton was damp.

When he released her nipple, intending to move to the other, he realized she was standing on her toes, lifting herself to him. The discovery both aroused and distressed him.

"Let's make you more comfortable, shall we?"

Then he straightened, reached behind her, and cleared the

table with a single sweep of his forearm, enjoying the clatter
and thud of the chess pieces hitting the floor.

Her uncertain, incredulous laugh became a gasp when he
encircled her waist in his hands and hoisted her onto the
table, then covered her open mouth with a kiss. Perhaps
there was something to this *playing chess* silliness after all.

"Aren't you afraid someone will come to see what caused
the racket?" she asked, when he let her have her breath.

He wasn't. They were at the far end of the house, only his
empty chambers above them, and it was well after midnight,
the servants surely sound asleep. But to oblige her, he went
to the library door and shut it, then twisted the key in the
lock with a *snick*. "And if anyone did hear, and asks about it
tomorrow," he said, turning back to her, "I intend to blame
your sister's cat."

Even in the dimness, he saw her lips curve in a smile.
"Poor Eileen. And for once, she's innocent."

Innocent . . .

She had propped herself up, with one hand behind her for
balance, the other splayed beside her hip. The dressing gown
was a puddle of silk on the floor above her dangling feet,
while her nightgown was hitched up beneath her, giving him
a view of her shapely calves. He watched her breasts rise
and fall with each unsteady, ragged breath.

Such an unstudied pose. Innocent, yes . . . yet unmistakably beckoning him back to the shadowy corner.

As he prowled toward her, he tugged the hems of his shirt
from his breeches, then paused a foot or so from her to pull
the garment off over his head and toss it to join the forgotten
chess pieces.

The candlelight caught the flare of her eyes, and she sat
up a little straighter, freeing both of her hands to reach for
him, just as he'd hoped. With a whisper-light touch, she
explored his chest and arms, tracing the curves and hollows
of his musculature, well defined by an active life. She leaned

forward to nuzzle the triangle of hair over his breastbone, to press her curious lips to one of his flat nipples.

He'd never imagined he would find being tortured into madness so enjoyable.

Before she pushed him entirely over the precipice, he dropped to his knees and took each of her cold feet between his hands in turn, chaffing warmth into her toes before kissing her instep. Then he skated his hands upward, over her ankles, her calves, pushing the hem of her nightgown higher, until her knees were bare. Urging them gently apart, he pressed his lips to the little hollow inside each of them.

Then he looked up, seeking her shadowed eyes. Did she know, could she guess, what he wanted?

Kisses, he'd offered her. And kisses he longed to give her . . . *everywhere.*

Just a little rakishness, as he'd promised.

For all it involved lips and tongue, to call what he had in mind *kissing* was, he supposed, a bit of a stretch—more the letter of the law than the spirit. If her barrister brother ever got wind of what happened tonight, Miles might swing.

But he'd die with a smile on his face and Daphne on his lips.

If she were willing . . .

He slid one hand higher, the nightgown bunching around his wrist. The movement hidden by the fabric, he brushed a thumb over the soft skin of her thigh. "May I kiss you here too?"

Her eyes widened and her chest lifted on a silent intake of breath. She didn't speak or, for a long moment, move. But at last, she parted her legs a few inches more.

The breath that he'd kept pinned in his chest rushed from him in a sigh of relief and gratitude. Inching the nightgown higher, he praised her with soft kisses against the delicate skin of her inner thighs, drawing in her womanly scent, sweeter than any rose garden.

Still beneath the shielding cotton, he grazed his knuckle across her private curls, feeling her body stiffen in anticipation. He pressed his thumb lightly to her hidden bud. She jolted at the sensation—and spread her legs wider yet.

Sliding his hands around her hips, he eased her body forward, closer to the edge of the table, and worked his shoulders beneath her thighs, so that she was utterly open to him when he shoved her nightgown to her waist.

He was shaking when he lowered his mouth to her mound, trying to restrain his hunger. Light kisses, then firmer, letting her grow acclimated to the idea, the sensation, but at last, he gave in and traced a fingertip along her seam, reveling in the discovery of her slickness, and followed the movement with his tongue. Ah, but she was sweet, so sweet . . . and all his. He set about devouring her.

As he skillfully ratcheted up her need, her legs trembled against his shoulders, and the fingers of one hand speared into his hair, tugging lightly. Perhaps playfulness, perhaps passion. But still, he lifted his head. He would not risk the possibility that it might have been a gesture of uncertainty, an attempt—however feeble—to urge him to stop. Daphne had shown him the most extraordinary gesture of trust tonight. And by God, he meant to honor it.

She was looking down at him, watching through hooded eyes. Though her expression was unreadable in the dimness, he locked onto her gaze. He wanted to plead with her to let him continue. But he waited as she worked to bring her labored breathing under control.

"Tell me what you want, Daphne," he whispered after a moment, wondering whether she even knew.

She blinked, twice, as if in disbelief, though whether at his words or his actions, he couldn't decide. Then her fingertips flexed against his skull, urging him back to his task.

He did not hesitate to comply. With tongue and lips, he drove her to a shattering peak, relishing her muffled cry and the feel of the pulsing tremors of her climax as they radiated from her core. When at last she sagged against the table, spent, he rose, surveying the scene of his triumph, her damp flesh glistening in the candlelight, clothes and chess pieces scattered at his feet.

She pushed herself upright again, the movement lowering her nightgown to mid-thigh. "I never . . . knew." She reached out a trembling hand, as if to snag him by the waistband and draw him closer, but he stepped nimbly from her grasp. Confusion, perhaps even hurt, wrinkled her brow. "Oughtn't I to—?"

"First of all," he said, catching her outstretched hand and bringing her fingertips to his lips, "I do not ever wish to hear you speak of *ought* or *must* when it comes to lovemaking. Understood?" She gave a wide-eyed nod. "And second, one touch from you and I would surely disgrace myself and ruin my rakish reputation," he teased.

"Would that be so very bad?" A naughty smile curved her lips. "Surely even a rake can be ruined."

"I can think of nothing I'd like better than to be ruined by you," he said, and meant it. "But not tonight. How long before your sister notices your absence, or Lady Stalbridge—?"

As if jolted back to full awareness by his words, she slid down from the table.

With a discreet adjustment to his breeches, he bent and retrieved her dressing gown and his shirt from the floor. "Now, back to your bed with you," he admonished, laying the garment around her shoulders, and then adding in a low murmur, "Only a few days more until you can join me in mine."

Her face was hidden from him as he pulled on his shirt and she slipped her arms into the sleeves of her dressing gown and bent her head to tie the sash. Something passed through her, a shudder, a shiver . . . whether cold or longing, he couldn't say.

He stepped to unlock the door as she retreated to the desk to retrieve her candle.

When she returned to his side, he could at last see her clearly, the faint blush of passion still staining her cheeks, the uncertainty flickering in her eyes.

Though there was no clock in the library, he swore he could hear its ticking. *Three days left . . . Three days left . . .*

Three days to persuade her—if kisses weren't enough—that having a rake for a husband wouldn't be all bad. That they could be good together.

That this marriage meant more to him than winning a bet.

"Tomorrow morning, I shall give you a tour of the house," he offered. "And then in the afternoon, we'll all take a carriage ride into the village. Will that suit?"

She nodded—a trifle hesitantly, he thought. "Just as you wish."

"Come." Cupping his hand beneath her elbow, he led her through the drawing room to the hall.

At the doorway, she paused. "It's best if we go up separately, I think."

She was right, of course. He watched as she ascended the stairs, taking the light with her. As she disappeared into the shadows, he licked his lips, tasting her there.

What he wished, what he'd *had* just a moment before, seemed once more far out of reach.

CHAPTER 21

Famished, Daphne piled her plate with eggs and sat down beside Bell, who was not so surreptitiously feeding Eileen bits of kipper beneath the table.

"You look well rested," Lady Stalbridge said to her while buttering her toast.

"It must've been all that fresh air she took in during her long walk in the garden yesterday," suggested Bell, with a sly, sidelong glance at Daphne.

Daphne managed, somehow, to keep her own expression mild. "I did sleep well," she admitted. "For whatever reason."

In fact, she'd not expected to sleep a wink, plagued by restless thoughts and wayward recollections. Instead, she had collapsed on her bed and fallen instantly into a dreamless slumber, without even pausing to remove her dressing gown.

It was just as well. If one had to remember and reflect upon the events of such a night, it was surely better to do so by the clear light of day.

Alas, it was a misty, cloudy morning. But no amount of sunshine could have prevented her from clenching her thighs together at the memory of what he'd done, and how thoroughly, wantonly she had enjoyed it. When, at the end, he'd mentioned joining him in his bed, she had hurried away, embarrassed by how much she wanted to do just that.

Her chiding conscience sounded remarkably like Miss Busy B.: *Of course you enjoyed it—who would be surprised to discover a rake knows the means of coaxing pleasure from a woman's body?*

But that prim voice was unexpectedly countered by another—softer, but surprisingly confident: *If he were nothing but a rake, wouldn't he be concerned first and foremost with his own pleasure?*

Daphne thought of how he'd paused more than once to ascertain her will and fulfill her desires, how the slightest pressure of her fingers—she'd hardly realized she had tangled them in his golden hair—had been enough to stay him, and how a single word would have been enough to stop him for good. Not rakish behavior, as she'd always heard it described.

And that was not even to mention the most important discovery of the evening. Miss Grey hadn't caught him in a moment of faithlessness, merely in the midst of losing an actual game of chess.

There was still the matter of the wager, of course, but her understanding of even that had begun to shift.

While her disparate thoughts wrestled with one another, Lord Stalbridge sauntered into the breakfast room and bent to give his wife a kiss on the cheek.

One could not be in their presence for long without some reminder that they were, in fact, newlyweds, childhood friends who had rediscovered one another only last winter. As a consequence, they sometimes indulged in open affection that would scandalize those of a certain social set. More often, they limited themselves merely to a stolen glance, a gleam of satisfaction in Lady Stalbridge's eyes and a catlike smile playing about her husband's lips. This morning,

Daphne read even those more subtle exchanges with new knowledge and found them more scandalous than the kiss.

"I've been speaking with Deveraux," Lord Stalbridge said, waving off a footman in favor of pouring his own coffee. "He proposes to show off his house this morning, and to take all of us on a jaunt into the village this afternoon, once the sun has had a chance to burn away this damp," he finished with a disparaging glance toward the window.

"That seems a thoroughly pleasant way to spend a day," said his wife. Daphne thought it might be a softening trick of the light, or perhaps of her own good mood, but Lady Stalbridge sounded less suspicious, less skeptical of Miles than she had done even the day before. "Don't you agree, Miss Burke?"

Daphne did, barring the unavoidable embarrassment of having to greet Miles after last night, and the potential peril of bursting into flame if he so much as sent her a conspiratorial wink.

Her anxiety over that first meeting was not prolonged, as Miles entered the breakfast room not five minutes later and called out a greeting to all. "Oh, no thank you, ma'am," he replied to Lady Stalbridge's invitation to take the seat beside her. "I breakfasted an hour ago, with my grandmama. I'm always an early riser at Lyneham—there's something about it that makes me eager not to waste a minute."

Despite his determined cheeriness, Daphne glimpsed a hint of shadow beneath his eyes, as if he had not passed a restful night. Well, she supposed she had not exactly sent him off to his bed in a state of relaxation. But then, why had he not simply, er, taken matters into his own hands?

Really! gasped Miss Busy B., thoroughly appalled.

Daphne smiled to herself, rather hoping the prim and proper half of her conscience would depart in a huff and leave her in peace for the rest of the day.

"What?" cried Miles, scanning the table. "No sign of

Ryland yet this morning? Well, I'll send Frost to wake him, and then I'm off to take care of a small matter Mr. Palmer brought to my attention last evening. But after that, I shall be ready to show you Lyneham. In an hour or so? Excellent— we'll meet in the winter parlor." And with a pair of crisp nods—one to the company and one to Daphne in particular, though he did not meet her eyes—he was gone.

"Such energy," declared Lady Stalbridge, more amused than chiding.

Bell nodded her agreement as she wiped kipper grease from her fingertips and then laid her napkin aside. "And for family portraits, elegant tapestries, some awful sculpture Great-Uncle So-and-So brought back from abroad?" She mimed a yawn. "Pass the coffee, please. I'm going to need it."

Long practice made it easy enough for Daphne to ignore her sister. After finishing her eggs, toast, and tea, she rose from the table. "I believe I will go upstairs and bid Lady Deveraux a good morning."

"An excellent idea," said Lady Stalbridge. "I shall join you shortly."

"By the way . . ." Daphne turned on the threshold and spoke over her shoulder. "Have any of you seen my writing desk?"

"Mm." Lord Stalbridge, in the midst of a noisy slurp of coffee, raised a finger. "It's in our room," he said when he could speak. "Must've been some mix-up in the flurry of unpacking yesterday afternoon."

"I'll see that it gets taken across the corridor to your room, first thing," promised Lady Stalbridge with a knowing smile.

Daphne nodded her thanks, though she had less and less of an idea how to finish her essay in a way that would satisfy Lady Stalbridge and the readers of the *Magazine for Misses* without hurting Miles. But if she gave it up entirely, she would be sealing her fate here. She would have no excuse not to marry him. . . .

There was a certain irony in her uncertainty about how to proceed—she who could give others such clear-sighted, unwavering advice. Suddenly she wished she hadn't been quite so eager to silence her inner Miss Busy B.

In her journey from the breakfast room, through the hall, to the winter parlor she glimpsed not another soul, except a housemaid carrying an armload of linens, who scurried out of sight at the sound of Daphne's footsteps.

She found Lady Deveraux and Miss Palmer in the winter parlor, seated at the round table on which tea had been served the day before. Daphne supposed that was where Miles had breakfasted. The dishes had been cleared, but there was still a silver coffee service and a cup and saucer before each lady.

Miss Palmer was reading from a duodecimo volume bound in dull brown leather. Something edifying and religious, by the sounds of it. Lady Deveraux had her needlework in her lap, but her hands were still, and she appeared to have fallen into a doze.

"Oh, it's Miss Burke. Good morning," called Miss Palmer with a welcoming smile.

Lady Deveraux's needle began to flash. "G'morning. Well, get on with it then, Palmer."

Her companion started at the reminder, then giggled and switched out the slender volume in her hand for a thicker one tucked in her lap, beneath the table.

"We were just about to learn the fate of Allora," explained Miss Palmer, opening the book.

"Aye, the brigand has just dragged her into his hideout and is puzzling over how to share his prize among his men," said Lady Deveraux with a gleeful cackle. "Couldn't be sure whose footsteps we heard in the corridor, so Palmer always has something less salacious at hand, just in case. Wouldn't want to shock Lord Ryland. But you strike me as the sort of young lady who appreciates good literature?" She gestured with her needle toward the chair to her left.

Daphne sat down beside her. "Indeed, I adore Robin Ratliff's books."

"We've read this one six times," confessed Miss Palmer, her cheeks pink.

"Seventh time's the charm," declared the elderly viscountess, with an impatient motion of one hand and a comical leer.

While Miss Palmer continued with the familiar tale of *The Brigand's Captive,* Daphne poured herself a cup of coffee and considered the day ahead. Miles was about to show her the estate of which he intended to make her mistress, just as he'd told her family. She'd accepted this invitation with the idea it would make her inevitable rejection sting even more.

But she had not considered how many others might be hurt by her callousness.

And it certainly had never occurred to her how much she might like Lyneham Park.

To say nothing of its master.

Lady Deveraux's needle slowed as Miss Palmer neared the end of the chapter, but it returned to its usual quicksilver pace as soon as the book was closed. "That Mr. Ratliff never disappoints, does he?"

"No indeed," agreed Daphne. "Though I confess I have wondered now and again whether the author might not be a woman."

Miss Palmer's eyes flared, but Lady Deveraux nodded contemplatively. "An interesting notion. It's a fact there aren't too many men who truly understand the appeal of the supposed villain to a gently bred young lady. I like you, Miss Burke."

"I'm glad, ma'am. Very glad."

"I should think you would be." The viscountess leaned

toward her and spoke in what was probably intended as a whisper. "Don't think I don't know what you and my grandson are up to."

Heat bloomed in Daphne's belly and spread upward through her chest, her throat, her cheeks with the speed of wildfire. "I don't know what you—"

"The party you're planning. At the week's end. For my birthday." She spoke as if each detail ought to be sparking understanding in Daphne's mind.

Which it had, though not precisely as Lady Deveraux had intended.

"Lady Deveraux fancies that his lordship intends to make a grand announcement at her birthday party," explained Miss Palmer, brimming with excitement herself. "I did tell her not to get her hopes up. A house party with new friends may be all he has in mind."

But her mischievous expression revealed as clearly as words could have done that she did not really believe that was the extent of it. She, too, expected an announcement, one pertaining to Daphne.

Thankfully, they were joined a few moments later by the Stalbridges and Bellis. Lord Ryland arrived shortly after that and greeted them in a raspy voice.

"Palmer," Lady Deveraux ordered, "ring for some tea with honey for Lord Ryland."

"That's not neces—" began the earl.

But Lady Deveraux dismissed his protest with a flick of her hand, yarn and all. "Now see what you made me do," she scolded.

The next half an hour was pleasantly spent. Lord Ryland took up the chair Daphne vacated, obediently sipping his honey-sweetened tea with one hand while he kept Eileen from Lady Deveraux's yarn basket with the other. Miss Palmer, Lady Stalbridge, and Daphne sat apart in a small group of chairs debating various theories about the identity of Robin Ratliff, while Bell leafed through the book itself, her eyebrows rising fractionally higher every few pages. Lord Stalbridge moved from window to window, admiring the view and remarking on the improving weather.

When Lord Deveraux arrived, it was a few moments before anyone noticed.

Lord Stalbridge spoke first. "It would seem the skies are falling in line with your plan, Deveraux."

Much as she had last night, Daphne glanced up to find him watching her from the doorway. Neither the present brightness of the room nor the fact that both of them were now fully dressed made as much difference as it ought; her cheeks still prickled with a flush of awareness.

"I should hate to interrupt your amusements here," Miles declared, breaking his gaze and sauntering across the room to clap Ryland on the shoulder.

"Pshaw," said his grandmother. "They are all restless to be doing something, I'm sure."

"Will you join us, ma'am?" asked Lady Stalbridge.

"To poke around my own house?" She pulled a face. "But I should like to go into the village this afternoon. Want a few words with the vicar—I'll have none of his sour sermons on my birthday."

Miles laughed and kissed her cheek. "Of course, Grandmama. Shall we be off?" he asked the others. They rose and obediently followed him from the room.

Daphne listened with interest, more to the pride in his voice when he spoke of his home than to many of the details. As Bell had predicted, there were old paintings galore, but some newer ones too. Daphne thought that Miles lingered for a moment over a portrait of his parents, a somber-looking young couple dressed in what was likely to have been their wedding finery. He favored his father, she decided after a brief study, though he had his mother's warm brown eyes.

In the drawing room, he pointed out a painting of the house as it had once been, small and relatively unassuming, before the addition and renovation undertaken in the time of Queen Anne. Only Lord Stalbridge expressed interest in seeing the old portion of the building, and Miles declared himself at the earl's disposal, after they had visited the library.

Daphne would have given much not to cross the threshold of that room at present, though sunlight revealed a warm, handsome space with mahogany wainscotting and damask-covered furnishings in deep shades of blue and green. She dared a glance toward the chessboard, only to discover that all appeared in perfect order, the pieces arrayed for play and two polished wooden chairs to either side, awaiting worthy opponents.

In a sort of trance, she approached the round table and traced an uncertain fingertip along its edge, as if expecting to discover it was a mirage. Perhaps she had dreamed the whole thing. The others were milling about, admiring the collection of books or the elaborately carved mantelpiece. Their murmured conversations gave cover to Miles's approach.

"Just one casualty," he said, slipping something cool into her hand.

She looked down at her palm to find the black knight, arm upraised, his marble broadsword snapped off at the hilt.

"I don't care to dwell too long on the symbolism," he said softly. A wry smile played about his mouth as he plucked the piece from her hand and returned it to its proper place on the board.

While the others filed from the library behind Miles, who had promised a cold collation in the dining room, Daphne hung back to speak with Lord Ryland, who was studying a pair of sketches done by Lady Deveraux in her youth.

"You have visited Lyneham Park many times," she remarked, coming to stand beside him.

"Too many to count," he agreed. "I came for the first time the summer I turned thirteen."

Daphne pretended to turn her attention to the pictures. "Is Lord Deveraux always so thoughtful about his grandmother's birthday?"

"Well, it is rather a special year—she will be eighty on the first of July."

"Remarkable. I wonder . . ." She paused, uncertain what to ask, or how much she really wanted to know. "It's quite a coincidence, is it not, with such a momentous family occasion on the horizon, that he should make a wager requiring him to marry by the end of June? And that he should choose to do so here, at Lyneham Park?"

He did not move, and yet she was aware that his posture had stiffened. "Quite," he acknowledged after a moment. "Young men do make rash bets, I'm afraid."

"So I've heard."

"My friend is fortunate—most fortunate—to come out ahead this time."

Understanding that he intended to pay her a compliment, Daphne dipped her head. "He did not want to disappoint Lady Deveraux." She still could not wrap her mind around the wager, but she was beginning to grasp that Miles had believed his marriage would make his grandmother happy, a sort of present for her, if not for himself.

A strange sort of sacrifice, made out of the love Daphne had once believed a man like him incapable of feeling.

"No," acknowledged Lord Ryland readily. Then he tilted his head just enough to meet her eye. "But I have known both of them for many years, and if I may say so, it is something else again to see both of them so well pleased."

Could he be right? Did the thought of marrying Daphne make Miles happy too?

With a bow, Lord Ryland turned away and left her to contemplate Lady Deveraux's pen and ink drawings, one of a building that was probably the village church, and another of a young man who looked like, but was not, Miles.

Oh, she ought never to have come here.

But then, countered the inner voice that was not Miss Busy B., *you might never have learned the truth. You might have missed seeing the real him.*

Was the man at Lyneham Park the real Miles?

Or was the real Miles the rake who held her secret, and her future, in his remarkably skillful hands?

From the doorway, Bell called for her. "Luncheon's ready, Daph."

"I'm not hungry," she replied. "I think I'll just go to my room for a bit." She hoped Lady Stalbridge had returned her writing desk.

She had an essay to write—a very different essay from the one she'd begun last week.

CHAPTER 22

Miles's high hopes for the drive into the village faltered when the arrangement of the two carriages somehow ended with Daphne in one conveyance with his grandmama and Alistair in the other with Miles.

The ladies had all declared that since the barouche seated four perfectly, they would not be separated, and Lord Stalbridge had preferred to ride on horseback, leaving Miles alone in his glossy curricle, with its snug seat for two. With an apologetic shrug, Alistair had climbed in beside him. "Could be worse, old man," he insisted.

But at present, Miles wasn't sure how.

Not a moment for private conversation between him and Daphne since last night—unless one counted those few seconds in the library this morning, which he had squandered with a bawdy remark about the broken chess piece. Not a moment to ascertain how she was feeling, whether she had any regrets. (He was confident she'd had at least some satisfactions.)

Two bloody hours he might have spent in wooing—genuinely wooing, this time—and he would have to bloody waste half the time bumping along the bloody road beside Alistair.

The heavy barouche traveled more slowly, so he'd opted

to let its driver set the pace, which now only increased his frustration. And when Stalbridge trotted past and drew abreast of the ladies' open carriage, chatting amiably with them as they rolled along, Miles muttered a string of epithets beneath his breath.

"I wouldn't curse him too heartily," Alistair advised.

Perhaps Miles hadn't spoken under his breath after all.

"If it weren't for Stalbridge, Miss Burke wouldn't even be here," Alistair reminded him. "It's not every gentleman who would leave Town in a rush to fetch his wife's friend's sister into the country."

"You don't believe the story about business at Ferncliffe, then?"

Alistair shot him a skeptical glance. "Do you?"

No. Stalbridge was dedicated landowner; if some urgent matter had called him home, he would have been there already.

"Why, then?" asked Miles.

"Can't say, really." Alistair watched the ladies chattering merrily amongst themselves. "Lady Stalbridge seems quite interested in her charge's happiness—more than one might expect of a mere acquaintance."

"Which is your excruciatingly polite way of telling me that she doesn't trust me and she'd sooner tell me to kick rocks than encourage Daphne to marry me."

One of Alistair's shoulders rose and fell. "I'm not sure what she wants—or rather, I would have agreed with you until dinner last night. Palmer's story about the ram had her in tears of laughter—"

"Don't you mean *your* story? And thanks for that, by the way. . . ."

"Well, if it softened up at least one of the women at that table, it did what it was intended to do."

"I had no idea humiliation was the way to a woman's heart," Miles scoffed.

"Oh, I hardly believe that—I've seen you play the fool for some female too often," he teased, though there was an edge to the words. But when he spoke again, his voice had softened. "I've also seen the hardworking landowner, the caring master, the dutiful grandson. Once in a while, it might be nice to let someone other than your tenants at Lyneham see *that* Lord Deveraux."

"Even if the rest of the world is content with the vacuous, pleasure-seeking rake?"

Alistair shot him another look but didn't argue.

They traveled the next half mile in silence. Miles considered whether to confess what he'd done. But Alistair wasn't the one who needed to hear it—hear his explanations, his excuses, his apologies.

He had to talk to Daphne. And soon.

Lyneham was an unassuming village, a hamlet really, as the name implied, with the River Lyne dividing the ancient settlement from the thousand or so acres of Lyneham Park. When they rattled over the little stone bridge, hardly wide enough to accommodate the barouche, Miles could see that Daphne was craning her neck—unnecessarily, truth be told—to see the extent of it: a blacksmith, a butcher shop, a dry goods emporium, two pubs, and the church.

The two carriages stopped outside the second pub, the Ram and Rooster. Stalbridge and Miles dismounted and helped the driver with the horses, while Alistair went to help the ladies down from the barouche. By the time Miles joined them, plans had already been formed. Lady Stalbridge had agreed to accompany Bellis to the emporium, to see what might be found there, while Stalbridge and Alistair had decided to duck into the pub for a pint. Miles tucked his grandmother's arm around his elbow, preparing to lead her toward the church, as she had requested.

Only Daphne stood apart.

"Come to the shop with us," her sister pleaded.

Daphne shook her head. "I'd like to see the church."

"I was married here," said Grandmama as they approached, leaning heavily on both Miles and her cane. "Sixty-two years ago. Don't believe it's changed one bit."

"Barring the new roof I had put on the year before last," Miles pointed out; both women ignored him.

"I saw your sketch of it this morning, in the library," Daphne said. "And the other picture you drew—was that your husband?"

A glow suffused her wrinkled face. "Aye. Handsomest man I'd ever seen. Miles favors him."

Daphne, rather than accept that blatant invitation to look at Miles, glanced down at her feet. He tried not to recall the way her gaze had raked over him as he'd stripped off his shirt last night.

Had he somehow managed, instead of improving matters between them, to ruin everything with his too-bold kisses?

"Now, where is Yearsley?" Grandmama cried, as they stepped into the church. It was a quaint old building, made of stone like the bridge, with pointed windows on one side overlooking the river as it wound past the village, and rows of wooden pews polished by the backsides of generations.

Mr. Yearsley, the vicar, bustled from the vestry. "My lord, my lady. How good to see you."

His jolly aspect—smiling face; round belly; bald, shining pate—were in sharp contrast to his frequently stern words from the pulpit. Miles had always considered him rather hard on the petty misdeeds of his flock, whose lives were not easy, despite Miles's best efforts. If the clergyman had had any notion of what Miles got up to in Town, it might have given him an apoplexy.

"Your text this week?" Grandmama demanded.

Mr. Yearsley looked taken aback. "The loaves and fishes, ma'am."

"Ah." She nodded approvingly. "Lovely story about

faith, generosity, and conviviality. The perfect start to my birthday celebration."

The vicar folded his arms over his chest while he reflected on her assessment of the Scriptures. "Yes, well. It's also about doubt, failure to plan, and a remarkable lack of—"

Grandmama had been tapping about the stone floor with the tip of her cane, the movement apparently aimless. But when she encountered the vicar's foot, she pressed down firmly on his toes.

Mr. Yearsley yelped. "But if you wish it, my lady, I can of course highlight the, uh, more p-positive aspects. . . ."

"Excellent," she replied, lifting her cane. "Now, all this chatter has given me a powerful thirst."

"I'm sure, if you cared to step over to our humble vicarage," said the parson, "Mrs. Yearsley could have a pot of tea—"

"Take me to the Ram and Rooster," she commanded Miles, who had to choke back a laugh at Mr. Yearsley's pinched expression.

Though they had already discussed matters, Miles had hoped for another private word with the vicar about the wedding. He wanted every detail to be perfect.

On Saturday morning, Ryland would bring Daphne into Lyneham to meet Miles at the church. Afterward, they would return to enjoy the lavish wedding breakfast the cook was already preparing, at which Miles would present his grandmother with her surprise. Following services Sunday morning, everyone in the village would gather on the green to toast the new Lady Deveraux and to wish the Dowager Lady Deveraux a happy birthday.

But any conversation on the matter was forestalled when Daphne turned away from the plaque she'd been reading and approached, wearing her Miss Busy B. expression. "Is there a school?" she asked, and her tone suggested she already knew—and did not approve of—the answer.

Mr. Yearsley, to whom the question had been directed, stammered a little. "I, er, I beg your pardon, Miss Burke . . ."

She looked vaguely taken aback that the vicar already knew her name, but it did not distract her from her inquiry. "Is there a school nearby? For the children of the village and Lord Deveraux's tenants?"

"Oh. Well, er. No, miss. Those with the means see to their children's education at home."

"And those without the means?"

Mr. Yearsley rocked back on his heels and fixed her with a chary, disbelieving look. "What need have they for education?"

Miles said a silent prayer—why not? they were in the proper place for it—that Daphne never smiled at him the way she was presently smiling at the vicar. And her eyes . . . My God, surely Yearsley could feel their steely chill piercing his soul?

Daphne said nothing further, however, and the vicar took leave of them with a bow. On the street, his grandmother took a half-dozen creaky steps before pausing to tilt her head in Daphne's direction. "I take it you're one of those radical reformers?"

Had Miles really tempted fate by suggesting that nothing could be worse than the earlier carriage mix-up? He would have given a great deal to be in his curricle now, racing away from impending disaster.

Though, to be fair, Daphne looked less affronted than she might have. "Well," she said, clearly considering her reply. "I believe our society has need of reform in many areas. I believe in education for all and rights for women, that slavery is an abomination, and that the poor ought to be treated with compassion. Is that radical?"

Such an innocent-seeming question . . . to which the answer could only be "Yes."

No matter how much Miles agreed with her, no matter how he had tried to improve things at Lyneham or how he voted in the Lords, there was no question such views lay outside those held by society in general.

Grandmama scrunched her mouth and furrowed her brow, which in Miles's experience was the prelude to a tongue-lashing. "You know it is," she began, in a scolding tone.

And then, tottering slightly, she released Miles's arm, shifted her cane from her other side, and reached for Daphne, patting her hand when she found it and then linking their arms to proceed down the street. "But you're not wrong, Miss Burke. You're not wrong."

Dumbstruck, Miles followed, listening as Daphne explained how her parents' unconventional educational theories had produced an important political novelist, a top barrister, a renowned botanist, and a much-lauded poet.

And you, he wanted to add. But didn't.

"And your younger sister?" Grandmama asked instead.

"She's something of a family pet," Daphne confessed. "But Bellis has a sharp mind and a good heart."

By the time Daphne had finished singing her siblings' praises, they had reached the Ram and Rooster. Grandmama was eager to sit down and enjoy a glass of beer in the cool, dimly lit pub, so Miles left her in the care of Ryland and Stalbridge and offered to walk a bit farther with Daphne.

He half expected her to refuse, but she fell into step beside him as he strolled past the blacksmith's forge toward a grassy patch that sloped down to the riverbank, the area that passed for a village green.

"What do you think of Lyneham?" he asked, apprehensive of her answer.

She was wearing the bonnet she had worn in the rose

garden. Walking beside her, he could see nothing of her face but the point of her chin. "It's prettily situated, certainly," she said, with a nod toward the sparkling river as it danced past. She turned around to see the village laid out behind her. "Charming, despite its small size. Rather cut off from the world, for being just twenty-three miles from London."

He couldn't decide whether she had meant that as a criticism, or merely an observation. Most of the people born in Lyneham would die there, many without ever having seen anything farther from home than the nearest market town.

"A school would improve things, I suppose? Bring the world here?"

"It might," she agreed.

"Some would say that educating the children of laborers will lead only to trouble and dissatisfaction," he pointed out.

The bonnet's brim dipped in a sort of nod—of acknowledgment rather than agreement. "People say many things."

"Yes." Miles scanned the water through narrowed eyes. "I ought to have done something in that line sooner, a regrettable omission—"

"But understandable, given your own experiences with schooling. It's the sort of thing I suspect your mother might have done, had she lived. Or perhaps Mrs. Yearsley, if her husband didn't hold such narrow views on the matter."

Or perhaps it's a task for the future Lady Deveraux? he was tempted to suggest.

Instead, he explained with a quiet laugh, "Mrs. Yearsley has been kept busy with eleven children of her own—she may fancy she's running a school already."

The corners of Daphne's mouth lifted in an answering smile, and then, to his shock, she reached out and laid a hand on his arm. "It's clear from the condition of the estate and the village you have been busy about other things. You have nothing to apologize for."

Nothing? he wanted to exclaim.

Perhaps not to his tenants, though even there, it was a matter for some debate.

But as to Daphne, well, he owed her an apology for his presumption, his arrogance, his foolishness, his selfishness. . . .

He'd wanted time to speak with her, but now that the moment was at hand, he realized it would never be enough. If he began his apologies now, he might be through half of them by the time they returned to Lyneham Park. But only if they walked. His curricle would speed them along far too quickly.

Some of his frustration must have communicated itself to her through the tension of his arm, but instead of dropping her hand, she tightened her grip. "I did not expect to like it here. But I do. Very much. The people, as well as the place."

Steady now, he warned the bubble of hope determined to rise into his chest. She was likely referring to his grandmother.

But wouldn't even that be a victory, unlooked for just a few days ago?

He laid a hand over hers. So many things he wanted to tell her, but his thoughts were tangled, the words caught in his throat. "You must at least allow me to make amends for my boldness last night, Daphne."

"And how, exactly, does one make amends for something so thoroughly . . ." Her other hand wove a small circle, as if trying to conjure a suitable word.

"Shocking?" he suggested. "Scandalous?"

"Yes," she agreed with a dip of her head. "But I was thinking of *enjoyable.*"

"Oh." His heart stuttered, perhaps a result of the sudden rush of all his blood farther south. Alistair could say what he liked about Miles's hidden depths, but in truth, he was a rake to his core. "I suppose in that case," he retorted with a sly grin, "one offers to do it again."

Daphne laid a finger at the corner of her mouth, as if considering. "Hmm." Then tipped back her chin and laughed.

He supposed he ought to be grateful that Stalbridge chose that moment to emerge from the pub and shout a halloo across the green. Otherwise, Miles might have dropped to his knees on the spot and proved his willingness.

As it was, he had to stop and pretend to dig a pebble from the heel of his boot to disguise his flustered and aroused state.

By the time he reached the carriages, Ryland and Stalbridge had already assisted Miles's grandmother to her seat in the barouche. The older man related how pleased he was by some tidbit about shearing he'd gleaned from an old farmer, and Alistair looked restored by an hour away from Hertfordshire's deceptively lovely flora.

Lady Stalbridge and Bellis joined them a few moments later. Bell clambered into the barouche and patted the spot next to her. "Come and see the ribbon I found, Daph—just the shade I've been looking for!"

With an apologetic glance toward Miles, Daphne nodded and sat down by her sister.

"I can't decide," Alistair said once they were underway, the curricle racing ahead this time, "whether you feel the trip went well or not."

"Almost too well," Miles replied, rattling the whip to urge the horses faster yet.

Uncertainty, however, was not so easily outrun.

He'd done everything and nothing he'd set out to do this afternoon. And despite Daphne's reassurances, doubt still plagued him.

Was it truly possible that a visit to Lyneham Park had transformed her reluctant proposal into something real, as her comment about liking the place *and the people* had suggested?

Or had he won the wager but failed the test? Had that hour in the library fully convinced her he could never be anything more than that devil, Deveraux?

CHAPTER 23

The trimmings of Daphne's pen lay scattered about her like bones in a predator's den. At breakfast, Frost had informed them that the master would be away for most of the day, called to an urgent matter some miles away. The butler had been more than usually tight-lipped about the details. Daphne had seen Lady Stalbridge exchange a glance with her husband when the news was delivered. Not a romantic glance. Not an irritated glance. Not a glance Daphne knew how to read.

But something about it had driven her upstairs, to her writing desk, determined to gather her thoughts and finish her essay at last, now less about rakes than about choices. It wasn't at all what she had planned, and it wouldn't be enough to secure her freedom—but she was less sure with each passing day that she wanted to be free of Miles.

She had not realized how many hours had passed until Bell opened the door and sailed into their joined rooms, Eileen in her arms. "Here you are! I've been to the library, the drawing room, the winter parlor, the—"

"And now you've found me," Daphne said, putting a point to her final sentence and waving the sheet in the air to dry the ink. "What's so important, anyway?"

"Cami and Gabriel are here," she announced with a little

jump that sent the cat leaping from her arms. "I think Eileen's disappointed they didn't bring Zwolf or any of the children."

Daphne felt a similar longing for some distraction. The memories of Gabriel's words the morning of her departure from London, and Cami's worried face two nights before, were still painfully fresh. Her family would support her through any scandal, but they had also come all this way expecting a wedding, in spite of their reservations. What would they make of her decision . . . when she finally made it?

After stacking the pages together and folding them, she slipped the completed essay beneath the lid of her writing desk and stood. "Where are they now?"

"Frost took them to the winter parlor to meet Lady Deveraux."

"Then we should join them."

"I'll be right there," Bell agreed, even as she moved toward the door to her room. "I promised Miss Palmer the loan of my copy of *The Highwayman's Hostage*. Can you believe she hasn't read it?"

"Boggles the mind," Daphne agreed, and stepped into the corridor.

In the winter parlor, she found Lady Deveraux, Miss Palmer, Lord Ryland, Lord and Lady Stalbridge, and Cami and Gabriel still making introductions.

"Ah, yes, the famous authoress," Lady Deveraux said, as she greeted Cami. "Haven't read any of your books, I'm afraid—my companion has developed a taste for the gothic and nothing else will do."

Miss Palmer flushed crimson but did not deny it.

"But I did read your brother's book of poetry . . . well, I heard some of the young ladies from the village sing a few of the pieces last winter. So romantic."

Cami looked as if she couldn't decide whether to be affronted on Galen's behalf or amused, but Gabriel laughed, coaxing her toward the latter. "Do you know," he said to Miss Palmer, "I have the distinction of being the hero of my wife's first novel?"

"And the villain," Cami reminded him, her scolding glance over the top rim of her spectacles paired with a poorly repressed smile.

"Oh!" Miss Palmer looked him up and down, her interest obviously piqued. There was no denying Gabriel still cut a dashing figure. He would not have looked out of place in one of the companion's beloved Robin Ratliff books.

"Do I hear Miss Burke?" asked Lady Deveraux, tilting her gray head toward the door.

"Yes, ma'am," Daphne said, approaching.

"Daphne." Cami reached out her hands and drew her into an uncharacteristic hug, then held her at arm's length to scrutinize her face, her clothes, her figure, as if they'd been separated for weeks or months and not days. "The country air agrees with you."

"Lyneham Park is a lovely place," she said. "You are both well now? And the children?"

At that veiled reference to their shared, itchy malady, Gabriel fidgeted and Cami raised a quelling eyebrow at him. "Never better."

"Have you met Lord Ryland, Lord Deveraux's friend?"

Gabriel and Lord Ryland nodded and explained they had been acquainted in Town.

"But where is Deveraux?" Gabriel asked the room.

"Called away, I'm afraid," said Lord Ryland. "I'm sure he will join us for dinner. If he can."

"You must be wishing for an opportunity for some family conversation," said Lady Deveraux, planting her cane and attempting to push to her feet.

"Do not let us displace you, ma'am," Cami insisted, without denying the older woman's supposition. "I'm sure there must be somewhere else—"

Bellis appeared in the doorway, looking flustered. "What did I miss?"

Daphne rose. "With your permission, ma'am," she said to Lady Deveraux, "we'll go down to the drawing room."

"An excellent notion," said Lady Deveraux, settling back into her chair. "But I'm sure our travelers must also have need of some refreshment. Shall we all join you in the dining room in an hour for a light luncheon?"

Murmurs of agreement passed around the room. Lady Deveraux sent Miss Palmer with a message for the cook, while Daphne gestured her eldest sister toward the door. As she passed Bellis, she said in a low voice, "Did you forget your book?"

A flicker of confusion crossed Bell's brow, and then she laughed. "Silly me. I'll fetch it and meet you in the drawing room. I won't be a minute."

In fact, the task took at least ten minutes—time Cami did not waste.

Hardly had the footman closed the drawing room door than she asked again about Miles's absence. "It shows a remarkable lack of manners. Did he not expect us?"

"The precise day of your arrival was not known," Daphne pointed out. "To say nothing of the hour."

Gabriel laid a soothing hand on his wife's shoulder. "And many things may demand a gentleman's attention."

"Doubtless some amusement called him back to Town."

Astonished even by the suggestion, though her own speculations would have run along a similar path not so long ago, Daphne hardly knew what to say. But Gabriel calmly reminded Cami, "We would have passed him on the road."

Rather than let herself be consoled, Cami began a different line of questioning. "What of the wedding plans? No one breathed a word upstairs—almost as if he has no intention of going through with it, as if he simply wanted to humiliate you, or—or drag you to the middle of nowhere, apart from your family, and have his way with—"

"Cami!"

No one had heard the door open, but Bellis stood just inside it now, mouth agape. "How could you say such things? I assure you, Lord Deveraux has behaved with perfect decorum since we arrived—"

Daphne managed, somehow, to keep herself from choking, though her cheeks prickled with heat.

"And Lord and Lady Stalbridge have been most attentive," Bell continued. "We have hardly been friendless here. *We* have not been gallivanting about the country unchaperoned."

Cami looked chagrined by that reprimand, a pointed reminder of her own past misdeeds.

Gabriel hid his smile with his hand.

Their eldest sister sank down on a chair, and her husband came to stand behind her. "I'm sorry," Cami said, looking from Bell to Daphne. "It's just that, for so long now, it's been my job to worry . . ."

"Your *job,* Cami?" Daphne came to sit in the chair next to hers and reached for her hand. "Did Mama, or Papa, ask you to—"

"No," she confessed with a shake of her head. "Of course not. It's just that, as the eldest, I—"

"Felt responsible," supplied Bell, still standing several feet away. "But we're not children anymore. We have to be allowed to make a few of our own mistakes."

Cami seized on those words. "So, you think it's a mistake, too, Daphne's decision to marry this—this—"

"Rake?" suggested Gabriel with a wry smile and a half-raised eyebrow, as if coaxing her to remember the things that had once been said of him. "Gambler? Ne'er-do-well?"

"That was different," Cami protested weakly.

He nodded. "I'm quite sure our situation was worse." Then

his smile widened. "At least Daphne hasn't been penning scandalous untruths about Deveraux just to advance her own writing career."

A terrible stew began to bubble in Daphne's stomach, a noxious concoction of guilt, disbelief, and self-doubt. Here was Bell arguing for the importance of learning from their own mistakes, while Daphne had been busily committing her eldest sister's over again.

Was there nothing she could do that wasn't simply a pale imitation of something another Burke had done already, and better?

"And for the record," Bell said, "no, I don't think it's a mistake. Someone who gives such good advice, who's honest with others, even when the truth stings . . ." She punctuated that remark with a surreptitious wink at Daphne. "Surely she would be honest with herself too." She took a step toward her. "So, this marriage must be what you want. I should hope you wouldn't go through with it otherwise."

Daphne leaped to her feet, threw her arms about her sister's neck, and tried not to sob. In Bell's words, it all sounded so simple. . . .

"But I still don't understand," said Cami, "why no one has mentioned any wedding plans. I thought this was all supposed to be a matter of great urgency on Lord Deveraux's part." Her voice had a familiar scornful edge. "Lady Deveraux doesn't even seem to know you're engaged!"

"Miss Palmer believes it's all to be a surprise," explained Bell, extracting herself from Daphne's damp embrace, "for Lady Deveraux's birthday."

"But surely *you* know the details, Daphne?"

Daphne could only shake her head.

"Well, I can't like this," Cami declared. "Secrecy combined with a rush to the altar—and to win a wager, at that! Sounds like a recipe for—"

"Romance," Gabriel declared, speaking over Cami, with

a sympathetic nod toward Daphne. "Which your sister would know all about if she—"

"Ever read any of Galen's poems," finished Bell with a laugh.

"All right, all right." Cami threw up her hands in mock surrender. "I can see it's three against one. So I'll hold my tongue. *For now,*" she added under her breath.

As the conversation shifted to other matters—their travels, the children, an update on Rosamund and Paris's baby, who had not yet deigned to make an appearance—Daphne's pulse slowly returned to normal and the knot in her stomach began to unwind. She hadn't realized Bell valued her advice or admired her honesty . . . or rather, Miss Busy B.'s. But it was something to be going on with, at least.

A few moments later, there was a tap on the door. "I do beg your pardon," said Lord Stalbridge as he entered. "I hope I'm not interrupting, but Lady Stalbridge wondered if she might have a word with Miss Burke before we go?"

"Go?" echoed Cami.

"Yes, now that Miss Burke and Miss Bellis have you and Lord Ashborough here to look after them, we should be on our way. This visit is really a family concern."

"Of course," said Daphne, rising to accompany him from the room. "You've been most generous with your time and attention."

"My wife thought you might have something for her," Lord Stalbridge explained at the bottom of the stairs, and then added in a lower voice, "some message you wished to relay . . . to Mrs. Goode?"

Something for the magazine, in other words. She was actually planning to return to London to publish Daphne's essay.

"Oh. Yes, of course. It's in my room. I'll just be a moment," she promised, hurrying up two or three steps.

Lord Stalbridge didn't follow. "I'm bound for the stables.

But you'll find her in our room, overseeing the last of the packing."

With a nod, Daphne turned and bustled up the stairs. Once in her room, she reached into her writing desk. Finding the folded pages of the essay by feel, she withdrew them, carried them across the corridor, and handed them to Lady Stalbridge. "Finished just this morning, ma'am."

Surprise sketched across the countess's features. "Oh?"

"Yes, I . . . I finally figured out what I wished to write."

Lady Stalbridge glanced down at the papers but did not unfold them. "I must say, Lord Deveraux's demeanor here at Lyneham Park is something altogether different from how he conducts himself in Town. I began to doubt . . . that is to say, I thought you might . . ."

"Yes?" She couldn't bring herself to confess that she hadn't written the essay everyone expected. Lady Stalbridge would discover that for herself soon enough. But Daphne would have given a great deal for some sign that the countess wouldn't be disappointed in her choice . . . along with a bit of guidance as to what that choice should be.

"Never mind," said Lady Stalbridge, waving away her hesitation. Her voice dropped to a whisper. "Our readers will surely benefit from whatever drops of honeyed wisdom Miss Busy B. has chosen to dispense."

Feeling a blush rising to her cheeks, Daphne dropped her gaze. "Thank you for coming all this way. And please, give Lord Stalbridge my thanks as well."

"It was our pleasure," the countess insisted, leaning in to press a kiss on Daphne's cheek. "I'm sure we'll see one another again soon."

Realizing she had left the door to her chamber open, Daphne stepped back across the corridor as Lady Stalbridge's door once more closed behind her. Voices came from farther along, near the top of the staircase. Miles and Lord Ryland.

Suspended on her own threshold, Daphne could not help but overhear.

"I've already told you, I had something to take care of." Miles's voice, tinged with good-natured annoyance. "I won't say another word at present, so it's no use asking."

"Not, I hope, more wild oats to sow before your wedding day," said Lord Ryland.

Miles laughed. "You know I prefer my oats carefully cultivated, old chap."

"Oh, I see. You were paying a call on that widow in St. Albans."

"Every bit as lovely as rumored," Miles said, not denying it. "But you mustn't— Daphne?"

She had shut her door—almost slammed it shut, to be honest—both to make them aware of her presence and to block out the sounds of their conversation with the noise.

"What are you doing up here?" Miles asked, wearing a smile that looked not at all guilty. If she hadn't known better, she would have said he was happy to see her. "I assumed you were with your family below. I was going to greet them after a quick word with my grandmother."

"Of course. They will be pleased to know you've returned from—wherever it is you've been."

"Alistair," he said, turning toward his friend, "would you tell Grandmama I've a message for her? I'll be along with it as soon as I've bid the Ashboroughs welcome to Lyneham Park."

"Certainly," said Lord Ryland with a dip of his head.

As he went on his way down the corridor, Miles took Daphne's hand and wrapped it around his arm. "This was well met," he said, as he led her back toward the stairs.

"Was it?"

"Yes. I have a surprise for you." Boyish charm beamed from him like sunlight. "Meet me at the rose garden gate tomorrow at dawn."

"At dawn?"

Was tomorrow meant to be her wedding day?

"If anyone asks, say you couldn't sleep and fancied a breath of fresh air."

"I don't think—"

They were almost to the last step. Miles turned before she finished speaking. "Why, Lady Stalbridge. Dressed for traveling?"

"Yes. Now that Miss Burke's family has arrived, Lord Stalbridge and I are eager to get back to—er, *on* to Ferncliffe," she fudged.

"Certainly," Miles said with a bow. "But please know, my neighbors especially are always welcome at Lyneham."

"You are too kind, my lord. Miss Burke," she said, inclining her head.

Daphne curtsied as Miles turned toward the drawing room door, calling out a greeting to Cami and Gabriel that sounded genuinely hearty to Daphne's ears. Out of his sight, Lady Stalbridge patted her reticule and winked.

Daphne watched as she left the house, carrying her words to the printer, and wondered whether she'd done the right thing.

CHAPTER 24

Though the sun hadn't even fully crested the horizon, Miles paced before the garden gate—a kissing gate, it was sometimes dubbed, for the squeeze required for two people to pass through it together. Daphne wasn't late for their dawn rendezvous, not really. But he was nervous, nonetheless, sweat prickling beneath his arms, despite the coolness of the morning.

There had been a moment, yesterday afternoon, standing in the hall, when he'd thought she meant to go after Lady Stalbridge. Had she wanted to beg to be taken up in their carriage and hurried away from the future that awaited her here?

If so, she hadn't given in to the temptation. She had followed him into the drawing room, sung the praises of Lyneham Park to her family over luncheon, over dinner, over tea. She hadn't run away.

Not then, at least.

He supposed it wasn't entirely irrational, this fear he had of being left alone. He didn't remember his parents' death, but he'd once overheard his grandmother describing the inconsolable child he had been, incapable of understanding why Mama and Papa wouldn't come back.

He'd carried that fear forward, in his desire to be popular among his peers, to be liked. He'd taken women to his bed, merely to avoid spending a night in his own company. And whenever it had been necessary to bid adieu after an entertainment, to move on from a familiar place, or to break things off with a mistress, he had always made sure he was the first to leave, rather than the one who was left.

He'd long suspected that Alistair understood the root of his weakness—why else would he have tolerated Miles's company, all these years? But even knowing for himself why he did these foolish things didn't make the days less bitter or the nights less dark.

At present, however, it was the hour of hope, suspended between darkness and day. He dragged in a shuddering breath and watched the door to the house, waiting for Daphne to appear.

"Miles?"

Her voice came, inexplicably, from behind him, and he spun on the gravel to find her watching him through the wrought iron gate. "I—I really *couldn't* sleep," she explained, as he reached out to lift the latch. "I c-came out an hour ago, thinking a walk through the garden might help me gather my thoughts, but I g-got t-t-turned around on the paths and had to wait until it was light t-t-to find my way out."

"You must be cold," he said, drawing her instinctively into his arms, wrapping his coat around her shivering body, laying his cheek against her hair. She'd come out, most uncharacteristically, without a bonnet, though she had at least worn a pelisse.

After a few minutes, the tremors subsided and she tipped her chin up to search his face. "What is it you wanted me to see?"

"Come this way." Tucking her arm around his elbow and knitting the fingers of his other hand with hers, he directed her toward the stables. By prior arrangement, a groom led out a small dapple-gray mare with soft black eyes, which she fixed on Daphne as they approached. "She's your wedding present," Miles said.

"A horse?"

"Well, more of a large pony, really." He released Daphne's arm and stepped forward to take the horse's lead from the groom, who returned to the stable. "The gentlest mount I could find in Hertfordshire. Lord Stalbridge gave me the tip. She's called"—he paused to tousle the mare's forelock and chuckled—"The Widow of St. Albans; for her gray hair, I suppose. But you can give her any name you like."

"A horse." Daphne approached warily, hand extended, palm up. Widow nuzzled, clearly hopeful for a treat, then blew out her nostrils in disappointment. Daphne giggled. "You got me a horse."

"I know you said you're not much of a rider, but Raynham was right—it's a necessity in the country. I've a stable of hunters, but I wanted a horse you'd feel secure on. You'll be safe as houses on this one," he said, slapping the horse's sound flank. "Why, I shouldn't even worry if you took a notion to go out alone."

"Alone?" Daphne drew back her hand and shook her head, as if she couldn't imagine such a thing.

"Well, best not to," he agreed. "But I thought, sometimes, you might like to be by yourself. And speaking of, it's time for the second part of your gift. Care to take a little ride?"

She glanced down at her clothes. "I'm really not dressed for it."

"No matter," he said, whistling for the groom, who led the horse away. "We can walk, though I hope we don't get soaked." The sun was surely fully risen by now, but its face was hidden behind dark, tumbling clouds. "It's not too far," he promised, and took her arm again, leading her through tall grasses, along the edge of the trees.

Just as the raindrops began to pelt down, they came to a clearing and a tiny stone outbuilding hardly worthy of the

name of cottage. Hurrying her to the door, he ushered her
inside and ducked beneath the lintel to join her.

"What is this place?" she asked, looking about her.

He hung his greatcoat and hat on a peg behind the door,
then held out a hand for her pelisse. "You asked to see my
favorite place at Lyneham."

He'd never know what the building had been meant for,
a storeroom or perhaps a shepherd's shelter. But when he'd
found it, some twenty years ago, it had seemed magical—
the only place he'd never minded being by himself.

He'd come out the day they had arrived to make certain
the roof and the hearth were sound, and the day after that,
he'd repaired some masonry and swept away the cobwebs
with his own hands. Yesterday, after he'd returned with the
horse, he'd come back and seen to its furnishing: a quilt-
covered cot, a desk stocked with paper and quills, candles
and a tinderbox on the rough wood mantel, and two chairs—
just in case she might ever be inclined to share the space.

He'd even laid a fire, for which foresight he was glad as
he knelt to light the kindling. "I used to hide away here," he
explained with a laugh. "I needed someplace my tutor
couldn't find me." And then, dusting off his hands as he
rose, he finished simply, "Now it's yours."

She glanced around again—it took but a moment to take
in every corner—and shook her head, clearly bewildered.
"A horse, a hideout . . . it's as if you're inviting me to run
away from home."

His answer, if there was one, caught in his throat. He
dragged a chair closer to the fire and gestured for her to sit
down in it, then sank into the other. It took three deep
breaths for him to gather the proper words.

"Maybe, in some way, I am," he confessed at last. "If I
were any sort of gentleman, I'd let you go, not hold you to
a promise, a proposal made under duress."

As he spoke, she watched the flames lick along the logs,

blackening them. "You did warn me, that first night, that you're no gentleman."

He turned his gaze to the window; just the day before yesterday, he'd filled the opening with a single pane of clear glass, now blurred with rain. "I did."

"In fact, when Lord Ryland asked you about a widow in St. Albans, I thought . . ."

Ah. He'd wondered whether she might have overheard their conversation, but he hadn't considered how Alistair's teasing remark might have sounded to her ears.

"You thought you'd caught me playing chess."

He saw her chin wobble in a sort of nod. "But why—why have you done it?" she demanded, her face still in profile. "When I see the man you are here, at Lyneham, so concerned with the welfare and feelings of others, I can't help but wonder why you've been content to play the part of a notorious rake in Town, why you let yourself be branded *that devil, Deveraux.*"

"Make no mistake, Daphne," he said, reaching for her hand, but settling for the arm of her chair. "Those aren't mere rumors. There have indeed been too many women, too much gambling, and far, far too few checks on my bad behavior over the years. Alistair says I'm constitutionally incapable of believing myself disliked, and I always avoid being alone. I suppose that's why I concocted this marriage scheme—though I told myself it was for my grandmama. To make her happy, and to do my duty to the title before I turned thirty. But the truth is, a wife, any wife, mostly meant to me that there would always be someone in my house. In my bed . . ."

She chewed her lip, then looked toward the window and the little cot beneath it. "And yet you gave me all this?" she asked, turning to face him again, her eyes the shade of the gray mare's coat and the stormy sky outside. "As a means of escape . . . from you?"

He managed a weak smile. "No one ever accused me of being clever."

"So it would seem," she answered, with narrowed gaze. "Certainly not that knuckle-rapping tutor you found it necessary to hide from."

"Well," he said with a shrug, "I don't blame him, now. I wasn't an easy student, by any means. Always preferred to be on the go, rather than settling to a book or applying myself to some problem to be worked out on a slate. Numbers and letters are more often a source of confusion than clarity for me, but if I can just *do* . . ." He made a motion with his fingers like tying a knot.

"'Lord Deveraux has never been a man for numbers, but he's right good with his hands,'" she said, evidently quoting someone. At his bemused expression, she explained. "Your steward said that to Lord Stalbridge, at dinner the night we arrived, and it struck me then, though I couldn't decide why. But I've been told my sister Erica was much the same as a child. When Bell and I were girls, most of our schooling was unconventional. Papa said once that Erica's resistance to all the usual lessons, the ones that had worked so well for Cami and Paris, had forced him to come up with a new plan."

"The old ways can't have been easy for her," he said, knowing how rarely girls had a chance to run and jump and play, but were instead expected to sit and stitch on samplers all day.

"No, I don't suppose it was. But it doesn't sound as if it was easy for you either," she said, softly laying her hand over his where it rested on the arm of the chair. "I've never understood why people refuse to see children as . . . well, as *people*. People aren't all cut from the same cloth, so it stands to reason they wouldn't all learn things the same way— whether boy or girl, rich or poor."

He thought again of her insistence on the need for a school in the village. "You're a wise woman, Daphne Burke," he said, dropping his gaze to watch her fingertip trace the back of his hand. "Surely too wise for me."

"That," she said, with a pointed look worthy of Miss Busy B., "may be true. But I'll argue with anyone who tries to claim you're not clever. You arranged all this." She got to her feet and walked around the small room, touching everything, lingering for a moment over the desk before sitting on the edge of the cot. "You understood, without my having to explain it, how I would treasure a room of my own, a quiet place to retreat to on occasion. I've rarely been alone either. Rarely had the chance or the choice. But all the same . . ." She smoothed her palm over the quilt. "I have sometimes been lonely."

He tilted his head. "Aren't alone and lonely one and the same?"

"Not at all," she insisted. "And I think some part of you must have always known that, or you would never have come here. Of course . . ." She hesitated, looking down at the toes of her walking boots, peeping beneath the damp hems of her skirt. "I suppose that also means that, even when you're a married man, you may still sometimes feel lonely, might decide to seek out—"

"No." He could plainly see what she had been about to suggest. "Because this is not about some nameless, faceless woman to manage my household and give me an heir. Not anymore."

"Not about someone who would help you win your wager?" She glanced upward but did not quite meet his eyes.

"No." He stood and would have paced if there had been room. "I thought I knew what I needed, but I was wrong." She was watching him now, and he latched on to her tenuous gaze and held it. "I need *you*."

The words, the most desperate plea he had ever uttered, seemed to hang in the air between them.

And then she patted the empty space beside her on the bed.

If she had needed any further proof that he was no gentleman, the speed with which he tore off his coat, tossed it aside, and crossed the cottage floor would surely have been sufficient. Setting his knee on the bed, he propped his forearm along the window ledge behind her, uncertain whether the cot would bear their combined weight—something he'd never dared hope for an opportunity to discover. He reached out his other hand to tip up her chin for a kiss, but she slipped easily from his grasp, sinking down to the mattress and inviting him with her expression to follow.

The ropes beneath the cot creaked ominously, but they held as he lowered himself over her. The bed was narrow and their bodies were aligned in such a way that it would be futile to try to disguise his arousal. As he cupped the back of her head in his hand and brought their mouths together for a searching kiss, there could be no question of his desire, his intent.

And no question of her willingness as she dragged a foot up his leg and hooked her leg over his hip.

"If we do this," he said, slightly breathless as he broke the kiss and tipped his forehead to hers, "you have to marry me."

He felt her smile against his jaw as her hands freed his shirt from his breeches and slid up his back. "I haven't been privy to all the details, but I did think that was the plan."

"Be honest." He lifted himself slightly, holding himself away from her, if only a fraction of an inch. "You had your doubts. You've been looking for a way out of it."

"I have," she agreed, pressing her lips to his throat. "But I'm not searching anymore. I want this." She tightened her arms around him, pulling their bodies together again. "I want you."

* * *

Somewhere in the back of Daphne's mind, Miss Busy B. cleared her throat.

But when she spoke, it was in that other voice. Not a scold, just a gentle warning.

This changes things, you know. Are you sure?

Perhaps Daphne's conscience wasn't as divided as she'd thought.

Well, she wasn't going to waste time arguing. She'd made up her mind—yesterday, at the latest, but almost certainly before that. And her decision had had nothing . . . well, almost nothing to do with what had happened in the library.

She had come to Lyneham intending to find proof of something she had already begun to doubt: that Miles was the worst sort of profligate, representative of a species of men whom women could never trust. The truth, as always, was rather more complicated.

He wasn't perfect. *Except perhaps at this,* she thought as his lips traveled down her throat, tracing a searing path. But his mistakes and misspent years mattered less to her than the decency she'd glimpsed deep inside him: his love for his friend, for his grandmother, for Lyneham Park.

And while young women might need advice from time to time, they didn't need a moralizing lesson, to be told again and again to guard their chastity and refuse to open their hearts. She had written as much, and sent it off to London with Lady Stalbridge.

After all, the goal of the *Magazine for Misses* was to empower young women to make choices for themselves . . . even if that meant choosing a rake.

"Wait."

For just a moment, she thought the rough voice belonged to Miss Busy B., urging caution once more.

Then Miles levered himself off her, off the bed. "This," he said, looking down at her, "isn't what you deserve."

She hoisted herself onto her elbows, prepared to argue, to explain her new philosophy on liberty of choice. But before she could speak, he had sat down in one of the chairs and begun to toe off his boots. Then he peeled off his stockings, revealing muscled calves dusted with fair hair. And after he had unknotted his cravat, he stood, stripped off his shirt, dropped it onto the chair.

Her mouth went dry. The darkened library, she realized, had revealed almost nothing at all. But now, she could see everything. His sculpted chest and arms. The V of muscles between his hip bones like an arrow pointing to his arousal, barely disguised beneath his low-slung breeches. The melting heat of his gaze.

Then he crooked his finger, urging her to rise, and she understood he wanted to look at her too.

Though nervous, she complied with his silent request. After all, one of the things that had helped her to make her decision was the realization that he truly *saw* her, just when she had decided it would be her fate to be forever overlooked.

She unfolded herself from the low bed and began to fumble with the fastenings of her dress.

"I have a better idea," he said, grasping her by the waist and turning her slowly so she faced the bed and her backside was to the fire. The window cast its pale, stormy light over her face.

"Now," he said with a devilish grin, stretching himself out on his side on the bed, one elbow against the mattress, his head propped up on his hand, "you may begin."

She set one foot on the seat of a chair to unlace her boot and remove it, then did the same with the other. "Leave your stockings on," came the rasped order when she began to reach up to untie her garters.

The dress was more of a struggle, though she had chosen it in the wee hours of the morning because it did not require a maid's assistance. Though she was sure she must look dreadfully awkward, his face revealed nothing but desire as she managed to undo the buttons and ties and eventually shimmied the dress down her arms and over her hips until it lay in a puddle at her feet.

And then just her shift remained, for she certainly had not bothered with a corset when she had dressed alone in hurried silence an hour before dawn.

When she reached down to grasp the hem, he sat up a little straighter. As she lifted her shift, inch by inch, he watched avidly—looking not just at the skin she revealed, as the garment rose over her knees and up her thighs, but at *her*. All of her.

She paused at the top of her legs, the hem of her shift drooping just low enough to cover her thatch of dark brown curls. His charming, boyish smile grew strained.

"What advice would Miss Busy B. give a man who's being slowly driven mad by desire?" he asked.

"Be patient."

Turning her back to him and her already flaming face toward the fire, she lifted the shift over her head and let it drop to the floor.

He sucked in a sharp breath. The rope cot creaked as he sat up fully. "Did you somehow imagine I wasn't aching to see this side of you too? My God . . ." She heard his feet strike the floor, and a moment later, his hand swept over her hip and the breadth of his chest was pressed against her back. His whispered voice was reverent. "You're beautiful— every inch of you."

"I'm just . . . ordinary," she insisted.

"I'm not going to waste breath arguing with you." He dropped an open-mouthed kiss at the base of her neck, in that spot that made her shiver with delight.

"If I'd said as much to you on the night of the Clearwaters' ball," she pointed out, "I'm fairly certain you would have agreed with me."

He wrapped an arm around her hip bones, nudging her backside with his erection. "Does it feel like I agree with you now?"

"I'll admit I have limited . . . well, *no* experience with the matter, but it's my understanding that the male anatomy will respond predictably to certain stimuli— Oh!"

He had lifted a hand to her breast and began to rub his thumb over her nipple, rousing it to an aching peak. His low, wicked laugh was hot against her ear. "Not just the male anatomy. Now . . ." He turned them both to face the bed. "I'm quite willing to concede that Miss Busy B. knows a great many things. Otherwise, how could she give such excellent advice? But she doesn't know more than I do about how much I desire my—my bride." The word sent a surprising shiver of longing through her. "Into the bed with you."

She practically scampered away at his command, her haste a combination of eagerness and nerves. As she fumbled to untuck the quilt so she could climb beneath it, he caught her hand. "Afraid you'll be cold?"

Heat radiated from him, warming her from shoulder to hip. He'd shed his breeches, she realized. She managed to shake her head. Still, he obliged her by reaching around and lifting the blanket for her. But as she turned to lie on her back, she didn't cover herself with it. She had no desire to hide from him.

And he hid nothing from her. Not the need in his darkened gaze, nor the tautness of his trembling muscles as he lowered himself over her. And not his . . . *cock,* she'd heard it called. She'd seen them on marble statues and, once, in a bawdy cartoon. She'd not been prepared for how different it would look on a living, breathing man.

Her man.

She'd expected, quite honestly, to be a little alarmed by the sight of it. After all, it was larger than she'd imagined, though thankfully not as large as the naughty picture had portrayed. She knew it was meant to fit, somehow, inside of her. She hadn't known it would be ruddy and beautiful, that the mere sight of it would make her pulse speed and her body ache with need.

Almost of its own volition, her hand reached for him, and this time, he didn't stop her, though he gasped a little when her cool fingers closed around his heated flesh. The contrast between satin skin and iron hardness was fascinating.

"Far be it from me to discourage you," he said in a shivery voice, as she would have drawn him closer. "But I don't see any reason to rush." His cock slipped from her grasp as he shifted the angle between them, lowering his upper body over hers so he could kiss her mouth, her throat, her breasts. "Pink as a rose petal," he murmured as his tongue came out to tease her nipple. "Here . . ." His hand slid up her thigh to her aching center. One fingertip traced her seam, where two nights past, his mouth had been. Where she hoped he would put it again. "And here."

His lips and his hands tormented her in concert, until she was slick and squirming with desire. "Please," she gasped, driving her fingertips into his golden hair. The slightest bit more would send her toppling over the precipice into bliss.

Her nipple popped from between his lips as he raised his torso and reached for her hand, shifting her touch from his leg to his cock. "Guide me where you want me."

Instinct took over, though not without a little uncertainty and awkwardness as she discovered how wide she had to spread her legs to accommodate him. He hissed as she brushed his heat against her wetness, and she almost let go, fearful she'd done something wrong, thought it felt so very right.

"Yes," he hissed again, nudging his hips forward. "Yes."

When their bodies were aligned, she withdrew her hand and tilted her pelvis, gasping as he entered her, inch by inch. As he surged slowly forward, stretching her, he murmured words of praise against her ear. Anticipating pain, she tried not to tense, though that part of her was already clenching around him.

Then he slipped a hand between their bodies, and his thumb began circling the sensitive spot at the top of her sex. She forgot to be anxious, forgot everything but her need as he thrust, the momentary pinch of discomfort overwhelmed by building waves of sensation.

Slowly, he withdrew and thrust again, rocking his hips to fill her over and over. "Come to me, my love," he rasped, and she moved to join him in the ancient, primal rhythm that drove out everything else, until she knew nothing but his heat and his scent and her own wild need.

"Oh, yes. Please," she whispered again, not knowing whether she begged for release or wished the pleasure might go on forever.

At last, the steady, skillful pace of his thrusts gave way to frantic eagerness, a climax impossible to deny—and yet, only a beginning. He stiffened, straining upward, and she felt a rush of heat at her core as he spent. Then she tumbled after him, crying out as she came.

"You see, I was right," he declared a few moments later, his breath still ragged. "Even on the night of the Clearwaters' ball, when you pretended you couldn't dance, I knew we'd be good together. Although . . ." He let out a low, incredulous laugh. "*Good* doesn't do this justice."

"Mmm," she agreed, snuggling against him as he drew up the quilt. "You *were* right. I did quite enjoy being ruined."

"So, I can expect a retraction from Miss Busy B.?" he teased.

She glanced past him, toward the writing space he had so thoughtfully arranged for her. She had already been thinking about the subject of her next essay, and today's events had indeed decided her on the topic, though not in the way he meant.

"I think," she said, giving his well-muscled shoulder a playful nip, "I'll need to conduct a bit more research first."

CHAPTER 25

Daphne woke on the last of June to bright skies and a troublesome cat.

"Eileen," she scolded as the sleek feline wove among the items scattered on Daphne's dressing table, trying to find a way to reach the feathered headpiece hanging from one corner of the looking glass. "How did you get in here?"

"Oh, did we wake you?" Bell asked innocently from the doorway dividing their rooms. "I never imagined you'd still be asleep."

"Why? What time is it?" Daphne pushed upright and stretched, aware as she did so of a pleasant soreness from yesterday's adventure. Thankfully, there had been few questions about her whereabouts, and a willingness to accept her story about an early stroll that had lasted longer than expected when she was forced to find shelter and wait out the rain.

"Half nine," Bell said, shooing the cat from the dressing table. "And I promised Lord Ryland I'd have you ready for a curricle ride in an hour."

"A curricle ride?" Daphne sent her sister a curious glance. "That sounds lovely."

"Doesn't it?" agreed Bell, disappearing momentarily into

her room and reemerging with something draped over her arm. "I thought you might want to borrow this for the occasion."

Daphne had eventually managed to tease the wedding plans out of Miles the day before. But she wasn't sure how much even her sister knew about how the day was to unfold, until Bell held up a dress so new she had not yet worn it.

The muslin was palest pink, almost white—the color of an apple blossom about to burst into bloom—and so delicate it seemed to float. Its only adornment was a band of dark brown silk at the hem, embroidered with pink roses. From behind her back, Bell pulled a high crowned chip bonnet, trimmed with more roses and the crisp green ribbon she'd purchased in the village.

For good manners' sake, Daphne knew she ought to protest her sister's generosity, to say *I couldn't possibly,* or some such thing. But when she imagined Miles's face when he saw her in that gown, her pulse began to thrum. "It's perfect, Bell. Thank you."

"Come on, then." Bell motioned with the armful of fabric. "Ring for the maid."

Daphne climbed out of bed and went to the bell pull. The maid soon arrived with hot water, so that both sisters could wash. Then the flurry of dressing began, with every detail suddenly more significant than it ever had been: the silkiness of her cambric shift; the clocked stockings that reminded Daphne of Miles's fascination yesterday with her legs, how he had eventually untied her garters with his teeth; the dress itself, airy perfection that made her feel . . . well, like a bride.

When it was time to arrange her hair, she sat down at the dressing table, and Eileen came, too, still eager to explore. While Daphne, Bell, and the maid were discussing which style would go best with the hat, the cat jumped on top of the dressing table—or intended to. The maid had pushed Daphne's writing desk aside; one edge hung over the front of the table, with the result that when Eileen landed, her weight caused the writing desk to tip. Without a quick reaction on the part of the maid, it would have been upended entirely and landed on the floor.

"Eileen," scolded Bell, though the cat had disappeared beneath the bed. "Not again."

The maid placed three hairpins while Daphne chewed on those words. "What do you mean, *again*?" she finally asked.

"Ohhh." Bell gave a rather nervous laugh and tried to wave her concern away. "It's nothing, really."

Four more hairpins. "Nothing?"

"Truly. She tried the same thing the other day, that's all. Though I suppose . . ."

Daphne knew a guilty look on her younger sister's face when she saw one. In the mirror, she sent a glance to the maid, who nodded and hurriedly placed three more pins, then bobbed a curtsy and left. Daphne spun on the dressing table stool to face Bell. "You suppose what?"

"Well, I suppose you might say she succeeded."

"She knocked over my writing desk, you mean. Did anything fall out?" She tried frantically to remember if she'd locked it.

Bell stood and paced a few steps away. She was wringing her hangs in front of her. "Only . . . everything."

"*What?*"

"When I was delayed, fetching that book for Miss Palmer? That's what took me so long. Papers were spread across the floor—you know how Eileen is with paper. And she'd been chewing on a quill. It's a wonder the cork in the ink bottle held—"

"Did you read anything?" Daphne demanded.

Wide-eyed, Bell started to shake her head. Then her lips parted and shaped a silent *well . . .*

"You did." She was on her feet without having realized she'd risen. "What—what did you read?"

"Just a few words, truly. Something about . . . about rakes. I . . . I . . . I assumed it must have to do with the magazine. And with Lord Deveraux?"

Daphne felt her nostrils flaring as she tried to draw in a steadying breath. "Yes. Miss Busy B. has been . . . on assignment, I suppose you could say. I was to let him court me. I came to Lyneham Park with the intention of learning enough to write an essay, something that would expose his worst flaws and make it impossible for him to humiliate some other poor young lady the way he did Miss Grey."

Bell was breathing hard, too, her shock evident. After a moment, she said simply, "But?"

Daphne sank back down to the dressing table stool, looking down at her lap as she knitted her fingers together. "But I . . . I changed my mind. I wrote a different essay instead. And I gave that one to Lady Stalbridge to take to, er, Mrs. Goode, for the magazine. I daresay it's already gone to print."

Bell swallowed noisily. "Oh, thank goodness." Daphne lifted her gaze to her sister's face. "Because I like Lord Deveraux. And I think he truly likes you too. But those few words I read? Well . . ." A dramatic shiver passed through her. "I should hope he never sees them."

"He won't," Daphne vowed, spinning around to face the dressing table and lifting the lid of the writing desk. "I'll just burn them . . . Bell?"

"Hmm?"

The contents of the box were in total disarray, once neatly folded stacks now shuffled together with scraps. "When you put things back, did you put them back exactly as they were?"

"Well, I . . . I wasn't really sure how to—I don't make a

habit of snooping, you know," she tried to defend herself. "And I was in a bit of a hurry. Afraid you'd come back and think—"

But Daphne hardly heard her sister. She was pawing through the box, unfolding pages and scanning them, searching . . . searching . . . "Oh, my God."

"What?" Bell demanded, her voice sharp with panic. "I swear I didn't take anything."

A folded set of pages clutched in her hand, Daphne spun back to face her and tried to form the word *no,* but in the end could only shake her head. She didn't blame Bell for what had happened.

Not knowing the contents of the desk had been re-arranged, Daphne had reached inside to retrieve the recently finished essay, expecting it to be on top where she had left it, and without looking, had handed those papers to Lady Stalbridge. Except . . .

"*This* is the second essay," she said, shaking the papers she held. "The one I wanted to publish."

Bell reached out and took the pages from her before she could crumple them. "So, then, if this is the right essay, you must have given Lady Stalbridge the wr— Oh."

Daphne could guess from Bell's expression that her sister had told at least one fib.

She had read more than a few words of the first essay. Enough to know that Miles would never forgive Daphne if those words saw the light of day.

"I have to—" Daphne jumped to her feet and paced toward the door, then back again. Her pale and frantic reflection in the looking glass startled her. A few moments ago, she had seen . . . well, some hint of the woman Miles saw, the one that filled his eyes with hunger and delight. She had seen herself as a bride. His bride. And now . . .

"I have to go to London and try to stop this," she said, knowing even as she said it how impossible it was.

"You can't journey all that way alone," Bell insisted. "I'll go with you."

"No." Daphne snatched up the bonnet and tied its green ribbons beneath her chin. "You have to stay here. Lord Ryland will be expecting—and you're the only one who can—"

"I'll manage things—don't worry." Bell leaned in to kiss her cheek. "But be careful."

Daphne nodded, though she hardly needed the warning. Despite her misgivings, and the fact that she was not dressed for riding, she was going to have to put the Widow of St. Albans through her paces—such as they were—at least to the next village, where she could hopefully board a London-bound stage and reach the printer in time to stop the essay from being published.

It was a mad scheme, hardly worthy of the name *plan*. But it had to succeed. Because if she failed, she would be left to cry over yesterday's dream of a future here with Miles like so much spilt ink.

Miles wasn't sure how many more of Mrs. Yearsley's mildly reproachful smiles he could bear. Did the vicar's wife fear his footsteps would wear a trench in the transept? Surely a bridegroom was allowed to work off a bit of nervousness by pacing—especially when the bride had been expected by ten o'clock, and the last notes of that hour had long since pealed.

But he paused to oblige her and was glad he did, for the clatter of his boot heels against stone had drowned out the jangle of harness.

They were finally here.

Miles hurried toward the door, but Alistair beat him inside, looking hurriedly around the church before meeting Miles's gaze. His expression was stark. He shook his head.

"What's that supposed to mean, old man?" Miles demanded with considerably more cheerfulness than he felt. His pulse was clattering, but his heart still did not seem to have the energy to move his suddenly congealed blood through his veins. He had to grip the side of a pew to keep from stumbling. "Where's Daphne?"

Alistair extended his hands, motioning him to stay where he was, urging calm. Then he shook his head at the Yearsleys, who stood huddled in the doorway to the vestry, watching anxiously. The vicar, seeming to understand the meaning of that gesture, led his wife inside and shut the door.

Turning back to Miles, Alistair said quietly, "She's gone. The stableboy said she asked for the Widow of St. Albans to be saddled just after nine this morning."

Remembering where he was, Miles didn't swear. But he did sink onto the nearest pew. "Gone?"

What a bloody fool he'd been, trusting her with a horse.

Trusting her with his heart.

"Yes. Bellis says she—"

The heavy oak door creaked open again, just far enough for Daphne's younger sister to slip inside the church. "I thought we'd agreed that I would explain. Since it's all my fault—mine and Eileen's." She stopped at the end of the aisle and stood, wringing her gloved hands, making the reticule dangling from her wrist dance, looking even younger than she was.

"Eileen?" Miles echoed.

"My cat. Well, *our* cat, really. Mine and Daphne's. But I was the one who insisted on bringing her to Lyneham. If I hadn't . . ."

Miles gripped the back of the pew on which he sat, to keep from shouting that he couldn't care less about the bloody cat.

But of course, he knew full well it was unfair to pin his agitated state on poor Eileen.

He had only himself to blame for what Daphne had done—been driven to do.

Unable to drag himself to his feet, Miles motioned for Bellis to sit in the pew behind him and twisted himself sideways to listen to her story.

"It's funny, really," she began, with a faraway look. "Eileen's also partly responsible for Daphne joining the mag—the, er, that is to say—"

"The *Magazine for Misses*?" Miles inserted wearily.

"You knew?" Bellis gasped. Alistair looked equally incredulous.

"I knew. From the night of the Clearwaters' ball."

"Oh." Bellis nodded. Then, "*Oooohhhh.* So, you must know that she—?"

"Advised Miss Grey to break our engagement? Oh, yes. That's why I insisted she find me a replacement bride. Under the circumstances, she had very little choice but to agree." He couldn't meet either set of eyes as he revealed the awful thing he had done. "Two nights later, she offered to marry me herself, on the stipulation that I courted her first. I agreed. Over the course of the next week or so, I . . ." He shoved his damp palm over his bent knee, smoothing the wrinkles there. "I fell in love with her." Bellis made a little squeak; Alistair said nothing. "I brought her to Lyneham, thinking, perhaps, she could come to care for me too."

"She did—she *does,*" Bellis insisted. "That's why she—"

"Left me at the altar?" Miles suggested, mustering a wry grin. "Funny way of showing it, that."

"No. You see, she was . . ." She fidgeted with the ribbons of her reticule. "She was working on an essay. About rakes. About . . . you. She wanted t-t-to expose you, she said. I think . . . I think she wanted to make you angry."

"So angry I'd refuse to marry her after all?"

One of Bellis's shoulders rose, a silent acknowledgment. "Lady Stalbridge was to pass it on to Mrs. Goode in London

for publication. She took it straight to Town from here."
Here, she paused to tug open her reticule and slid some
folded papers from it. "But unbeknownst to her, Daphne had
begun a second essay. Because she had realized that the
more she saw of you, the more she . . . she . . ."

He didn't realize she was sobbing until the a few teardrops
pattered onto the papers she held. Alistair whipped out a
clean handkerchief and gave it to her—a typically gentlemanly gesture, as well as a significant sacrifice on his part,
as his own eyes were distinctly red, though the church was
free of flowers.

Bellis dabbed at her eyes and quickly pulled herself together. "She does care for you, Lord Deveraux. And here"—
she handed him the folded papers—"is your proof."

Miles shook his head, even as he took the papers from
her. "I would have preferred she deliver any message to
me in person. Even if she has decided she can no longer
marry me."

"It's not a m-message," she hiccuped. "It's the second
essay, the one Daphne intended to give to Lady Stalbridge.
But she accidentally gave her the first, b-b-because I let
Eileen get into her papers and m-m-mess up everything."

Her explanation almost defied belief. "Where is she?"
Miles demanded, when he could find his voice.

"Bellis says she's gone to London," Alistair chimed in,
since she was now crying too hard to speak for herself. "To
try to stop the essay from being printed." He sighed. "I think
she hopes to spare your reputation."

Those words were a punch to the gut, driving a sound
from Miles's lungs that might have been either a wry laugh
or a sob. Even he did not know. It echoed against the
church's rafters as he dropped his head to his hands.

And then, "Wait," he cried, squaring his gaze to Alistair's.
"When you first came in, you said she'd left on horseback."
Good God, why had he told her the horse was docile enough

for her to go for a ride alone? Absently tucking the papers Bell had given him into his breast pocket, he pushed to his feet. "Surely she doesn't mean to ride all the way to London?"

Had she been that desperate to get away?

"She was devastated when she realized the mistake," Bell said. "I think she'd do whatever it took to get there."

"Your curricle stands right outside," Alistair reminded him. "With two of the fastest goers in the kingdom between its traces."

Needing no further encouragement—whatever Daphne thought of him, he would make sure she came to no harm—Miles slid from between the pews and started down the aisle. Only when he laid his hand on the door did he pause. "But what of my grandmama and the others? They'll wonder what's happened."

"I'll tell them," Bellis offered, then added reassuringly, "as little as I can. If you hurry, you can still be back for Lady Deveraux's birthday celebration, at least. As for the rest, I'll explain to the vicar that there's been a delay."

A delay. Miles wished he could believe her choice of words was significant, but a twice-jilted bridegroom had little cause for hope.

"And then you'll accompany her back to Lyneham?" Miles demanded of Alistair, who stood between them.

"No." His greatcoat flared as he turned toward the door. "Yearsley will have to do the honors. Because I'm going with you. A hundred things might go wrong on the journey. I would not want you to be alone."

Miles's shoulders sagged as he nodded, grateful as always for Alistair's friendship and understanding, though it wasn't the journey that worried him.

It was what he might find at journey's end.

CHAPTER 26

Daphne arrived at Porter's just past midday to search for the name and direction of the printer, praying she was not too late.

The key to the back room was not on its usual hook, which meant she would find someone in the magazine's makeshift office. With growing apprehension, she approached the door. If she could have brought herself to face Lady Stalbridge's disappointment, she would have gone to Berkeley Square instead.

But once more, the room's only occupant was Constantia Cooper, sketching away, though from a quick glance, it did not appear to be one of her usual outlandish cartoons.

With the tip of her pencil still pressed to the paper, Constantia looked Daphne up and down. "No animal companion this time? Or do you keep a dormouse in your pocket, in case of emergencies?"

Daphne tried to smile, but her lower lip began to wobble instead, thinking of how Eileen had brought her to this very room, and how the cat's love of mischief had brought everything crashing down in the end.

Constantia's expression changed. "Miss Burke?" She dropped the pencil, pushed away from the table, and stood. "Are you quite well?"

This time, Daphne managed to shake her head. "I've made a terrible mistake."

Constantia came around the table to stand before her. She did not lay a consoling hand on Daphne's arm or offer an encouraging smile. "Sit down," she ordered. "Before you faint."

"I won't," Daphne promised, though she did rest a hand on the back of a nearby chair for support. "I haven't time—to sit down, or to faint. I need to know whom Lady Stalbridge employs to print the magazine."

"Why?" Constantia asked, her fair brows knitting together. "What's happened?"

"The essay on rakes," Daphne explained. "I . . . I had a change of heart."

Constantia only blinked. Daphne knew she had never regarded hearts as reliable barometers for decision-making. She had announced as much at their very first meeting.

"It's too late," she said after a moment. "Lady Stalbridge delivered your text and my illustration yesterday. I daresay it's already printed, perhaps even distributed to the book-sellers."

At least, Daphne consoled herself, she hadn't heard any boys in the street hawking a broadsheet that promised to deliver the latest scandal about *that devil, Deveraux*.

"I have to try," she insisted to Constantia.

Constantia only shook her head. And then, to Daphne's shock, she picked up the key to the room from the table, snatched her pelisse from the coat rack, and gestured Daphne toward the door. When Daphne didn't immediately move, she tapped her toe. "I thought you were in a great hurry."

"Oh. Oh, yes," Daphne agreed, moving past her. "It's just that I did not expect—that is, I thought you would just tell me the direction, or write it down."

"If I did that," she answered in a low voice as they passed

through the bookshop, "I wouldn't be able to press for details about what happened."

Constantia's presence will be a comfort, Daphne told herself, although she wasn't sure it was true. She was surprised to think that Constantia merely wanted to indulge in gossip—or perhaps she wanted to indulge in faultfinding, which would be no surprise at all.

She watched Constantia return the key to its usual place and ask the clerk to signal for a hackney. "They won't stop for two women," she said, with a roll of her eyes, "though I'm sure my coin spends as well as anyone's."

Having spent part of the day being jostled among strangers on a public stage, after first wrangling over the matter of purchasing a ticket for herself, Daphne was quite familiar with the ways in which young ladies' movements were restricted. Perhaps she ought to suggest it as an issue for the magazine to take up.

Though after today, she doubted her voice would carry much weight among these women—or any weight at all.

The shop clerk was quick about his business. After Constantia had given the cab driver an address, the two of them were soon watching the familiar scenery of Mayfair slide by as they traveled eastward.

Constantia leaned against the squabs of the forward-facing seat, folded her arms over her chest, and regarded Daphne skeptically. "So. It would seem Miss Nelson was right." At Daphne's look of confusion, she elaborated. "She believed it would be dangerous for you to get close enough to Lord Deveraux to write that essay, remember?"

Daphne's chest ached, pierced by the realization of all that she had likely lost. Perhaps Theodosia had been right, though she had been concerned more with ruined reputations than broken hearts.

Then again, it wasn't just her heart. Her whole body felt

heavy with the knowledge of the harm she had done, the pain her words would cause Miles and his grandmother. Her essay would confirm his own worst beliefs about himself, perhaps propel him away from Lyneham Park and the man he was there—the man he might have been everywhere, if she had not set out to prove that rakes were never to be trusted, because they could never truly be reformed.

"I'm not sorry that I let myself get close to Lord Deveraux," she said to Constantia. "If I had not let him court me, if I had never gone to Hertfordshire, I would never have known the man he really is. I wrote that essay from a place of ignorance, ignorance and anger."

Constantia considered Daphne's answer. "In other words, you fancy yourself in love with the man now."

It wasn't a question, but Daphne nodded nonetheless.

"If you changed your mind about the essay, then why didn't you tell Lady Stalbridge you couldn't go through with it?"

"Because I feared disappointing her," she said, plucking at the green ribbons to her—Bell's—bonnet, which, like her sister's dress, were somewhat worse for wear after the morning's adventure. "She will see both my reluctance to expose Lord Deveraux and my willingness—no, eagerness—to marry him as feminine weakness."

When Constantia made no answer, Daphne eventually made herself drag her eyes to the other woman's face, expecting to see disgust etched there.

What she saw instead was something like pity. "You misjudge her," she insisted. "But even if that were the case, you certainly did not have to supply her with such damning words about the man."

"I didn't intend to," Daphne answered sharply, and explained the mix-up in her papers, without implicating the cat.

As she finished the story, the carriage jolted to a stop. Constantia glanced out the window. "We're here," she said.

The two of them stepped out. Constantia began to wrangle with the driver, who proved reluctant to wait. Meanwhile, Daphne approached the door of the printer's shop, unsure what she would find on its other side.

Miles steered the curricle toward Berkley Square, on Alistair's direction. "Lady Stalbridge lived with her stepson before her remarriage," his friend had explained, his feet pressed to the floorboards, as if he could slow the carriage by sheer force of will. "And I have it on good authority that when the earl and his countess are in town, they stay in Manwaring's house still."

Good authority meant one or more of Alistair's seven sisters, but Miles knew they were rarely wrong about such matters.

"One would think that living in such close quarters with his stepmama would interfere with Manwaring's wilder tendencies," Miles observed, desperate to think about anything but his own present dilemma.

But Alistair was not inclined to oblige him. "Perhaps," he suggested, with a sideways glance, "the viscount is not as wild as he's rumored to be"—a remark that applied at least as well to Miles as it did to Manwaring.

Manwaring's servant showed them in, and in a few moments, they were joined by Manwaring himself. The viscount, only a year or two their junior, wore his brown curls in an unruly, artistic mop and ordinarily favored clothing just this side of foppish. This afternoon, however, he looked unusually subdued.

"Gentlemen." He took in their road-weary appearance

before bowing his head in greeting. "To what do I owe the pleasure?"

"We are—" Miles began, and then corrected himself. "*I* am looking for Lady Stalbridge."

A slight frown of surprise notched the space between Manwaring's brows. "She is from home, paying calls."

Miles muttered an oath beneath his breath, but Alistair laid a staying hand on his shoulder and wagged his head to urge restraint. "Perhaps, sir, you could help us?"

"Certainly, if I can." Manwaring gestured toward a grouping of chairs, but Alistair refused.

"We have come down this morning from Hertfordshire on a matter that requires both discretion and haste," he explained. "We are given to understand that Lady Stalbridge is acquainted with . . . Mrs. Goode?"

An expression, not quite amusement, curled Manwaring's lips. "Of *Mrs. Goode's Guide to Homekeeping?*"

"More to the point, the *Magazine for Mischief,*" interjected Miles, who had to cross his arms behind his back to keep from fidgeting—or from reaching for Manwaring's elegantly tied neckcloth, just to drive home the urgency of the situation.

Manwaring seemed to guess the direction of his thoughts and gave a sly smile as he adjusted the knot in his cravat. "As it happens, she is."

"We need to find out where the magazine is printed," explained Alistair.

"I'm not sure that's information Mrs. Goode would readily part with," Manwaring said. "The magazine has its detractors, as you may know."

Miles's snort made Alistair dig his fingers deeper into his shoulder. "We do. But it's a matter of—"

"Life and death?" Manwaring interjected with a smirk.

"Love and happiness," said Miles, with one lunging step

toward him, shaking off Alistair's grip. "And a birthday surprise for an eighty-year-old woman, to boot."

Manwaring didn't blanch. Or laugh. "Well, in that case . . ." He turned away and stepped to a table piled with books and papers. He picked up a pencil and jotted down something in the corner of a page, then tore the note free. "Here."

It was an address in Fleet Street, written on a fragment of paper that looked for all the world like a portion of the banner that headed Miss Busy B.'s advice column.

"Much obliged," Miles said, snatching it from him even as he wondered how Manwaring had come by the information.

"Yes," echoed Alistair. "My friend will be eternally grateful—"

"That," said Miles, already headed toward the door, "remains to be seen."

"And if you could also extend our thanks to Lady Stalbridge," Alistair continued, ignoring him, "it would be most appreciated."

The not-quite-amused expression returned. "Oh, rest assured. Both Lady Stalbridge and Mrs. Goode will hear about your visit." Once more he inclined his head. "Ryland. Deveraux."

Miles was already seated in his curricle, reins in hand, when Alistair clambered up beside him. Though slightly breathless, he clasped his hands around the lines and tugged them free of Miles's grasp. "In the state you're in, you'll overturn us—and probably every cart and pedestrian we pass between here and the Strand."

Thankfully, Alistair set aside at least some of his usual caution while driving, meaning that Miles's shouts and curses fell on a more limited audience than they might otherwise have done: a pack of raucous boys oblivious to their surroundings and prone to jostling one another into the roadway, and the driver of a brewer's wagon, who flexed a fist the size of a small ham at him in response.

They pulled up beside a parked hackney cab in front of the printer's address, and Miles sprang from the carriage before it had even come to a full stop.

"Wait," Alistair said, jumping down and tying the reins. Miles narrowly stopped himself from pounding on the shop door. "I'm sure you've already given a great deal of thought to what you wish to say. . . ."

Had he? As usual, his mind had been spinning faster than the curricle's wheels, almost from the moment Bellis had delivered the news in the Lyneham church.

"You didn't read what Bellis gave you," Alistair observed.

It had been too much to take in, Daphne's words, her feelings about him, all contained in black ink that would swim before his eyes if he'd dared to unfold the paper. He couldn't bear to think what she might have written. So he'd kept it tucked safely in his pocket instead.

"I don't care," he lied.

I love her, and no essay can change that.

As if he'd heard those unspoken words, Alistair nodded, partly in understanding, partly to urge Miles to knock.

The door was opened by a small, balding man, about fifty, with spectacles perched on his forehead and a nose too large for his face. He was wiping his hands with an ink-stained rag. "How can I help you gents?"

"We're looking for a young lady," explained Alistair.

"Mrs. Goode sent us," Miles added, which earned him a skeptical glance from the older man.

Nevertheless, the printer stepped back and let them enter the shop, the small front room of which was papered with samples of the man's work. He nodded them toward a door at the back, past a wooden counter.

The next room was dominated by a large press, the scents of paper and ink strong in the air. The press clattered and clanged as a younger man cranked the handle with surprising speed, churning out sheet after sheet. Bundles of broadsheets, tied with twine, were piled on a narrow table and on the floor around the perimeter. On the far side of the room, atop one of those bundles, sat Daphne, knees drawn up to her chest, head down.

Miles would have gone to her, but Alistair reached across him for one of the freshly printed pages. Surrounded by text, a man's face stared up at them, smirking, with the tips of a pair of horns peeking from beneath his hair. Exaggerated features, to be sure, but identifiably Miles.

"It would seem that the artist behind the Unfashionable Plates has expanded her repertoire," said Alistair in a dry voice.

"I have," said a voice, and from behind the door appeared a woman, perilously close to thirty, tall and thin, with frizzy hair between red and blond.

"Ah, so you are Miss C." Alistair dipped his head in her direction. "Intrigued to meet you."

"Likewise, Lord Ryland," she said, and did not curtsy.

The noise of the press must have drowned out the sound of their conversation enough that Daphne could not hear it; at least, she did not look up.

"Like I told her already," the printer said, nodding first toward Daphne's huddled figure and then toward a clock on the wall, "they go out at four, unless I hear word to the contrary from Mrs. Goode direct."

It wanted but twelve minutes to the hour.

"Surely, some small delay won't matter . . ." pleaded Alistair.

Miles pulled from his greatcoat pocket the leather pouch of guineas he'd intended to scatter among the village well-wishers following the wedding and dropped it on the nearest bundle. "How much?"

The printer glanced between the sketch on the broadsheet

and Miles, assumed self-preservation was the motive for the bribe, and shook his head. "I'm paid by Mrs. Goode."

Snatching up the purse, Miles dropped it back into his pocket as he crossed the room to Daphne. Here, closer to the clank and creak of the press, he could hardly hear himself think. He stopped just a few inches from the bundle on which she sat, and though he didn't speak and she didn't look up, she scrambled to her feet and spread her skirts with her hands, evidently an attempt to hide the contents of the pile of broadsheets on which she had been sitting.

The press clattered to a stop as the last page slid off the stack onto the floor beside them. His ears rang with the sudden stillness, but he nonetheless heard Daphne sigh.

"I've ruined everything," she said, releasing her skirts and then taking an ineffectual swipe at the inky fingerprints she'd left behind. "Including Bell's dress."

Miles reached beneath her chin with his forefinger and lifted her face to his. "I liked the blue one better anyway."

"I'm sorry," she whispered. "I . . . I tried. . . . Nearly four." Her eyes were pinned on something just over his shoulder, evidently the clock. "At least there's still a few hours left in the day. You haven't yet lost your wager." She drew in a ragged breath. "Though perhaps you no longer want . . ."

"No," he agreed. "I don't."

Tears welled in her eyes, and her lips began to quiver as she nodded her understanding.

Slowly, gently, he slid his fingers along her jaw, until he was cupping the side of her face and could wipe the tears from her cheek with the pad of his thumb. Reluctantly, she looked up and met his gaze.

"We'll wed on Monday," he said. "The second of July. I don't ever want anyone to say I married to win a bet, or even to please my grandmother. Let there never be a question in your mind, or anyone else's—I love you, Daphne, and I always will."

The strangled noise that burst from her as she launched herself into his arms muffled the chime of the hour—and the arrival of Lady Stalbridge and Lord Manwaring.

"I say," said Manwaring, snatching up one of the broadsheets and studying it, "that's a handsome fellow. Vaguely familiar face."

With Daphne still clinging to his chest, Miles turned in time to see Lady Stalbridge fixing him, or perhaps Daphne, with an assessing look. Then she reached into her reticule and handed something to the printer. "There's been an error. On behalf of Mrs. Goode, I ask you to stop the distribution of this broadsheet. There's an additional payment there to ensure you destroy all copies."

The printer looked bemused, but he nodded his acceptance of the new orders and motioned for his assistant to begin collecting the bundles that lay about the room. Miles reached out a hand to rescue one copy from the nearest stack. "For posterity's sake," he explained with a grin. "The artwork alone may be worth something one day."

The red-haired artist, Miss C., still stood beside Alistair and appeared unable to make up her mind whether to be flattered or affronted by his comment. Color flushed across her freckled cheekbones as she adjusted her spectacles.

"Here," Miles said, extracting himself from Daphne's embrace just enough to reach into his breast pocket. He held up the folded pages Bellis had given him. "Print this in its stead."

"You haven't even read what she wrote," Alistair protested.

Miles glanced down at Daphne. He could see by the look in her eyes that she recognized the paper, though as Alistair's words sank in, her expression shifted to something almost chiding.

"She didn't write it for me. This is what she wanted to tell the world." He waved the papers toward Lady Stalbridge, who stepped forward to collect them from him with a smile. "And while I won't deny that the truth may sometimes sting, in the end, I trust Miss Busy B."

CHAPTER 27

After Daphne had washed her face and hands, combed and re-pinned her hair, and let the maid refresh Bell's dress as best she could, she joined Lady Stalbridge in the stylish drawing room of Lord Manwaring's town home. The countess stood at the window, watching the carriage being loaded on the street below.

"Ah, there is Lord Ryland," she said, "back from escorting Miss Cooper home. I wonder what they discussed?"

"That presumes they spoke to one another at all," said Daphne.

"Too true." Lady Stalbridge turned from the window and smiled. "I do not think you and Lord Deveraux will suffer from any such awkwardness."

"Will I not be riding in *your* carriage, ma'am?"

Once more, Lord and Lady Stalbridge were preparing to escort her from London to Hertfordshire, and as the next day was Sunday and not a day for travel, they had hurried their servants around to be ready to leave yet that evening. On an early summer night, the sunset would be late enough that they would have daylight almost to the end of their journey.

"Oh"—she waved off Daphne's concern with a flutter of her fingers and came to sit down in a gold-and-green striped chair—"I don't think we need to worry overmuch about propriety. You'll ride in Lord Deveraux's curricle, and Lord Ryland may come with us. We shall soon be on our way to the wedding of the Season . . . again."

Daphne sat down near her, perched uncertainly on the edge of her chair. "I was afraid you would be displeased with me."

"Why should you think that?"

"Because . . ." She stared down at her fingers knotted in her lap. "In the end, I was as susceptible as any young lady—perhaps more so—to a rake's charms." At Lady Stalbridge's laugh, she jerked her chin up. "Ma'am?"

"It was easy enough to see the way the wind was blowing at Lyneham Park. Your looks, and his, gave the game away. I felt sure you would declare you couldn't go through with the essay. You could have knocked me over with a feather when I read what you had written. I nearly insisted on Lord Stalbridge turning the coach around."

"I rather wish you had," Daphne interjected with a weary smile.

"Ah, but if it were not for today's turn of events, you might always have had lingering doubts—"

"About Lord Deveraux?"

"Perhaps," she said, with a tiny shrug of uncertainty. "There was still the matter of the wager. But I was referring to doubts about yourself."

Daphne started.

"I've watched you give thoughtful, sensible advice to those around you, drawn from wisdom and shaped by a firmness of character beyond your years. The only one who didn't seem to trust Miss Busy B. . . . was you. Now, however, I hope you realize your own insightfulness. There is nothing more valuable than curiosity and a willingness to learn."

Once more that afternoon, Daphne found herself blinking back tears. "I always assumed you would frown upon any of us doing something so ordinary as falling in love and getting married."

Lady Stalbridge looked genuinely taken aback. "Why should you think that?"

"Well, you are the head of a magazine for *misses*."

"True," she conceded with a tip of her chin. "And I do hope catching a most eligible husband won't be the only use to which you put your gifts. I hope a part of you will always be Miss Busy B. at heart, even when the world knows you as *Lady Deveraux*. But marriage can be a wonderful thing. I know that now, though I didn't always. I'm not sure I even believed in the sort of starry-eyed love one reads about in books . . . until I found Kit—Lord Stalbridge—again, and I was free to choose for myself." A faraway look spread across her face, bringing an unusual softness to her ordinarily sharp features, curving her lips in a gentle smile, and misting over her blue eyes.

After a moment, she shook herself, as if remembering where she was, and to whom she was speaking. "So, no— I'm not disappointed. I'm happy that you're happy. I only ever intended to object to the notion that a young woman is a mere satellite, orbiting around the world of men, nothing to do but sparkle and shine, moving from her father to her husband as if drawn by gravity, rather than moving of her own free will—or capable of spinning off in another direction entirely.

"And speaking of liberty of choice . . ." She picked up a thin stack of folded papers from the table beside her. "I didn't give your new essay to the printer yet—I wanted to have a look at it first. I read it while you were freshening up. *Mrs. Goode's Magazine for Misses* will be happy to publish it," she said, handing it to Daphne, "under whatever name you choose. But I do think Lord Deveraux should read it before it goes to print—not because the decision is his to make, but because he deserves to know how you feel."

Daphne nodded, hoping the movement of her head would disguise her blush. "Yes, ma'am."

"All set?" Lord Stalbridge spoke from the doorway.

"Of course, my dear," said his wife, rising from her chair and donning her pelisse while Daphne tucked the essay away and put on her bonnet.

Below, Miles waited to hand her into his curricle. "Home, ma'am?" he teased.

But the warmth in his eyes and the pressure of his fingers was real. Lyneham Park would be her home from now on— the home she would build with him.

"Yes, please," she said, and then added, with a mischievous wink, "my lord."

Ah, there it was, that rakish smile. "I begin to think, my dear, that you are reluctant to tell the world what a devil I am, because you would prefer to keep me all to yourself." He raised her fingers to his lips and kissed her knuckles one by one, a clear promise of more kisses to come, when they weren't under the watchful eye of a chaperone.

Once the lightweight curricle had put some distance between them and the Stalbridges' carriage, Daphne twisted slightly on the seat and threaded her arm through his. She could feel the strength of his forearm beneath her hand as he guided the horses northward.

"Do you regret sending me that bundle of quills?" she asked, half playful, half serious.

"Daphne," he scolded, shifting the reins into one hand so he could cover hers with the other. "I hope I've made it clear today that you may write and publish whatever you wish— so long as it is, in fact, what you wish." He glanced down at her. "My lady."

A shiver of anticipation slipped through her. One day more, and she would be his lady indeed.

"And if what I wish to write is a treatise on education," she went on, "something that challenges the received wisdom on

how children should be taught and what girls in particular
should learn, something that will no doubt be branded outlandish and radical . . . ?"

"Then," he answered without a moment's hesitation, "I
will be glad to think of all the children whose teachers and
parents are wise enough to listen to your good advice."

When they arrived at Lyneham Park, the daylight had
been reduced to a hint of dusky purple on the horizon. Against
that backdrop, the candlelit rooms blazed a welcome.

"It would seem your grandmother is still awake," Daphne
said, looking up at the gleaming windows of the winter
parlor. "But it must be nearly midnight."

"Well, as I understand it, she and Miss Palmer had just
begun a new book, something they borrowed from your
sister."

Daphne giggled, grateful to discover she could laugh
at anything to do with Bell's copy of *The Highwayman's
Hostage,* given everything that had followed on the heels of
her offer to lend it.

Frost opened the door and bowed them into the house,
neither surprised by their late arrival nor discombobulated
by the sudden influx of guests. "Lady Deveraux is in the
winter parlor, my lord."

"Yes, thank you. We saw her light." Taking Daphne's
hand in his, he led her upstairs and called out as they crossed
the threshold, "Happy birthday, Grandmama! I have a surprise for you."

As it turned out, however, Lady Deveraux was not listening to Miss Palmer read breathlessly from one of Robin
Ratliff's adventures. She was playing piquet with Gabriel . . .
and, from all appearances, she was winning.

She shushed Miles with a flutter of her fingers. "One
moment, boy." And then she snapped down her final card.
"Ah ha! Three games in a row. You owe me a shilling."

With a self-satisfied smile, Gabriel began to rake in the cards with a practiced hand. "I do indeed, ma'am."

"But . . . how?" asked Miles, looking from the deck to his grandmother's near-sightless eyes.

"Lord Ash said he knew of a way to mark the cards with pinpricks, both number and suit—an old sharper's trick, in reverse," Lady Deveraux explained. "I can feel the cards in my hand." She lifted one to show him, running a fingertip over the face of the card, then turning it over. "But the pattern on the back makes it impossible for my opponent to identify them."

"Brilliant," declared Miles, with a look of genuine gratitude at Gabriel.

"It would be a shame if all my time at the tables couldn't be put to some good use," he replied, taking the last cards from Lady Deveraux's hand.

"Now," she said, turning toward her grandson, "you said something about a birthday surprise?"

"Two, actually. First, there's to be a celebration in your honor on the village green tomorrow afternoon, and everyone at Lyneham is invited," he said, sweeping his gaze around the roomful of pleased faces, and settling finally on Daphne beside him. "And then, first thing Monday morning, Miss Burke and I are to be married."

Miss Palmer squealed and so did Bell. Lady Deveraux's face split into a smile as she reached for Daphne's free hand and squeezed. "I couldn't be happier for you both," she said, and then tilted her head in Miles's direction, "but your being head over heels for Miss Burke hardly qualifies as a surprise, my boy."

Everyone laughed good naturedly except for Cami, who had come to stand near her husband and still regarded Miles with suspicion. "The wedding date is certainly unexpected," she said. "I thought—"

Gabriel looked up at her, and though Daphne could no

longer see his face, his expression did something to melt away at least some of Cami's lingering reservations about the match. "Sometimes," he explained, with a knowing glance at Miles, whose fingers were still tangled with Daphne's, "a fellow loses a trifling wager deliberately, to be sure of winning the hand that really matters."

Monday morning found Miles once more pacing the transept of the small stone church, this time out of eagerness rather than nerves. Even Mrs. Yearsley did not scold him.

Instead of a private ceremony, guests now dotted the pews: Grandmama; Lord and Lady Ashborough; Bellis, soon to be the sole remaining Miss Burke; the Stalbridges; the Palmers. Alistair stood patiently at the rail, ready to witness the momentous occasion of *that devil, Deveraux* pledging himself to love and cherish one woman for the rest of his life.

Nothing had ever seemed so easy to Miles in his life.

Because there she was, at the end of the aisle, clad in that shimmering steely blue gown he admired so much, now softened slightly by the addition of his grandmother's lace veil, pinned to Daphne's brown locks with a circlet of dewy roses plucked that morning from Lyneham Park's garden.

She stepped forward, smiling a trifle uncertainly, still unaccustomed to being the center of attention, the focus of everyone's gaze. But when she locked eyes with him, that hint of nervousness fled . . . or perhaps made its way to her feet, which hurried her onward with almost indecorous haste.

Side by side, they faced the vicar, who nodded first at them, and then at the assembly. "Dearly beloved," he intoned.

And then Daphne tipped up her chin beneath the veil and said, "Wait."

Miles's pulse, which had been cantering along at a steady enough pace, ticked up to a gallop.

Daphne smiled up at him reassuringly, then turned to face their family and friends. "Before we begin, I have something I wish to say."

"This is most irregular," declared Mr. Yearsley.

Miles heard Alistair murmur behind him, "Get used to it."

When she began to unfold a familiar slip of paper tucked into her palm, he finally understood. His first impulse was to stay her, to tell her it was unnecessary. But he had already vowed that any decisions about her writing would be hers.

"This is from an essay, soon to be published in *Mrs. Goode's Magazine for Misses,*" she explained, and then began to read.

"'Marriage, young ladies are told, is a sacred duty and an honor, by which it is unfortunately too often meant that she has a *duty* to align her family's interests with another's, for which she is to be rewarded with the *honor* of being addressed as 'mistress' or 'my lady,' and little more. Even in this modern day and age, young ladies are still married against their wishes. Not—or perhaps, not only—because their fathers or brothers are tyrants, but because the young ladies themselves do not know their own minds, or have been taught not to trust their own hearts. They have been instructed time and again to disavow rakish charm in favor of good character, and it was, at first, the intention of this author to advise as much again. But may a young lady not have both?'"

Here, she turned to glance at Miles, her cheeks pink. "'She must be given the freedom to learn both human nature and her own nature, to study the workings of society, as well as her own soul, for only then will she know what she truly desires. In the matter of her own happiness, she must be at liberty to choose for herself.'"

Carefully, she folded the paper once more and tucked it away with fingers that had begun to tremble.

For a long moment, silence hung over the small congregation. Then his grandmother rapped her cane on the stone floor. "Hear, hear," she said, then turning to Miss Palmer added, "I liked that girl from the start."

Mr. Yearsley cleared his throat disapprovingly. "May we proceed?"

Daphne nodded.

And when they reached the point at which she looked up into Miles's eyes and said, "I do," he understood the full meaning of her little speech. Maybe she *had* written it for him, after all.

She was marrying him today not to help him win a wager. Not because reformed rakes really made the best husbands. But because she loved him, flaws and all.

She had looked beneath that mask of rakish charm, as she'd called it, and seen him—just as he had seen her. And now she was choosing him freely, with her clever mind and her generous heart and her lush body. He would never let her regret that choice.

They walked out, arm in arm, to face their family and friends beneath the bright summer sky. But he had eyes only for his wife.

Starting today, he had a lifetime to prove the truth of another old saying: the lady knows best.

EPILOGUE

One year later

Though the door of the little stone cottage stood open to admit the warm summer breeze, Miles tapped with one knuckle against the wooden frame to ask admittance. He never disturbed Daphne here without an invitation, but today's post had brought several items she would want to see right away.

"Come in," she called softly, without turning her head, which was bent over her work, revealing that spot at the back of her neck he so loved to kiss.

The interior of the cottage looked much as it had on the day he'd first shown it to her, barring the addition of a bassinet in the corner, by her desk. From it, he heard the occasional coo and gurgle from his son.

Taken together, it was a sight he could hardly believe—more than he imagined he would ever be fortunate enough to see, certainly, and better than he deserved.

"You know, love," he said, approaching them, "there's no shame in leaving little Geoffrey Alistair in the nursery. This is supposed to be your retreat."

"It still is," Daphne insisted, putting the point to something before she turned and beamed up at Miles over her shoulder. "He's no trouble. The fresh air is good for us both, and this way when he's hungry, I'm nearby." She shifted the other way to lean toward the bassinet and bent to scoop the baby up.

Unable to resist, Miles swooped in to kiss and nip the soft skin at her nape, peeking from beneath her loosely arranged hair. "And when *I'm* hungry?" he teased.

"It seems you know where to find me," she retorted with what she had perhaps intended as a sidelong scold but was in fact a glance rich with longing.

His pulse began to thud. "Daph?" The weeks since the baby's birth had been some of the longest of his life. He wanted his wife, and her newly softened, plush curves, with a desire so strong it alarmed him. He would wait as long as she needed, of course. But he could not keep himself from asking, "Does that mean . . . ?"

Her answering smile was tinged with wickedness. "It might."

"Minx!" He watched as she gathered her papers into a neat stack, somewhat hampered by the baby on one arm. "Here," he insisted, holding out the post and reaching for the baby. "You've got me forgetting why I came here in the first place."

"What's this?" She motioned for him to deposit the small stack of papers on the desk, and once his hands were free, handed him his son, bundled in the purple blanket his grandmother had been crocheting the day Miles had brought Daphne home—though it hadn't been a baby blanket then. At least, he didn't think that had been Grandmama's plan. One never knew.

Geoffrey Alistair looked up at him, his round face topped by a bit of golden brown fuzz, and regarded him with solemn blue-gray eyes. That trust, the sacredness of that bond, made Miles's heart squeeze every time.

"Miles?" Daphne prompted him softly, even as she

reached to pull the edge of the blanket back to join in his admiration of their child.

"Hmm? Oh, yes. The post. Well, you can see there's the latest issue of the *Magazine for Misses,* containing Miss Busy B.'s usual words of wisdom."

"Did you read it?" she asked, as she picked up the magazine and began to thumb through the pages.

"No—but since when do you dispense anything but words of wisdom?"

"Since I chose to answer the letter from a young lady desperate for advice about how to persuade her parents she didn't want a London Season."

Miles shifted the baby slightly so he could lay a hand on Daphne's shoulder. "You're afraid you gave her the wrong answer?"

"I'm afraid I didn't really give her an answer at all. I told her all the usual things—that she must be guided by her own sense of the matter. She knows herself better than anyone. That if a husband was wanted, he might just as well be found elsewhere. That sort of thing. And then I added that if she opened herself to the experience, she might surprise herself—might be surprised at what she discovered. As I had been."

"Ah. Miss Busy B. doesn't usually refer to her personal experiences."

"Not often, no."

"I don't see the harm," he said after a moment's reflection. "Experience is one of the things that produces wisdom, and isn't that one of the goals of the magazine?"

"Yes, of course. But I—"

"And giving a young woman ample information to help her make her own choice seems to me perfectly consistent with Miss Busy B.'s philosophy."

A blush of pleasure and pride lit Daphne's cheeks. "I hope so. But then I got to thinking of the young ladies I've

known who were genuinely miserable during the Season. . . .
Vivi, for example."

He might have guessed that the Duke of Raynham's
bluestocking sister wasn't one for the mindless social whirl
of Town. "Speaking of Lady Viviane, there's a letter from
Hawesdale Chase in the stack."

The pages of the magazine fanned shut, and Daphne
began to shuffle through the post once more. "Here it is."
She broke the seal with eager fingers. "I hope everything is
all right." He watched as she scanned the page. "Oh, baby
Izzy has begun to toddle around after her brothers . . . she'll
soon be leading them into trouble, I'm sure." She paused to
read a few more lines. "Vivi sounds genuinely happy to be
a maiden aunt—says she's taking on a new project, a chari-
table endeavor . . . oh." Daphne sank into the chair behind
her, so distracted she nearly missed the seat.

"Is something amiss?"

She stared a moment longer, then raised her gaze to him,
her eyes wide and bright. "Just the opposite. Vivi wants her
name put down as a subscriber to my new book, and she's
offering . . ." She gestured weakly with the letter. "It's
enough to send the book to press."

Publishers had been so wary of the radical theories
Daphne espoused in her educational treatise that they had
shied away from buying the manuscript. Miles believed in
the book and would gladly have borne the expense of printing it, but Daphne had insisted on doing it herself, by going
the more old-fashioned route and raising subscriptions
among the well-to-do.

The subscribers' names would appear in a list inside the
book, as a sort of stamp of endorsement of Daphne's
ideas. Both Lady Stalbridge and Mrs. Goode—though
Miles suspected they were one in the same person—had put
their names down. But Daphne had sedulously refused to
allow her sisters, or her husband, to give enough to fund the

project outright. Instead, she had reached out, with endless letters and even visits, to those whose notorious skepticism would lend the book credibility. It had seemed, at times, as if the project would never see print.

"She also offers to write a preface," Daphne went on, once more studying the letter, "drawing on her own childhood experiences with a string of governesses and explaining why she supports my ideas. She wouldn't do it just for me, you know." She glanced up, and he glimpsed tears of joy sparkling in her eyes. "She wouldn't put her name on something she didn't believe in."

"Of course not," he agreed, bending to kiss her. "We all believe in you." Geoffrey Alistair joined in with a well-timed burble.

Daphne laid the post aside and took the baby back. "I don't deserve all this happiness. Is it dangerous, do you think—tempting fate, perhaps—to have too many marvelous things happen at once?"

"I hope not," he answered with a laugh, "because if it is, I'm at far greater risk than you." He began to stuff her papers, including Lady Viviane's letter and the magazine, into the little satchel Daphne carried back and forth between her desk in the library and the one in the cottage. "But just to be safe, I'd better not tell you the other piece of news."

"Miles!" she demanded, thrusting out her lower lip.

"Now, what sort of example would I be setting," he said with a nod toward the baby as he tucked the satchel beneath his arm and ushered his wife toward the door, "if I simply indulge you every time you pout?"

On the threshold, she rose up on her toes and whispered into his ear, painting a delectable picture of all the ways in which she intended to indulge him as soon as they were back in the house and their son had been safely deposited with the nursemaid.

"That's hardly fair," he protested.

Her lips quirked in a naughty smile. "I know."

"Very well," he said with an indulgent sigh, shaking his head in mock disappointment. "Palmer told me when he dropped off the post that the school building in the village will be finished by the end of the week, and that the final crate of supplies was delivered to his sister just this morning. Stroke of genius, your putting Miss Palmer in charge—the children will love her."

"Yes," Daphne agreed immodestly, "but I'm not sure your grandmama will ever forgive me for luring her companion away."

"Perhaps not, especially given that the last three women she interviewed for the post have steadfastly refused to read Robin Ratliff novels aloud."

Daphne laughed, the most marvelous, musical sound in the world. "She needn't worry about that. I'd be more than happy to read to her in the evenings."

"Are you certain? Your sensibilities won't be overwhelmed by those scandalous tales of erotic adventure?" he asked, lifting his brows.

"If they are, I shall simply have to take to my bed afterward," she said, threading her arm through his and giving his biceps a squeeze. "My lord."

Miles shook his head. "Why, Lady Deveraux," he said, pretending to be shocked. "What would Mrs. Goode say?"

"She would say that a properly made bed is a work of domestic art," Daphne replied, "reflective of a great deal of feminine labor, and thus ought to be appreciated."

"And Miss Busy B.?"

She tilted her head coyly as she glanced up from beneath her lashes and winked. "She would be forced to acknowledge that, as with courtships, what's improper is usually more fun."

She glanced toward the quilt-covered cot in the corner. Because he had been determined to keep this space hers alone, they hadn't indulged in a tryst on that bed since their first one—the occasion on which he suspected Geoffrey Alistair had been conceived.

His breath caught. "A wise woman, indeed. And my darling Daphne? What would she say?"

Her expression grew more serious, more thoughtful. "She would say, 'I love you, Miles. For many reasons. But most especially for loving me enough to see me, *all* of me. And for trusting me enough to show me who you really are.'"

"A reformed rake?"

"Far from it, I hope," she teased. "At least, not thoroughly reformed."

"I love you, Daph," he said, as he leaned down and whispered across her lips, just the promise of a kiss. "And to show you how much, I plan to take you back to the house and ruin you properly all over again."

As he closed the door of the cottage behind them, Daphne laughed and scampered ahead through the tall grass, with the baby wrapped in her arms. Beneath the warm summer sun, Miles followed them home to Lyneham Park, his whole world—or rather, the corner of the world that contained all the small but crucial pieces that had come together to make him whole at last.

ACKNOWLEDGMENTS

Many thanks to those who supported me through the writing of this book: my family, especially my infinitely patient husband; my friend Amy, who knows just when to nudge; and the ladies of the Drawing Room group. Thanks also to my agent, Jill Marsal, and all the folks at Kensington who turned this dream into reality, particularly the three editors who worked with me on various stages of this project: Elizabeth Trout, Liz May, and Esi Sogah.

Keep reading for a special excerpt
of the prequel novella . . .

NICE EARLS DO
by
Susanna Craig

To readers of her popular book
Mrs. Goode's Guide to Homekeeping,
"Mrs. Goode" is an expert in all domestic matters.
Household management, home décor, entertainment . . .
there is nothing about which she lacks an opinion.
Who better to assist the Earl of Stalbridge,
newly appointed guardian to his niece and nephew,
in turning his house into a home?

The widowed Lady Manwaring is the furthest thing from a
domestic doyenne, so when asked to pose as
Mrs. Goode on behalf of the book's true author, she
warily agrees. On arrival, she's surprised to discover that
Lord Stalbridge is actually her childhood friend,
Kit Killigrew. Tabetha might be an imposter,
but her attraction to Kit is all too real . . .

After years separated from the woman of his dreams,
Kit's eager to do more than play house.
Will Tabetha's big reveal ruin everything, or lay the
foundation for true love?

CHAPTER 1

Kit had already read the letter a dozen times at least. Looking at it again would tell him nothing new—not least because he'd left his reading spectacles downstairs. Nevertheless, restless, he withdrew the paper from his breast pocket and unfolded it.

The blur of indistinguishable words might just as easily have belonged to another, similarly life-changing letter, one he'd received almost a year ago, announcing his younger brother's death.

That news hadn't come as a surprise, by any means. A lifetime of rebellion and risk-taking was not likely to lead to any other outcome. Nevertheless, Kit had mourned, was still mourning, his loss. The world's loss. Edmund's gifts might have been turned to better uses. Kit found himself now, as then, grateful his parents had not lived to see what had become of their favorite.

Amid the clatter of his thoughts, he hadn't heard Mrs. Rushworth's footsteps.

"Lord Stalbridge?" the housekeeper prompted, a hint of worry in her voice.

Kit folded the letter, returned it to his pocket, and glanced toward her before surveying the boxes and crates that surrounded them, the sundry relics of another man's life.

"I want this room cleaned out, thoroughly scrubbed, and set to rights, Mrs. Rushworth."

"Of course, my lord," she replied, inclining her head. But she did not immediately turn and go. He had not really expected it of her. "May a body ask why?"

The previous earl, a distant cousin Kit had never met, had been a noted traveler and a collector. The uppermost floor of Ferncliffe had been devoted to storage of his treasures. In the four years since his unexpected inheritance, Kit had focused his attention on other parts of the estate and spared little thought for the house itself, and even less for this particular room. He had had no need for the space. Until now.

"Because, Mrs. Rushworth, the nursery is soon to be occupied."

"Oh?" A note of speculative interest replaced the previous concern in Mrs. Rushworth's voice.

"Edmund's children will be arriving by the end of the month," he explained.

Silence hung on the air, mingling lazily with the dust motes. "Beggin' your pardon, my lord," she said at last, "but I never knew your brother had taken a bride."

Kit cleared his throat. The housekeeper's respectability fit her even more neatly than the charcoal-colored woolen dress she wore. If he weren't careful in his reply, she'd tender her resignation—or at least leave him to clean out the nursery by himself.

"Oh, yes," he told her, though he, too, had his doubts. The wedding ceremony had probably been conducted under the watchful eye of some poor girl's father—or at the end of his hunting rifle, or the point of his sword.

"The children and their mother were living with Edmund in Sicily. She contracted his fever while nursing him, it seems, and died some months after," he said, patting the letter inside his coat. "But her friends did not initially know to whom the children ought to be sent." The only marvel, really, was how much time had elapsed before someone had asked him to clean up another—and hopefully the last—of his brother's messes.

To his surprise, Mrs. Rushworth sighed. "Then the poor things are orphans."

"Yes." He surveyed the dismal, dirty attic. "I'd like to arrange a suitable welcome for my niece and nephew, Mrs. Rushworth."

"Of course, sir," she said, though the enormity of the task had stripped away some of her usual confidence. And his.

How could a man of forty-five, with no wife of his own and no intention of acquiring one, no experience with children, and a house in which even he did not feel welcome, ever hope to give two young children the home they needed?

"You need Mrs. Goode," the housekeeper declared.

Was this another of Mrs. Rushworth's matchmaking schemes? Since he'd come into the title, the housekeeper had hinted mercilessly about the need for a Lady Stalbridge.

Kit, who had sworn off marriage twenty years before when the girl he loved had married another, had learned to smile and nod and politely ignore her. This time, however, he blurted out, "I beg your pardon?"

"Mrs. Goode," she repeated, as if the woman's identity must be self-evident. "Of *Mrs. Goode's Guide to Home-keeping,*" she added by way of explanation, though clearly incredulous at the necessity of providing it. Finally, his baffled expression forced her to concede defeat. "It's a book, my lord. Very popular. Indispensable advice on how to design, decorate, and prepare the household for any guest or occasion."

"Ah. A pity this Mrs. Goode cannot come to us in person," he joked, then sobered as he looked once more about the room. "We need all the help we can get."

Mrs. Rushworth made a noise in her throat, the meaning

of which was indecipherable to him. "I'll get right to it, sir." With a curtsy, she bustled away.

Though wintry wind whistled through the cracked window, chilling the air around him, Kit remained behind, thinking not of the work that lay ahead but of Edmund and the adventures they would have had in such a room when they were little boys, when guarding his brother from cuts, torn clothes, and splinters was the biggest challenge he faced.

People had always thought of Kit Killigrew—he thought of himself—as a serious, predictable, orderly sort of man.

Why then had nothing in his life turned out as he had planned?

Tabetha Holt Cantwell, Dowager Viscountess Manwaring, stared down at the gray pavement three stories below and sighed. London in November tried her patience. Her friends had long since decamped for the autumn entertainments of the countryside, and the promised amusements of the Christmas season were still weeks away. She was in danger of succumbing to ennui.

Truth be told, she was beginning to find it equally difficult to fend off boredom in the other eleven months of the year.

Early in her widowhood, London had held an allure nothing could match. Her late husband's country estate, in which she'd been immured for the better part of twenty years, hadn't even had much of a library. In London, she'd found plays and lectures and books and people. She'd devoured the town's pleasures like a starving woman presented with a plate of cream puffs.

And now, she had a stomachache.

From the opposite end of the room, her stepson Oliver, Lord Manwaring, echoed her sigh. Or perhaps it would be more accurate to call the noise he'd made a gasp. Oliver had a tendency toward the dramatic, to be sure, but when she'd gone to the window, he'd been lazily leafing through his correspondence, and he was not the sort of young man who generally exclaimed over the post.

In any case, the sound made her turn. His posture, usually teetering on the brink of indolence, was as rigid as she had ever seen it, though his head was bent over his letter. No, *two* letters, one in each hand. As she watched, he shoved the papers together in one fist and pushed the shaking fingers of the other hand through his dark brown curls.

She began to hurry toward him, then forced her steps to a more sedate pace. She'd been Oliver's protector for so long, first from his father and later from the world, that the impulse to smooth his hair from his brow and solve his problems was second nature. Sometimes she forgot he was a grown man and might no longer appreciate the interference.

"What is it, dear?"

She had to repeat the question before he looked up from the papers, and when he did, his brown eyes verged on wild. "It seems I've landed in a spot of trouble, Mamabet," he said, twisting his lips into a self-deprecating smile. He'd chosen the name for her on the second evening of their acquaintance, combining the address upon which his father had insisted with a lisped version of what she'd always been called by family and friends, which she'd told Oliver he might use in private.

She laid a hand along the curved back of a green-and-gold striped chair. "What sort of trouble?"

"The 'detrimental to the name of Manwaring' sort, I'm afraid." He punctuated the sentence with a humorless laugh.

Detrimental to the name of Manwaring. His father's phrase—they'd both heard it often enough. Applied variously to Oliver's mannerisms, to his lack of athletic prowess and distaste for shooting a rifle, and most recently to his failure to choose a bride and "do his duty by the title," Oliver's own desires and future happiness be damned.

The late Lord Manwaring had not been an ideal husband, by any means, but he'd been a truly awful father to Oliver.

She'd entered the marriage in possession of all the desirable accomplishments a young lady might acquire—dancing, drawing, modern languages—and with a clear understanding of what was expected of her.

Or so she'd thought.

As it had turned out, she'd been better prepared by the books on philosophy she'd sneaked from her father's library and by the childhood games of hide-and-seek she'd played with the boys next door. The old viscount had married her for one reason: to produce a second, more acceptable, son. Tabetha, who liked children very much and who had looked forward to motherhood, had not mourned her inability to give her husband what he most wanted. When he'd died, she had made the proper observances, but she had not mourned him in her heart.

Oliver sank back in his chair, the partner to the one against which Tabetha now leaned, and flung one leg over the rolled arm, in something approximating his usual relaxed pose. Only his death grip on the letters betrayed him.

"You've heard, I suppose, of *Mrs. Goode's Guide to Homekeeping*?" he asked, not quite meeting her eye.

Tabetha was the sort of person who happily left decisions about the weekly menu to her housekeeper. She preferred the role of guest to that of hostess. And she had given carte blanche to Oliver when it came to redecorating the town house they shared.

But one would have to have taken up residence under a rock not to have heard of *Mrs. Goode's Guide*, not only because of its ubiquity but because of the controversy it had engendered by making the secrets of elegant design and epicurean delights accessible to anyone who could afford the book; six shillings in paper, ten and sixpence bound.

Who would have suspected that homekeeping could inspire such passion?

She nodded, and though Oliver was not really looking at her, he seemed to have anticipated her answer.

"Well, *this*," he said, shifting his thumb to push the uppermost letter forward slightly, "is from a devoted reader, the housekeeper of a bachelor gentleman who has recently been named guardian to the children of his dearly departed brother. He would benefit from Mrs. Goode's assistance in the preparation of his nursery, she says."

"And what, may I ask, has that to do with you?" As she spoke, Tabetha stepped around to the front of the chair and sat down, fearing Oliver's answer might require it.

He favored her with a lopsided smile and lifted one shoulder. "I'm Mrs. Goode."

Her mouth popped open, as if the hinge of her jaw were powered by a spring beyond her control. But no words came. Only a strangled noise of astonishment in her throat.

"That is to say," he went on smoothly, ignoring the fact that she was gaping at him like a fish floundering on dry land, "I wrote the *Guide to Homekeeping*."

Still wide-eyed, Tabetha glanced around the room. Four years ago, following her husband's death, both she and her stepson had been eager for a change. Oliver had suggested the rarely used family town house in Berkeley Square and promised to make it ready for them to inhabit by the time her mourning ended. He'd always had a flair for colors and textiles, for arranging things *just so*—much to his father's chagrin. Tabetha had agreed to remain in the country while Oliver chose every finish, every fabric. He'd overseen the workmen. And he'd recorded the adventure in a series of amusing letters to her that had made a long, dreary winter bearable.

Perhaps his revelation about the book should not have surprised her as much as it did.

"Does anyone else know?" she asked, dragging her gaze back to her stepson.

His lips quirked in a chiding smile that carved a dimple into one cheek, as if he suspected she must already know the answer. "Not even my publisher. We've been negotiating plans for a companion volume, you see." He held out the two letters to her. "And before those plans are finalized, they're insisting Mrs. Goode go to Hertfordshire. They believe it will be excellent publicity."

Tabetha scanned the letters. The threat—for what else could it be called?—wasn't explicit. But clearly the publisher's willingness to purchase Oliver's future work depended upon Mrs. Goode's compliance with this, this . . . *request*. She suspected it was at least in part a ploy to find out the identity of Mrs. Goode. But the publisher wouldn't be happy with what their little scheme uncovered.

Oh, it wasn't just that *Mrs. Goode's Guide* had been written by a man. Gentlemen were forever involving themselves in ladies' affairs, telling them what to do or wear or buy. That a man would proffer a book of advice on such topics was unremarkable. But gentlemen weren't actually supposed to be *interested* in such feminine trifles as home décor, recipes, and furbelows. If word got out that Oliver had written *Mrs. Goode's Guide* from a place of genuine enthusiasm for its subject matter, he could expect ridicule, scorn, or worse. He would be driven to set aside yet another of his passions to keep someone else's peace.

"What will you do?"

He shrugged, as if the matter were of complete indifference to him. As if a measure of his happiness didn't hang in the balance.

She'd seen that shrug before.

"I'll go in your stead," she offered rashly. "I can pretend to be Mrs. Goode."

One eyebrow shot skyward. "You know I love you, Mamabet. But no, you cannot."

Did he hesitate for her sake or his own? Was he reluctant to participate in a deception that might damage his stepmother's character? Or fearful her taste was so execrable that Mrs. Goode's good name would be ruined?

"We could come up with some pretext for you to accompany me," she suggested. "That way, you could still make all the important decisions, while I simply play the public part."

"If I were able and inclined to disguise myself as a lady's maid," he scoffed, "I daresay I could also manage a passable Mrs. Goode."

"Not as my *maid*," she said, pushing to her feet and beginning to pace. "As my . . . my groom?"

His lips pursed, and distaste shuddered through his lithe frame.

"My manservant, then. Or—oh, I know! My secretary. Surely someone as successful as Mrs. Goode would have a secretary?"

She held her breath, waiting for his reaction. After an impossibly long moment, his long leg slid down from the arm of the chair, and his glossy boot settled on the floor beside its mate. "Go on . . ."

"We will travel to Hertfordshire and present ourselves to . . . to . . ." She sat down and scanned the letter again. "To this Lord Stalbridge's housekeeper as the esteemed Mrs. Goode and her secretary, Mr. Oliver. A day or two of discussion and sketches should be sufficient, wouldn't you say? Surely your publisher cannot expect more. And then we'll be free to return to town. You can make all the actual arrangements for the nursery renovation from here, in the name of Mrs. Goode, and no one will be the wiser."

Oliver leaned toward her. "You would do that? For me?"

"Can you doubt it?" The hurt in her voice was not put on.

Certainly she wasn't doing it for Lord Stalbridge, whoever he might be. She'd heard the title but could put no face to it. Under ordinary circumstances, her curiosity might have been piqued, particularly when she had so little to occupy her at present. But now, her irritation outweighed her interest. Being a bachelor gentleman did not excuse a total inattention to matters of household management.

Oliver snatched up her hands, heedless of the papers crumpling between them, pulled her to her feet, and planted a smacking kiss on her cheek. "Bless you, Mamabet. I'll see to everything," he promised before departing in a whirlwind.

A house in mourning, buried in the country, undergoing improvements, and soon to be filled with the noise of children, was not exactly the cure for the doldrums she'd been hoping for. But she would go gladly, just to help Oliver.

And perhaps for the added pleasure of giving this Lord Stalbridge a piece of her—or rather, the indomitable Mrs. Goode's—mind.

Not quite a week later, Kit looked up from the account ledger he'd been reviewing to find Mrs. Rushworth standing in the doorway of his study, her starched linen handkerchief stark white against her dark dress. He had to peer over the tops of his spectacles to see her expression clearly, a mixture of apprehension and surprise.

"Is everything all right?" he asked. For a moment, she didn't answer, leaving him to picture any number of catastrophes. "Something in the attic?" Perhaps, against all odds, one of the late earl's crates had contained something interesting, even shocking. . . .

"No, my lord. That is, everything is fine. It's naught to do with anything upstairs . . . exactly."

He closed the ledger, laid his spectacles aside, and folded his hands on the desktop. "Then what, *exactly*, is the matter?"

"It's Mrs. Goode, sir." Mrs. Rushworth's mouth moved oddly; he suspected her of chewing on the inside of her lip. Her voice dropped. "She's here."

His brain suddenly felt as thick and impenetrable as the crust of an overdone plum pudding. Her whispered words could not seem to pierce it. *Mrs. Goode?* He'd assumed the name was nothing more than a polite fiction, manufactured to sell books.

Before he could muster even simple questions—*How? Why?*—Mrs. Rushworth went on. "I wrote, you see, to her publisher. It was you, my lord, who put the notion into my mind. I thought perhaps, if she weren't too busy, she might offer a little free advice. But I never dreamed . . ." Now she began to twist her handkerchief with agitated hands.

"She's here." In his stuttering attempt at comprehension, the words came out half statement, half question.

"Yes, sir. With her secretary, Mr. Oliver. To help us," she finished, brightening. "Shall I show them in?"

He didn't think he'd answered her. He still didn't think Mrs. Goode was real. But the housekeeper turned from the room with a purposeful stride, and he found himself unfolding his hands, laying them flat on the desktop, and pushing to his feet, just in case.

A moment later, he heard steps along the corridor. Mrs. Rushworth reappeared and curtsied. "Mrs. Goode to see you, my lord."

A lady entered behind her. A flesh-and-blood lady, clad in a china-blue pelisse. More, he could not say, for her head was turned in such a way that he could see nothing beyond the brim of her bonnet, not a glimpse of her profile, not even the color of her hair.

She was speaking low to someone behind her: her

secretary, he presumed. He could not make out her words. But the voice . . . Its huskiness sent a spark along his spine, like the sensation of a touch tracing the contours of each vertebra. *A familiar touch* . . .

He kept his hands planted firmly on his desk, suddenly conscious that if he lifted them, he would reveal two perfect prints, the sweat of his palms dark against the leather blotter.

The secretary, Mr. Oliver, entered behind Mrs. Goode. He was a tall, slender young man with a veritable mop of curly dark brown hair, his coat and greatcoat gaping open to reveal the flash of a pink-and-green checked waistcoat. One of Mrs. Goode's gloved hands rose to brush a few raindrops from Mr. Oliver's shoulder, a surprisingly intimate gesture between a lady and her secretary.

Before Kit had succeeded in tamping down a rush of jealousy, to say nothing of examining the absurdity of such a reaction, the woman turned, and his brain—moments before, as solid and impervious as a kiln-fired brick—turned to mush.

Beth—unmistakably *his* Beth, though twenty years had passed since his parting look at her—was stepping toward him.

She extended that same hand in greeting, and though her steady blue gaze appeared to be focused on him, he could tell she hadn't really *seen* him. Not yet.

He knew precisely the moment she did. The flicker of recognition. The flash of disbelief. Her cheeks paled, then pinked, and the outstretched hand drew back and fluttered to the base of her throat. "Lord Stalbridge?"

The necessity of coming forward and helping her to a chair prevented him from giving in to the temptation to sink into one himself. He curled his hand beneath her elbow and eased her to a seat, bending close enough that he could smell her perfume, an inviting mixture of pear blossoms and vanilla.

"Are you quite well . . . Mrs. Goode?" She had never been far from his thoughts, but the address was strange on his lips. *Manwaring* had been the fellow's title, the dour old hermit her father had insisted she marry, all so he could hear his only daughter addressed as "my lady."

She didn't answer, merely searched his face, her eyes wide with aching wonder. Then her gaze dropped to his hand, which had slid up from her elbow to curve around her upper arm, a forward gesture, even in spite of their history. He tried to marshal his mind—more custard than pudding, more mortar than brick—to order his fingers to relax their grip.

But every instinct told him never to let her go again.

Look for **NICE EARLS DO** *available now in ebook!*

Visit our website at
KensingtonBooks.com
to sign up for our newsletters, read
more from your favorite authors, see
books by series, view reading group
guides, and more!

Become a Part of Our
Between the Chapters Book Club
Community and Join the Conversation